CHARING CROSS

CLAIRE RAYNER

CHARING CROSS

BOOK CLUB ASSOCIATES

London

For George 'Rog' Rogers
who has read more of my work than any man should have to

FAMILY TREE I

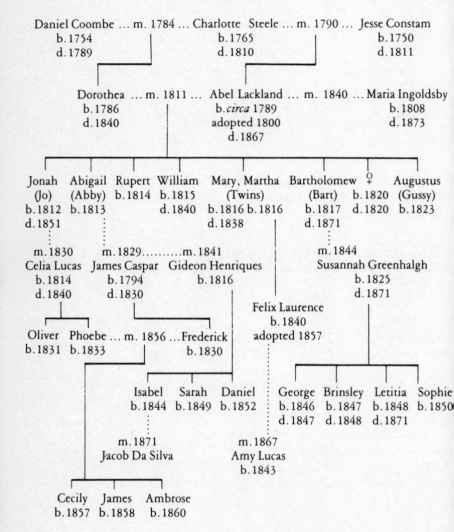

FAMILY TREE II

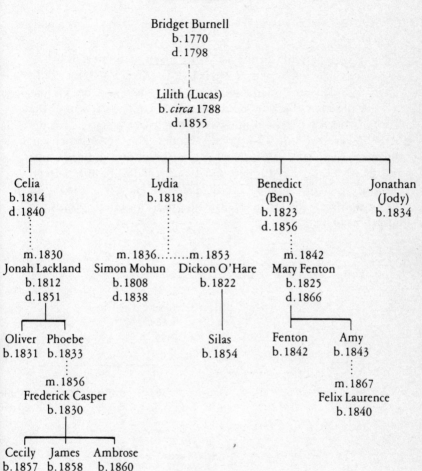

Bridget Burnell
b. 1770
d. 1798

Lilith (Lucas)
b. *circa* 1788
d. 1855

Celia
b. 1814
d. 1840

Lydia
b. 1818

Benedict
(Ben)
b. 1823
d. 1856

Jonathan
(Jody)
b. 1834

m. 1830
Jonah Lackland
b. 1812
d. 1851

m. 1836.......m. 1853
Simon Mohun   Dickon O'Hare
b. 1808   b. 1822
d. 1838

m. 1842
Mary Fenton
b. 1825
d. 1866

Oliver   Phoebe
b. 1831 b. 1833

Silas
b. 1854

Fenton   Amy
b. 1842 b. 1843

m. 1856
Frederick Casper
b. 1830

m. 1867
Felix Laurence
b. 1840

Cecily   James   Ambrose
b. 1857 b. 1858 b. 1860

ACKNOWLEDGEMENTS

The author is grateful for the assistance given with research by the Library of the Royal Society of Medicine, London; Macarthy's Ltd., Surgical Instrument Manufacturers; The London Library; The London Borough of Camden Libraries; The London Museum; The Victoria and Albert Museum; Westminster City Library; Leichner Stage Make-Up Ltd.; Raymond Mander and Jo Mitchenson, theatrical historians; Miss Geraldine Stephenson, choreographer and dance historian; Museum and Library of the Brontë Society, Haworth; J. Geoffrey Moore, Local Historian, Haworth; The Public Records Office; The Archivist, British Rail; and other sources too numerous to mention.

CHAPTER ONE

Halfway up the steep cobbled high street Sophie Lackland stopped, as she always did, ostensibly to catch her breath, but really to stare back down the valley to the cluster of roofs far below by the railway station.

She did it for the same reason that she would prod an aching tooth with the tip of her tongue; to remind herself of the pain. For, dearly as she loved her home here in the grey Pennine village of Haworth, she felt an almost constant longing to get away from it. Haworth was familiar, Haworth was safe, Haworth was filled with the scenes and the people she had known all her life, but Haworth was so dull and stifling and boring that sometimes she could have shouted her frustration aloud.

But of course she never did, for how could she? Who was there to understand such absurd longings, when she could hardly understand them herself and did not even know what it was that she wanted so much? So, this morning, as on every other morning, she pulled her shawl more tightly around her shoulders and turned to complete the climb that would bring her to the Black Bull, where she was to arrange for a jug of porter to be sent down to old Nehemiah Moore, the butcher who lived in Town End Bottom and who was beginning to recover from his bronchitis as last, and then to the druggist to persuade Robert Lambert to give her some embrocation for poor old Mrs Binns in Back Lane whose rheumatism was so much worse this year.

And perhaps she should call in at the Parsonage to pay her respects to Mr Wade, though like all right-minded Haworth residents she was annoyed with him for having altered the Parsonage as he had. Building that new wing on the side last year had been a dreadful thing to do — and now rumour had it that he was actually planning to pull down the old church and rebuild that as well — but it would be a kindness, for he was a lonely man, and the Pastor, after all. And he needed someone to show him friendship

1

when most of the villagers plainly showed their disgust with cold Yorkshire disdain.

She shivered and walked faster, even though that made her even more breathless. It was bitterly cold although not as cold as it would become when the year turned, and the wind was whirling down from the moors with ice on its breath. Her shawl, for all it was knitted of good-quality locally spun yarn sheared from the dull-faced sheep that grazed the high tops, was no defence against it. She needed a thick woollen mantle, if the truth were told; but there was no sense in thinking of such things, for where was Sophie Lackland to find the wherewithal to buy such a garment? She must just be glad to have her shawl, for in its possession she was vastly richer than the people down in Town End Bottom where she had spent so much of the morning. They, poor things, had barely bread enough to call their own, let alone a shawl.

She was rosy and rather warmer by the time she reached the top, and Moses Baldwin, the baker, clattering by with his cart loaded high with new round loaves, gave her a nod and the faint grimace that can only be interpreted as a smile by those used to the taciturnity of the moor people, and which made her smile widely back at him. His bread smelled good on the cold air, and she felt a sudden pang of hunger. It must be close on time for luncheon, and here she still was with her rounds, as she liked to call them, not yet half complete.

She hurried through her errands, grateful for Mr Sugden's ready willingness to send some restorative porter down to old Nehemiah, for he was a generous man and as landlord of the most prosperous inn in the village could afford to gratify his taste for philanthropy; and then she went to Mr Lambert, who was equally generous with a bottle of his embrocation.

Not that she really liked having to smile and be grateful to Mr Lambert; there was an eager knowingness in his expression as he looked at her that made her recoil a little. Sophie had no airs and graces about her — who could in a village like Haworth? — but she knew herself to be a reasonably personable young lady, and disliked extremely the marked favours Mr Lambert paid her. He must be forty-five if he was a day, a small leathery man of no sensibility whatsoever; not at all the sort who would appeal to her, with her tastes for books and music and scientific enquiry. But with her poor

2

old friends waiting so hopefully at Town End Bottom for her help she could not indulge her own humours, but must be polite to Mr Lambert, while yet chilly enough to repel any unseemly advances.

She escaped from the shop as soon as she could, clutching her embrocation in her hand and glad to leave the dusty interior with its tall bottles filled with coloured water and its sickly smell of sassafras and quassia chips, and stood on the stone kerb outside to take a deep breath of the bitter air. It tasted fresh and good, and she felt better; she would hurry home now, going up through Changegate to the rough moors' edge above the village, and would finish her rounds this afternoon; for if she delayed much longer, she thought, as the church clock struck the half hour, Bessie would be waiting with her arms akimbo and the rough edge of her tongue ready to complain about her hoydenish, gormless ways.

But before she could step down into the roadway the sound of hooves and wheels came clattering past the grey stone houses and a most elegant equipage, drawn by two glossy black horses, drew alongside her. She shrank back against Mr Lambert's shop doorway to allow it to go past, for the roadway was narrow and not really meant to accommodate quite so splendid a vehicle and pair. Such might be seen on the wider, busier streets of Bradford, or even Keighley, but here in Haworth it was all out of place.

But the horses were pulled back on a tight rein and the carriage stopped and Sophie blinked and looked up as the door opened and a voice came ringingly through the folds of her shawl which she had pulled over her head, ready for the cold walk home.

'My dear Miss Lackland! What *do* you think you are doing, standing there like that?'

'Good morning, Mrs Brotherton. Good morning, Wilfred,' Sophie said calmly after a moment, and she pulled her shawl back down to her shoulders, so that her brown hair, drawn to each side of her head in neat wings, was slightly ruffled. It was not a fashionable style, although it suited her round face well enough, and generally she did not care much about fashion anyway. But looking up now at Mrs Brotherton staring down at her from her splendid carriage, she was keenly aware of her deficiencies.

Mrs Brotherton's own hair was dressed in a series of convoluted curls and waves which were piled high on her head, surmounted by a small hat so lusciously trimmed with feathers and flowers that hardly any of the glossy black plaited straw of the brim could be seen. A charming hat, in many ways, thought Sophie, although over Mrs Brotherton's rather too red cheeks and rather too jowly jaws and heavy-lidded eyes it lost some of its attraction.

Not that Mrs Brotherton seemed aware of the fact, for she was clearly very pleased with the way her hat became her, as well as with her striped mantle of purple cloth trimmed with rich sable, and her tiered, massively frilled crimson skirt, welling up around her large shape as she sat very straight backed in her velvet upholstered carriage.

'You look too absurd, my dear, you really do, standing there like some mill girl in that dreadful shawl! You really are very naughty, is she not, Wilfred?' And she turned her head and smiled with bright archness at the young man on the facing seat.

But he was already on his feet and jumped out on to the cobbles to stand beside Sophie, his curly-brimmed round hat held in one leather-gloved hand.

'How pleasant to see you, Miss Sophie,' he said in his usual rather stilted way, and smiled at her, his lips closed and rather stiff. 'I trust you are well?'

'Very well, thank you, Wilfred,' Sophie said, and then raised her voice a little. 'I enjoy better health, I am happy to say, than most of the mill girls I know, however much like them I might look!'

'Oh, Sophie, pay no attention,' he muttered, and then loudly enough for his mother to hear, added, 'My dear Miss Sophie, you look, as ever, precisely as you should — I imagine you have been about some of your benevolent affairs in the village? It is wisest always to dress for one's occupations, and you clearly are *very* wise on this score ——'

'I do my best,' Sophie said, and now she made no effort to hide her irritation with Mrs Brotherton, staring up at her with her chin set at a sharp angle and her lips in a hard line. 'I am sorry if my appearance displeases you, ma'am,' she said loudly and bobbed a curtsy, the sort of deferential curtsy the village children were taught to produce for the gentry, and then added with even greater mock humility, 'I am sure I would not wish to offend you in any way but you know, the weather is very cold, and I have not the means to purchase any garment more suitable. I trust you will forgive me for it.'

4

'Oh, do not distress yourself, child!' Mrs Brotherton said and produced a chilly smile. 'I am not upbraiding you, you know. I have not the right, after all —'

'Have you not, ma'am?' Sophie said sweetly, but Mrs Brotherton went on, choosing to ignore the edge in Sophie's voice, '— I simply find it sad that a young lady of breeding should set so poor an example to the village people.'

'They are more interested in my deeds than my appearance, Mrs Brotherton,' Sophie said, and deliberately pulled up her shawl and set it over her ears in exactly the way the clog-wearing girls from the Eburs Mill did. 'I doubt they are as concerned with fashion as they might be. They are often too hungry, or too ill, you know.'

'Yes — no doubt —' Mrs Brotherton said vaguely and tweaked at her mantle. 'Wilfred, we must get on, you know. I have a host of things to do at The Hall —— Good morning, Miss Lackland ——'

'Mamma, you seem to have forgotten why we stopped!' Wilfred said sharply. 'I am sure you would not wish to do so.'

'What was that, my dear boy?' Mrs Brotherton said, and looked wide-eyed at her son, and shook her head slightly; but he ignored such obvious signals and turned to Sophie. 'We wish to ask you to join us, Miss Sophie, at a small gathering at home ——'

This was too much for Mrs Brotherton. 'We are having an evening party, Miss Lackland, at The Hall, you know, for a few select people — no more than thirty or so, I do promise you, just for a few *select* people, you understand. Some music, a little conversation, a cold collation ——'

'It sounds very agreeable,' Sophie said. 'And most select.'

'Please come, Miss Sophie!' Wilfred said, and then in an undertone, 'It will be a dead bore for me if you do not!'

'I am afraid I cannot, Mr Brotherton,' Sophie said, and smiled at him, but there was little of friendship in it. 'I have not a suitable toilette, you know, for so — *select* — a party. You must forgive me.'

'Oh, you need not concern yourself unduly with that, Miss Lackland,' Mrs Brotherton said graciously. 'I am sure people will understand and forgive you. And it will be an agreeable evening for you, and it would be a pity for you to miss the opportunity to ——'

'Even if I had a suitable gown, Mrs Brotherton, I am afraid it is out of the question.' Sophie was thoroughly nettled now and made

5

no effort to hide the fact. 'I have promised Mrs Ribble I will take on the care of the people down in Town End Bottom from Friday noon until Monday morning, so that Doctor Tom and she can go to visit their married daughter in Sheffield, who has just been brought to bed of a fine son —' and her lips quirked as Mrs Brotherton drew back in distaste from so blunt a statement of such unmentionable matters as childbirth, '— and I would not disappoint her for the world.'

'Oh, Sophie, surely Dr Ingham can take his share of such a burden! He is a physician after all, and you are not. Although I know, of course, you are a very careful and experienced nurse —' Wilfred added hastily as Sophie turned her sharp gaze on him. 'I was so hoping you would be one of our party.'

Sophie shook her head. 'I really am sorry, Wilfred, and I am sure you mean kindly,' she said quietly. 'But it is quite true that I have made a promise and Dr Ingham, you know, has a heavy cold himself, and is getting old now, after all.'

'The evening will be a dreadful bore without you,' he said softly, turning his shoulder slightly so that his mother could not see his face as he spoke. 'Could you not come, and if any of the people there need you, let me send you down in the carriage?'

Again she shook her head. 'Please, Wilfred, don't be so tiresome! If I cannot, I cannot. But I am sure your invitation was kindly meant,' and the little emphasis she put on 'your' made his face redden a little.

'Indeed it was,' he said shortly, and turned back to the carriage. 'Mamma, you go home. I shall escort Miss Lackland to her home, and then walk back.'

'Walk all the way to The Hall?' Mrs Brotherton said, scandalized. 'Oh, really, Wilfred, this is sheer quixotry! I never heard of anything so ——' But Wilfred had slammed the door closed upon her expostulating face and signalled to the coachman and the carriage went off with a rattle, the cold horses eagerly pulling away towards a warm stable and hot mash.

'I am sorry, Sophie, I truly am,' Wilfred said after a moment and put his hand on her arm. 'I would not have your feelings hurt for the world! I try all I can to make my Mamma behave, but you know, she is a strong-minded woman and ——'

'Oh, it is not your fault, Wilfred!' Sophie said and smiled and

6

tucked her hand comfortably into the crook of his elbow. 'I should not let her airs and graces irritate me so, but it is difficult, when I have known you so long and know quite well that you are a dear good friend, of sterling worth and so many good qualities, but far from being a member of a family of any great renown ——'

He laughed at that, and they started to walk, continuing on up the street towards the church and the path behind the Parsonage that led to the moors, and to Tansey Clough. Sophie was glad to have him beside her, for his sturdy body was warm and kept the wind away in a most agreeable manner, and he was, after all, a very old friend. Had they not played together in the stones of the becks in their childhood days? Had he not brought her home many times in her torn and muddy gown and stoutly lied to Bessie that it was all his fault, and that he had led her into wicked ways, when it had been quite the other way about?

She hugged his arm against her body suddenly, in an access of pleasure, and smiled up at him. 'Dear Wilfred! I'm happy for you that your Papa made so much money with his wool affairs, but you know, it has been shocking bad for your Mamma! It has quite ruined her character. Some people should never be rich, should they? They cannot handle it as it should be handled ——'

'You would handle it well, Sophie ——' he began, and at once Sophie started to chatter. She had become adept at knowing when Wilfred was about to declare himself, and equally adept at preventing him. And today was no exception.

'But let us talk no more of riches or select evening parties or clothes! Tell me what you are doing at the mill and how it is you can spare the time to accompany me home in this way. You will be scolded dreadfully by Joseph Barraclough, will you not, for such dereliction of your duties?'

'Joseph Barraclough is an excellent spinner and foreman, Sophie, but I am master of my own mill and never you think otherwise!'

She laughed at that, and looked at him, and bowed her head in mock deference. He was as comfortable to look at as to be with, with his square face and the sleek brown whiskers that framed it; while he was far from being a follower of fashion, Wilfred Brotherton was by no means lacking in self-esteem, and when the Bradford dandies began to appear in mutton-chop whiskers, he soon followed suit, for the style suited him well. His brown eyes above a strong nose were large and bright and the whiskers balanced his face. He had thick broad shoulders — for he was not above hauling bales of wool and yarn about, for all he was master of his own mill — and was altogether an agreeable specimen of twenty-eight-year-old Yorkshire manhood. He might be a bit stiff in his ways sometimes, but he was a good friend and she was glad of him.

'I cannot think where the morning has gone,' she said, a little breathless now as they climbed sharply up past the grey stone walls and on to the rough moorland path that led to the old house in which she had been born. 'I spent no longer, I swear, in each house, but here I am, with half the visits I meant to make not yet done. I shall have to return this afternoon, for they will be sorely disappointed ——'

'Why do you set yourself so disagreeable a task, Sophie?' Wilfred said. 'Those Town End families are hardly your sort of company, and the houses are disgustingly kept ——'

'Oh, not at all,' she said, loyalty triumphing over truthfulness. 'They do all they can to be clean, but it is not easy when you share a pump with five other households, and one midden, too, must serve five families' needs, and the wretched thing overflows and carries stench and disease everywhere it wills! They try so hard, and they are so much in need of care and ——'

'Well, of that I am sure. But why *you*? Dr Ribble, after all, is the Town End physician and it is his affair, but you are a lady and ——'

'Oh, pooh to being a lady,' Sophie said and laughed, turning her gaze on him and shaking her head so that some of her hair flew loose, and tendrils wrapped themselves around her throat. 'To be a lady requires money, and I have none since Mamma and Papa died. And even if I had, I would not wish to use it to be ladylike, you know. Your Mamma would give me up as completely lost if she knew that, would she not? You must understand, Will, that I *like* what I do for the families there. I have learned so much from Doctor Tom of illness, and the workings of the human body. I am quite fascinated by — well, let us just say it is work for which I have a natural bent ——'

Not even to Wilfred could she confide the way she really felt about working with Doctor Tom, about her gratitude to the frail old man for all he had told her over the years since she had been a hoydenish fifteen-year-old, bursting with energy and curiosity and having no way in which to use such qualities.

He had opened more to her than the doors of the poverty-stricken houses at Town End. He had awakened in her a hunger for knowledge of the human organism which sometimes maddened her in its intensity. Why? How? For what purpose? She would watch ill people get well again, or sicken and die and ask the same questions over and over, and Doctor Tom, bless him, would answer them to the best of his ability, for all she was a girl, and a lady at that. Whatever a lady might be. For from all she had seen — and she had seen much these past eight years — the mill girls' bodies and pains and needs were little different from her own. But none of this could she explain to Wilfred, friend of her childhood though he was.

'Anyway, there is a need for me there and it is agreeable to be needed, is it not? You would have been most unhappy, dear Wilfred, if your Papa had not died so opportune and left you the mill to run. Oh, do not look so shocked! You know he was an old tyrant and bullied you shockingly! I cheered for you when he died, and I am not ashamed to say it. It was one of the few good moments in those bad times. And it pleases me greatly now to see you so happy with your workers and your wool. You are needed there, and it is splendid indeed that you are, for otherwise, imagine! You would have to be with your Mamma even more than you are!'

He shook his head at her, trying to look disapproving, but he could not. Not with Sophie, who had always, as long as he had known her, said what she thought to him, and hidden no secrets from him at all.

And she was right, of course. His father had been as tyrannical as his mother was empty-headed and frivolous and given to putting on airs of gentility, although she had started life as no more than a hatter's daughter from Bradford and a hatter in a very small way of business at that. Many times Wilfred would bless the day when he had met the wild, leggy young Sophie and become her friend, for she had opened his eyes to so much, to so many different ideas and feelings and attitudes. She had made him a better man than he could ever have been without her friendship, he would tell himself in the long dark nights when he lay wondering how he was ever to

9

persuade her to become his wife, as he so dearly wished her to. But how was he to succeed when somehow she always managed to prevent him from speaking his heart?

Oh, a very special person was Sophie Lackland to Wilfred Brotherton, and had been these fifteen years. Perhaps too long, he sometimes thought, for how could she regard as a romantic figure a man she had seen grow from an awkward twelve-year-old to his present masculine maturity? Not that the fact that he had known her since she was an eight-year-old scrap — with hair that hung down her back and got tangled in the heather when she rolled down the beck sides, and narrow green eyes that worried him dreadfully, so lively was their glance, so disturbing their depths — had affected him. He loved the grown-up Sophie quite desperately and did not know what to do about it.

They were almost at the top of the rise now, and the buildings of Haworth were no more than a cluster of grey roofs far below. A mist was rising and her hair was beaded with little globes of moisture and he put his hand out to touch her. At once she smiled brilliantly at him, but somehow contrived to read his mind, to hear the words he had been about to speak, and pulled away.

'Oh, Wilfred, I am such a fool! I am quite the greatest fool in all the West Riding. Do you see what I have here? Mrs Binns's embrocation! And the poor old dear will be waiting and wondering and aching for want of it! Please, dear Wilfred, please, will you take it to her? If you hurry back down the moor she will have it as soon as I would have taken it to her had I not so cruelly forgotten and set off home for my luncheon. Please, will you, Wilfred?'

He sighed and held out his hand unwillingly. 'Well, if you have made up your mind to it that I must do so, then I have no choice. I know that well enough! But surely it could wait until ——'

'Oh, indeed it cannot, Wilfred. She hurts all over, she really does! Her poor old joints, you see, are so arthritic. Please?'

He stood there for a moment with the embrocation in his hand, and then nodded and smiled wearily and turned back down the path.

'Well, as I say, I have little choice! I am sorry you cannot be with us on Friday, Sophie — but I will contrive to visit you, perhaps in the next day or two? May I do so?'

'Of course you can, you foolish creature,' Sophie said, and

10

laughed, and began to climb further up the path. 'You know I am always glad to see you, for you are my oldest friend, are you not? Goodbye — away w'ye, lad ——'

And with that little scrap of the local dialect ringing in his ears he had to be content, as she went on up the greying misty moor towards Tansey Clough, the old grey house that stood tucked between two folds of the hills waiting for her.

CHAPTER TWO

She slipped in quietly through the back door, praying Bessie would be elsewhere in the house, in the hope of convincing her that in fact she had been home for some time; but she should have known such subterfuge would gain her nothing. As soon as her foot touched the scrubbed stone flags of the kitchen floor Bessie was there in the doorway, her arms folded across her chest and her face set in a scowl.

'An' what sort of a time does tha call this to be comin' home for tha food, then?' she demanded. 'Half an hour Ah've bin stood here, with as fine a bit o' mutton as we've seen this twelvemonth drying out in th'oven, and you givin' it no more thought than if it'd ——'

'Oh, Bessie, I am so sorry!' Sophie sat down in the big rocker by the wide range, and began to unlace her shoes. 'I did not mean to be late, you know ——'

'Nay, tha never does, does tha? 'Alf an hour! I've bin that worritted ——'

'Oh, worried, worried! You worry if a fly goes sideways instead of straight up. What on earth is there to worry about, for heaven's sake? I've been in Town End Bottom, and ——'

'That's enough to worrit anybody,' Bessie said darkly, as she carefully took a dish from the oven on the range and set it on a tray. 'Those folks dahn there — no better than they ought to be, and as dirty an' feckless a lot as ever ——'

'I've told you before, Bessie,' Sophie said sharply, 'that I won't listen to you complain about those people. It is no sin to be poor — and they are *very* poor. To be clean is a luxury and if you are ill most of the time and you have no conveniences at all, it is small wonder you cannot be as perfect in your housekeeping as some are.'

'Conveniences!' Bessie said, and slapped the tray down on the kitchen table. 'Conveniences is it? An' me runnin' this house wi' no help apart from me own two 'ands, and fetchin' every drop o' water from t'beck, and no 'ope of ever gettin' t'gas up here, and all those oil lamps to be fettled up an' —— '

'Oh, Bessie, please let us not quarrel! I am late, and I am sorry. Let us leave it at that.' Sophie came over to the square figure and hugged her, and kissed her cheek, and after a moment Bessie sniffed.

'Well, just you remember, my lass, as there's others in this world beside thissen, an' that some o' those others is concerned wi' thy wellbein'. An' now come and sup thi food. 'Tis a good dish, mutton an' apples, the way tha likes it.'

'Lovely,' Sophie said, 'An' I'm fair starved — no, don't look at me like that! Why shouldn't I speak good Yorkshire if I choose? Come, Bessie, let me eat in here, by the fire, and you sit down and have some with me —— '

'I'll do no such thing!' Bessie said, scandalized. 'Away an' wash thissen and into t'dinin' room at once! Eat in here! I never heerd o' sich a thing!'

Obediently Sophie went, climbing the wide wooden staircase to her room where a polished brass can full of hot water stood waiting for her, cooling now but still warm enough to be pleasant to use. As she washed and dried her hands she looked about her, enjoying as she always did the sight of the neat half-tester bed with its white counterpane, the well-made if simple oak furniture, the green and white dimity curtains that framed the window and its view of the moors, yet at the same time feeling herself filled with a mixture of guilt and shame. That she should enjoy such comfort while those others with whom she had spent her morning should live in such squalor — it was all wrong. She caught the scent of hot mutton, savoury and rich, as Bessie went clattering across the hall downstairs towards the dining room, and the guilt sharpened. They were lucky to eat sour bread, while she ate butcher's meat. All *wrong*.

But for all that, she ate with relish, under Bessie's watchful eye, for she waited at table, insisting always that the house be run 'like a gentleman's house should' for all there was only Sophie and herself there. It had been years now since any new furnishings had been bought for Tansey Clough, and the curtains and carpets had been darned and turned so often there was hardly a patch that was not worn to its last threads. But it sparkled, the whole house sparkled under Bessie's unremitting labours. Brass doorknobs and fireplace

13

fittings gleamed in the grey afternoon like small suns, and the furniture glowed with a satin richness from hours of polishing with beeswax. The table cloth was snowy white, and beautifully darned, and the plates from which Sophie ate — she had now started on a piece of sugar-sprinkled pie fluffed with pastry and plump with apples — positively shone.

'Oh, Bessie, we are so *rich*, are we not?' she said impulsively, her mouth full. 'We have so much to be grateful for.'

'Rich, is it?' Bessie said and snorted. 'Wi' t'house fair fallin' about our ears for want of a bit of attention, and grocer's bills as'd put t'fear o' God into a heathen? Tha's daft to think so!'

'Oh, I know we are not rich as — as the Brothertons are rich, but when you see how it is for some of the people in the village, oh, Bessie, we are indeed fortunate!'

'Thou'll be called to join t'saints if tha goes on that road! Tha's soundin' too good to live! Ah've told thee before this, Miss Sophie, an Ah'll tell thee again, Ah don't 'old wi' all this lakin' about in Town End, wi' folks as feckless and as mucky as a lot o' pigs! Tha should stay at 'ome and mind thy manners, and visit wi' t'other young ladies and gentlemen and live a proper life!'

'And I've told you, Bessie, that I cannot. It would be too insipid to be borne! If I must live here in Haworth, I must do *something* — and that it all there is for me. What else could I do?'

'Find thissen a husband!' Bessie said, and put a platter of cheese on the table with a thump. 'Nay, don't thee throw looks like that! Ah know what ah knows, an' that's what's right. Thy mother must be fair spinnin' in 'er grave to see 'er last remaining lass be'avin' as you do! A respectable married lady as was Susannah Greenhalgh — if she were 'ere, it'd all be different, that Ah know. She'd never 'ave let thee go on this road ——'

'Would she not, Bessie? I am not so sure. She did not have so wonderful a time as a married lady, after all — and *her* family ——'

'Aye well, less said about them, soonest mended,' Bessie said sharply, and her face reddened a little and from her place behind Sophie's chair she reached out with one big red hand and touched the girl's shoulder awkwardly. 'Tha knows my feelin's on that score. Ah told 'em, aye, that Ah did, told 'em fair an' square, but — eh, lass, it were a sorry day when you was left alone in the world wi' none but a parcel o' selfish, wicked ——'

14

'I am not alone in the world, Bessie, for I have you,' Sophie said, and stood up and put her arm about the older woman's shoulders. 'I have always had you, have I not? So I have no need to be anxious for my care. Though why you will not do as I bid you and wed your Josiah ——'

'Ah've told thee,' Bessie said flatly, and began to collect the dishes. 'Ah've told thee till Ah'm blue, I stop 'ere wi' thee, where Ah've bin since thee were nobbut a baby in short coats until such time as thee sees sense and gets thissen a husband. Then Ah can tak' mine. Not before.'

'Oh, Bessie, that is blackmail, and well you know it! How can I marry, just like that? And who is there to marry, anyway?'

'Who? Why there's young gentlemen in these parts and in Bradford as'd tak' thee so fast — there's young Mr Booth — Edwin, that one, and there's the Reverend Patchett as teaches at the Grammar School — now 'e's a right gentleman 'e is, an wi' a fair income of 'is own, I'm told, for all 'e spends 'is time teachin' those 'eathen lads ——'

'Me? A reverend schoolmaster's wife? Oh, Bessie, can you see it! I am much too frivolous for such a one. He would shake his head over my hoydenish ways even more than you do.'

'Well, then, what abaht Wilfred Brotherton, then? 'E's bin sweet on thee these past dozen years or more, and 'e's thine for the askin', or my name's not Bessie Pighills! Now, 'e'd be a grand husband for thee, as warm as they come, they tell me, wi' that mill fair coinin' brass ——'

'Now, Bessie, that is enough! I will not talk of this another moment. I do not wish to marry anyone, not now or ever. From all I see, people wed each other in these parts with more concern for what is in their pockets than what is in their hearts, and I couldn't bear it! But you should marry, for Josiah Oldenshaw and you have been walking out more years than I can remember and ——'

'Well, we can go on the same road as long as it suits us. An' it suits me to stay as I am until I get thee off 'ands. So, there's all about it. Now, will you go and settle to some sewin' in the drawin' room an' ——'

'No, Bessie, I'm going out again. I was not half finished this morning, for there was so much to do at Mrs Ackroyd's house, for the baby is very sick, and ——'

'Not again!'

'Aye, lass, again!' Sophie said and laughed. 'You'll never be used to me, Bessie, will you? Or I to you! Ah well, it stops us being bored with each other. Come, let me help you with those dishes and then I must be on my way.'

'Tha'll do no sich thing! Ah'll fettle me own pots — but if tha'll wait nobbut a few minutes, Ah'll walk down to t'village wi' thee. Ah must go to t'post office — there should be a letter from me niece in Leeds — go and put on tha heavy boots, now! There'll be more rain on the way, Ah'm thinkin' and tha needs to keep thy feet dry, if tha's dead set on muckin' abaht in Town End Bottom ——'

They walked side by side in amiable silence down the moor path, fifteen minutes later, on the way to the village, both wearing their thick shawls and heavy boots to keep out the bitter cold. Already the November afternoon was shortening to darkness, and the sky sat over the moors as heavy and threatening as a headache. Sophie shivered and tucked her hand into Bessie's elbow, and the older woman grinned at her and they walked on, still in silence, but happy to be in each other's company.

Bessie Pighills had been part of Sophie's life as long as she could remember. She had come to Tansey Clough, a gawky red-faced country girl, to be nursemaid to the sickly Lackland boys, first George, and then Brinsley; but both had died before they were in short coats, and lay now among the cluster of infants' graves in Haworth churchyard. Sophie could remember her mother's dependence on Bessie, who, as the years had gone on and two more children had arrived at Tansey Clough, had become more and more important to all of them. Sophie smiled reminiscently into the folds of her shawl as she thought of the way Letty, lovely, naughty, beautiful Letty, so clever in her two years' seniority, had taught her to tease Bessie, and how to cozen out of her pieces of sticky parkin on baking day. It had been so lovely in those years as the two girls had grown up, even though Mamma had spent most of her time on her sofa, ailing and devoting herself to her Bible study, for there had been, as well as comfortable Bessie, Papa.

Papa. Her face tightened, remembering Papa. Such a funny man, such a delight to be with, such heaven for a child to love and grow up with. But such misery in these later grown-up years, when

16

his daughters had to face the fact that for all his charm he was a feckless lazy man, much given to gambling, with a taste for such low sports as cock-fighting and whippet racing. First Letty and then Sophie had realized that life at Tansey Clough was much harder than it need be because of the way Papa went through money.

And then had come the shame of discovering from Mamma's hateful pompous brother Nathan Greenhalgh that they lived on Greenhalgh alms.

'For as long as my sister lives, she'll not want,' Uncle Nathan had boomed at Papa at the height of one of their frequent arguments. 'But I tell you now — to your face I tell you, Bartholomew Lackland, that not a penny shall you see of mine from the day Susannah dies. You and your airs-and-graces brats will starve before I'll lift a finger to help you!' And nineteen-year-old Letty had sneered at him, and mocked him, and Sophie had too, for Papa's face had looked so stricken — oh, that had been a dreadful day. Dreadful.

But not so dreadful, she thought now, as the day when first Mamma had gone down with the typhoid fever, when the epidemic hit the village like a tornado; and then Papa; and then, oh then, dear darling Letty, so full of life and hope and beauty ——

Her eyes suddenly pricked with pain as a picture of Letty rose before her eyes. Not Letty with her dark curls falling over her shoulders and her great grey eyes alight with wickedness, but Letty lying so still and ugly on her tumbled bed, Letty exhausted and ruined by the speed with which the fever had attacked her, as dead and as empty as the sheep carcasses Sophie sometimes found on the high tops, when the weather had been particularly bad. To lose Letty had been dreadful, and she could not even seek comfort from anyone else, for with both Papa and Mamma sick of the same fever and Bessie red-eyed and grim as she tried to nurse them both and yet protect Sophie from being infected, who was there to turn to? Not even Wilfred, for his father had fever too. And his father had died of it.

She had wanted to go and see Wilfred, to seek his comfort because of Letty, for he had known and loved her well, but how could she, with his mother 'carryin' on alarmin'' as Bessie reported, having been told by the baker's roundsman of Mrs Brotherton's exaggerated grief.

'For all she's treated 'im like dirt these past twenty years, and wanted him for nowt but 'is brass all along ——' Bessie had snorted. 'Oh, Miss Sophie, will you tak' this down to t'village for me? Ah'm needin' it filled for thy Ma. An' the walk'll do thee good. Tha's lookin' right peaky ——'

So Sophie had gone down to the village, walking along this very path they were walking now, carrying the empty medicine bottle to be refilled by Mr Lambert at the druggist's shop, and feeling only numb inside, trying to remember that Letty really was dead, and would never be alive again, no matter how many tears were wept for her.

And when she had come back, climbing up the moor through the darkening evening, she found Bessie sitting in the kitchen, rocking, with her apron flung up over her head, and both her parents dead upstairs. And she had stood there dry eyed and cold and not been able to care, for it was Letty who had used up all her grief, Letty's loss which had pre-empted all other losses.

Again she shivered, walking down the moor this afternoon with Bessie beside her, and the older woman looked at her sharply and said, 'What ails thee, lass? Goose walked over thy grave?'

'I was remembering,' Sophie said. 'Mamma and Papa ——' But she did not talk of Letty. She never did. She never could, not even to Bessie.

'Well, there's no use in dwellin' on past miseries. We've enough to fret us over what's here and now,' Bessie said sharply, but she pressed Sophie's hand for all that and resolutely Sophie marched on, enjoying the clump of her boots on the heathery path.

As the village roofs lifted into view below them, Bessie said awkwardly, 'Since we've mentioned times past, Miss Sophie, Ah might as well tell thee — Ah've bin in touch wi' them Greenhalgh folks ——'

Sophie stopped sharply and pulled on Bessie's arm, and made her turn to look at her. 'You did what?'

'Nay, lass, don't try to frighten me! Ah knew thee'd not be best pleased, so Ah did it off my own bat. Ah'm not one to sit around whingein' when a few words in the right direction might make all the difference.'

'I'm not taking a penny from them, not if they were to try to force it into my hands,' Sophie said passionately. 'You hear me, Bessie? I'll not take ——'

'Well, there's no call to get thi rag up. It won't be necessary to tak' owt, for Ah got nowt but abuse for me pains. Ah told 'em as 'ow we was livin' on nowt minus tuppence a week, with the little yer Pa left an' all, and only a few of thi Ma's bits and pieces left to be sold, an' that man — dost tha know what that man said?'

'Something hateful, I'll be bound.'

'He said as 'e'd buy Tansey Clough from thee, for two hundred pounds — two hundred!'

'I always knew he was hateful,' Sophie said, with a sort of satisfaction in her voice. 'Now I know he's wicked as well. Why, Tansey Clough is worth an *enormous* amount more than that. It's a fine old house, been standing there close on two hundred years, and solid as the day it was built, and with all those fine rooms — how dare he make such an insulting offer! If I hadn't sworn never to speak to him again, I'd go there and I'd — I'd ——'

'Well, the only reason Ah told thee what Ah'd done was because 'e said as 'e'd be comin' round to Tansey Clough to make the offer 'issen. I told 'im not to bother — to go find another orphan to rob ——'

Sophie giggled and they started walking again. 'Did you say that, Bessie? Good for you! He is a robber, of course, but to tell him so to his face — oh, lovely!'

'Aye, that Ah did,' Bessie said, and grinned as well. But her face still bore a worried look. 'Thing is, Miss Sophie, we've got to face up to t'problem. We're down to the last of our brass, near enough, and I'm getting mortal worritted, that I am. Everythin' costs so much these days, an' it's not as though we could even raise any food of our own — not so much as a cabbage could we grow up at Tansey Clough, could we? Though Ah dessay we might run to a pig or two, or mebbe a few sheep, and see if we can ——'

'Oh, please, Bessie, don't worry. I shall go and see Mr Fordyce. He may know of other resources upon which Mamma and Papa drew, or other ways in which we can manage. He is a very good lawyer, I know, and I am sure he will think of something.'

'Aye, well, as long as it's not a matter of sellin' Tansey Clough to yon Greenhalgh crew, then Ah'm content. Ah'll turn washerwoman first, that Ah will!' Bessie said, and then, as they reached the top of the village pulled her shawl more firmly about her shoulders, and nodded briskly at Sophie.

19

'Well, Ah'll go to t'post office first, and then spend a few minutes wi' Josiah — an' see to it that thee's back at a proper time tonight, now, for big as thou art, I'll give thee what for if th'art late again ——'

'I won't be, Bessie, I promise. Oh — good! There's Dr Ribble's gig — Doctor Tom — Doctor Tom! —' and she ran down the cobbled street towards the Black Bull, leaving Bessie shaking her head in disapproval behind her.

The next three hours were contented ones for Sophie. Doctor Tom was his usual comfortable self, though obviously tired and in much need of a few days' rest, and was as glad to see her as he always was.

'For, Sophie, you are without doubt the best nurse there is in these parts! If some of Dr Ingham's richer patients could have the sort of care you give our poor friends down here at Town End Bottom, why, they would think themselves in very heaven! I tell you, my dear child, you're a credit to an old man's teaching.'

She laughed at that, and jumped lightly from the gig, holding her hand up to the old man to guide him down. As one of the urchins led the horse away to rest its weary old bones in the lee of one of the houses, the two of them went into the first of the cramped hovels that housed so many tired and ill-fed people at this end of the village.

The Ackroyd baby was still very ill, fretful and yet floppy, lying in a heap of ragged blankets on a table top, his mother — a girl of little more than seventeen, with a face as pale as a pudding and eyes which were heavy and dull — sitting lumpishly beside him.

'I got him to take some water this morning from a spoon, Doctor Tom,' Sophie said softly. 'But he still seems to be very short of fluid, does he not? So hot and dry to the touch ——'

Doctor Tom was peering at the child, and then after a moment lifted him and carried him to the doorway, to look at the red face and snuffling nose in the bleak daylight.

'Hmmph,' he said after a moment, and then, turning the baby's head even more into the light looked more closely at his face.

'See this, Sophie? Look now, at his skin — you see? A fine granular rash is beginning — d'you see? Now, what would you say ——'

'Measles,' Sophie said, and looked back over her shoulder at the baby's mother, still sitting dully at the table, staring into space. But she seemed not to have heard. 'Oh, dear, measles. Is there anything we can do?'

'Nursing is the only answer, and good food and a clean fresh bed and — all the things he cannot have. The question is, how many other children will get it now? Oh, drat it and damn it, if you'll forgive the language, Sophie, but this is all I needed to fill my cup to overflowing with anxiety. Measles in Town End Bottom ——'

He turned to Mrs Ackroyd. 'My dear, how many others have been in to see you since young William here took ill?'

'Eh? Oh, nobbut the lasses from Mrs Stoney's — and then Mrs Reddihough, she come in wi' her little lad — Eh, Doctor, but t'babe's been that mardy! I can't get 'im to take nobbut a sip o' water once or twice, for all Miss told me as I should keep on — but 'e's that mardy ——'

'I'm afraid he has the measles, Mrs Ackroyd,' Doctor Tom said gently. 'No, do not look so alarmed, my dear. While there is yet life, you know — but we must try to get him more care than you can give, for you are still not well yourself, are you? When will your man be back?'

''E's away over to Colne, doin' a job 'e reckons'll tak' till Christmas, and bring in some reet good brass, too, if all they've promised be true — but Ah could send for me mam, if it's measles. She understands measles, does me mam ——'

'I'll see she gets a message,' Doctor Tom said and, putting his head outside the door, whistled. One of the many small boys who hung about the narrow reeking street came running, barefoot in spite of the bitter cold.

'Take this message up to the post office,' he said, scribbling on a piece of paper. 'Now, the direction, Mrs Ackroyd —'

While he dealt with the message and the careful instructing of the child, Sophie busied herself about the tiny dark room, sweeping the floor with a worn-out besom she found behind the door, and making up the fire with the last scraps of coal piled beside it.

'I'll send some more coal up tonight, Mrs Ackroyd,' she promised, trying not to think of how low their own stocks were at Tansey Clough.

In the next two houses there were old people to be looked to; Mrs

Whitaker needing a new dressing to her leg, which had a hideously oozing ulcer, and then Mr Murgatroyd, a difficult old man whose crippled hips filled him with such rage he could hardly bring himself to be civil to anyone, even Doctor Tom and Sophie, both of whom he knew well and trusted. But they understood him well enough, and interpreted his grunts with equanimity.

And then there were the women recovering from their confinements, three of them, who needed comforting washes and attention of so intimate a nature that they would never allow Doctor Tom to give it, even though he had delivered their babies for them; and one of them needed poultices made for the breast abscess which was causing her to be so ill and feverish. Sophie mixed the poultice from bread and linseed oil and heated it over the struggling fire in the little stove, wishing not for the first time that she could carry these sick women away to Tansey Clough and care for them where all was so clean and comfortable.

She said as much to Doctor Tom, but he shook his head at her. 'No, my dear, it does you credit that you have so generous a wish, but to take people away from their homes, however poor those homes might be, is no answer. My house, you know, suits me as yours suits you, and these folk are suited well enough here. It would be better if they had good water, and decent drains as they have in some parts of Bradford now for the poorer houses, but the houses themselves, poor as they may seem to you, are right for them. Remember that always, my dear, if you wish to care for the sick. Good as it is to have hospitals and such like establishments for their care, it is home which is always the best, however mean a hovel it may be ——'

It was quite dark by the time they had finished the last visit, where they had drained an abscess in a child's ear, with Sophie holding the frightened screeching three-year-old firmly on her lap while Doctor Tom wielded his blade as best he could in the flickering light of an ill-trimmed oil lamp. When the lancing was done, and the child had settled to rest on his grateful mother's lap, they made their way out into the street, and Doctor Tom whistled and the urchin who had been so patiently guarding his gig and horse all afternoon came hurrying to deliver the reins into the doctor's hands, and receive his penny reward.

'I will take you to the top of the village, Sophie, and then I shall walk with you the rest of the way. It is getting bitter now —— ' and indeed the wind was howling cruelly past the buildings, sobbing and keening like a sick child.

'You will do no such thing,' Sophie said firmly. 'For you are tired out yourself and need to be at home by your own fireside. To Changegate you may take me and glad I'll be of the ride — but after that my own feet are good enough ——'

'I'll not hear of it ——'

Arguing amiably they sat side by side as the horse clopped wearily up the steep ill-lit street, and at the top, just as the street turned towards the Parsonage, Sophie gathered herself together and made to jump down.

'I'll not wait for you,' she called cheerfully. 'So you might as well sit tight, for I will be half way over the moor before you have tethered the nag. Good night, Doctor Tom ——'

'Oh, Miss Sophie, is that thee? Miss Sophie!'

She turned her head to peer into the dimness, and then saw her. Bessie, one hand clutching her shawl close beneath her chin and the other hand hidden in its folds.

'Bessie, whatever is the matter? You must be frozen solid — whatever has happened that you are out here at this hour of the evening?'

'Oh, Miss Sophie, Ah've bin waitin' that long for thee! Oh, Miss Sophie — there's a letter for thee from *London*! A letter ——' and she held out a thick white envelope.

'A letter? For me? But no one ever writes me letters!' Sophie said, staring at the envelope and making no attempt to take it. 'It must be some mistake, surely ——'

'I said th'same, that Ah did — but look for thissen ——'

Sophie looked. 'The Family Lackland'. It was written in a fine cursive script on the heavy envelope. 'The Family Lackland, Tansey Clough, Haworth, Yorkshire,' and the postmark, just decipherable in the flickering light thrown from the window of the Black Bull, was 'Lincoln's Inn'.

'I think you'd better take it and read it, don't you?' Doctor Tom's voice came equably out of the darkness. 'For there is none other but you to be called the Family Lackland, is there, my dear? So whatever it is, it is your concern.'

CHAPTER THREE

Sophie would have been willing to wait till she had made the climb back up the moor to home to read the letter, but neither Bessie nor Doctor Tom could countenance that. Bessie in particular, who was chilled to the marrow from her long wait for Sophie's return from Town End, was insistent that they use Mr Sugden's private room in the Black Bull to warm themselves while Sophie read her letter.

So, there she sat with her feet stretched comfortably to the blaze in Mr Sugden's great fireplace and a glass of hot negus beside her — for Mr Sugden, as agog as anyone else over the mysterious letter, had insisted she be his guest — and turned the envelope over and over in her fingers, curiously unwilling to open it.

'Well, sitting there fretting won't give you any information,' Doctor Tom said reasonably, from the other side of the fireplace. 'It won't bite you, lass. Open it!'

So she did. There was another envelope inside and also a single sheet and she unfolded it, and smoothed it out and began to read.

The address at the top of the letter was 'Eustace Vivian and Alfred Onions, Attorneys-at-Law, Lincoln's Inn, London', and the date, Monday, November the twenty-fourth, 1873.

'Read it aloud, do, Miss Sophie,' Bessie said impulsively, and then flushed brick-red and drank a great deal of her hot ale to cover her confusion. 'Eh, Ah doan't know what coom over me, Ah don't that! 'Tis none o' my business, after all. Read it to thissen, lass, and tell us aught you choose to after ——'

'Not at all, Bessie,' Sophie said warmly. 'You are as much a member of the family — what there is of it! — as I am. We two are now the Lackland family, for I know of no others. Of course I shall read it aloud.'

Holding the letter to the light of the oil lamp on the table, she began.

'"Sir, Madam, We trust we do not in any way offend the reader of this letter in using this form of salute, but we cannot know to whom we directly address the following words. We also cannot know whether or not the message of these words is germane to yourself, since we cannot be sure that yours is the Lackland family we seek. However, we trust you will bear with us.

' "In short, we the undersigned are concerned in the matter of the Will of Mrs Maria Lackland, of Gower Street in London, deceased, who was the relict of Mr Abel Lackland, Surgeon, of Gower Street in London.

' "In order that the terms of this Will should be carried out, it has been necessary for us to search for the family of one Bartholomew Lackland, a younger son of Abel Lackland, and for whom Mrs Lackland had formed a particular attachment when she had charge of him while a governess in the house of the said Abel Lackland during the lifetime of his first wife ——" ' '

Sophie broke off and looked up at Bessie who was listening with her lips parted, and her eyes wide.

'Bessie! Papa never spoke to us of his own family, did he? I remember Letty asked him once and he laughed and said it was all too unedifying to tell so young a lady, and not to concern herself. And when she asked him again, he became quite angry and bade her not to speak of matters which did not concern her ——'

'Aye, Ah remember that well. 'E were always a close man, was thy Pa. Never said nowt more'n 'e could 'elp about personal affairs, like, on account o' the way those Greenhalgh folks were. ''Never give t'Devil an 'andle 'e can use agin yer, Bessie,'' 'e'd say to me. But I tell thee this — 'is name were Bartholomew right enough, as well you know, an' 'e did once let slip as 'ow his Pa had been a medical man. And o' course we knew as 'e wasn't a local man. Come from — well, we never rightly knew. I allus reckoned it were down south somewheres ——'

'Abel Lackland?' Doctor Tom said slowly, staring at the firelight. 'Damned if that doesn't mean something to me — beggin' your pardon, m'dear — indeed it does — d'you know, when I was a student, all those years ago, there was a surgeon we had there at Bradford Royal Infirmary, splendid chap he was, told us he'd been trained in London. Now, where was it? I must be getting old, for my memory deserts me — ah, of course! Queen Eleanor's Hospital in Covent Garden in London, and the surgeon who taught him was — Abel Lackland!' He finished triumphantly and turned and looked at Sophie. 'Now, why did I never recall that when your poor dear Pa was alive? Why did I not connect the name? For I never did, you know.'

'Well, I think that it is clear that my Papa could well be the Bartholomew Lackland mentioned in this letter,' Sophie said, and bent her head towards it again. 'Although I imagine they would need more evidence that — ah! Now! Listen to this part! — "We have been apprised by our colleagues, Messrs Wishfort and Routledge, Attorneys-at-Law of Bradford, that they had dealings with Mr Bartholomew Lackland when he first went to live in Yorkshire a number of years ago — some time in the 1840s they say, regrettably unable to be more precise — and that they acted for him in some slightly acrimonious dealings with his father, Mr Abel Lackland. However, the younger Mr Lackland married a Miss Susannah Greenhalgh, and transferred his business affairs to the hands of her lawyers after his marriage. They were nonetheless able to give the name of the house Miss Susannah Greenhalgh had taken into her marriage as a dowry, and it is the house named on the envelope in which this letter has been sent.

' "If we have in fact found the family for which we seek, then we would ask you to open the enclosed envelope, read it, and act as you see fit upon its contents. However, if it should transpire that we have sent this missive to the wrong persons, we trust you will forgive us for so wasting your time. You will, we feel sure, understand that we felt it would be less distasteful to use this method of seeking the legatee under the Will of Mrs Lackland, rather than advertising in newspapers. This we may have to do in the future if we have been unable to succeed on this occasion. May we say, however, that we are reasonably confident that we are not in error, and this is why we have taken the step of enclosing the other envelope and its information.

' "We trust to hear from you in due course, and would enjoin some haste if in fact you are the family we seek, since this matter has been before us for some time.

' "Your most obedient servants . . ." — Well!' Sophie said and let the letter fall on to her lap. 'Well!' and could say no more at all.

'A legatee! My dear Sophie, you are a legatee!' Doctor Tom said, and leaned over and clapped her cheerfully on the shoulder. 'There can be no more delightful experience than to benefit under a will and when that will is of a person who is a relation one has never known and for whom one has certainly no ties of affection, then one can indeed rejoice without any hint of impropriety. I do congratulate you, my dear Sophie, I do indeed.'

'I — well — I do not — I cannot — I mean —' Sophie said and then shook her head. 'Oh, the cat has quite got my tongue and my senses as well! How can I be a legatee of someone of whom I have never heard, let alone knew? It does not seem possible.'

'Tha'd better read t'other letter, hadn't thee?' Bessie said, her practicality taking charge. 'It might turn out ye're gettin' no more'n a couple o' Staffordshire dogs and a set o' fire irons, which is what happened to me, you'll remember, Dr Ribble, when me Uncle Enoch died over at Bingley. There's no call to be gettin' excited, Miss Sophie, an' that Ah tell thee, on account it mak's it that much 'arder to tak' what's been given wi' a good 'eart. So open t'other envelope, do!'

'I'm afraid,' Sophie said, and shook her head in bewilderment. 'I know it is mad, but I cannot help it. I am *afraid*. It may — it could be that — oh, I have a feeling deep inside ——' and she clasped both hands over the bodice of her gown with unconscious theatricality, '— that all this means something very — oh, please, Doctor Tom, will you do it for me? I cannot bear to open it, and yet I cannot bear not to know!'

Nothing loth, Doctor Tom reached for the other envelope and then with what seemed maddeningly slow precision, took from his pocket his spectacles and unfolded them and hooked them over his ears and nose.

And then he too bent his head to bring himself nearer to the lamplight, slit the envelope with one gnarled thumb, removed the letter and began to read.

'"Sir/Madam, Since you are reading this, we take it you are the son or wife of the son of Abel Lackland, deceased, of Gower Street in London. It is our melancholy duty to inform you that his wife, Mrs Maria Lackland, your stepmother, died on August seventeenth last of an apoplexy.

'"The terms of her Will are very precise. It is her wish that her considerable fortune, which amounts to some fifty-seven thousand pounds net, be the inheritance of whichever of your offspring chooses to accept the conditions under which the fortune is left.

27

If more than one seeks to claim, then the inheritance shall go to whichever shall be deemed the most suitable by public examination, in a manner laid down by a clause in her Will with which we need not at this point concern ourselves since the clause becomes germane only in this special event.

'"It was the express wish of Mrs Lackland that the profession of surgeon be carried on by a person with the name of Lackland, as a memorial to her late husband, and also that such a person should, once suitably qualified, work in the profession of surgeon, thus maintaining the name of Mr Abel Lackland at the hospital which he founded, that is, Queen Eleanor's Hospital, in Endell Street, Covent Garden.

'"Mrs Lackland was well aware that this condition would be a lengthy time in the fulfilment thereof, and would demand of the accepting legatee considerable effort of spirit and intellect, but was persuaded, from her long acquaintance with Mr Lackland, and from her previous understanding of his children in their infancy, when she acted as Governess to them after the death of their mother, Mrs Dorothea Lackland, that such effort would be made.

'"However, she made provision should it transpire that the conditions of the Will could not be fully observed. In such case the fortune will become the property of a most respectable and worthy charity in which the Lackland family have long held an interest, viz. The London Ladies' Committee for the Rescue of the Profligate Poor.

'"We now await, dear Sir/Madam, some notification of a possible legatee. If one of your offspring or (should it be the melancholy case that both Mr and Mrs Bartholomew Lackland be deceased, and this letter is being read by one of the offspring themselves) yourselves as such offspring feel entitled to inherit, we require further instructions. If, of course, it should transpire that there are no living offspring of Mr Bartholomew Lackland then of course arrangements must be put in hand to put the fortune in the hands of the Committee aforementioned.

'"We remain your obedient servants . . ."'

Slowly, Doctor Tom folded the letter and slipped it back into its envelope, while Sophie sat and stared at him with her mouth open and her eyes so wide and staring that she seemed almost to be in a trance.

'Oh, Doctor Tom,' she said at length almost in a whisper. 'Oh, Doctor Tom!' and it was as though she could say no more.

He took off his glasses with as much slow deliberation as he had put them on, keeping his head bent, and still Sophie sat and stared into space, her face white with excitement.

Bessie and Doctor Tom exchanged a glance then, and Bessie shook her head slightly, and then stood up, and picked up her shawl.

'Well, love, like Ah said, doesn't do to get too excited afore there is aught to get excited about, does it? There was 'ope there for a bit, and now there ain't. Well, man proposes, as they say, and God disposes. Let's away up to Tansey Clough then, and forget all about it ——'

Sophie seemed hardly to have heard her at first, and then she moved her head and looked at Bessie and blinked. 'What did you say?'

'Ah said, let's away to Tansey Clough. There's nowt to be 'ad sittin' 'ere any longer, is there? Eh, these fancy London lawyers gettin' a body that stirred up ——'

'But it is wonderful news, Bessie! How can you be so sour about it? Did you not hear what Doctor Tom read out? Fifty-seven thousand pounds! Why, it is a vast fortune, an impossible fortune — even Uncle Nathan Greenhalgh would have to admit that to be a handsome competence! How can you be so ——'

'But did thee not hear, neither? The conditions, thi daft ha'porth! The conditions!'

'What about them?' Sophie was on her feet, marching about the room with a sudden restless energy that made the flames in the grate dance as she went sweeping past, and even the heavy red curtains move in sympathy with her plunging steps.

'What about them? Did'st tha not *hear*? To inherit this brass, tha's got to be a *surgeon*! Wheer's tha common sense, thi gormless gurt nowt!' Bessie, in her own bitter disappointment, was lapsing further and further into the dialect of her childhood. 'Did'st ever 'ear such carryin's on from a lass as is supposed to 'ave a bit o' eddication? Tha's clean off tha rocker, that's what! Theer's no brass for thee in this will, an' the sooner tha gets that in tha thick skull and comes away 'ome, the better for all of us!'

'Of course I heard, Bessie! There's no need to shriek at me that way! I heard every word and it's marvellous, it is so marvellous I can hardly think! Not only all that money, but the chance to do something that I would value above all others. To be a *surgeon*! It will be quite, quite marvellous!'

'Now, wait a bit, m'dear, wait a bit!' Doctor Tom said. 'You to be a surgeon? Come, you have let your hopes go to your head and addle your wits! Bessie is quite right. It is not possible for you to benefit under this will, cruel though that must seem to you. Had your brothers lived, it would have been different, so very different — but ——'

Sophie was standing very still now in the middle of the hearth-rug, her body framed in the firelight and her face almost entirely in shadow, and he peered up at her, at the taut lines of her figure, and could have wept for her. Had she only been a man! How could fate be so cruel as to offer this delightful girl of whom he had become so fond over the years a fortune in one hand, only to snatch it away with the other?

'I am so sorry, my dear, dear child,' he said gently. 'But you must face reality. You cannot inherit this money.'

'Doctor Tom,' Sophie said in a voice so calm and controlled that she might have been discussing nothing more important than the weather. 'Doctor Tom, tell me this. Have I not, on many occasions, heard you say to me that I am as gifted when it comes to the care of the sick as any person with whom you have ever been?'

'Aye, I have said that,' Doctor Tom said, 'But that does not mean ——'

'And have I not been helping you in every way a fellow physician might have helped you this past — oh, eight years and more?'

'That is true, indeed. You have been an excellent nurse, in many ways, and ——'

'Was I being an excellent *nurse* when you had that infection in your thumb and could not hold a scalpel, and you watched me and guided me while I bled Mr Clapham and lanced that abscess? And when I delivered Mrs Gawthorp of her baby, and he in a breech position?'

'Oh, come, my dear!' Doctor Tom threw an embarrassed glance at Bessie who was looking at Sophie with her face set as hard as the granite outcrops on the moors. 'That was a matter between our-selves and the patients. It was not my fault I got the erisypelas, was it? Nor that it lasted so long. I was grateful for your assistance, and indeed still am, but that does not mean ——'

'I am not speaking now of gratitude! I ask but facts of you, Doctor Tom. Did you not say then, as on other occasions, that I was as good as any physician, and with more teaching could make a great go in your very own profession?'

'Well — oh dear, but this is — well, yes, I suppose I did,' Doctor Tom said unhappily, looking again at Bessie who glared back at him.

'And are you sitting there and branding yourself a liar, Doctor Tom?' Sophie said even more softly. 'Were you trying to cozen me with sweet words? You, who so pride yourself on your Yorkshire honesty?'

'Damme, Sophie, but you go too far! Of course I did not lie! I do not lie, ever, and well you know it.'

'Then there is no reason why I should not make as excellent a surgeon as anyone else? Why I should not take this legacy?'

'There's every reason!' Doctor Tom roared, and jumped to his feet. 'You foolish girl, you are a *female*! Whoever heard of a female surgeon? You must be clean out of your attic. There is no other explanation for it! These damned lawyers and their letters have stolen your sense from you!'

'Oh, pooh as to that! Of course I know it is not *usual* for a woman to study surgery, but that does not mean to say it is impossible! Have you forgotten Miss Garrett? Why, I recall, if you do not, how we spoke of her when there was all that in the newspaper of the way she had persuaded the Society of Apothecaries to admit her to their examinations, and ——'

'Aye, I remember it well enough. It was many years ago, before your poor parents died, and would to heaven they were here now to exercise some control over you! I recall more, also — that they changed their rules at the Society, so that no other foolish woman could ——'

'Oh, Doctor Tom, please, do not play the turncoat with me!' She ran across the room and stood before him, her hands holding each of his coat lapels beseechingly. 'We talked of it, and I said would it not be wonderful if I could do as Miss Garrett had and you said it would indeed, child though I was at the time, and you said that women could be as good physicians as any men, with their

31

tender feelings and deeper understanding of the human soul and ——'

'Oh, my dear, of course I remember! And I do not seek to swallow my words now. I supported the bravery of Miss Garrett, indeed I did — but I was saddened by her foolishness, for it seemed to me, and still does, that to set one's face against the tide of all popular feeling is to court misery. To be so unwomanly — it cannot be! Not in my time, that is sure! I know the world is changing fast, my child, but not so fast that women can ever hope in our lifetimes to be admitted to the mysteries of the craft of the physician. And anyway ——'

'Anyway nothing! You agree, you agree!' She almost danced away from him, once again marching about the room in a great burst of excited energy. 'You agree that I am a suitable person to do this work, that I have helped you in such ways that you have admitted me to be capable of being your equal, though yet much in need of teaching, of course, and now I have the opportunity to follow the path blazed by Miss Garrett — why Bessie, my dear Bessie, I might even yet gratify your ambition, and find myself a husband, for Miss Garrett for all her *unwomanly* ways has done so! Did she not wed two or three years ago? I know I saw it in the newspapers — a captain of a steamship line, Captain Anderson was it not? So you see, it will be — oh, *splendid*!'

'She is a physician, not a surgeon, Miss Sophie,' Doctor Tom said almost despairingly. 'Can you not understand that it is impossible for you to become a surgeon, as the will insists? Where will you gain your training? Where will you take your examinations? You must remember that your precious Miss Garrett — Mrs Anderson — succeeded only by a flaw in the rules of the Society at that time, and those rules have now been changed. There has been much talk in Parliament this year, I know, but it has not yet changed the situation by so much as a jot or a tittle. No woman can possibly become a physician in this country, while as for surgery — it is unthinkable! And do not forget that those women who sought to force themselves on to the Edinburgh University examiners quite lost their appeal. And what would you live upon while you studied, even if it were possible? You have no money, no affluent friends in London. Believe me, dear Sophie, the time is not yet ripe for your desires to be satisfied. You must accept the pain of the loss of this legacy, and seek to expunge all thought of it from your mind. You cannot be happy otherwise ——'

'I shall do no such thing!' Sophie said, and whirled on him, and stood with her fists on her hips, in unconscious imitation of Bessie's familiar stance. 'This chance has been dropped in my way, and I would be a weak and foolish thing indeed if I were to miss picking it up simply because there are some difficulties. Pooh to difficulties! I shall go to London, I shall see these attorneys, and I shall claim my legacy. If I am to inherit such a sum they cannot refuse to advance me a few meagre shillings to maintain myself until I reach my goal. I have great expectations, after all! And one of them is that I shall be a surgeon. And I *shall* be a surgeon. You see if I don't! Just you see!'

CHAPTER FOUR

Sophie sat in the train, her hands crossed tightly on her lap and her booted feet set neatly side by side on the drugget-covered floor of the carriage. Above her on the rack sat her carefully tied bandbox, and in the luggage van at the end of the train her corded box was stacked somewhere amid the trunks and crates and sacks that had been piled on at the train's starting point at Colne. In less than five minutes the door of the carriage would be slammed shut by the self-important, heavily brass-buttoned guard with the green flag, and the sound of steam would increase and the train would move ponderously out of Keighley Station, on its way to London ——

She almost stood up, almost hurled herself out on to the stone flagged platform below into Bessie's arms, but she took a deep breath and clasped her hands even more tightly than they were, if that were possible, and smiled at Bessie, a little tremulously perhaps, but a smile for all that.

'Don't look so woebegone, Bessie, for heaven's sake!' she said with a rallying note in her voice. 'You would think from your face that the world was about to fall in — not at all becoming in one that is to be wed before Christmas is past, and ——'

'Nay, wed! As if that matters, when tha's so set on throwin' thyself into such trouble as ——'

'Now, Bessie, we've been through all that! Over and over — and you heard what Mr Fordyce said did you not? It is really the only answer! And it is not the end of the world I am going to after all. Only to London ——'

'It could be t'end o' t'world for all the good it'll do thee! 'Tis a wicked place, from all I've 'eard, and you nobbut a girl, an' all alone — eh, Miss Sophie, get thee off that there train, do! 'Tis not too late, an' we'll manage well enough, some road or t'other. Come away, do, an' ——'

'Here we are, my dear! I had them pack it close and with plenty of hay, so it should remain hot well into the afternoon! And there's

a little something to keep you extra warm when you need it ——'
Doctor Tom had come panting up the platform, his thin twittery
wife running behind him, holding in both his heavily gloved hands
a large wicker basket.

'Nay, she's got comestibles enough to last 'er from 'ere to — to
France!' Bessie said sharply, staring at the wicker basket with great
disfavour. 'Tha'd never think as Ah'd send 'er off on sich 'eathen
traipsin's wi'out plenty of good food to keep 'er, dost tha?'

'Not food, this, Bessie!' Doctor Tom said and winked at Sophie
as he handed the wicker basket up to her in the train. 'Liquid
refreshment! If she is to be a medical student, why, she must learn
to take her liquor like a gentleman! No, don't look so scandalized,
you foolish woman! I've given her nothing she should not have!
There is in there but a jug of hot soup, and another of hot coffee,
and the smallest of bottles of brandy. Purely medicinal, I do
promise you — oh, dear me, is that the time? It cannot be so soon
— oh, my dear dear Sophie, take such care of yourself! Remember
we are always here and will be waiting so eagerly for news of
you ——'

The button-bedecked guard was making his ponderous way
along the train, busily slamming the doors and looking quite
horridly portentous as the great engine at the front of the train took
its huge steamy breaths and began to puff with the excitement of
imminent departure.

Sophie jumped up, feeling her chest tighten with anxiety and
was about to jump down on to the platform to give both Bessie and
Doctor Tom a great hug, but the guard was there, shutting the
door between them. She struggled for a moment with the heavy
leather strap that held the window and then, at last, managed to let
it down and leaned out holding both hands out to Bessie.

'Goodbye, Bessie, my dear — I will write — I will think of you
on your wedding day and ——'

'Oh, Sophie, my little love, tak' care o' thyself — mak' sure that
tha' never does owt as'd worry me, now, an' keep that brass sewed
into thi stays, remember — 'tis thy train fare back 'ome when
thee's got this maggot out o' thi brain — eh, lass, but Ah shall miss
thee ——'

There were tears running down her weather-reddened face and
Sophie felt her own eyes prickle but she had promised herself she

would not weep, and savagely she bit her lip and managed a grin.

'I'll remember, my dear Bessie, I will remember — Goodbye, Doctor Tom! Goodbye, Mrs Ribble — and Doctor Tom, tell Mrs Blalock I'll send her that book of stories from London that I promised, as long as she goes on exercising that poor leg of hers — oh, we are going — goodbye, my loves — goodbye — I shall write at once, I promise you — goodbye!'

The train was gathering momentum, and the platform was moving past so fast now that it was not possible for her three friends to keep up as she leaned out of the window, blinking in the bitter cold air, peering back up the lamplit platform through the trails of steam at their dear familiar figures. Now she could allow herself to cry, and she did, feeling her tears hot in her eyes and then cold on her cheeks as the chill snatched the heat from them. She was going into heaven alone knows what, leaving all she knew and loved far behind her, and she was doing it because of her own wilful stupidity. She was getting exactly what she had wanted for years and years and years and she could not have been more miserable about it than she was at that moment.

There was a hurrumph from behind her, and then a loud cough and, as the train took the curve between the coalyards and the great overhanging warehouses and the friendly lights of Keighley platform at last disappeared, she pulled her head in, and looked around.

A middle-aged man in a heavy ulster, a scarf pulled close around his head and ears and a Norfolk cap perched rather ludicrously on top was glaring at her from one corner, while on the other a thin angular lady, wearing pince-nez and the ugliest bonnet Sophie had ever seen over a straight grey coat that was almost equally hideous, looked at her with cold scorn on her face. It was the only other passenger, a ruddy-faced young man well upholstered in a coat of very heavy tweed, who jumped to his feet to help her, taking the leather strap and pulling up the window.

'A bitter morning, is it not?' he said cheerfully. 'Not at all the ideal for travelling! May I put your basket on the rack for you, ma'am? There — just say the word when you want it, and I'll have it down in a trice for you. Would you care to share my hot brick? It's a lot harder to keep small feminine feet warm, I'll be bound, than great hulking boots like mine! Ha, ha, wouldn't you agree?

Are you going far, ma'am?'

Deeply conscious of the disapproving stares of the thin-faced woman, and with Bessie's warning utterances about Evil Men ringing in her ears, Sophie acknowledged her would-be protector's help as coolly as she could, and declined his offer of a foot warmer with an incline of her head. Regretfully, however, for indeed her feet were bitterly cold and, inexperienced travellers as she and her friends were, none had thought of providing this vital adjunct for the seven hours of journeying that lay ahead.

She settled herself in her corner as cosily as she could, pulling her rug over her knees — at least they had realized she would need that — and tucking her hands into its folds, fell to staring out of the window at the gradually lifting sky. It was still grey out there, for even though it was now almost half past eight in the morning the Yorkshire day was barely up, for it was now the second week in December and the days were pitifully short as well as wickedly cold.

The warehouse and coalyards dwindled away and now the rolling hills that dominated the landscape between Keighley and Bingley took over, ghostlike with their skin of snow. As she stared out at it, at the dear familiarity, again her eyes filled and she sniffed hard, trying to pretend it wasn't happening, her head turned resolutely to the window. No one should see that she was at all distressed. They must all be led to believe that she was the most insouciant traveller imaginable, taking journeys to London every week of her life and thinking nothing of it.

But it had all been so exciting this last two weeks that she could hardly absorb all that *had* happened. There had been the interminable discussions with Bessie in which Bessie had insisted that they'd manage to go on as they always had, somehow, and averring with every atom of spirit in her that the notion that her Miss Sophie should go gadding off to London on such a mad chase was out of the question, while Sophie argued back equally heatedly that she had no choice but to go, for were not their small resources quite exhausted?

She had gone over it all time and again; the long discussions with Mr Fordyce, her lawyer in Keighley, who had told her flatly if sadly that her money was quite gone.

'For the fact of the matter is, my dear Miss Lackland, that your parents subsisted on the smallest of annuities and the — ahem —

37

generosity of your poor dear Mamma's family, both of which sources of income died with her. I have done all I could to temper the wind to you, I do promise you, but there is little enough left but Tansey Clough itself. It is a good house and I am glad that you have it, but it offers you little more than a shelter, in all truth, and you cannot eat that, can you? I have been sadly put about for some time now, considering your problem, and I must tell you that this — ah — missive from Vivian and Onions comes at a most opportune time, most opportune ——'

'Then you agree I should go to London and claim the inheritance and become a surgeon, Mr Fordyce?' Sophie had said eagerly. 'Oh, I am glad to hear that, indeed I am! For you know Doctor Tom — Dr Ribble, I mean — and Bessie have set their faces against it so that ——'

'Become a surgeon?' Mr Fordyce had said, quite horrified at the mere suggestion. 'Oh, dear me no! Far from it! No, it was my idea that you should — ah — contest this will. If you lay claim as the sole surviving relative of Bartholomew Lackland, why, then you may be able to persuade the courts to put aside this charitable bequest and ——'

Sophie had shaken her head at that. 'I would never *never* contest the wishes of a dead person, Mr Fordyce,' she said with decision. 'It would be wrong. I will gladly accept any honourable bequest, and I promise you I will fight with every bit of — of *energy* I have to persuade any who need such persuasion that I am a fit person to benefit, and I will become a surgeon at Queen Eleanor's no matter what any of you say! Even you, my dear Mr Fordyce. But I am not going to go cap in hand begging from these London lawyers for the will of an old lady I never knew, and who clearly had never heard of me, to be overset in my favour. That would be a very wicked thing to do, I do believe.'

'Not wicked,' Mr Fordyce had said mildly. 'Not wicked at all, though your sentiments do you credit. But, my dear child, you cannot eat sentiments, can you? I think the answer perhaps may be to close up Tansey Clough and set about seeking an — ah — position for yourself elsewhere. I dare say you could become a governess, eh? It is, I cannot deny, not always the happiest of occupations, but with good fortune you may find a family that is kind and thoughtful, and certainly I will do all I can to find you such a one. And then, perhaps, one day —' and he had become positively arch, twinkling at her in what she later described to Wilfred as the most hateful manner possible, '— one day, perhaps, you will find a charming and — um — pecunious young man for whom the chance to live with you in Tansey Clough will seem the most delightful thing he could possibly conceive of and ——'

'As if,' she had said wrathfully to Wilfred, 'I would marry any man merely for the sake of securing a competency for myself! And,' she had gone on hastily, believing she could see words positively trembling on Wilfred's lips, 'as if I would not despise any man who offered for me out of pity for my *im*pecunious state! It is no sin to be poor, as I am always telling Bessie, and if one has energy and common sense and a — and a little *application*, then there are always answers to problems. Mr Fordyce thinks my answers lie in governessing — well, pooh to governessing, say I! I can think of no activity more disagreeable. I will seize this great chance that has come to my hands, and a surgeon I will be, even if all my friends, including you, Wilfred, hate me for it.'

'I could never hate you, Sophie, no matter what you did. And anyway, why should I agree with Bessie and Doctor Tom and Mr Fordyce? Did you expect me to?'

She had looked at him then, her head on one side and her forehead a little creased. They had been sitting in the small parlour at Tansey Clough, a fine fire burning the last of their sea coal in the grate and a comfortable Bessie-cooked dinner inside them. Minding her manners, Sophie had invited both Mrs and Mr Brotherton to visit her for, as she had put it, a farewell dinner; and she had been not a little put out when Mrs Brotherton had thanked her graciously but declared herself far too occupied to come, and anyway, to venture so far and to so cold a house would not be beneficial to her health. A message that had so enraged Sophie that when Wilfred had arrived she had set about him with her tongue until he had pointed out mildly enough that he could not be blamed for his mother's ill behaviour, and that he had left her tonight in high dudgeon in order to be at Tansey Clough himself. At which Sophie had felt ashamed of her own bad manners and begged his pardon, and they had settled to a cosy prosy evening.

Until she had been so surprised by him; for he had listened to all her reports of all that the others had said, and listened to her own decided views on the subject of a woman — notably herself — becoming a surgeon and had said nothing. Until this point, and then what he did say left her almost speechless.

'I believe that every one of us must do what is right for what we perceive to be our own talents. It is often difficult for we must do so without distressing others more than we need, and this is where sometimes pain arises. There is much that I might have wished to do, but any joy I would have found in following my own bent would have been quite overset by the knowledge of the distress my parents would have suffered on my behalf. That made it impossible for me. But for you, Sophie, — what you choose to do will offend some people's notions of propriety perhaps, but can it do them any harm? I think not. You tell me that Bessie has agreed that if you go away she will marry her Josiah, so she will be well enough, and as for Dr and Mrs Ribble — why, I am sure they care enough for you as friends, but they cannot suffer if you choose to go to London, can they? As long as you are not aware of causing pain to any other person, then you are right to do as you feel is right for you. Of this I am convinced ——'

She had stared at him, at the familiar square face with the comfortable lines around the eyes and mouth, at the brown eyes, so warm and friendly in the lamplight and tried with some confusion to take in all he had said. Had she been wrong all these years? Had he not after all been on the brink of declaring himself as she had fondly believed? This was not the speech of a lover, this encouragement to go away and seek her fortune in a manner that flew in the face of all conventional ideas of good behaviour for a respectable young lady of good family. This was the counsel of a friend, undoubtedly, but no more than a friend — and for one amazing moment she felt a faint twinge of pique. So he did not wish to wed her? How dare he be so? Until her own good sense took over again, as well as her amazement, and pushed that foolish thought into the oblivion where it belonged.

'You do not think I am mad to seek to take up this legacy, Wilfred?'

'Mad? Of course not! Brave — to the point of foolhardiness even. Unusual, to the point of being outrageous. But mad, never. In your shoes, feeling as you do, I hope I would have the courage to do the same.'

She had jumped to her feet then, allowing her sewing — she was busily making over her old gowns to take them to London — to fly all over the place, and hugged him, and she had felt his shoulders tense suddenly under her hands and was again amazed. Did he find her touch so unwelcome that he pulled away? Absurd thought! And she hugged him closer and this time he set his arms about her own shoulders and hugged her too, just as he had when they had been children together, playing silly games high on the moors on summer afternoons.

'You are a dear, good friend, Wilfred, and I am grateful to you for your good will. You have cheered me more than you will ever know,' she said and smiled at him, her eyes brilliant in the lamplight and he had smiled soberly back, his own face quite unreadable.

She had settled to her chair again and then prattled on, explaining how Mr Fordyce had at last agreed, if unwillingly, to accept her decision to go to London to claim the legacy. He had also agreed to sell the very last vestiges of her father's property in order to furnish her with the cost of her train journey to London, and some prudent purchases to set herself up with (and although Wilfred said not a word, he shrewdly suspected that Mr Fordyce had dipped into his own pocket for these funds) and all was set afoot. She had spent her busy days alternately looking after her old friends in Town End Bottom, as she always did, and in getting ready; and Tansey Clough, she told Wilfred, had been such a bustle of sewing and preparing this past two weeks he could not imagine!

'Sophie,' he said then, carefully. 'I would wish to be, as an old friend, a small part of these preparations.'

She had looked up again from her sewing and smiled at him. 'But you are, dear Wilfred! I could not go away without apprising you of all my doings. And are you not here tonight, to bid me farewell?'

'Aye. I'm here tonight — but I would wish to send away with you some small — memento. I doubt you'd forget me altogether — you were never one to shed old friends — but it would make me feel happy to know that you had something of me by you ——'

There had been a small silence then as she looked at him soberly and he had sat there in the opposite armchair, foursquare and sensible, staring back.

'What had you in mind, Wilfred? For understand me well, I will not allow you to ——'

'Eh, but tha's jumpin' 'igh in thy mind, lass!' he said and she laughed then, and reddened.

'Well, yes, I dare say I did leap to a conclusion. For one dreadful moment I thought you were going to offer me money. And old friend or not, I would show you the door so fast if — well, let be. Forgive me for thinking it. Just tell me what you did think.'

'I would like to give you a length of my own cloth, if you would but take it, Sophie,' he said. 'I have a bolt of fine green nine-ounce velours, woven specially by me in my own mill from my finest first shearings. It would please me beyond measure if you would let me give you a length of this, for it would become you well, and it is a warm and very hardwearing cloth which would stand you in good stead.'

There had been a further little silence between them and then she had said soberly, 'That is very kind in you, Wilfred. It is the most generous and most charming of farewell gifts, for the makings of a man's own hands — that is a gift that is very special. I thank you warmly for it.'

Sitting now in the rocking rattling train as it pushed its way under its great plume of steam through the snowy, gradually lightening countryside to Bingley, she looked down at her mantle, at the rich dark green folds of it, and felt the warmth of it across her back. Dear, good Wilfred. Without him, she would have had to go to London either cloakless or wearing a shawl, and both possibilities were unthinkable. As it was, she was travelling there looking every inch the lady — and much more interestingly dressed than the formidable thin-faced dragon in the opposite corner of the carriage — for all that her gowns and underclothes and boots were well-worn, and often mended.

Bingley lifted her mood a little, for there was a small bustle as other people got into their carriage, making them all move up. The young man in the tweed coat chose the opportunity to sit beside her, for a mother of somewhat ample proportions and her even more ample children wished to sit together. This attempt at friendliness Sophie easily kept at bay by taking a warm interest in the mother, and offering to hold her youngest, a stout and active child of some four years, upon her lap. Which, since the family did not leave the train for almost another hour and a half, at Leeds, showed him clearly that he was to gain little from Miss's company in the succeeding part of the journey.

The morning wore on heavily. At Barnsley she allowed herself the luxury of taking some of the coffee Doctor Tom had provided, and she was grateful for it, for it was indeed hot and strong and very revivifying. She was tired already, truth to tell, for it was a long time since the journey had started on the little Worth Valley railway which had carried her and Bessie and Dr and Mrs Ribble from Haworth to meet the London train on the Midland line at Keighley.

So, it was not surprising that she fell into a light doze, and slept until the train came puffing into Trent station at a quarter to twelve. To her relief the tweedy young man left then, as did the angular lady, to be replaced by a party of foreigners of some sort; and she sat there in the corner of the carriage, eating the mutton pie and cheese that Bessie had packed in her basket for her and drinking Doctor Tom's hot soup, and listened to them babble, and decided they were Swiss, although she could not imagine what Swiss people could want in Trent at such a time of the year, and was amazed at herself to be in such cosmopolitan company. All of which beguiled her well enough to keep her apprehensions at bay.

But they were there, for all that. When the train at last steamed out of Trent Station — for it had stayed there long enough to allow the better-off passengers the chance to buy themselves a hot dinner at the station restaurant — she felt very low as well as very anxious. Home seemed an eternity away, for the landscape through which they were now passing was so bleak, so very miserable, that it offered her no comfort at all. Oh, there were mills and coalyards and warehouses enough at home in Yorkshire, but there were also moors and hills and snow-softened trees. Here there were just black chimneys and row after row of mean little houses, nothing to gladden the eye at all ——

But then her spirits lifted, for the train seemed to gather momentum as the landscape eased, became less and less industrial as first Birmingham and then Leicester and Northampton were left behind, and they steamed busily southwards through the gentler rolling fields on the way to Luton and St Albans and Hendon.

By now the carriage was full of people, the Swiss party having left at Kettering to be replaced by an eager family going to London, she soon gathered, to spend the Christmas holiday with Grandpapa and Grandmamma. For a while she sat and listened to the six children chatter about the fun they would have at the pantomime, and their pious hopes that Grandpapa would take them all to the music hall as he had last year, and perhaps to eat ices afterwards in that lovely Italian place; she found pleasure in overhearing their happiness and yet a sort of bleak self-pity too, for to whom was she to go? Just to a lawyer. No joyous Christmas awaited her in the great metropolis ahead.

At which she mentally rapped her own knuckles and set herself to staring out of the window as the train pushed its vainglorious way through the neat London suburbs, passing the rooftops of Kilburn and Finchley, Haverstock Hill and Kentish Town. And then, suddenly, all was bustle and excitement as the children in the family party surged to their feet and began to jump about, and their fussing Mamma and irritable Papa collected them and their piles of luggage and coats and muffs and shepherded them to the door.

For they had arrived. The great expanse of St Pancras station lay on each side of them as the train took a huge shuddering breath, let out the last of its steam in a great shriek of triumph and sank into silence.

Sophie, struggling out after the noisy children with her bandbox in one hand and her wicker baskets and travelling rug clutched somehow in the other stood there bewildered and unsure as the heedless passengers surged round her on their way to the far distant ticket barrier and their homes and comfortable destinations.

She had arrived in London. The hope she had entertained for all these years, of getting away from Haworth to do something different, something special, had come true at last. She was here — and she was very frightened, and very alone, and very, very tired indeed.

CHAPTER FIVE

Quite what she had expected on her arrival in London she did not know. In all her imaginings — and there had been many — she had of course seen herself in the middle of many buildings and busy streets, like Bradford writ large, but this was beyond anything Bradford could offer. This mad hubbub of people and horses and cabs and vans and more people, people, people left her stunned.

Worse even was the fact that she found so much of the speech that was directed at her so difficult to comprehend. That the people at home spoke in rhythms and patterns unique to themselves of course she knew; had she not grown up with the sound of Yorkshire speech wrapping her round and yet been taught herself to speak in an 'elegant' manner? Had she thought of it at all, she would have assumed that the ordinary people in London spoke in their special rhythmic patterns too, but that at least it would be comprehensible.

But it was not. She had come struggling to the van to see her big corded box handed down, and then looked about for a porter, and having found one, followed him and the luggage to the barrier where she gave up her ticket. He stopped there and looked back over his shoulder and said loudly, 'Keb, lidy?'

'I'm sorry — what did you say?'

'Where're yer goin', lidy? D'yer want the kebs, bein' met, wotcher want?'

She stared at him and shook her head and then said, 'I — er — I need a hansom, I think ——'

'Not wiv this lot, yer don't, lidy!' the man said cheerfully. 'Won't take it, not no'ow. Growler's what you needs ——' and he went on his way, pushing through the crowded concourse as easily as she would have walked across the open moor at home, leaving her to follow him as best she might.

Once in the growler, with her luggage perched awkwardly on top of it, and sitting in the dusty musty interior and trying to tell the

45

jarvey where she wanted to go, it was even worse; she repeated the address from the letter from Messrs Vivian and Onions and the man shook his head and shouted, 'Eh?' above the unending hubbub all around them and she tried again and quite failed to make him understand, until at last he took the letter from her hand and saw the address for himself and nodded his head and clicked his tongue at his horse, and they were off.

At which point Sophie almost gave in altogether to her sense of strangeness. She could have been in another world, and not just the capital city of her own country, so alien was it all. Not that the buildings and the vehicles were all that different from those at Keighley, or even Bradford. Admittedly, all the main buildings at home were built of heavy grey stone, and here black seemed to predominate, and at home there were many wool carts and spanking merchants' carriages while here great drays and smaller swifter equipages seemed to be much more common, but it was an English city after all. It was just the sheer size and numbers involved that made it seem so strange. The pavements were thronged with foot passengers and the streets with vehicles to such an extent that she seemed to spend all her time shrinking back into her corner as the heads of horses drawing other carriages came so close to the windows she was sure they would come inside. By the time the growler reached its destination, wheeling suddenly into a wide and much quieter open space, she was almost shaking with the tension it had all created in her.

So she was not at her best when at last she found herself in the handsome and heavily furnished waiting room of Vivian and Onions' chambers. Not knowing what else she could do about it, she instructed the jarvey to unload her luggage and leave it near the doorway that led from Lincoln's Inn to the set of rooms the lawyers occupied (greatly to the disapproval of their Clerk who stared at her modest possessions with a disdainful air) and then marched into the waiting room and sat herself down, holding her reticule firmly in both hands.

It soon became clear to her that the Clerk, bustling pompously in and out, was deliberately ignoring her, and after waiting some five minutes for his attention she got to her feet and marched over to the door through which he had last vanished and rapped on it sharply. A rather scared small man, in an excessively high collar and with inky fingers, came out and said breathlessly, 'Can I 'elp you?'

'I hope someone can!' she said in as lofty a tone as she could manage. 'I wish to see Mr Vivian or Mr Onions. At once.'

'Both the Partners are heavily engaged all afternoon, Simmonds!' A voice came from the room beyond, making the high-collared little man look nervously over his shoulder. 'Tell the young person to return on another occasion. Make an appointment. Next week perhaps ——'

This was too much for Sophie, for she was quite unaccustomed to being treated in so cavalier a manner. At home in Haworth everyone knew her to be poor, perhaps, but she was a lady, nonetheless and was always treated so. To be regarded by a clerk in a lawyer's office as a 'young person' to be sent peremptorily away was not at all Sophie's idea of the way such a one as herself should be treated.

So, she pushed on the door behind the little man, who scuttled after her like a frightened rabbit, and marched into the Clerk's room.

'Be so good, my man, as to tell your *masters* that I am here to see them on the matter of the Lackland will. Tell them at once, d'you understand me? I have no time to waste further on you.'

The Clerk leaned back in his large chair and looked at her over his spectacles. 'The Lackland will? Now, what would you know about that?' He had clearly chosen now to be indulgent rather than frosty, and he was looking at her with a most avuncular air, but by now Sophie was in a state of great wrath, and found this even more insulting than his previous manner.

'That, sir, I venture to suggest, is none of your affair. Tell your master at once that I seek discussion with him. And mind your manners, or I shall be constrained to speak to him about the disgusting way in which you have behaved to me here this afternoon!'

The Clerk lifted his brows at that, and said haughtily, 'As to that, Miss — er — I have no doubt Mr Vivian or Mr Onions will soon decide whether or not they wish to waste any of their time on such matters — Simmonds, by all means tell the Senior Partner of this — person's — demands. I have no further time to waste on such ——' and he waved his hand and bent his head to his desk again, leaving Sophie to march out behind the now almost paralysed Mr Simmonds into the waiting room beyond.

Which was where Mr Onions found her a few moments later. He had stared at Simmonds, bobbing his head at him in his doorway and muttering about, 'A person to see you, sir, says it's about the Lackland will, sir — Mr Buckman most put out by it all, sorry to disturb you, sir ——' and had at once got to his feet.

'Someone about the Lackland will? Then we did find the right people. From Yorkshire, by any chance? Hey? Come, man, you must surely know how they speak in those remote parts.'

'Couldn't say, sir — hardly spoke to me — I mean, sir, very put about by bein' kept waitin' by Mr Buckman — very irate indeed, you might say — talked like a — well — hard to say, really sir. Sounds educated you know, but a bit different to what — I can't really say, sir ——'

Mr Onions grinned then. 'Sounds different, and put out by being kept waiting. That's a Lackland all right. Dear me, we seem to have found what we sought. Well, well, I'll come out and see him immediately, Simmonds. Just put this box back, will you? And get out the Lackland box forthwith. This young man and I have much to discuss — a great deal indeed to discuss ——'

And quite ignoring Simmonds' attempts to say something — for everyone in the chambers nearly always did ignore poor Mr Simmonds, who worked inordinately hard but was too nervous to be able to speak properly to anyone — he went surging out of his office to the waiting room.

And then stood and stared at the sight that met his eyes.

A girl. Tall, rather gangling, wearing a heavy green mantle of somewhat dowdy cut, though obviously of good cloth, her hair escaping from under her black straw bonnet to lie in untidy tendrils across her forehead and shoulders. A pleasant face with long narrow green eyes, but smudged now with the soot of a long railway journey. And an expression of fury that tightened every muscle and left spots of high colour in the cheeks.

'Ah — I was expecting to see — ah, well, now, Miss — er — ma'am — won't you take a seat? I dare say my Clerk will be able to advise you — I was looking for a gentleman I expected to see here. Simmonds!'

He turned on the shrinking little man. 'Where is Mr Lackland?'

'Tried to tell you, sir — not Mister. This lady — this is the one

48

what said she was here about the Lackland will. I never said nothing about a gentleman ——'

'I am Sophia Lackland, of Tansey Clough in Haworth in Yorkshire,' Sophie said with some grandiloquence, drawing herself up to her not inconsiderable height, fortunately quite unaware of the ludicrous effect created by the smudges on her face. 'And I am here in response to a letter from you, sir, which I have here —' and she gave it to him, pulling it from her reticule with an air of decision which Mr Onions found a little amusing, '— which I preferred to answer in person. That is why I did not write. I am here, sir, to inform you that I am the last remaining child of Mr Bartholomew Lackland and Susannah Greenhalgh, both of whom I am sad to say are dead, and that I am here to lay claim to the legacy of my — er — my step-grandmamma.'

Mr Onions had been looking down at the letter in his hand in a slightly bemused state, but now his head snapped up and his eyes seemed to shutter themselves, like a hawk's.

'To lay claim to the legacy — my dear Miss Lackland! I trust there is no thought in you of contesting. That cannot be, I do assure you! You cannot possibly ——'

'Oh, you are as bad as Mr Fordyce!' Sophie said irritably, and sat down. She was beginning to feel the long weariness of her journey creeping up on her again. 'He immediately talked of my contesting this will — as if I should! Why, I never knew Grandmamma Lackland. So how could I contest her will? But she wished me to become a surgeon at Queen Eleanor's, and that I shall undoubtedly do.'

Now it was Mr Onions's turn to sit down, and he did so, almost with a bump. A large man, with a round face plentifully whiskered, and a gold-chain-bedecked expanse of well-fed belly, he looked as taken aback as any experienced attorney possibly could.

'You? Become a *surgeon*? Come, Miss Lackland — I can well understand your pique at losing so splendid a bequest, but you cannot, you really cannot, expect me or anyone else to take you seriously.'

'Mr — Onions? Yes. You did not actually tell me which of the partners you are. Mr Onions, let me at this point disabuse your mind of any misapprehensions under which you may be labouring. I am a person who has, for many years, been much interested in the

49

practice of medicine. Ever since I was quite a child I have, under the aegis of an excellent physician of our village, Dr Thomas Ribble — he learned his own medical practice in Bradford, a not inconsiderable town, I am sure you will agree — been working with sick people. No, *not* in the usual manner of benevolent ladies offering soup and suchlike to the sick —' She over-rode his attempts to interpose a few words, '— I have no use for such activities. They are for the sort of lady who wishes merely to discharge her religious duties easily, but who would never actually dirty her own hands in giving direct care. I *have* so soiled my hands, and proud I am to say it! I have with me a letter from Doctor Tom — Dr Ribble — which will act as a reference for my character, my interest and my determination to become a surgeon. This letter of yours about this legacy excited, Mr Onions, not my cupidity as you so clearly believe, but my deepest ambitions. A surgeon I will be, and you cannot stop me. So there!'

And ending on that positively childish note she sat and glared at him, her mouth set hard, and somehow not looking nearly as absurd as she might, though the sooty smudges were still there on her face.

'I see,' Mr Onions said slowly. 'I see. But — no, you really must let *me* speak now, my dear Miss Lackland! Let me tell you first of all that I am not unsympathetic to young ladies of spirit. Bless my soul, I admire 'em! It is fortunate, to tell you the truth —' and here his voice dropped a little to a more confidential note, '— that it was I and not m'partner who came out to see you. For he is a much more — well, let us say he lacks my own heart. I am a most compassionate man, Miss Lackland, and yet I venture to think an astute one. I believe that I can read character as well as anyone, and I read in your visage and your most earnest words steadfastness and honesty and a spirit that does you credit. So do not think I seek to stand in your way out of any —any flaw in my own character. But I must tell you, Miss Lackland, that this cannot be. It really cannot be!'

'Why not?'

'Why not? Because you are a female, Miss Lackland. That is why not.'

Sophie's voice was low and almost conversational, as she sat back and folded her hands on her lap and smiled at him with a sudden sweetness that made the lawyer blink.

50

'Tell me, Mr Onions, in the actual words of this will, are any exclusive conditions laid down? As regards sex, I mean?'

'Exclusive conditions? I do not quite understand ——'

'Does Mrs Lackland's will at any point say specifically that a female is to be barred from inheriting?'

'I — well, I cannot — that is a most —' Mr Onions stood up suddenly. 'D'you know, Miss Lackland, I do not know! In drawing up this will for Mrs Lackland — who was a most charming and gentle lady, though somewhat of a recluse in her later years being much distressed by the death of her husband your late grandfather — it was always assumed that we spoke of the sons of Bartholomew Lackland. Never once did the mention of a *daughter* — well! I think perhaps we had better read it, do you not agree?'

'Indeed I do,' Sophie said firmly, and suddenly yawned, quite spoiling her picture of a woman of determination and attack at which she had been working so hard ever since she had arrived in these chambers. She looked up at the great clock on the wall and marvelled. It was but five o'clock. Could it be possible that she had first seen St Pancras station only two hours ago?

'Come, Miss Lackland, we will repair to the Partners' Room, and see if Mr Vivian, m'partner, you know, is available. Er —' He stopped then and shook his head a little ruefully. 'You will find him a — er — a rather different man to meself, m'dear. Not given to compassion, you must understand. An excellent fellow, in every way,' he added hastily, 'but not given to any sort of compassion.'

Or, Sophie thought shrewdly, having so strong a taste for the company of young ladies. Clearly Mr Onions was a most susceptible man, and it would be exceedingly easy to work upon him, by the use of the feminine wiles she had always most despised in other ladies of her acquaintance, to obtain her own way. But she would not do that, not Sophie Lackland. Or not, she amended her thoughts prudently as Mr Onions led her into a large and most comfortably furnished office, not until I find there is not another course open to me.

The next hour went by in a blur. Mr Onions, fussing a little, offered her, with charming tact, the use of his closet to tidy herself after her journey, and she accepted with gratitude, though was most chagrined when she discovered how crumpled and dirty she looked. But then, with her usual common sense, she told herself

51

that she had managed well enough with Mr Onions for all her travel-worn state so there was no point in fretting over it now; and she washed her face and hands quickly and tidied her rumpled hair.

By the time she returned to Mr Onions's office he was sitting on one side of his great desk with his partner facing him on the other, and she was introduced with great punctiliousness to Mr Vivian, who looked remarkably like Mr Onions yet carried with him a chilly air that made him much less agreeable company.

And then the two men fell to reading the will, each solemnly perusing a page and then giving it to the other, and she sat there, with a glass of sherry thoughtfully provided by Mr Onions and watched them and waited and hoped.

The clock hands crept round and the sky outside the red-curtained windows which had thickened to a velvety darkness pushed against the glass and she sat in an agreeable semi-doze. She had known she was tired but she had not realized just how weary she was. Now she had arrived, and was sitting here actually facing the lawyers it seemed to her that she could at last relax. No more apprehension, no more doubts. She was here, and soon all would be settled and she would start on the road that would take her to a surgical career at Queen Eleanor's Hospital.

She almost jumped when at last Mr Vivian's voice broke the silence.

'Well,' he said, and there was a sharpness in his voice that woke her up completely. 'It is in fact the case that there seems to be no mention at any point in this document regarding the — ah — sex of the beneficiary. All the conditions are based on family connection and a willingness to undertake the course of action laid down. However —' and here he stopped and fixed Sophie with a very severe gaze. 'However, even though sex is not mentioned in this document it is implied ——'

'It has always been my understanding that legal documents deal always and only with what is actually stated, not with what is implied,' Sophie said equally sharply, sitting up very straight.

'Yes, that *is* so! Vivian, you know, Miss Lackland is quite right, that is so.' Mr Onions sounded quite struck and beamed most approvingly at Sophie, as though she were a bright pupil, fast learning the ways of the law.

'Furthermore,' Sophie went on inexorably. 'If the wording of the will is at all like the wording of your letter, then at no point is gender even *implied*. You referred in your letter to the offspring of Bartholomew Lackland. You never said 'he' or 'she' — though sometimes 'they'. And that is a most general word indeed. So, you cannot stop me from claiming. I can prove my birth — I have brought documents from ——'

Mr Vivian waved that away. 'I am not concerned with that. We have no anxiety on that score — were you an imposter we would rapidly identify that fact. No, it is the deeper implications here ——'

'There are no deeper implications! I am the offspring of Bartholomew Lackland. The only surviving offspring. I am ready and willing to embark upon the course of action demanded by Mrs Lackland in her will ——'

'Ah, ready and willing you may be!' Mr Vivian said with sour triumph. 'But are you able? That's the important question. Are you *able* to become a surgeon? It is on this point that I have the gravest reservations. The gravest.'

'I too, I must confess.' Mr Onions shook his head mournfully, looking at Sophie with sheep's eyes full of compassion — which was beginning to irritate her as much as Mr Vivian's bloodless cut-and-dried approach. 'It will not be easy. Indeed, will it even be possible?'

'Of course it will,' Sophie said stoutly, but a qualm of doubt was beginning to stir deep inside her. The opposition of her friends in Haworth had seemed to her but gnat-bites to be swept away and laughed at, but these sophisticated Londoners, with their knowledge of the way the world wagged were a different matter. If they were both so sure it could not be, was it possible, was it just dreadfully, terrifyingly possible that they were right? No, that most certainly could *not* be, she told herself firmly. It could not. I must and I will ——

'I think, you know, Vivian, that we must take further advice on this. It seems to me that the best thing we can do is seek the opinion of some — ah — informed member of the medical profession, hey? Now what say you to that? If he can suggest a way in which Miss Lackland can do as she says she wishes to do, and qualify for this legacy ——'

'It is not just because of the legacy, you must understand!'

53

Sophie said swiftly. 'It is because I want to be a surgeon. I truly do. As long as I have been able to think at all I have thought about illness and the care of the sick and the uses of physic.'

'Your motives are well understood, I do promise you, Miss Lackland,' Mr Onions said soothingly. 'Do not fret yourself on that score. Do you not agree that the advice of some sensible man of knowledge is what we need?'

'Yes,' she said after a moment. 'Yes, perhaps you are right. But I of course know of no one who could ——'

'Mr Caspar,' Mr Vivian said suddenly. 'Frederick Caspar. He's the man to ask.'

'Mr Caspar? Why, of course! The very ticket. Mr Caspar!' Mr Onions said with great good humour, and stood up and looked at a large watch which he removed from his waistcoat pocket with a great air. 'Well, tomorrow, I think, hey, Vivian? Perhaps if you will wait upon us here tomorrow at two in the afternoon, Miss Lackland ——'

'Tomorrow?' Sophie looked at him blankly. 'But why not tonight? Something must be decided tonight, for you know I have nowhere in London to stay, and very little money. It must all be settled very quickly, really it must. If I am not set upon my studies within the week, then to tell the truth I do not know what I shall do. I had thought — I had hoped ——'

She lifted her chin then and looked at them with some defiance. 'I had hoped to draw upon my expectations under this will to give me sustenance until such time as I finish my studies and can embark upon my work at Queen Eleanor's, so there is no time to be lost in making all arrangements, gentlemen. Why can you not speak to this Mr Caspar tonight? Now, in fact?'

CHAPTER SIX

'Out of the question!' Freddy Casper said firmly. 'Positively out of the question. How could you possibly imagine, my dear young lady, that the estate would provide you with the wherewithal with which to lay claim to it?'

'That is precisely the point I made, Mr Caspar,' Mr Vivian said and to Sophie the note of self-satisfaction in his unctuous voice was even more annoying than the much more important content of Mr Caspar's words. How dare he be so complacent, when it meant the loss of all that mattered to her at this moment?

'Well, of course,' she said somewhat spitefully, shooting a sidelong glance at Mr Vivian's round face. 'No doubt it does give you pleasure to see a young female put down in her aspirations, but for my part, I would have thought it more important to concern yourself with the spirit of Mrs Lackland's bequest, rather than this pettifogging ——'

'You were swift to point out to me earlier, Miss Lackland, that legal documents are involved with what is actually written rather than what is implied,' Mr Vivian said. 'So let us please hear no nonsense about the *spirit* of this document.'

'I am the executor of this will, Miss Lackland, and the decision, I believe, rests largely with me,' Freddy Caspar said, turning his shoulder slightly towards Mr Vivian, which made Sophie feel a little better; clearly this pleasant man liked the lawyer as little as she did. 'And I assure you that were it possible to see any way in which I could accommodate you I would. Clearly a little more thought must be given to the matter — the urgency of all this caught me a little unprepared, you must understand ——'

Sophie reddened. 'I am sorry about that. I dare say I was somewhat precipitate in insisting that Mr Onions and Mr Vivian seek you tonight, rather than tomorrow morning. But, you know, I have come a very long way to deal with this matter and I am feeling a — it is of great importance to me.'

They were sitting in a small cluttered room in Queen Eleanor's Hospital, to which place Mr Vivian and Mr Onions had agreed to accompany her when she insisted yet again that her affairs be dealt with this very evening. Mr Onions, ever the gentleman, had supervised the loading of her luggage on to a growler and had it sent to a 'respectable small hotel where I think you will be tolerably comfortable — it is very convenient for the station —' while Mr Vivian, icy and uncommunicative in his disdain, had accompanied her in another cab, a hansom this time, to Mr Caspar's hospital.

'I do this under some duress, Miss Lackland,' he had said repressively. 'I would wish you to understand that. It is in no part my duty to give in to such importunings as yours. However, since it is clearly imperative that you be disabused as soon as may be of these foolish ambitions you entertain, I am willing to go with you to the hospital to see if Mr Caspar will see you. Be prepared, however, to be disappointed. He is a man of great importance and excessively busy. He may not choose to be disturbed by your request for an interview.'

But Mr Caspar had indeed agreed to be disturbed, and the white-capped and aproned nurse who had taken their message to him returned to show them into the little room to one side of the echoing entrance hall to wait here for the surgeon's arrival.

Sophie had been glad the nurse had left the office door open. While Mr Vivian stood with widely straddled legs before the struggling coal fire in the little grate, thus effectively cutting off any heat from her, she stood beside the door and stared out into the expanse of marble-floored and marble-pillared splendour that was the hospital's main entrance, and was struck with admiration. It glittered with cleanliness and well-scrubbed shiny paint in the light of several gas lamps, and sparkled with polished brass, and there was a strong reek of carbolic and ether and good yellow soap in the air. She sniffed it and thought suddenly of Bessie, redding up her kitchen with energy and dispatch with her great bars of home-made soap, and her eyes prickled. Bessie. So far away, and so missed already. She would give a lot, Sophie had thought suddenly, to be in her chair by her own fireside at Tansey Clough, with a cup of one of Bessie's rich broths in her hand and her mind quite free of all this nonsense about surgery.

But then a man of medium height, in a neatly cut though not

excessively fashionable black coat and trousers, had come across the hallway towards the little room and she had looked at him with great interest. Was this Mr Caspar?

He had reddish hair, rather faded in colour, and a broad sandy face, with a few freckles across the cheeks that gave him a rather endearingly young air, although he was clearly well into his forties. He had looked at her with an enquiring air, as he walked in to the office, and at once Mr Vivian had sprung into business.

'My dear Mr Caspar! I trust I see you well? I am sorry indeed to disturb you at this late hour of the afternoon, but Miss was, you know, more than a little importunate! I am sure when I explain all you will be able to find it in you to forgive me ——'

Mr Onions had come panting into the hospital and been brought to the little room by the time Mr Vivian had, with some circumlocution, explained the situation to Mr Caspar, who had sat silent and attentive throughout, one knee crossed over the other, and Sophie had sat and looked at him, and liked what she saw. There was something of Wilfred about him, something solid and sensible, and she felt hope begin to rise in her again as she tried to see beyond his quiet expression to whatever thoughts might be behind that broad brow. And been dashed again at his decided, 'Out of the question! Positively out of the question —' response.

He turned and looked at her then and smiled. 'You will be thinking me most churlish, Miss Lackland, to greet you in such a manner. It is not precisely my fault, however — you came upon me quite unawares! But I must welcome you now in a manner proper to a connection. We are, of course, related. Did you know that?'

She flushed. 'Why, I — no. I had not thought of the matter. I had thought that we were to talk to you as a medical man who could advise me on the — the possibilities of my studying the subject of surgery. Mr Vivian did not say ——' and she shot the lawyer a dismissive look. 'Only that your name was Caspar, and I did not think that — well, you understand, I am sure.'

'Indeed I do. But for all that I am named Caspar, related we are. My grandfather on my mother's side was Abel Lackland. And he was yours on your father's!'

'Oh! So we are — cousins?'

'Indeed we are. Welcome to London, cousin! I am sorry to hear of the death of your father my uncle, though I must confess that I never knew him. To tell the truth, the family to which we both belong is not one that is noted for its — um — closeness. We are no better and no worse than some, I dare say, but there it is — I do not know of all the family's past history, so I do not know why it was that your father parted company from his relations as he did. My mother, now, Mrs Gideon Henriques — she will know. She is the repository of all family affairs!' He smiled indulgently then, and Sophie liked him even more. 'She would greatly enjoy a comfortable prose with a new-discovered niece, I am sure!'

'I should enjoy it myself, Mr Caspar!' Sophie said warmly. 'And ——'

'Well, you will forgive me, I am sure, Mr Caspar, if I suggest we settle matters regarding this — um — legacy now.' Mr Vivian had removed a large gold watch from his waistcoat pocket and was comparing it with some punctiliousness with a small clock ticking on the mantelshelf behind him. 'I am sure you will not wish to waste any more of your valuable time on this affair ——'

Freddy's face straightened and he nodded, and turned to look again at Sophie. 'Well, yes, to our muttons. I am afraid, my dear Miss Lackland, that there can be no question of the estate permitting moneys to be released until such time as the conditions to inherit are fulfilled. I am sure Mr Vivian and Mr Onions here will agree with me ——'

'Eh? What?' Mr Onions had been dozing a little in the only comfortable chair in the room, and jumped a little at the sound of his name, and turned a look of blinking enquiry on to Sophie's face. 'What was that?'

Freddy repeated his words, a little louder, and after a moment Mr Onions looked at his partner, and then nodded.

'On that score I must agree. I do not think it would be proper at all to risk any of the bequest in such a way. Why, suppose Miss Lackland were not to achieve her ambition? It is one thing, Miss Lackland, to wish to become a surgeon — and I have already told you that I much admire young ladies — young people — of spirit. But it is quite another to achieve it. Suppose we were to release this money and then you failed to fulfil the conditions? It would be most irregular, and the London Ladies, you see — we have to consider them, do we not?'

The three men sat and looked at her and she looked back at them and felt herself suddenly filled with a huge weariness. It was as though every atom of spirit and energy in her had died, as though hope itself had flickered and gone out and she was too tired to care.

'So even if I were to find a way to receive my medical lectures and training, I could not have any money on which to subsist while I was studying? There is no way in which this could be arranged?'

Freddy shook his head, and said again, but with great gentleness, 'Out of the question. I am so sorry, my dear, for I too admire spirit and ambition, but in your case I fear ambition has o'erleaped itself ——'

She stood up after a moment and began to pull on her gloves, and smoothed the folds of her mantle over her hips.

'Well,' she said as bravely as she could. 'Then there is little more I can do. I would fight for ever to have the right to study — but I cannot fight with no ammunition. And with no source of income, a student I can never be.'

'I am sorry,' Freddy said again and stood up and held out his hand.

'I too,' Sophie said, head bent, and then she lifted her chin and smiled shakily at him. 'Well, at least I have my return fare on the railway sewn into my stays,' she went on, rather cheekily. 'Bessie — my old nurse, you know, and now my housekeeper — insisted upon it! I thought her too fussy, but she was right, was she not? I must return to Haworth.'

'Not before you have met your other relations, I trust, Miss Lackland,' Freddy said.

'Would there be any point, Mr Caspar? It has been most agreeable meeting you, sad though it has been to hear your decision regarding — well, never mind now. What is done is done. But to meet new relations now and then have to leave anyway to go home — it would be sadly dispiriting, I think. I thank you for your kindness, but I will go now to the hotel Mr Onions has arranged for me, and then, I suppose must telegraph home and follow the message myself as soon as may be ——'

Mr Caspar led her to the front door of the hospital himself, and held it wide for her, in spite of the disapproval of the large porter in pewter buttons who hovered nearby.

'I am indeed so sorry, Miss Lackland,' he said earnestly. 'I really am. Do not be too precipitate in making arrangements to return to

Yorkshire. See something of our great metropolis while you are here. There is much of interest — the Tower, you know, and the Waxworks and so forth. And if you tell me of the hotel where you are staying I will arrange for my mother to call upon you, if you will not call upon her, for I am sure she will be most put out if she does not meet you ——'

'I have taken a room for Miss Lackland at the Eastern Star Hotel, near St Pancras, Mr Caspar, and I trust she will find it comfortable, though it is a modest establishment,' Mr Onions said, and Freddy nodded.

'Thank you. Well, au revoir, Miss Lackland. I hope we can meet again.'

'Thank you. I too. Goodbye,' Sophie said drearily and turned and walked down the steps to the street, too depressed to feel even a twinge of regret. Half an hour ago she had walked up those steps so hopefully, imagining herself, for one brief moment, as a busy surgeon there, and now she was leaving, her last flicker of ambition quite extinguished under the quenching problem of money. Oh, hateful, hateful money! It meant so little in reality, and yet could blast the hopes of a whole lifetime! Never mind the preaching of the Pastor at home about the vanity of possessions — without them, life was a sorry business.

Indeed Sophie Lackland was a bitter as well as a very weary young woman that December evening, and she stood on the pavement outside Queen Eleanor's breathing the acrid, slightly foggy air, heavy with soot, and aching for the clean honest breath of her moorlands, while Messrs Onions and Vivian made their careful farewells of Mr Caspar.

Freddy Caspar watched her go away down Endell Street, her long back swaying elegantly, for all it was drooping with fatigue, between the bulky shapes of the lawyers, and felt more than a little depressed himself. Such an eager, vivid creature, so young, so bubbling with hope. It had given him no pleasure at all to so blight her dream; and he had felt more than usually irritated with Mr Vivian, to whom it so patently had. But what could he have done? Quite apart from the problems surrounding the whole question of medical education for women, there was the matter of the money. And it would be wrong to allow so much as sixpence of his dead grandmamma's money to be deflected from its rightful beneficiary.

And it was patently obvious that that beneficiary would have to be the London Ladies. He would have to call on Aunt Martha on Sunday afternoon, and talk to her about it ——

He hurried back to the Women's Surgical Ward, looking at his watch as he went. Close on seven o'clock, already, and Phoebe waiting at home with one of her splendid dinners especially ordered for him, and becoming more and more annoyed at the delay, for they were to go out tonight — and there was still that girl with her pain and bleeding that would have to be dealt with.

He sighed softly and beckoned the hall porter, and taking a notebook from his pocket scribbled a note to Phoebe, telling her not to wait for him, to take her dinner, and that she would have to go on to the opera alone, for he was quite sure he would be late. He signed himself as her loving husband, flattening a twist of wry amusement as he did so, and folded it, and told the porter to see it was taken round to his house in Tavistock Square.

She will be annoyed and I will suffer for that, he thought, as he went hurrying along the echoing green-painted corridors, but for all that he did not find himself as distressed as he once would have been at the thought of upsetting his Phoebe. In recent years she had become more and more as she had been as a girl, much too occupied with the fripperies of fashion and silly socializing. There were times when he looked back on his young self, so besottedly in love that he could hardly think straight, and would wonder if, had he known what he now did of life with Phoebe, he would have suffered quite so much — and then would push the thought aside as ignoble. And anyway, absurd. He was married to Phoebe, for good or ill, and must learn to tolerate her more irritating ways as best he could. There was no other choice for him.

He pushed the big door that led to the Women's Surgical Ward and stood for a moment in the embrasure, looking along the expanse of room that stretched ahead. It never failed to give him pleasure, such a sight of one of the hospital's eleven wards, on a winter's evening like this.

The serried ranks of beds, all thirty of them, stretched down to the far end and in the middle the big double fireplace, with its burnished chimney stretching up till it pierced the ceiling, glowed with a bright sea coal fire. The polished wooden bedside lockers with their few flowers and jugs of water under beaded covers, the beds with their crimson blankets, the curtains neatly pulled back against the walls between the long windows — it breathed of comfort and peace, for all its occupants were all sick and ailing and in pain.

In many ways it was for Freddy a more homelike and comfortable place to be than his own home in Tavistock Square. There all was style and elegance and deeply buttoned, heavily upholstered crimson velvet sofas and chairs, and little gilded tables and fringes and pictures and statues and ornaments, ornaments, ornaments, till sometimes he felt there was nowhere he could set his foot without being at imminent risk of causing grave damage to some expensive gewgaw. Here at least all was clean and quiet and simple. No luxury ever tainted these busy wards, for Queen Eleanor's budget was a small one, with little enough money to spare for essentials, let alone fripperies.

There was a faint sound from the end of the ward, rising above the low buzz of women's voices which was coming from those patients who were fit enough to be sitting beside the fire engaged in desultory conversation, a sharp little wail of pain, and he shook his head and went hurrying down the ward to the bed at the far end, round which the curtains were drawn.

'Oh, Mr Caspar, I was about to come and fetch you, truth to tell!' A nurse, well wrapped in a calico apron and with her hair pulled back tightly beneath her old fashioned cap, bustled importantly up to him. 'For she's really in a bad way, and getting more feverish by the minute. We've applied the cold compresses to her as you said, sir, and she's had the syrup and we've packed her with ice to staunch the bleeding, but she's clearly in great pain, sir, and ——'

'Will she let me see her now, d'you think?'

'Poor soul, she's barely fit to think of aught but her pain now, I'm thinking,' the nurse said, and drew the curtain to one side to let him reach the bedside. 'I doubt she'll trouble now that you want to examine her.'

But she was wrong. As Freddy sat down on the bed beside the girl lying there with her knees drawn up and her face twisted with pain she opened her eyes and stared wildly at him for a moment, and he leaned forwards and touched her forehead. She was wet with sweat and her eyes were red-rimmed and bloodshot, and her lips dry and cracked.

She was, Freddy knew, about twenty-two or three — about the same age as that girl he had just seen walk away down Endell Street, yet this one looked old and worn out, long before her time. Her face was pulled into a grimace of pain, and her forehead was creased with anxiety.

'I am sorry you feel so poorly, my dear,' Freddy said gently. 'I really think, you know, that you must let me examine you now and decide what shall be done for the best ——'

'No ——' the girl wailed it, thinly, almost as a cat mews, but there was sharpness in her tone for all that. 'No — you shall not — I could not bear it — no — it is dreadful to consider ——' and then she moaned again and drew her knees even more closely up to her chin as another twinge of pain swept her.

'This really will not do, my dear,' Freddy said with determination. 'I know it to be of great importance not to distress any patient, and I would not distress you for the world, but this is modesty run mad. You must let me examine you, and decide on your further care — if you do not, you may die of your ills, and leave your husband and poor baby alone in the world — and all for misplaced modesty ——'

'It is not misplaced.' The girl on the bed was gasping a little now, and the beads of sweat on her brow could be clearly seen.

'She's bleeding,' Freddy thought, staring down at her. 'That pallor — she's bleeding, damn it all ——'

The girl rolled her head restlessly on the pillow. 'Indeed 'tis not right to allow a man to — I cannot bear it ——'

But Freddy nodded crisply to the nurse who leaned forwards and with a firm movement folded back the blankets to reveal the girl's belly and thighs. Her nightgown was pulled up close to her waist, for her abdomen was covered with a strip of wet flannel, and between her thighs was a bag of ice.

The girl moaned and with a pitiful gesture of shame tried to cover her body with her hands, but her strength was not enough, and as gently as he could, Freddy removed the wet compress and then, easing her knees apart with firm yet gentle hands, removed the ice bag.

At once a spurt of crimson blood shot out from the little patch of coarse pubic hair and Freddy, moving fast, put one hand on the girl's belly, and slid the other under her, two fingers advanced, so that he could slip them inside her, and she moaned and rolled a little and the blood ran even faster.

'Keep still, you foolish creature!' the nurse said sharply. 'Would you try to kill yourself? Mr Caspar will not hurt you ——'

Again the girl moaned and tried to pull away from Freddy's exploring hands, and the nurse lifted her chin and called sharply, 'Biggins! Snell!' and after a moment two more nurses appeared round the curtains and at a jerk of the older woman's head, set themselves on each side of the now almost distraught patient, holding her firmly.

Freddy was hating it. That this girl was bleeding dangerously was clear, and if the bleeding was not stopped soon then she would be dead. But to have to force himself upon a woman who shrank so miserably, as did this girl, from being touched by a man in the way he had to touch her to examine her, distressed him deeply. He was not angered by modesty as were many of his colleagues in similar situations. They would fulminate quite often against these 'damned female megrims' finding it impossible to enter into their feelings, but not Freddy. Women needed their dignity protected, and should be able to trust their medical men to do so, even though they were men.

Once again the girl pulled away from him, and her distress seemed to give her strength for she managed to evade his hand and this time the blood spurted so strongly that his black jacket was spattered with it.

'Drat the girl,' Nurse Biggins said, and pulled her back roughly and Freddy said quietly but with unmistakable edge, 'Remember that you are dealing with a sensitive lady, nurse. Treat her as you would wish to be treated yourself — my dear — can you listen to me?' He turned back to the patient. 'I must tell you that you are bleeding badly. I suspect that you have much of the afterbirth of your baby held in your body and it must be removed. Please do not be frightened. We shall give you chloroform and ——'

'The midwife!' the girl on the bed gasped. 'Let the midwife — a good woman — let the midwife do it ——'

'No,' he said quietly, and put the ice bag back between her groins. 'The midwife lacks the necessary skills and knowledge,' and intelligence too, he thought savagely and signalled to the nurses to wrap the girl up in her blankets, ready to be carried to the operating theatre. Any doctor would have seen long before that damned midwife had that this girl had retained the placenta and was bleeding fit to die, but she, stupid hamfisted creature had done nothing for her for fully twenty-four hours — a piece of laxity which the girl's young husband had for all his concern allowed, knowing as he did how much his sensitive wife shrank from the attention of any man other than himself, doctor or not.

But then he had brought her in despair to Queen Eleanor's when the midwife, at last alarmed by her patient's deteriorating condition, had decamped, leaving him helpless and bewildered. Freddy had seen him and gladly taken the young mother in, even though she had protested weakly, clinging to her husband with all the tenacity of the very ill. The baby had been sent to the ward kept for sick children at the back part of the hospital — where their cries could be less easily heard by sick people in the wards — and work was set in hand at once to solve the mother's problems.

As far as Freddy had been able to determine, faced with the girl's steadfast refusal to allow any man's hand to touch so intimate a part of her body, she had been badly torn by the mismanaged birth, and the placenta had separated but been trapped inside the torn vaginal tissues. The girl's state was parlous, and her intense anxiety whenever Freddy approached her had made it even worse.

He had hoped the ice packs and the wet compresses would help staunch the bleeding, but had in his heart known they would not. And now the time had come when, will-she, nill-she, the girl would have to reveal her body in all its detail to his masculine mind and eye and hands.

But it was too late. For all he spent two hours labouring over the damaged uterus and cervix, for all his struggles to clamp down on the bleeding from the placental site deep inside, the time when intervention could have helped was long since gone — had probably gone even before she arrived at Queen Eleanor's.

When Freddy left the hospital that night, walking home with great strides through the silent midnight streets, the baby in the back ward was motherless, and the young husband who had tried so hard to protect his wife's modesty was weeping alone in his big double bed in his house in St Catherine's Street. And Freddy was deeply, furiously angry.

As he reached the flight of steps that led to his own house in

Tavistock Square he lifted his chin and stared up at the blank sky, unbroken on this bitter night with a single glimmer of starlight.

'She should have had a woman to care for her,' he thought. And then, with apparent inconsequentiality, 'Tomorrow, I shall go to see Martha about that Yorkshire cousin. Tomorrow, before I go to Nellie's. First thing ——'

CHAPTER SEVEN

'Do tell me, Freddy — does she bear any family resemblances?'

'Oh, Aunt Martha, how can I say? She is a girl, you know, like any other ——'

'Come, Freddy, do not pretend with me to be so lofty! You are as interested as anyone else in the appearance of girls. You have always had a very pretty taste in ladies. Indeed, every time I look at your Phoebe I find myself wondering how it was she never escaped your clutches to marry a duke at the very least!'

'She might have liked that,' Freddy said absently, and then, as his aunt flicked a sharp glance at him, laughed. 'Phoebe would dearly love me to be the sort of man who would work for preferment! But there, I am happy enough at Queen Eleanor's, after all ——'

'About this girl — Sophie, you say her name is? Sophie — you are perturbed in your mind about her, are you not, Freddy?'

There was a little silence and Freddy drank some more coffee, staring out of the window at the sky above Bedford Row with a blank expression on his face. Sitting here with Aunt Martha at her breakfast table was very agreeable. There she sat, her small square shape encased in a cotton wrapper, and her hair concealed under the most respectable of morning caps — such a lovely old-fashioned thing to do, to wear a cap! — surrounded by her coffee equipage and composedly eating toasted bread sippets and quince jam. At home Phoebe would be barely turning into her second sleep; her morning chocolate tray would not be delivered to her handsome bedroom until well after eleven had struck, and Cecily had been busy for the last two hours in the schoolroom with Miss Fuggle struggling with French. Ever since James and Ambrose had gone away to school at Winchester, Phoebe had become more and more indolent, and Freddy was finding it more and more irritating.

Especially when he thought of that young cousin with her narrow green eyes and her fine country complexion and her hair constantly escaping from the confines in which she tied it. And her energy. It had been that of which he had been most aware last night; the girl had been tired, clearly — considering she had made the long journey from Yorkshire that very day, she was entitled to be — but there had still been a strength in her, a sense of controlled power that he had found very attractive.

Yes, he was mixed up in his feelings about her, and he put down his cup with a little clatter and turned to his aunt and smiled at her. 'Aunt, you are a wise and downy old bird! Are you not? You always have been. Yes, I am perturbed in my mind about her. She is kin, of course, and that should give her some claim on my interest, but there is more to it than that. She has — oh, I do not know! Yes I do. She made me think of Grandpapa. Now is that not very strange? A slip of a girl, and she made me think of Grandpapa!'

'Indeed, I must meet this young person,' Martha said after a moment, looking closely at her nephew. 'That must be a strange likeness indeed. Is it her colouring, perhaps? Papa was very dark — hair as black as a crow's wing when he was younger, though in his later years of course as white as ——'

'No — although he had the same sort of green eyes, I think. But hers are much stronger, somehow, in colour. Brighter, you know — quite piercing green. No, it was not the look of her — at least I do not think so ——'

'Well,' Aunt Martha said briskly and stood up. 'There is no answer for it but that I must see for myself. I will soon be able to see what this likeness is — and I long to speak to her of her father. Oh dear, imagine silly little Barty a father! It is so many years ago — but still whenever I think of him I see that indolent foolish delightful boy that he was — why it must be — oh, he could not have been above twenty when I last saw him! Not that I guessed for a moment that that would be our last meeting. How could I? How could any of us have thought so? But away he went, and then Papa took one of his absurd notions, you know, and decided to be bad friends with poor Barty — they had never been precisely soul-tied, after all — and there we were. Oh dear! Time goes so quickly ——'

And she stood there for a moment holding her wrapper around her and staring back down the vista of her fifty-seven years.

'And you look exactly as you did twenty years ago, my dear Aunt! A slip of a girl who went cavorting off to the Crimea —

perhaps it is you I saw in that young woman yesterday!' Freddy leaned back in his chair and grinned up at her. 'Wilful, outrageous, quite set on her own ideas ——'

'Oh, as to that, pooh!' Aunt Martha said, but she looked pleased none the less. 'You say, Freddy, that she has given up all notions of becoming a surgeon and claiming Maria's legacy?'

Freddy nodded, sober again. 'I cannot see she can do otherwise. I cannot allow her to take money from the estate in order to qualify, and there is no one who can support her while she does seek a medical career. And even if she does, how can any of us know what will happen? This Jex-Blake girl — you know her, do you not? Yes, I thought you did — well, she is making a great pother and to-do up there in Edinburgh, and of course there is Dr Garrett — Mrs Anderson — a splendid lady, that. I have met her, and like her well. But she was admitted to the profession by a mere fluke, and it is no longer possible for any other girl to enter that way — so what is to be done? She must give in — which should please you, Aunt!'

'Please me?'

'As the leading light of the London Ladies, of course.'

'Oh yes.' There was a little silence and Aunt Martha stood in the window and stared down at the street below. The London Ladies. They were poor enough, heaven knew. This hostel here in Bedford Row cost more and more to run each year, and the new one just about to be started in Villiers Street would cost a pretty penny. The legacy of that house had been a dubious benefit, she now realized. Old Mrs Deering who had left it to them to be used for a hostel for young women alone in London had meant well enough, no doubt, but it would stretch the Committee's slender resources greatly to fit the place out, let alone to run it as it should be run, and to find the wages of a Lady Warden. So, a legacy of over fifty-seven thousand pounds would be received with the warmest welcome at the present.

And yet — she stared down at the street, seeing a shadowy vision of herself down there. Herself twenty years ago, brave yet terrified, standing on the curb on a misty early morning with Sal piling her luggage into a growler, on their way to the great adventure in the Crimea. Alexander had been there waiting for her too and ——

She shook her head at that and turned back to Freddy. 'We would want no legacy that was not fully ours by right. Maria I know had it as her dearest wish that a surgeon named Lackland should carry on to follow in Papa's footsteps. I think she saw the idea as a memorial to him that would be much longer lasting and more important than that statue the Hospital Governors had made could ever be — dreadful great thing! Were she alive she would applaud this child's idea of taking on the task, I am sure of it. She was, for all her old-fashioned ways, a very special lady, was Maria. She had much bottom to her ——'

'If she were here, dear Aunt Martha,' Freddy said dryly, 'we would have no problems. But she is not, and has left an ambiguous will behind her, clear though its stipulations may appear to be on the surface. Oh dear, I *will* be glad when this girl is gone. As it is, she — oh, she nibbles at my conscience in some absurd way. It is quite ridiculous that I, of all men, should applaud the ambitions of a chit of a girl who wants to poach in my river, but there it is — I am not as horrified as I might be at the suggestion ——'

There was a little silence and then Martha said quietly, 'Freddy, is it possible for her?'

'Eh? Is it — how do you mean?'

'If she really chose to put her mind to it, is there a way she could become a surgeon, could qualify? Have there not been these dreadful problems in Edinburgh? And are not questions being asked in the House of Commons and ——'

'I don't know, Aunt,' Freddy said slowly. 'I really do not know how it will all turn out. The world is changing so fast these days that sometimes I think I cannot keep track of all that is happening in it. When I was a student at Nellie's, when Grandpapa was there, the mere notion of a woman student would have been unthinkable. Yet, now it is not so shocking after all. Though still, I cannot see how — the anatomy classes, you see, and the practical work — and what about the matter of teaching men and women *obstetrics* together? It is bad enough that the patients are all women and the doctors are all men ——'

He stopped then and his gaze blanked and Martha looked at him and felt a wave of warmth for him fill her; after her own dear Felix, her adopted son, there was no one she loved more dearly than Freddy. And sometimes when Amy was being particularly irritating and captious, and Felix more than usually defensive about his wife's behaviour, it was Freddy who found himself in first place in his aunt's affections.

'There was a girl last night,' he said then, painfully. 'Died. I cannot say she might not have died anyway — shocking bad confinement by some idiot woman of a midwife — but the girl was one that could not bear the idea of a man near her at her time, and held me back until it was too late. Had she had a doctor of her own sex to care for her, would it have been different? I don't know — but there is a dead girl and a motherless babe and I feel so — well, let be! I learned one lesson in my early days at Nellie's, and that was not to repine over what could not be undone. Only to learn from it. I am trying still to learn —— Aunt, I must go. I have several operations before me today, and the hospital will be in a fine old ferment if I am late. Let me know what you think of our new young relative, will you? I will be more than a little interested ——'

And he was gone, leaving her to dress in her usual sensible if rather dull clothes, and settle the morning affairs of the hostel. She spent some time worrying over Villiers Street as well, but to little point. The architect had finished his work of converting the rooms in the upper stories of the old house to make them fit to be used as dormitories for up to four or five girls at a time, the kitchens had been handsomely extended, the big dining room painted out and the drawing room papered. All that remained now was to pay for all, and to see the furniture in, furniture bought with great care by Martha herself at various auctions in Somers Town warehouses where she had struck some shrewd bargains. The problem was finding someone to be there to accept the deliveries, arrange where the items were to be placed, to wash the floors, fill the shelves in the kitchen and generally set the place to rights. There was Sal of course, her old friend of the Crimean days, but she was busy enough running her prosperous public house in Camden Town. She would come if Martha sent for her to help, albeit with much grumbling, but it would cost her dear, for Sal ran her tavern single-handed, and when she was not there herself had to close doors. So Martha would not ask her to help, if she could possibly help it.

But, she told herself, setting the piles of papers relating to Villiers Street to one side, I will think no more about that now. I will concern myself with visiting. I shall go to see my niece: 'Mary!' — and as her little parlour maid came scuttling up to the drawing room — 'Fetch me a hansom! I am to go to the Royal Eastern Hotel, in St Pancras. Immediately, now!'

And if she had a glimmering of a plan already at the back of her practical mind, she did not, at this stage, admit the fact to herself.

* * *

'It is strange, really!' Sophie said ingenuously. 'I would have thought, you know, that you more than anyone would want to see me give up my ambitions. After all, you stand to gain so much when I do.' She reddened suddenly and her hand flew to her mouth in embarrassment. 'Oh, I am so sorry! How dreadfully rude of me! I did not mean to suggest — to make any implication that — it's just that I know that the charity and — oh dear, I do beg your pardon!'

Martha laughed aloud, with genuine pleasure. She had wanted to see the girl out of simple curiosity; was she not her own brother's child? But she had found herself captivated almost at once by Sophie's transparent ways. Not for her any of the drawing room tricks so many young London ladies indulged in. Not for her the posing prettiness that was designed to bewitch — and if for a moment she thought with disapproval of her adoptive daughter-in-law, Amy, she soon pushed that away — or the fencing with words that seemed so de rigueur these days. Just a blunt straight-forwardness that was very refreshing.

She had found her in her modest hotel bedroom mournfully putting the last of her possessions into the little basket that Bessie had packed with food for the hopeful journey down to London, and with the corded box standing ready by the door to be collected. She had looked neat and pleasant to Martha, standing there in the doorway, and for a moment she saw the hint of family likeness that Freddy had mentioned. There was something about the set of her long back, the way her head was poised on her neck, that was deeply familiar. But then she had looked up and seen her visitor and cocked her head to one side in an enquiring way and at once had looked quite different.

'Ah — Mrs Henriques?' she had hazarded.

'Dear me, no,' Martha had said briskly, and came into the room, taking off her gloves to settle herself, uninvited, on the bed. 'You and I share the same name, my dear — I am Martha Lackland — Mrs Henriques is my sister, Abby. Did you expect her?'

'Not really. It was just that Mr Caspar said she would like to meet me — as a member of the family, you know. But I did not wish to disturb her, for there seems so little point. If I am to go home again at once.'

'Are you?'

Sophie had looked at her very directly then, her chin up. 'You must surely know, since you are here at all, that I have no other choice. Mr Caspar is the executor of the will, and he and both those lawyers say it is not possible for me to be — supported in any way while I study, so ——' She had shrugged, and turned back to the fastening of her little basket.

'Have you sent a message home to say you are returning?'

The busy hands stopped but Sophie did not look round. 'No. Not yet.'

'But if you are sure you are going, why not?'

There was a little silence and then Sophie shrugged. 'Oh, perhaps I was hoping that — well, never mind. I will send a telegraph message directly.'

'You give up rather easily, then? I would not have thought it of you. Any girl who has the temerity even to think of becoming a medical student must surely be one of no ordinary stamp and who has a little more tenacity than you appear to be displaying. When I heard from Freddy of the way you had arrived yesterday and made your claim I was vastly entertained, I do assure you!'

'Entertained?'

'Indeed, yes! It seems to me that the world has gone milk and water in far too many ways. That girls become less and less interested in reality, more and more involved with nonsense such as clothes and parties. We are all so *rich* these days — there is so much there for the young to enjoy that they have no — no *energy* any more! To hear of a girl who was — dare I say it, more as *I* was when I was young — well, it warmed me. And it entertained me. If you give up this easily then I shall be sorely disappointed.'

That was when Sophie had made her faux pas about Martha's standing to gain so much for her abandonment of her ambitions, and Martha had enjoyed that enormously, and after a moment Sophie had caught the infection of her laughter and joined in, until the two of them were sitting side by side on the tumbled bed in the dismal little hotel in St Pancras and sharing their pleasure in

73

each other with unashamed delight. It was a moment that Sophie was never to forget.

'I think, you know, that we must talk sensibly,' Martha said at length. 'Amusement is all very well, but it is practical that we must now be. Tell me the situation as you see it. Never mind what the lawyers and Freddy said — let me hear your thinking.'

So Sophie told her. Of the long years of apprenticeship in Haworth, looking after the rag, tag and bobtail of the village, with their aches and pains and births and deaths. Of the years of dreaming of a world bigger and better and altogether more exciting, beyond the boundaries of home, beloved though home was. Of the enormous hope that had surged in her, of the bitter disappointment when she discovered that all that stood between her and her ambition was lack of money. All of it.

And Martha listened and nodded and never took her eyes from the girl's face. Not a pretty face precisely, but a strong one, with its broad cheekbones and firm mouth and chin, and those fascinating narrow green eyes of which Freddy had been so aware. Martha could see ever more clearly with every moment that passed just how it had been that this girl had made so strong an impression on her middle-aged cousin.

'Hmph,' she said, when Sophie stopped at last. 'I see. Had you made enquiries about how you were to prosecute your medical training, if money were available to keep you while you studied?'

'Not in any detail,' Sophie admitted. 'But I was sanguine. I was very sanguine. Here is Miss Jex-Blake and her friends pushing all before them in Edinburgh to qualify and then Mrs Anderson — if they could do it, so can I! Why not! I know it is surgery that I seek and this is much harder for a woman than being a physician, but never mind. Someone has to try first, and it might as well be me! Or so I felt,' she amended soberly, some of the fire dying out of her. 'But money, wretched hateful money — that is an insoluble problem. To tell you the truth,' she went on disarmingly, 'I am not sure what will happen when I go home. We were already on our last legs, so to speak, for Papa, dear and funny as he was, was a poor provider, and Mamma's family — well, the less said about them the better for all of us. And I suspect I must sell Tansey Clough and take a cottage somewhere if we are to live at all. Not that it is as bad as it was, for at least Bessie will be married and she will have her husband to keep her — oh, it is all so dispiriting.' And she sat and looked down at her hands clasped on her lap, and let her shoulders droop with the weight of her anxiety.

'Well!' Martha said briskly after a moment and got to her feet. 'I think we must do something practical about this situation. Sitting here repining will get us nowhere. Come along, my dear. Out! Put on your mantle and your bonnet, and we must be away.'

'Away? Where?' Sophie stared up at her, a small line forming between her brows. She had warmed to this friendly bustling little lady as soon as she had seen her standing there at the doorway in her dull but rich-looking mantle and heavy bonnet, and had found some comfort in telling her of her woes, but, after all, she was in a sense her adversary. Sophie's own loss was definitely her gain — or at least, her Committee's gain.

'I told you! To find a practical answer to your dilemma. I thought you wanted to stay in London? To become a student? Well, then — put on your mantle and bonnet!'

'I will not,' Sophie said mulishly, now thoroughly alarmed. 'Why should I? What do I know about you, after all? You came here and said you were Miss Lackland, and my aunt, but really, there is no reason why I should believe you! And anyway — no. I am sorry I did not ask you to leave me as soon as you arrived here. My affairs are my own and ——'

'Oh, foolish child!' Martha said, and laughed again. 'While I applaud your caution in one way, you really are doing it up rather too brown to display it now, when we have been sitting here talking so comfortably for so long. My dear, all I wish to do is take you to a house our Committee owns in Villiers Street. It is to be run as a new hostel for girls alone in London — there are far too many of them, you know, who fall into the most dreadful evil ways because of lack of a decent place to live and a decent person to care for them and guide them — and I have need of a Lady Warden to run it. It seems to me that with your past experience and your good sense — which is clear in all you say — that this is a post you could usefully adorn. Now, what do you say? To accept this offer would provide you with a roof over your head and food to eat, and a small competence. Not a great deal,' she added with prudent haste, 'for the Committee is hard pushed for funds, but enough to allow you to live decent if not fancy. Now, if that appeals to you, you will have a home to call

75

your own, the chance to earn your bread, and time — if you plan it right — to prosecute your studies. What do you say to that, then, Miss Lackland? Hey? What d'you say to that?'

CHAPTER EIGHT

If the day before had been breathless with excitement, today promised fair to be downright suffocating. Once Miss Martha Lackland took matters in hand, Sophie discovered, there was no holding her, and events piled up with such speed that even hard-working eager Sophie was left marvelling.

They took a cab to Villiers Street, and all the way Martha treated Sophie to a commentary on all they saw, and all that was of interest. She pointed out old buildings thick with the accretions of history, and new ones lifting their proud Gothic fronts — for the Gothic style of architecture was all the rage in London at present — to the heavy December skies. She animadverted on the problem of the traffic, complained about the bad manners of cab drivers and draymen, poured scorn on the sort of clothes some of the more fashion-conscious passers-by were parading, and altogether was so entertaining as the cab went spanking up the Marylebone Road towards Regent Street, before curving left to make its busy way towards Charing Cross, that Sophie was enchanted.

She began to feel for the first time some of the magic of London, the raw pulsing drama of success and prosperity that filled the streets and piled the shops up high with the riches of the world. She felt the first stirrings of the deep excitement she had dreamed she would find in this city, and yesterday had suspected was all a mirage. But now she knew, as she looked out at the thronged streets and the busy traffic, that it was all real, all important, and she was part of it. London was as modern as tomorrow, and she was young in it. What more could any girl want? She was one of the new generation of women. One who would set the world on its ears, in spite of her skirts. It was a very heady feeling, and she revelled in it.

Villiers Street brought her down to earth with a little thump. A narrow street, running straight down from the Strand to the embankment and the river, with the great bulk of Charing Cross station and its adjoining hotel rearing up on the western side, it looked a little sleazy, with its close-packed narrow houses and noisy pushing people. But then she looked again, and it began to seem a little more interesting, for many of the houses had small restaurants on the ground-floor level, jostling with customers at this busy time of the day, and there were public houses with gilded painted fronts and great expanses of engraved glass windows, and tea shops and little exotic groceries where foreign cheeses and sausages were piled high on marble counters. There was a little fruiterer's where oranges and lemons glowed with vivid colour and the smell of onions and carrots came appetizingly floating out into the cold air. But above all there was the scent of coffee. Somewhere one of these shops was roasting beans and grinding them, and she lifted her head and sniffed appreciatively. Martha, who had been paying the cab driver, turned then and smiled. 'I daresay you could find it in you to enjoy a little luncheon? Perhaps we could deal with that first and then I will show you the house which will be your domain. Over here, then — Gatti's.'

She led the way across the narrow thoroughfare to a small glass-windowed restaurant and pushed open the door and led Sophie into the noisiest, busiest and most delectable-smelling place she could ever remember being in. Everywhere was bustle; waiters ran between the tables, coat-tails flying, napkins over their arms equally busy in the rush of air, and customers, clustered round small marble-topped tables, chattered and gesticulated and roared at each other through the steam and clatter of glasses and dishes. She could have laughed aloud with pleasure at the exuberance of it all.

'Have you ever eaten Italian food, Sophie? No? Then this is an excellent opportunity for you to try some. The people here are in fact all Swiss — but from that part of Switzerland which abuts on to Italy. So the influence is there. Shall you leave the choice to me?'

'Oh, yes, please. I could never know what to select,' Sophie said, staring with wide eyes at the large sheet of white paper one of the flying waiters had thrust into her hand. It was covered in spidery blue handwriting and was almost illegible, but Martha coped well enough, and soon Sophie was dipping her spoon into a great bowl of minestrone soup, and relaxing blissfully under the influence of the good food.

They ate in companionable silence, following their soup with a pile of spaghetti, which alarmed Sophie at first, for she stared at the wormlike pile with great dubiety, until Martha showed her how to twist her fork through the slippery strands; and then she enjoyed it all hugely.

They ended their repast with multicoloured ice cream, which was also a great treat for Sophie who had only ever had it twice before, on both occasions at Mrs Brotherton's house, 'where,' she confided in Martha, 'it was not nearly as nice as this, for Mrs Brotherton, for all her airs, is a mean-minded creature who makes all she can out of the least of ingredients. Her parties are unsupportable unpleasant, they really are ——'

She prattled artlessly on, revealing more than she knew of herself as she talked of Haworth and her friends there, and, a little wistfully, of dear old Wilfred, who was always so reliable and kindly. And Martha, listening, was amused and thought of Freddy and his Phoebe and then sighed a little.

And then it was time to see the house, and Martha took Sophie across the street to number twenty-two, a tall narrow-fronted house with a solid front door under a fan-shaped transom, and opened the door with a large iron key and showed Sophie over every inch of it. She was now the complete businesswoman, and so crisp in her instruction and information that Sophie found she fell into a much more deferential pose; where before she had talked to Martha easily, as an equal, if older lady, now she felt herself very much the servant, but not in any disagreeable way. She was here to learn a new task, and learn it she would.

It was agreed that she should stay at the hotel for the remainder of the week, with the London Ladies paying her bill (Sophie demurred at first but Martha had overridden her objections; this was the way the matter was to be arranged and it was none of Sophie's affair) and attending at Villiers Street from eight in the morning till six at night to set it to rights.

'You will work hard,' Martha warned. 'Never think otherwise. I can provide no house servant until the first girls come to stay here — it would not be possible. So every scrap of work is yours alone. I depend upon you to do it properly. If it should transpire — which I doubt — that you do not do it well enough, well, rest assured I will give you your congé forthwith. I will not be sentimental, I can promise you, and keep you on if you prove to be less than I

79

expected. Niece you may be, but in the matter of this house, you are employed by the London Ladies, to whom my responsibility stands first.'

'I am glad to hear it,' Sophie said with some dignity. 'I want no charity for myself. The opportunity to work for my bread and keep myself while I study is one I greatly value — but you can rest assured you will not lose by it! I was reared by Bessie Pighills, you know, and she taught me the right and wrong ways to set about work. It will be done right, I assure you.'

And so it was. They spent the afternoon purchasing brooms and buckets and mops and dusters and soap and the following morning at half past seven sharp Sophie climbed aboard the omnibus at St Pancras to make her first journey to Villiers Street alone.

From then on she worked as though all the fiends of hell were after her. Each bedroom — and there were seven of them in the tall narrow house — was scrubbed to within an inch of its life until her hands were raw with the task, and had to be rubbed each night with big dollops of goose fat to make them comfortable again. The windows were polished to a glare, the curtains — for which Martha came to help — were carefully starched and hung in each neat window, and the furniture when it arrived was polished and burnished in a way that would have made Bessie proud of her nursling.

At first Sophie found it all exhausting. She worked grimly through each day, subsisting on many cups of coffee and bread and cheese from Gatti's across the road, and each night she tumbled into her narrow hotel bed to sleep heavily and dreamlessly before starting on yet another day of unremitting toil; but after a few days it got easier. The worst of the heavy work was done, and she began to take real pleasure in seeing the rooms take on a comfortable homely look. The beds that she made up in the dormitory rooms, four to each one, looked spartan but inviting, and she bought out of her own pocket flowers from the little old woman who sat regularly at the top of the street, to decorate each room as it was done. The floors were covered with blue drugget, plain and serviceable but cheerful enough, and the stairs with the same material, but in a more practical brown.

In her own room — and she was to have one to her own use entirely, a privilege which Martha insisted upon and for which

Sophie was very grateful — she had a deep crimson drugget. It suited her, she told Martha, who professed to find it rather too bright, and certainly the little room, high in the attic, looked most inviting. Martha had provided from Bedford Row a handsome marble washstand and elegant china bowls and jugs, and had found from somewhere a nicely made patchwork quilt which enlivened the room greatly. There was a big skylight window and a small cosy fireplace with a little hob where a kettle could easily boil to make a comforting bedtime posset, and a well-made brass oil lamp.

Altogether, Sophie thought when she looked round at it, it was all a girl could ask. There might not be the lovely views of the climbing moors which her window at home framed, no acres of purpling ling as the year turned, but there was all the drama and excitement of the street below with its cosmopolitan London inhabitants, and she felt that was a fair exchange.

As the days passed towards Christmas she discovered more and more about her neighbours, for they were at some pains to get to know her. First it was the waiters in Gatti's, who soon showed her their differing personalities; there was morose but essentially gentle Luigi Marionis, who longed all the time for his home in Switzerland, and cheerful impudent Pietro Pagani, as swift on his feet as any of the London sparrows that filled the gutters with their chattering. There were Giandelli — the only Italian among all these Swiss — and Jean and Giuseppe, as like each other as peas in a pod with their shining black hair and drooping black moustachios, and Daniele Togni and Antonio Maddalena who never ceased fighting with each other, but who were the closest of friends at bottom — she got to know them all, and liked them all. She heard all about Monsieur Gatti himself, who spent most of his time at his music hall at the end of Villiers Street, but who was at present at home in Milan, visiting his family, and at the same time seeking new waiters for his growing business.

She heard about the brothers Monico, who had started out as ordinary waiters just like themselves, working for Gatti, but who had managed to save enough money to have their own restaurant now, and whose example they all longed to follow. She heard about wives and children at home, about old mothers still yearning after widely travelled sons; and above all she heard their pithy views on the London populace.

81

'Such pipple!' Luigi would say scathingly. 'They eat robbish, you know dat? Robbish dey eat all de time — mutton pies and cold beef, de robbish — den I give dem a good plate of rigatoni and dey maka da faces! Such pipple!'

'Ha! Bad enough da food dey don' unnerstan' — but de vino!' Antonio would join in. 'Mamma mia! — dey drink beer, beer, beer, and spit out da good vino! Barbaro! All, all barbaro!'

Exciting and unusual though she found these people, and much as she enjoyed their company — and as the house became more and more the orderly place she wanted it to be, she was able to leave it to eat her luncheon at Gatti's, and that gave her time to get to know them — she also found much pleasure in the other people who lived in Villiers Street. There was the family that lived almost next door at number twenty-four, James Chamberlayne who was a licensed victualler and ran his little house with great economy, and his plump and pretty wife Lucy who ran James and their children, fifteen-year-old Charlie and eighteen-year-old Alice — as pretty as her mother but much cheekier — with an easy hand. They were cheerful and friendly people, and James came and told her on the second day that she was 'never to 'esitate to call on any one o' my 'ouse'old should the need arise. We knows as you're takin' on a big job 'ere, and right glad we are as yer adoin' of it. Don't like empty 'ouses, we don't, dahn Villiers Street, an' though we was a bit put aht at first, 'earin' as 'ow the place was to be used for gels alone, fearin' if you'll pardon me mentionin' it that it was to turn into little more than a bawdy 'ouse, we know nah as it's to be done right by them London Ladies so we got no fears. So if you ever needs a bit o' neighbourly care, jus' you say the word, my duck, and Jim Chamberlayne'll be there like a shot.'

That was not the only offer of support and help she had. Similar visits were paid by Robert Neal, the butcher from round the corner in Duke Street, who came to offer help and stayed for hours, while she washed china, to tell her of his loneliness since his wife had died three years before; and by a young man, who needed some chilling glances to control him, who came pretending to have received a letter meant for her, but in fact trying to discover the new young resident's name. He was a journalist, he told her self-importantly, one Thomas Forster, and well on his way to a great career, and she nodded a little frostily and wished him well in it. Then Joseph

Twigg, a rising young architect, in lodgings at number twenty-seven, came to admire the way the house had been arranged, for he knew the firm which had been involved in the original work on it — altogether, callers were many and she soon felt very much at home in her new establishment.

Until the third week of December turned and suddenly, it seemed, it was Christmas Eve.

She had by now moved all her possessions from the hotel in St Pancras and settled into her attic room, and on the afternoon of the twenty-fourth she pinned up the skirts of her gown and tied up her hair in an old kerchief and set out to go from the very top of the house to the bottom, to make sure all was finally set to rights, for Martha had announced that the Committee of the London Ladies would make their official visit to the hostel on St Stephen's Day, the twenty-sixth of December, and she wanted all to be perfect.

It was. She found little enough in the way of dust anywhere, and was proud of her handiwork by the time she reached the little hallway of the house, her brooms and dusters clutched in her hands, and her face, as often seemed to happen to her when she was busy, smudged and shiny with effort. Bessie would be proud of her, she thought, admiring the gleam of her own brass fixtures, especially the pole that hung over the front door and from which a cosy draught-excluding curtain was looped. Bessie herself could not have redded up the house better in the time.

Bessie, she thought, and stood there leaning on her broom in the dwindling afternoon light, and let a great wave of homesickness wash over her. At home in Tansey Clough on Christmas Eve there would be greenery hanging everywhere, hard-found greenery, culled from the beck sides, for little other than heather ever grew on these dank moors, but the fires would be high and mince pies would be fragrant in the kitchen. A great ham would be boiling over the range and a goose would be lying ready to be sacrificed next day, naked and glassy-eyed in the larder. And the plum puddings and the comfits and the sugar loaves — her eyes filled with tears and she sniffed.

At which point there was a loud knocking on the front door, and rather inelegantly wiping the tears from her face with the back of her hand — and so smudging it more than ever — she opened it.

The vision which stood there made her take a step back in

amazement. A tall handsome woman — of some forty years, Sophie suspected, though dressed to look rather younger — stood there encased in sable furs, her bonnet, a most fashionable scrap of straw bedecked with so many birds and feathers and imitation fruits it looked fair to fall off the piled-up sleek dark hair and with a rather chilly expression on her face.

'Good afternoon,' the vision said in a remote voice, and surged forward with such confidence that Sophie perforce took a step back, pressing herself against the open door, and she swept in and past her, and then, loosening her furs around her throat said in the same dying fall of a voice, 'Tell your mistress I am here to see her. Mrs Frederick Caspar.'

'Oh!' Sophie said, in surprise, and came to stand in front of her visitor, quite forgetting how tatterdemalion she looked in her apron and tied-up working clothes. 'How nice of you to come! Freddy — Mr Caspar — did say that his mother would want to visit, but not that you — well, this is kind!'

The woman turned then and looked at her, her glance moving slowly from the crown of her head to her feet, which were encased in rather shabby old slippers.

'Am I *addressing* Miss — ah — Lackland?'

'Why, yes, indeed!' Sophie said heartily, and held out her hand, at which Mrs Caspar drew back in some dismay, and then, for the first time Sophie realized just what sort of a picture she must be presenting.

'Oh, I'm mortified!' she gasped. 'To greet you so — what must you think of me? Do, please forgive me, but you know Aunt Martha — Miss Lackland told me to address her so — Miss Lackland set me the task of preparing the house for its new use, and we cannot employ servants until the occupants arrive you know, so there it is! I must do all myself. But there, I dare say as a mother of a family yourself you will have had similar contretemps!'

'I? I think not!' Mrs Caspar said. 'Really, it is too bad of Aunt Martha to — well, she is a law unto herself. Dear Aunt Martha! I will not keep you then, as you clearly have much to do. I came but to wish you the greetings of the season and to bid you take your dinner with us tomorrow. Unless you have other plans, of course.' Again that rather scathing glance slid down Sophie's long untidy shape.

Sophie was redder than ever now, and her chin was up. She had expected some amusement from Mrs Caspar, perhaps, but not continuing scorn. It was one thing to have confused her with a servant girl, quite another to go on being so top lofty when her error had been put right.

'It is kind in you to think of me, ma'am,' she said frostily. 'But I will not disturb you, I believe. I have other plans for spending Christmas. My regards to your husband, however. I was glad to meet Cousin Freddy — I found him most charming.'

And she marched to the front door and held it open, and after a moment Mrs Caspar, her own cheeks rather flushed, bent her head graciously and took her leave.

Sophie closed the door firmly behind her and then ran into the big dining room so that she could watch her from behind the Nottingham lace curtains hanging there. There was a large and handsome carriage waiting and Mrs Caspar climbed in with a great swirling of her very fashionable flounced skirts and a twirling of her sables, and angry though she was, Sophie had to admit she looked magnificent. A most handsome woman, full of style. And so easy to dislike! Poor Cousin Freddy, she thought suddenly. Such a nice man to have so horrid a wife.

But then after the carriage had gone rattling away up the street towards the Strand and the little boys who had been standing about admiring the matched pair of bays had wandered off to torment the hot-chestnut seller who stood beside the steamship pier at the end of the street by the river, dolour set in thoroughly. Sophie sat herself down on one of the new shiny horsehair sofas in the dining room, and wept bitter tears of loneliness and fatigue. It was Christmas and she was a long way from home and very miserable indeed. She had come to London to be a lady surgeon. And what had happened? She had spent a succession of long painful days scrubbing and cleaning all on her own, and had been mistaken for a slatternly housemaid by one of her own relations. It was too bad! And for two pins she would go back to Haworth forthwith, and forget all this nonsense about being ambitious. Even if it meant she would have to sell Tansey Clough.

At which thought she wept harder than ever. Suddenly life in raw exciting London was anything but what Sophie Lackland wanted.

CHAPTER NINE

In the event, Christmas was not as bad as Sophie had feared it would be. Not an hour after Mrs Caspar had left her mortified and smarting with rage, a message arrived from Bedford Row bidding her to present herself there first thing in the morning, to accompany Miss Lackland to church and then to celebrate the day with her.

'We shall be quiet, just the two of us, but if that will not bore you unduly, it will give me much pleasure to welcome you,' Martha had written. 'The rest of the family choose to make great parties of themselves and spend all the hours of the day in each other's pockets, but for my part, I find that exhausting and likely to be the cause of some strife. But I would never choose to be completely alone. So if you will gratify my old-maidish desire to share your company, I dare say we will sort well enough.'

Sophie had gone gladly, and been deeply grateful. She had received letters from home, full of news and admonitions from newly married Bessie — who from all accounts already had her Josiah even more firmly under her thumb — and gossip and eager questions from Doctor Tom, and to have been alone with just those close-written sheets for company all Christmas Day would have quite worn down her spirits.

The more she saw of Miss Martha Lackland, the more she liked her. She had a rather dry way with her, Sophie decided, but was far from lacking in humour. Her round face was serene enough, but she had a look of a woman who had lived and experienced a great deal, and that whetted Sophie's curiosity. Not that Miss Lackland was prepared to gratify it very much. She answered some of Sophie's questions about the rest of the family, but not in a way that invited any further probing, though she was willing to enlarge a little on her experiences in the Crimea. This Sophie found enthralling and the short December afternoon seemed to race by as she listened to accounts of Miss Nightingale and Scutari and Martha's own doings there.

So Christmas passed agreeably enough, and then St Stephen's Day, busy with the Committee, was upon her. She was both amused and alarmed by the congerie of ladies who descended upon twenty-two Villiers Street; each one seemed more heavily upholstered than the next, each more expensively gowned, more lavishly coiffed, and more shrill of voice. They looked everywhere, poking into cupboards and running gloved fingers along shelves seeking for signs of dust and checking the newly made-up beds for dampness. And Sophie trailed behind them trying to control her nervous giggles as she watched one particularly solid Committee member bounce solemnly on a bed to 'test the springs' and then shaking in her shoes as another checked over the contents of the china cupboard, for Sophie had in fact broken two cups and three plates in putting the new items away, and this lady, she was sure, was the sort who counted every penny spent.

She gave them all coffee in the dining room when they had finished, with little ratafia biscuits she had hurriedly purchased from the little shop at the top of the street; and then she waited, hands folded on her lap, to hear their verdict.

Which was favourable. She positively beamed as the ladies nodded at each other and at her and voted the new hostel excellently arranged and fitted out, and fell to discussing which of the inhabitants of the overcrowded Bedford Row establishment should be given the opportunity to come to Villiers Street.

Sophie listened to this part of the discussion with keen attention, for she had yesterday met several of the women at Bedford Row, for Miss Martha Lackland, although she kept her own establishment there separate from the rest of the house and its inhabitants, was on excellent terms with most of them, and they had all taken tea together after church. And she was more than content as she heard the list of eight names for she remembered four of them at least as bright and cheerful young women who would be agreeable to have about the house.

It was not until Martha had shepherded her Committee away, leaving Sophie with extra cash and firm instructions to employ servants at last, and also to buy food for her larders, that Sophie really stopped to think at all. And then marvelled a little at herself.

She had come to London to study to be a surgeon, and yet she had given little thought to that matter for at least two weeks.

She had become quite absorbed in her new tasks as Lady Warden of twenty-two Villiers Street, and somehow the prospect of becoming a student seemed to have receded into the distance.

She stood there in the kitchen staring down at the list she was making of foods to be bought and frowned a little at herself. This would not do, it really would not do! She must take matters in hand — and she suddenly remembered Mr Caspar, Cousin Freddy. For all his inability to help in the matter of the will, and allowing her support from it while she studied, he had been, she felt, sympathetic towards her. And he, if anyone, should be able to put her on the right road.

She came to a firm decision; she would get the hostel running smoothly, and the new residents settled in, and then, and swiftly too, she would go and see Mr Caspar. And if the thought of Mrs Caspar slipped into her mind as she framed her resolution, she soon pushed it away again. *She* had no place at all in Sophie Lackland's plans.

It took her in fact almost four weeks to settle the hostel as it should be settled; the first servants she employed proved to be the worst possible kind, slatternly and drunken, and had to be put summarily out of doors — and she was grateful for the help of James Chamberlayne there, for the one employed as cook had been most abusive — and finding suitable replacements not as easy as she had hoped. There were plenty of servants available for hire, but good ones — that was the problem. When compared with the sturdy hardworking Yorkshire people to whom she was accustomed, Sophie found these Londoners a sorry lot.

So, she had to cook and clean and scrub as hard as ever for several days, fitting in discussions with the various people sent by the servants' agency when she could, while the eight girls who had come with their few belongings to the new hostel were joined by four more, and then another three, until there was only room for another five, and four of those places were taken soon after the New Year.

The girls were cheerful, noisy, bouncy creatures, most of them working as actresses in the theatres around Covent Garden and in the Haymarket. If some of them had garish tastes in dress, with a predilection for feathers and bright colours, and a relish for gin which sometimes made them extra cheerful, noisy and bouncy, they were good-natured creatures at heart, and did all they could to help her. They kept their dormitories reasonably tidy, and agreed willingly enough to put their belongings neatly in the wardrobes provided, instead of spreading them all over the rooms, and were not above taking brooms and brushes in hand to assist her. Which she knew was good of them, for they paid for their accommodation as much as they could afford, the Committee making up the difference only where absolutely necessary, so they were entitled to expect some service for their payments.

But at last a good cook, practical and hardworking, was obtained and settled in the kitchen, and Sophie relinquished the commissariat to her gratefully, and when a couple of industrious maids were found to join her and take on the responsibility for the heavy cleaning, Sophie felt her lines were indeed falling in pleasant places.

Her daily duties now consisted of the shopping, after she had discussed with the cook the food that was to be provided, and the checking of such mundane matters as laundry and mending of linen and the very important matter of book-keeping, for every penny of the London Ladies' money had to be accounted for most meticulously. She also still did some simple housework such as dusting the drawing room, and took it upon herself also to supply flowers for the rooms from her own meagre salary, for the blooms the old woman at the corner sold were so cheering, and she was so grateful for Sophie's daily custom.

By the end of the third week in January, she felt ready to take stock of her situation and to seek an interview with Mr Caspar. But once again a stop was put in her way, this time in the person of Miss Madge Gunn.

It was one of those icily cold blue days in January which look so delightful when gazed upon through the window of a cosily firelit room, but which bite the fingers and nose cruelly as soon as a foot is set out of doors. People went by huddled in heavy overcoats, scarves wound round their faces until only watering eyes could be seen gleaming over them and every passer-by was wreathed in the steam of his own breath. Sophie had already been out to fetch fresh milk for breakfast from the dairy, for their own supply had frozen hard in its small churn in the scullery, and then she went hurrying home to wrap up warmly before setting out to walk to Queen Eleanor's, there to seek an interview with Mr Caspar.

But even as she reached for her mantle — and never was Wilfred's warm gift more appreciated than during these cruel winter days — she heard the doorbell jangle far below, and sighed. Whatever it was, she would have to see to it, for the maids, good enough girls though they were when it came to housework, lacked any presence of mind when faced with anything else.

By the time she came down from her attic, the door had in fact been opened and the sight and sounds that met her were startling.

Just inside the wide open street door a girl lay in a little heap on the doormat, with the little housemaid standing over her and wringing her hands and crying. Several of the girls, hearing the maid's keening cry, had come tumbling out of their dormitories, their hair still in curling papers and with their wrappers only just pulled around them, to see what was going on and avid for information, for life was usually a peaceful enough affair at number twenty-two, enlivened only by a squabble between the girls themselves.

'Whatever is going on, Eliza?' Sophie called sharply. 'Do stop that foolish din at once and tell me what this is about!'

'Oh, Miss Lackland, miss, I dunno, that I don't, miss, I opened the door and this girl was stood there, pale as a sheet and she opens 'er mouth an' says 'elp, she says, an' then falls flat on 'er face! Fair turned me up, she did, me 'eart's beatin' like an engine, that it is, an' I think I'm goin' to 'ave one o' me turns an' I think she's dead, miss, an' I don't know 'oo she is, miss, that I don't, and oh dear, Lord 'ave mussy on us!' And she threw her apron up over her face and howled more loudly than ever.

Sophie, tutting irritably, set one of the girls to lead Eliza to the kitchen and to tell Cook to restore her with some strong tea, and turned her attention to the girl on the floor.

She was still not stirring, and Sophie was a little puzzled for a moment, for she was breathing steadily enough, and her colour was reasonably good, however pale she may have looked to Eliza when she came tumbling in. But she knelt beside her, and turned the fair head, very gently, and lifted the girl slightly, and at once the lids fluttered and opened to reveal very blue eyes.

'Oh — oh dear —' she said in a soft voice and closed her eyes again. 'Oh dear, I do feel — oh, dear ——'

With the help of two of the eager onlookers, Sophie carried the girl into the dining room, and set her on one of the horsehair sofas, and began to chafe her hands — which were very cold — while one of the others waved smelling salts beneath her nose, and after a short while the girl stirred and opened her eyes again.

'Well, now, and what can we do for you, young lady?' Sophie said, and smiled at her. She was obviously very young, not more than seventeen at the most, and most delightfully pretty. In addition to the fair curly hair and the absurdly blue eyes she had a deep dimple in her chin, and a soft pouting mouth of the sort that most men admired above all others. She was wearing a low-cut gown of blue taffeta, and a thin silken shawl across her shoulders, and was obviously chilled to the marrow, for she was shivering and her small white teeth beat a tattoo against each other.

'Please — I am s-so sorry — I — I did not mean to — I sought only sh-she-shelter — I do hope you can h-help,' she said, and looked up at Sophie appealingly. 'This is the hostel for — for actresses is it not? I can come here and find a b-bed to sleep in and f-food to eat?'

'If you apply to the Committee of the London Ladies, who run this establishment, you may perhaps find what you seek,' Sophie said. 'And if you are a girl alone in London, with no means of support, then it is almost certain that they will accept you — if you are moral in your ways, of course. The London Ladies will have no truck with bits o' muslin, you know!' Sophie had learned a lot in her few weeks in London, and she bent a stern gaze on the soft round face on the horsehair sofa. But the girl stared steadfastly back, her eyes limpid with honesty and after a moment Sophie nodded. 'And it is in my power to accept a new resident, if I have room, and feel her to be a suitable person and allow her to apply formally to the Committee later. And it so happens we have a spare bed in the second floor back ——'

'Oh, thank you, miss, thank you, thank you!' the girl said, and seized Sophie's hand and began to kiss it with huge gratitude.

Sophie pulled her hand away at once. 'There's no need for that, now! Just tell me more about yourself, and then we'll see what we can do.'

'Please, miss, can I have something to eat first?' The girl looked at her piteously. 'For I am famished and have had nothing past my lips this past two days and ——'

'Oh, of course!' Sophie said, filled with compunction. To fuss about the rules of admission when the girl was half starved was not Sophie's way at all. 'Jenny!' She looked over her shoulder. 'Jenny, go at once, will you, to the kitchen and fetch some beef tea and toasted sippets, and ask Mrs Mildmay also if she has some of the blancmange we had last night. That I think will serve ——'

For the next half-hour there was much bustle, as the dining room fire was built up and the little fair girl — who announced herself to be Madge Gunn — was wrapped in a warm blanket and plied with food. And then at last Sophie shooed the eager onlooking girls away, and settled to talk more to Madge.

And as she listened to the girl's story, she felt her rage rise, for it was as sad a tale as she had ever heard.

'I come from Croydon, please, miss,' Madge began, snuggling back in her blanket and peeping over the top of it with wide blue eyes. 'D'you know it, miss? Well, it's a good enough area, I dare say, but it don't offer much to a girl as is ambitious, you know. My Pa's a butcher there, got a nice little business, and does well, and we all lives — me and my Ma and my two brothers who are still at school — over the shop. My Pa always said as I was to be a good girl, and stay home with Ma and mind my Ps and Qs until such time as Mr Right come along, but oh, miss, I didn't want to do that! I can sing and dance, and I wanted always to be on the stage. But when I told my Pa that he flew right off the handle, that he did, and gave me such a dressin' down, but my Ma she stood up for me and said as every person ought to have a right to try, an' she arranged for me to go and see Mr Hollingshead at the Gaiety, you know ——'

'The Gaiety?' Sophie asked.

'Up to the top of the Strand, miss, a nice theatre, where Nellie Farren is at, you know, and J. L. Toole — don't you know it, miss?'

'I have not lived long in London myself,' Sophie confessed, 'and have not yet visited a theatre — so you must forgive my ignorance.'

'Oh, miss, that Nellie Farren — she's as funny and as lovely a dancer and a singer as ever I saw! To be on the same stage with her, and see her doing her "I'll strike you with a Feather" number — oh, it'd do your heart good!'

'Well, that may be — but what about you?'

'Oh, well, miss, my Ma came with me and we saw Mr Hollingshead and he said I could be one of the walk-on supers, and

I was that happy! And my Ma said as I couldn't lodge at home no more, for my Pa'd go wild, so she said would they pay me enough to live in decent rooms o' my own, and Mr Hollingshead he said yes — and so Ma went away home — and oh, miss ——' and she burst into tears, her eyes overflowing prettily.

'And then what happened?' Sophie said, giving her a hand-kerchief, and Madge sniffed and swallowed and said piteously, 'Well, he didn't keep his word, did he, miss? He paid me only half of what he told my Ma he'd pay me, and when I tried to get a room on that, all I could find was —' here her voice dropped '— *bad* places, miss, where they thought a girl who was on the stage was no better'n she should be — so I had to move out and last night miss, I slept at the theatre, behind the flats where no one could see me and it was that cold, and when I woke up all my luggage had been stolen and me with no cloak to my back, and Mr Hollingshead said as he wouldn't give no more money not nohow, and didn't care if I *did* walk the streets, for I told him there was nothing I could do, and I wasn't going home for Pa to go on at me — well, can't you see how Pa would be! So I'd heard about you, miss, and I came to you ——'

By this time Sophie was on fire with rage. She knew little enough about the workings of the theatre, for there was none in Keighley, and she had visited the one in Bradford but three times in all her life. But she had heard enough of the chatter of the girls in the hostel to know it was a hard life, and that the managers were shrewd self-seeking men. But that one of them should treat an innocent girl, little more than a child, with such casual cruelty made her blood seethe in her ears.

And she was warming rapidly to the fair-haired child huddled on the sofa in a rug. There was an engaging perkiness about her, an innocent impudence that was very beguiling — and there was also her ambition. That her ambition to sing and dance upon a stage was not one into which Sophie could enter her own feelings made no difference. No doubt Madge would not be able to understand her own desire to be a lady surgeon. But that both yearned for difficult-to-achieve success — *that* they had in common, and impulsively Sophie put out her hand and said, 'That is infamous! That man should be whipped for such behaviour! I shall go and tell him so myself!'

'Oh, miss!' Madge's blue eyes became even wider and bluer, if that were possible. 'Do you really mean that? For it would do him all the good in the world if someone did, of that I am sure! My Ma always says that bullies are only bullies 'cos someone lets 'em be!' and she sniffed away a tear at the thought of her far distant Ma, and looked eagerly and with hope-filled eyes at Sophie.

'I will go now,' Sophie said, and stood up with great determination. 'Indeed I shall ——'

'Oh, miss, he won't be there now!' Madge said, in shocked tones. 'Not till past one o'clock, for there is a matinee today — but if you went at one o'clock you'd find him then, I'm sure.'

'Then at one I shall go — and you will be able to rest, for as you say, today is one when all the girls are working in the afternoon — they too have matinee performances. So the house will be quite empty, for I know Mrs Mildmay and Eliza and Annie are going to the Haymarket to see the play, for Jenny obtained passes for them. So all will be peaceful for you ——'

'That will be lovely,' Madge murmured, and slid further down on the slippery sofa, her eyes closing. 'Really lovely — ta ever so, Miss ——'

'Call me Miss Sophie, Madge,' Sophie said and bent and kissed the soft round face. 'All the other girls do, for we are one happy family here. Now you rest, and I will soon see to it that you will be treated right. Don't give it another thought.'

And at half past twelve precisely, Sophie donned her green mantle and her best bonnet and set off to walk up the windswept ice-cold Strand to the Aldwych and the Gaiety, there to give Mr Hollingshead a piece of her mind. She had hoped to be setting out upon her own affairs this morning, but they would now have to wait until tomorrow. Tiresome, but duty called first, and her undoubted duty at this moment was to poor little Madge Gunn.

CHAPTER TEN

By the time she arrived at the theatre, battling her way along the crowded Strand, her eyes were watering and her nose was red with the cold. But although her face was so chilled her hands and feet were warm enough with her exercise, and her own hot anger filled the rest of her body with an agreeable warmth. So, when she stood at last outside the building, staring up at its façade, she felt ready to cope with anybody, including cheese-paring selfish theatre managers who battened on lonely ambitious girls from the suburbs.

It was a handsome building, she had to allow; four big windows at street level were framed by fine Corinthian columns while a most elegantly fretted frieze ran the whole length of the frontage under a sign made of huge gilt letters which read 'Speirs and Pond's Gaiety Restaurant'. In the centre front rose a curved half-dome of glass elegantly inset with coloured panes, and here the proclamation 'The Gaiety Theatre' seemed prouder still. All very Frenchified and fancy, she decided, but not nearly as handsome as the Alhambra theatre at Bradford — at which thought she had to be a little amused at herself. To be so annoyed at the management that she could not admit that their building was a grand one was really rather childish, and not at all like her usual sensible self. She was, she had to admit as she marched in through the big double doors under the splendid glass canopy that led into the theatre, more irritated by having to spend time dealing with Madge Gunn's problems than she ought to be. The itch to be about her own affairs was getting stronger all the time, and had to be controlled. It is selfish, she told herself sternly, as she stood just inside the doors and looked about her, to think of oneself so much that one forgets one's duties to one's fellows. You must forget your own concerns for the present ——

It was not difficult to do so, once she set her mind to studying her surroundings. Such a glitter of gilt, such a splendour of red plush, such a shimmer of cut glass from mirrors and chandeliers met her eyes that for a moment she was almost dazzled by it all. And then her anger rose again; clearly this was a rich management. There was no shortage of money here — yet they treated one of their actresses so shabbily.

There was no one to be seen anywhere, and after a moment she coughed, loudly. But there was no response, and the shutter on the ticket office window remained tightly closed. All she could hear was the roar of traffic from the Strand outside, and, from somewhere deep in the bowels of the building, faint strains of music.

She frowned then, and moved towards one of the doors that led from the foyer where she was standing to the main body of the theatre, and pushed on it. It opened slowly and a great gust of hot, scented air poured out, together with a sudden roar of sound, and she jumped and let the door go.

But now someone was aware of her, and again the door opened, and out came a man in a very splendidly braided uniform and a shining top hat, and once again she heard the roar of sound as the door swung, and this time identified it as laughter.

'Sorry, madam, but the show's started — ten minutes into the first act, we are, an' anyway, not a seat to be 'ad in the h'entire 'ouse,' the braided one said loftily. 'Ticket office'll be open agin at five o'clock for this evenin's performance, so if you'd care to come back then, I dessay there may be a few seats available ——'

'I do not require a seat,' Sophie said, equally loftily. 'I wish to see Mr Hollingshead.'

'Ho, wish to see Mr 'Ollingshead, do yer? An' might I make so bold h'as to enquire for why?'

'No, you may not!' Sophie said, nettled. Why were so many minor functionaries in London establishments so tiresomely pushy? 'I have business with him concerning him and only him. So tell me at once where he is to be found!'

The man grinned then, his stringy moustache lifting on each side of his mouth with an insolence that nettled her even further. 'Well, well — got a right one 'ere, ain't we? I'll tell you this much, ducky — 'e ain't lookin' for no actresses at the present — this show's doing well enough and 'e won't be auditioning for ——'

'Mind your manners!' Sophie said wrathfully. 'How dare you assume I am an actress! That is a most impertinent, outrageous — tell me at *once* where Mr Hollingshead is to be found and do so

96

politely, or you will soon find out the weight of my temper!'

The insolent grin faded and the man looked at her dubiously. 'Well, sorry, I'm sure — but we gets so used to it, see — gals comin' 'ere lookin' for work all the time, an' 'alf o' them a right lot of — well, I'm sorry, I'm sure. 'E'll be backstage, I reckon, this time of the afternoon — an' there's bin trouble with the first act, so I dessay 'e'll be keepin' an eye on it — round the back, miss, in the alley down by Exeter Street ——'

She swept out and round the corner, seething, all her original anger now compounded by the rage she felt about being mistaken for an actress; how dare that jumped up jack-in-office think she was such a one? It was disgusting, infuriating, and she luxuriated in her indignation.

She found the alley easily enough, and the stage door, and here the atmosphere was quite different. Its sleazy little entrance led into a narrow corridor reeking of oil and glue size and the sick effluvium of gas from a hissing dilapidated lamp that burned over the little cubbyhole where the stage doorkeeper sat. He was a scrawny little man with a few wisps of grey hair snaking over an otherwise bald pate and he was sitting awkwardly in a straight-backed chair, snoring heavily and giving out a powerful odour of bitter beer and pickled onions and cheese. Clearly he had lunched well, and Sophie looked at him in disgust and marched past him into the bowels of the theatre. To wake such a one and ask him to find Mr Hollingshead for her would be sure to expose her to yet another maddening episode with an impudent employee, of that she was certain. She had put up with enough for one day; she would find the egregious Mr Hollingshead for herself.

It was like being in another world; narrow corridors snaked away into the distance, each smelling as unpleasant as the next to her fastidious moor-bred senses, for someone had grilled kippers here not long ago, and toasted some cheese as well, and the mixture of old food, beer and oil and gas was a queasy one.

She pushed open the doors here and there, emboldened by her own still simmering anger, but all she saw were cluttered little rooms where tawdry finery was hanging on nails in the walls, and tables were littered with pots and jars and sticks of what she assumed were greasepaint, so brightly coloured were they. But no people, apart from another sleeping figure, this time a portly woman in black bombazine and a very grubby apron, who sat close beside a smoking fire with her feet up on a straw hamper, snoring even more loudly than the stage doorkeeper, if that were possible.

But all the time, Sophie could hear the distant sounds of music and that occasional roar of laughter coming from far inside the building and by casting along first one corridor and then another she gradually made her way to its source.

And at last came out, through a heavy door, into a big shadowy area where the noise beat against her ears like a drum. The music was thumping heavily and the sound of the invisible audience was huge, and she moved forwards through the shadows until she was standing close beside a great patch of vivid light — and realized she had penetrated to the stage itself.

She stood there, entranced, staring. On the stage was a great collection of people in extraordinary clothes, vivid in colouring and dripping with feathers, but the one who held her eye was a little woman wearing simply black trousers and a white shirt.

Sophie stared at her, her eyes wide, and felt first a shock of disapproval — a woman, in *trousers*? — and then a sharp twinge of envy. How often, when she had been a child running on the moors and scrambling over the high tops had she yearned to share the same freedom that Wilfred had, to have her legs free to climb rather than tangled in those tiresome skirts? And there, on the stage, capering about like a little goat, was a girl throwing her legs about with delicious freedom. Lucky, lucky girl, thought Sophie, and then shook her head in irritation at herself. This was not what she was here for ——

The girl on the stage cut an even more outrageous caper, almost twisting her little body in two as she turned a cartwheel and another great roar came from the velvety blackness on the other side of the stage, and Sophie shrank back, almost as though she had been threatened by a wild animal. It was odd how this place made her feel, half exhilarated, half frightened ——

'And what in the name of the devil d'you think you're doing there?' a voice hissed at her and she whirled, peering into the shadows, quite unable to see, for her eyes had been dazzled by her staring at the vividly lit stage.

'What's going on here, for heaven's sake?' the voice whispered again. 'We've got a performance going on — how the devil did a stranger get in — Jim! Get this person out of here — at once — do you hear?'

'I'm looking for Mr Hollingshead,' Sophie said loudly. 'And ——'

'Hush, you fool!' The whisper came again more sharply. 'I told you — there's a performance going on here! Are you quite mad? Now be off and about your business ——'

A hand came out of the darkness and grasped her firmly at the elbow and first pulled and then pushed her back the way she had come. She tried to get away from it, but the hand and the person to whom it belonged were equally determined, and will-she, nill-she, she found herself on the far side of the big door again and in the narrow smelly corridor beyond.

'How dare you treat a lady so ill!' she said wrathfully, at last able to pull her arm away, and rubbing it with her other hand, for the fingers had pinched her shrewdly. 'How dare you be so — so — insolent!'

'And how dare you come meddling back stage in the middle of a performance?'

He was a tall youngish man of perhaps thirty years, with a shock of very dark tightly curling hair which seemed to crown his head like a furry cap, and wide, extremely dark eyes with ridiculously long lashes. His face was an odd one, very mobile, with a narrow mouth and full round cheeks — a face that would not be easy to forget. And it was at this moment bearing an expression of such scorn that she wanted to slap it.

'I came looking for ——' she began, but again his hand shot out and seized her elbow.

'Ye gods, woman, you have a voice like a foghorn on the river! They'll hear you clear to the dress circle at this rate! Come on — if you can't keep your voice down then you'd better come to the office and explain yourself there ——' and he set out along the corridor in a swift lope, never letting go of her arm, and half pushed and half pulled her up a narrow flight of stairs at the far end. And she had to go with him, too breathless in the headlong rush to say a word.

The office into which he finally pushed her was a small one, with a huge desk covered with papers on one side of it, a couple of rather battered chairs and very little else on the other. She looked round with a sneer on her own face as she pulled her sleeves to rights, and caught her breath.

'Well, if this is the best place you can find, it will have to do,' she said with what dignity she could muster. 'And now, fetch Mr Hollingshead, or tell me where he is to be found, for I have business with him.'

'Have you indeed?' the young man said, and went and flung himself into the chair behind the desk and put his feet up on the edge of it. 'That's agreeable for you!'

'I have no time to waste on underlings,' Sophie said witheringly and turned to go back to the door whence they had entered the room. 'And if you will not fetch him, then I shall return to seeking him for myself ——'

She pulled the door open and then stopped, feeling her face fill with colour. On the centre panel was a small piece of white card, on which was written in a fair copperplate hand 'John Hollingshead, Manager'.

She turned and glared at the man behind the desk. 'You, sir, have no manners at all!' she announced in ringing tones. 'How dare you behave so ill! I seek Mr Hollingshead, and I said so, and you choose to play the coxcomb and pretend you are not he ——'

'Oh, come, miss! You never said above a word to me about who you sought! How could you! I did not let you get a word in edgewise, as I recall! With a voice as powerful as yours, how could I? You would have interrupted the performance shockingly! Tell me, d'you sing contralto? And what is your range?'

'I am not a singer or an actress and would lie dead of starvation before I would dream of occupying myself in such a way!' Sophie said loudly and then, suddenly self-conscious about her voice — which had always been deep, but had never seemed to her to be as loud as this unpleasant man said it was — added more quietly, 'I came here to deal with the matter of one of the poor wretches who was misguided enough to think she *could* follow such a career under your management.'

'Oh? And who might that be?'

'Miss Madge Gunn.'

'Madge Gunn?' He stared at her with his big dark eyes very wide and then, suddenly, spluttered with laughter. 'Madge Gunn! The terror of Croydon! The Angel of the — oh, madam, tell me, do, all

100

you can about Madge Gunn! I cannot wait to hear it!'

'How dare you, sir, be so — so ribald about one whom you have used so ill? Have you no shame?'

'I have a great deal of shame,' the young man said promptly. 'When it is justified — but as for Miss Gunn — well, tell me, do, all you can! How do you know her? What has she told you?'

'I am the Lady Warden at twenty-two Villiers Street,' Sophie said, very formally, folding her hands in front of her as primly as she could. This man was discourteous beyond belief, but that did not give her permission to behave as ill as he did; she would be a lady, however little he was capable of playing the gentleman. So she kept her eyes firmly on his face, ignoring the ankles crossed on the desk and the lounging insolence of his posture as he sat there, his hands hooked together behind his head and his wide dark eyes fixed on her. 'It is a hostel run by the Committee of the London Ladies ——'

'I have heard of it. There is little we do not know here of such establishments and we were glad enough when we found there was to be another — Bedford Row was used by some of our girls and they spoke well enough of it ——'

'I should hope so!' Sophie said wrathfully. 'For great care is taken by the Committee to provide well for these poor girls, and to offer them decent lodgings at minimal cost, and they would have no cause to complain of any treatment they received, of that I am sure! As for Villiers Street — I run it to the best of my ability and ——'

'Oh, pooh!' said the young man and swung his feet to the floor. 'Do come down from your high horse! I am sure it is a most admirable establishment and you are very admirable in it. I am being most lax — forgive me — I must say I thought at first you were just another of these foolish little misses who haunt us here, and did not wish to make you too welcome. But I can see I am wrong and would wish to see you take a seat and ——'

'Thank you, no,' Sophie said frostily. 'I have as little time as you to waste on courtesies.'

The young man bowed rather elaborately and came round the desk to stand in front of her. 'Well, if you will not sit, then neither will I. Now, you were saying — Madge Gunn — I am all agog!'

'You know perfectly well about Madge Gunn! You do not need

me to tell you again of your — iniquitous treatment of the poor child! It was sheer good fortune that she reached my door and I was able to take care of her. I dread to think what might have happened had she not known of our establishment and ——'

A slow grin appeared on the young man's face, curling the corners of his mouth in a most agreeable way, and his dark eyes narrowed to slits so that his whole visage was lit with good humour. 'Tell me, ma'am — would it amaze you to know that I in fact have told many of our actresses of your hostel? That Madge Gunn probably heard of it from that source in the first place? To be accurate it was Bedford Row that I knew about, but all the same ——'

'You? Indeed it would! Or — no — now I think of it — did you imagine that by sending her to us to find lodgings we would allow her to pay so little that you would not need to give her a decent living wage? Was that your intent? Well, Mr Hollingshead, you may disabuse yourself of any such notions forthwith! I shall see to it that Miss Gunn goes home safe and sound to her parents and you — you may whistle! I will see to it that no actress employed by this theatre will ever live with us and so make it possible for you to cheat them — and us! It is infamous, it is ——'

'Oh, silly, silly — what did you say your name was?'

'I did not say it! Nor shall I ——'

'Sillier still! How can I know that you are what you claim if you refuse to tell me ——'

'This is absurd! I am Miss Lackland, Miss Sophia Lackland, and can be attested to by the Committee at Bedford Row and — anyway, it is not my accreditation we are here to discuss, but your shocking treatment of Miss Gunn.'

The young man perched on the edge of the desk now, folding his arms and looking at her with his head set perkily to one side and his face once again alight with laughter.

'Our shocking treatment of Miss Gunn! Oh, but it is sad, is it not? I dare say she told you that we promised her a greater salary than we gave her? That she was forced to seek such cheap lodgings that she nearly found herself in a house of ill repute? That she saved her honour by the skin of her teeth, wandering the streets in the cold night with no cloak, for we had stolen her luggage? Yes? I see from your face I am right ——'

'You — you *evil* man!' Sophie spluttered, her words almost falling over themselves in her fury. 'You have the brass effrontery to — to *boast* of your ill treatment of this poor creature? You sit there mopping and mowing like some — some street tinker, you and your great ugly face and your stupid hair that makes you look like some sort of sheep, and your nasty lazy lounging ways, you stand there and dare to ——'

She stopped then and stared, for the young man had thrown his head back and was — to her amazement — laughing so hard that tears were running down his face and his eyes could barely open. His laughter was rich and bubbling and in any other circumstances would have been agreeable to hear, but at this moment she found it so infuriating she wanted to hit him — and even, to her own distress, actually found her fists were clenched and her arms raised.

At last the laughter stopped and he pulled a large white handkerchief from his pocket and mopped his eyes and shook his head, and peered at her over the top of it as he blew his nose.

'You must forgive me, my dear Miss Lackland, for what will seem to you to be unseemly mirth, but you know, you have been sorely misused. Sorely misused! How ill you will not know until you return to your hostel. I collect you left Miss Gunn there?'

'Of course I did! I am not heartless! I will not put a penniless creature out of doors ——'

'Oh dear, oh dear ——' The young man shook his head. 'Just wait till Mr Hollingshead hears about this — he will ——'

Sophie's head snapped up and she stared at him. 'What did you say?'

'I said — oh, yes. Well, I suppose — oh, Miss Lackland, I am sorry, I meant no harm, indeed I did not! Mr Hollingshead has gone off on a matter of business with his old friend Richard D'Oyly Carte and left me to keep an eye on matters here this afternoon. I am Gilbert Stacey, ma'am, a poor singer and performer in this theatre, but standing for Mr Hollingshead at this moment and at your service. I trust you will forgive me for ——'

'I will forgive you for nothing,' Sophie said strongly. 'How dare you allow me to waste my time in this fashion? How dare you treat me so ill, and allow me to — oh, you are the outside of enough, sir, and I shall see to it that when your principal does return he will hear of this affair and will be told in no uncertain terms of your behaviour.'

'And will you also tell him your views on the way he has behaved to Miss Gunn?'

'Of course I will! That is why I came here. I am shocked beyond belief to discover that Christian gentlemen in the capital city of this great country could ever behave in so reprobate a manner, could be so wanting in any of the attributes of ——'

'Miss Lackland,' Mr Stacey said gently, and put out one hand and set it on hers. 'Please, Miss Lackland — you are entitled to feel some temper at the moment, but hear me out, will you? Miss Gunn, I have to tell you, is a notorious lady among the management of many London theatres. She has a way of — well, let me tell you that in truth she is no actress.'

'Well, not all the people who seek to follow a career are as gifted as they might be, I dare say,' Sophie said. 'But that does not mean they are lesser people, to be ill treated, and ——'

'You misunderstand me. Not to put too fine a point on it, ma'am, Miss Gunn has much acting ability — a great talent in fact. But she does not use it as an *actress*.'

'You do not explain yourself well — Mr Stacey, was it? — Mr Stacey,' Sophie said witheringly. 'I am accustomed to dealing with gentlemen who use words with intelligence and skill, and are able to directly communicate their thoughts ——'

'Well, if it is direct speech you want, Miss Lackland, you shall have it. Miss Gunn, my *dear* Miss Lackland, earns her living — and a very comfortable living too, by all accounts — from prostitution. She has a most handsome set of rooms near the flower market and there entertains men of all sorts and kinds, allowing them full use of her body for high fees. Is that direct enough for you?'

Sophie stared at him. 'You are making this up,' she said uncertainly.

'Indeed, I am not! She has been on that game this past four years to my certain knowledge. For the past two, however, she has added to her income, which is far from inconsiderable, by lying and cheating her way into the establishments of respectable persons, telling them great cock-and-bull tales of being a poor little girl from the suburbs struggling to save her virtue in the teeth of rapacious and evil theatre managers — and when her would-be benefactors leave her alone in their comfortable homes for the first time, they return to find she has made the most of her opportunities. In short, Miss Lackland, you have been ensnared by one of the most experienced and effective young thieves in Covent Garden and when you return to Villiers Street — where no doubt you left her peacefully resting after her *dreadful* experiences here at the Gaiety — you will find your bird flown and a good many of your feathers with her. I hope you have not many valuables there, Miss Lackland. She has been known to flush out every hiding place for money or jewels ever devised!'

CHAPTER ELEVEN

'And what of yours is missing?' Sophie said wearily, and looked up at Jenny. 'And please, Jenny, do not embroider at all! It is tiresome, indeed, for you all to have lost your things in this manner, but it is just as bad for us, and you cannot expect the Committee to allow you actually to benefit from what has happened ——'

'As if I would, Miss Sophie,' Jenny said, opening her eyes very wide. 'As if I would!'

'Well, I do not mean to insult you, but we have already discovered that several of the other girls have not been above claiming that that wretched Gunn creature took more than she did. Bad enough she robbed us as much as she did — no need to add to it ——'

'Well, Miss Sophie, I told 'em it was wrong to let you list things as bein' missin' when I knew for a fact they was worn out or sold, but there, some o' the others are not as well brought up as they might be! Me, I promise you, Miss Sophie, I'm tellin' the truth. And she's took me amber beads what my grandmother left me in 'er will, and a bandbox and seven handkerchieves, and my best taffeta jacket and ——'

The list went on and on and Sophie sat there at her desk, writing down each item in all the detail she could, trying not to think of the painful interview that lay ahead of her. For Miss Martha Lackland would have to be told, and some discussions entered into on how the girls who had been robbed by the reprobate Madge Gunn could be recompensed.

It had been a dreadful afternoon. She had come hurrying back from the Gaiety Theatre, firmly rejecting the hateful Mr Stacey's offer of a hansom cab, and almost running all the way, praying under her breath all the time that he would be proved wrong, but knowing, deep down, that he was absolutely right. Had she not herself had a moment of doubt of the girl's veracity when she had seen her lying crumpled on the floor, apparently in a dead faint but breathing normally and of a reasonable colour? Usually when people faint they recover almost at once and this was a fact that Sophie well knew; Doctor Tom had taught her that the faint was due to a loss of blood in the brain, and that fainting restored the vital fluid to those delicate tissues by ensuring the person lay down. And Miss Gunn had lain there crumpled on the floor looking quite delectable, but showed no signs of recovery until Sophie had lifted her head. That had puzzled her a little at the time, but not enough to alert her suspicions.

But if only it had! When she hurried into the house and ran straight into the dining room where she had left Miss Gunn, to see only the empty sofa there before the dying embers of the fire, her heart had sunk like a stone, and then gone even deeper into her boots as she set out to search the rest of the house, not even stopping to remove her mantle.

And found that the soft-faced blue-eyed little heap of sadness who had so touched her heart had decamped with a great deal of other people's property, and done so with efficiency, first helping herself to four large valises, and then packing them methodically with everything upon which she could lay her hands. Clothes and trumpery jewellery belonging to the girls, cutlery and table and bed linen belonging to the house; even her own bits and pieces of possessions were gone, including the little gold and garnet brooch which had been her mother's.

Sophie had wept a few tears over the empty velvet-lined box when she discovered that had gone, but not for long. Soon her anger and resentment hardened in her to a resolve to deal with this matter forthwith, and she set to work listing the missing property with great punctiliousness, and, once the girls came home for their evening meal in their usual rush between performances on matinee days, adding their losses to the lists.

Now, with the girls chattering and exclaiming as they hurried to set off again for their theatres, she collected her lists together and looked at them almost with despair. They were so long, so very long, and somehow these items would all have to be replaced. And where was the money to come from?

She asked Mr Chamberlayne to keep an eye on things for her while she went to Bedford Row, and he agreed at once, clucking like an old hen over her account of what had happened. 'Oh dear, oh, deary me! To think I saw that baggage goin' out o' here, into a cab, an' saw her handing all them valises in, an' never thought for one minute — well, it just shows, don't it? Never you worry now, Miss Sophie — I'll watch an' see all right and tight while you're gone — don't you worry ——'

But of course she did. All the way to Bedford Row in the hansom, swaying from side to side as the horse went pushing its way through the crowds of vans and growlers and omnibuses she sat staring unseeingly out of the window, quite oblivious of the busy pavements with the strolling theatregoers on their way to the evening performances, or to the dish-clattering mutton-flavoured restaurants that seemed to occupy every other building she passed.

By the time her hansom turned into Theobald's Road, almost reaching her destination, she had made up her mind what was to be done. It would be difficult and painful, but there was no other answer for it, she told herself as she stepped out of the cab and paid the jarvey. Nothing else could be done.

And so she prepared to tell Miss Martha Lackland, sitting unhappily on the edge of the chair she had been shown to as soon as she entered Martha's comfortable sitting room at the front of the top floor of the house, her hands folded primly on her lap, and her face set.

'Well, my dear, whatever it is that brought you here on this chilly evening, it is clearly worrying you,' Martha said mildly, and unhooked her spectacles from her ears, and, folding them neatly, put them in their embroidered case. 'So you had best tell me all about it, and then we shall settle for a comfortable prose. I am delighted you have come here tonight, for in fact I am expecting my nephew Freddy to call in — we have some small matters to discuss — and I wish to talk to him also about — well, let be. Let us get whatever your problem is out of the way first, shall we? Well, what is it? Has one of the girls misbehaved? Tried to bring a man into her room? Oh, do not look so surprised! I have not been running such a refuge as this house here for all these years without learning a good deal more about human nature than I would wish to know!'

'Oh, it is nothing to do with the girls, Miss Lackland — or not precisely ——'

'I told you to call me Aunt Martha!'

'I am sorry — I was so — I forgot. And anyway, I feel at the moment that — well, I am not sure that you will wish to acknowledge me as your niece after what has happened. I think you will be far too angry!'

'Dear me, how dramatic!' Martha said easily. 'I will be very surprised if it is quite as bad as all that, you know. Now, tell me what it is all about.'

So, Sophie told her. She made no effort to exculpate herself, and indeed dwelled at some length on her own stupidity at not heeding her own doubts about the veracity of Madge Gunn's 'faint' and went on to describe quite mercilessly how easily she had been hoodwinked.

'And,' she finished, 'I am well aware that I must take full responsibility for all this. So, ma'am — Aunt Martha — it is my intent to return forthwith to Haworth — and sell Tansey Clough and then send to you the money to recompense the losses. I ask only that you help me by finding enough money, if you can, to pay back immediately the girls who were robbed, instead of waiting for me to send the money, for I fear it may take a little while to set my hands upon the actual cash. But rest assured that I shall, indeed I shall and ——'

'Oh, pooh!' Aunt Martha said calmly, and took out her spectacles again and put them on, and then holding out one hand, 'I never heard such a fuss! Show me the lists you have made of missing property.'

Obediently, Sophie handed them over and waited quietly while Aunt Martha sat with bent head studying them. The room was tranquil and comfortable, with its grandfather clock ticking heavily in the corner and the fire burning with a cheerful crackle in the wide grate, and she let her shoulders relax for the first time since she had left Villiers Street for the Gaiety Theatre that afternoon — was it just six hours ago? And realized just how weary she was.

Somewhere far below she heard the doorbell ring, and the sound of someone going to answer it and then the soft burr of a deep voice and footsteps on the stairs, and then, just as Martha folded up the sheets of paper and once more took off her spectacles the door opened and Freddy Caspar came in.

His face lit up at the sight of her, its rather heavy lines seeming to disappear in a wide smile. 'My dear Cousin Sophie! How very agreeable to see you. This was a pleasure I did not expect at all.'

'Good evening, Mr Caspar — er — Cousin Freddy,' she said formally, and he looked a little puzzled.

'Are you out of sorts, my dear? You look a little peaky, you know. Is our London air disagreeing with you? I would not be surprised to find you taking ill to it, after the fresh cleanness of your home. London is a sorely sooty place, I am afraid.'

'She is bouleversée because she has been robbed,' Martha said cheerfully. 'It is good of you to come, Freddy dear. Are you well? And Phoebe? And the children?'

'Very well thank you, Aunt,' Freddy said and went across the room and bent and kissed Martha's cheek. 'As are you, I trust.'

At the mention of Phoebe's name Sophie's face had flamed. In her distress over the Madge Gunn incident she had for a moment quite forgotten what had happened on Christmas Eve but now she remembered with a vengeance and was mortified.

'I am sorry I was not able to — er — accept your kind invitation at Christmas, Cousin,' she said a little stiltedly.

'Oh, I was sorry too, as were we all,' Freddy said easily. 'But it could not be helped. Phoebe told me that you had a disagreeable cold and were tied to the house — I hope you are quite better now?'

'Oh!' Sophie said blankly. 'Oh — er — yes, of course ——' And she reddened as Martha gave her a sharp look.

'And now what is this about being robbed?' Freddy said. 'That sounds very worrying.'

Succinctly, Martha told him what had happened, and he listened, his pleasant face inscrutable. And then, when Martha had finished he turned to Sophie. 'And it is for this reason you are looking so down in the mouth, my dear? Come, you must not be, must she, Martha? Why, such experiences are ten-a-penny in London, ten-a-penny!'

'They are not ten-a-penny to me,' Sophie said. 'And I could never regard such an experience as anything but most — most distressing. As I was saying, Aunt Martha, I will return to Haworth and ——'

'You will do nothing of the sort!' Aunt Martha said vigorously, and stood up and twitched her shawl more firmly about her shoulders. 'I will ring for some tea, I think. Freddy — would you wish for tea, or would you prefer something a little more restorative?'

'Tea will be splendid, Aunt Martha — Now, Sophie, what are we to do about you? I am most concerned to see you looking so upset. There is no need, is there, Aunt Martha?'

'Not the least need,' Martha said equably, and bent to throw some more coal on the fire. 'We are often robbed in such a way, my dear — by the way ——' She straightened up and turned and looked at Sophie very seriously. 'Did you call the constable about this? Or send a message to the police station at Bow Street?'

Sophie looked at her blankly. 'Why — oh dear, I did not! Oh, I am such a fool! Such a stupid, ridiculous — how could you ever have considered employing me for this position? I am as useless as a sick headache and should be ——'

'Thank heaven for that!' Martha said, looking piously upwards. 'I would have been most angry if you had ——'

'You would?' Sophie said blankly.

'Indeed yes. The police create so many problems, I find, in such matters. We know that the girls to whom we offer refuge are not all as good as they might be. That is why they come to us. If we were to encourage them to fear that every little peccadillo or minor robbery was going to result in policemen marching about they would be very unlikely to stay with us. They would just melt away and disappear into the rookeries there in St Giles or in the nastier stews down in Covent Garden — and never forget that the disorderly houses in Haymarket are always on the look-out for likely new girls — no, my dear, we prefer to close our eyes to some things, and allow small sins to go unpunished for fear of the girls falling into greater ones. It is not so dreadful to be a thief when you have grown up in bitter poverty and never been taught better — but it is dreadful when a girl with no real taste for the life becomes a street woman. Thieves deal only in property — things that do not matter too much — but street women — they are dealing in their own bodies and — well, I for one do not worry about a little stealing. But if ever you find the girls are trying to use the house there in Villiers Street for assignations — ah, then, you may be as strong and harsh as you wish. But not over property ——'

'I really do not understand,' said Sophie bewildered and looking it. 'I was so upset about this — about being so stupid and ——'

'Well, you must now forget it! I will see to it you have the necessary funds to replenish the cutlery and linen and so forth, and to replace the girls' property — and watch them or they'll cheat you blind! — and then we will all forget about it. I will not have you running away to Haworth for any such feeble reason. I have plans for you, my child, and I intend they shall reach fruit. Ah, tea! Thank you, Susannah. Put the tray there, if you please — yes. Now, my dear, will you consent at last to remove your mantle and bonnet and be cosy with us?'

For the rest of the evening, Sophie was indeed cosy. She settled comfortably in her chair, and told both her listeners with much graphic description of her afternoon, especially of her adventures backstage at the Gaiety, and described her brush with Gilbert Stacey with such drollery that both Freddy and Martha laughed until they wept.

Freddy, wiping his eyes at last, said, 'I think I know the young man you mean. I have been several times to the Gaiety, for the children love to see Nellie Farren, and I recall him — very long legs and dances with great skill. I find myself wondering what sorts of joints he has, he throws his limbs about with such ferocity!'

'Is he a good performer?' Sophie said casually, sipping her tea. Why she was interested she did not know, she told herself. Mr Stacey had been abominably rude and disagreeable and very poor company indeed. Yet for all that she had a very vivid picture of his amusing mobile face in her mind's eye, and found herself filled with an interest in him that belied her attempts to deny any concern with so unpleasant a man.

'Oh, very good! I'm sure he will become most successful. My brother-in-law — he runs theatrical supper rooms not far away from the hospital, you know, in King Street — he says he has been trying to get him to join his company for some time, for he is a performer of great promise. And Oliver should know: he has been a theatrical producer these twenty years and more. By the by, Sophie, I feel it is high time you met the family, do you not agree, Aunt Martha? I feel we have been most remiss these past weeks since you arrived in that we have made no effort to arrange — though of course Phoebe did come and call, did she not, but you had that cold ——'

'Oh, it is no matter ——' Sophie said hastily at the same time as

Martha said, 'I think we really must talk about ——' and then they both stopped and indicated that the other should continue.

It was Martha who picked up Sophie's invitation. 'More to the point, dear boy, is Sophie's studying, do you not agree? It is her wish to be a surgeon, and though I know there are problems in the way of such an ambition, it is my firm intention to help her prosecute them in any way that I can.'

Freddy put his cup down with a clatter. 'Is it, by George!' he said softly, and stared at his aunt. 'Well, well. You surprise me.'

'Why?' Martha said calmly, and refilled his cup. 'It is not so strange, is it, that I should wish to help my own brother's girl?'

'Not strange, that, no — but to follow on such a — and anyway, what of the legacy? Grandmamma's money comes to your Committee, does it not, if ——'

'Freddy, let us hear no more about that wretched legacy!' Martha said strongly. 'The London Ladies exist at all because of my Mamma's — your Grandmamma Dorothea's — money. There is no reason they should expect to inherit from both of Papa's wives! That would be greedy. No, I have already told the Committee that it is likely that a beneficiary will be found for this legacy, and they are to seek elsewhere for further funds. And I can tell you that they are having a splendid time, organizing routs and picnics and balls and heaven knows what else besides, all to raise the extra money. Indeed it does them a service, this refusal — for they are all far too idle to be comfortable. To raise the money the Committee needs will do it *good*. So let us talk sensibly about Sophie, shall we? The question is, how is she to study? Hey? Will you take her as a student at Queen Eleanor's?'

'At Nellie's?' Freddy said blankly, and then laughed. 'My dear Aunt Martha, you must be mad! Can you imagine the Governors there accepting a woman medical student? This is not Edinburgh, you know. The Scots do many mad things, but here in England — bless you, no. I am sorry, Sophie ——' and here he turned back to a somewhat bemused Sophie, who was listening to this colloquy with her lips apart, '— but you must make other plans, I am afraid.'

'I — yes, I can see that,' Sophie said, and then shook her head. 'I must say I have been concerning myself a good deal lately about how I was to set to work, and had indeed made a plan to come and

113

see you and ask your advice. Now it seems I need not waste your time ——'

'Oh, you must come and visit me at Nellie's any time you wish,' Freddy said immediately. 'I would be glad to see you there, and would happily show you all I could. We could always pretend that you have an interest in nursing, should any of the Governors object.'

'But you cannot allow me to study as I wish? In the anatomy rooms, for example?'

'Indeed, I could not! I am the most senior of the surgeons at Nellie's but that does not allow me to be the complete autocrat. I must consider the needs and feelings of others — and the other surgeons and the patients and the physicians — well, they would agree with the Governors, of that I am sure. And the fact that we are related, you know, that would bring a charge of nepotism, would it not? All very difficult ——'

'Then we must make our own arrangements,' Martha said equably. 'There is no other answer. But tell me this, Freddy. If we can arrange for Sophie to find somewhere else where she can study, will you be willing to teach her privately as well? I believe there is much that you could help with, without the Governors or anyone else knowing much about it. If you are willing that is ——'

Freddy turned his head and looked at Sophie, sitting in the light of one of Martha's handsome oil lamps, her hair shining richly in the brightness and her face a little pale and shadowed tonight but still very fresh and young, and felt that sudden tightening of the chest he had experienced the last time they had met.

'Private teaching? Well, yes, I think that might be possible — on my rounds, you know, of my patients in their own homes.'

'But anatomy?' Sophie said, looking at him very directly, and her narrow green eyes glinted in the lamplight. 'Could you — would you teach me anatomy?'

'I would find it difficult. It is not as easy as it might be to have access, you know, to cadavers ——'

'But suppose I could arrange that,' Martha said. 'Suppose I knew someone who would be interested in teaching Sophie, and arranging a place for her to learn? Would you help?'

'Yes,' Freddy said after a moment, and then hid his face in his cup again. And did not look at either Sophie or Martha, in case

114

they could see just how much the idea of teaching this pretty young cousin appealed to him.

'Splendid!' Martha said heartily. 'Then I now have a weapon I can use. Miss Jex-Blake will be arriving in London next week, Sophie, after her Edinburgh adventures. Her friend Miss Hill is a friend of mine, and that is how I know. We shall contrive for you to visit her and discuss your ambitions with her. What do you say to that?'

CHAPTER TWELVE

'Well, I suppose I must believe you to be serious in your intentions, since you come equipped with good support. But I am still concerned about this matter of the money. How can you convince me that you do not seek to enter upon a life as a medical student merely in order to benefit in a pecuniary way?'

Sophie sat very upright and stared at the woman standing in front of her. She had a rather heavily built body surmounted by a strong face with a pair of the darkest, most penetrating eyes under the thickest, straightest brows Sophie could ever remember seeing on a woman, and she was looking at Sophie now very sternly indeed. An abrupt manner and rather gruff voice added to it all made her seem a very formidable person indeed.

But Sophie was not prepared to be intimidated. She had fought hard and long to get as far as she had, for the past weeks had not been easy. Tracking Miss Jex-Blake down had been one of the hardest things of all. Martha indeed knew Miss Octavia Hill, her one time great friend, but it appeared, when an approach was made to her for an introduction, that the two ladies had parted some time before on acrimonious terms.

'I am afraid that when women develop passionate feelings for each other, they can become exceedingly vitriolic,' Martha said. 'It is the fashion at present for women to enter into these ardent friendships, but for my part, I find them all rather overheated. I trust you are not the sort of female who is seized of these tendencies, Sophie?'

'I?' Sophie had said, startled. 'Why, I never thought about — really, Aunt Martha, I cannot say ——'

'Oh, come my dear! You are not a baby. You must know by now whether or not you have easily aroused tender feelings and to whom they are most likely to be directed. Have you never been in love, my dear?'

Sophie had stared at the lined round face and the steel-rimmed spectacles over which her aunt was gazing at her, and suddenly wanted to laugh aloud. It seemed so odd to be quizzed in such a way by a maiden aunt of such apparently settled ways. What could this spinster lady possibly know of love, after all? And then she remembered some of the tales Martha had told of her time in the Crimea, the casual mention of a man she had known there, her adopted son Felix's father, and she wondered. And shook her head.

'I have not, Aunt,' she had said sedately. 'I am always somewhat irritated by the excessive attention some young ladies pay to affairs of the heart, and try to avoid them.'

'Then you have never had lovers? Never been approached by any man who ——'

'I did not say that, Aunt,' Sophie had said, a little red in the face now. 'Indeed, there have been — there is Mr Brotherton, a most — an old friend, you know and — really, I do not like this conversation, Aunt Martha!'

Martha had laughed then. 'Well, I am impertinent, I dare say. I just do not wish to waste any more energies in arranging for you to become a student if in fact you are going to throw it all away the first time a man looks at you! I would also not wish to encourage any girl in a tendency to passionate friendships with other women, for this life you are planning for yourself will throw you much among women, you know. And it is important that you be — shall we say of an *equable* nature, if you are to be happy and successful in your efforts.'

'You need have no fears about me, Aunt Martha,' Sophie had said firmly. 'I am a Yorkshire woman, you know, and we are not much given to silliness of any sort!'

But looking now at Miss Jex-Blake with her arresting eyes and powerful personality Sophie could see just how easy it would be to be silly about such a one. The strength in her was almost palpable and Sophie took a deep breath. This was someone to stand up to, she felt, and also someone who would despise those lesser mortals who crumbled in front of power. So she lifted her brows as coolly as she could.

'I cannot convince you with any evidence,' she said calmly. 'You must take my word for it, that is all. I am here to tell you that I wish to become a medical student. I am told on good authority that you, as a newly qualified doctor yourself, are planning to start a medical school for women in London. So, I am applying for a place. Will you take me?'

The square woman looked at her for a long moment and then, suddenly grinned. 'Yes,' she said and turned sharply and went back to the desk at which she had been sitting when Sophie was shown into the room, and bent her head over her papers again.

There was a silence and then Sophie said, 'Well?'

'Well what?' Miss Jex-Blake did not look up.

'You say you will take me?'

'I have said so.'

'Then what happens now?'

'Ah, that is up to you!' Miss Jex-Blake put down her pen and leaned back in her chair. 'The school, we hope, will open its doors in the autumn. There will, we all hope, be legislation going through the House of Commons to enable women to take the examinations and study to that end. But until the end of the present session and the outcome of Mr Russell Gurney's efforts we cannot be sure. However, we intend to fight on in the meantime.'

'And what do *I* do in the meantime?' Sophie said blankly.

'You study, my girl, you study! What d'you think I did while waiting to be accepted at Edinburgh University? I can tell you — I applied to every class I could, in chemistry, in mathematics, in philosophy. You do the same. Then, when the school opens in the autumn you will be ready to work in the wards we will hope to have access to to give you your practical training. Also —' she picked up from her desk the letter Freddy had given her as a reference, '— can you not put some pressure upon this relation of yours and obtain some entry to the wards at Queen Eleanor's?'

Sophie shook her head. 'He says the Governors will object.'

'To a woman medical student, perhaps. But suppose you sought to study as a lady nurse?'

'That would be dishonest!'

'Oh, pooh to dishonesty! There are times when ends justify means, and this is one — and I say that as a thoughtful careful Christian. Go and tell your cousin you will work in his wards as a nurse when you can, and come back to me in the autumn. Then you may become a medical student, God and Parliament willing. Good afternoon.'

And that was the end of the interview. Sophie found herself

outside pulling on her gloves in the March rain in Henrietta Street almost before she realized she had been shown out of the house. All these weeks of searching among Martha's friends for some news of Miss Jex-Blake's whereabouts, all those weeks of persuading Freddy to give her a letter of reference, all to culminate in one short interview? It was absurd, she told herself, turning and staring up at the tall house from which she had come. I shall go back inside and tell her so ——

But she did not. Instead she took herself back to Villiers Street, for it was late in the afternoon now, and her duties there called her. The evening meal and its serving had to be supervised before the girls set off for the theatres, and Sophie took her post as Lady Warden very seriously indeed, for quite apart from the fact that it provided her with the wherewithal to live at all, Martha's support and generosity were important to her, and nothing would ever prevent her from fulfilling all her responsibilities to that lady.

So, later that evening, when the house was quiet and empty but for the servants, she once again sallied out, this time to Martha's house in Bedford Row.

The question of Sophie meeting her other relations had come up once or twice in the preceding weeks, with Freddy showing some anxiety on this score. He had taken to visiting Martha on most Thursday evenings, which happened to be the selfsame evenings on which Sophie regularly went to Bedford Row to deliver the week's accounts and collect her funds. They had become accustomed to seeing each other there and had fallen into a very easy comfortable relationship, with Freddy bantering a little and Sophie enjoying the chance to display her own sharp wits. But whenever he brought up the question of family meetings, both Sophie and Martha shied away. It was almost, Sophie sometimes thought, as though Martha knew that there had been that fracas with Freddy's wife. But they never talked about it.

But now Sophie wanted to talk to Martha without Freddy's company, so, although today was Wednesday, she collected up her books and account sheets and settled herself in Martha's drawing room with an air of determination.

They dealt with the business of the hostel with dispatch and then Sophie set her books aside and told Martha of all that had happened at the meeting with Miss Jex-Blake.

'And,' she finished, 'the problem now is that she has advised me to set about arranging my own classes, where I can, and to work as a nurse at Queen Eleanor's. But I am worried about this ——'

'Because of Freddy,' Martha said.

There was a little silence. 'I like Freddy,' Sophie said. 'I like and admire him. I am fortunate to have his help. But I am concerned that I am pushing him too hard. He was not too happy, was he, about giving me that letter of reference. We did bully him rather, Aunt Martha, did we not? And now I fear I must bully him again. He said I could visit the hospital, and I am sure he meant it, but he is not entirely in sympathy with my aims, is he? And I would not wish to — to override a man's wishes in any way.'

'My dear child, no one overrides Freddy, unless he chooses it,' Martha said, but she was a little abstracted, looking down at her clasped hands as Sophie went on with some earnestness. 'Then what am I to do? I must set about some hospital work, I feel — I cannot just wait until this autumn and my place at Miss Jex-Blake's school, can I?'

'No. I can see that you cannot,' Martha said.

'So?'

There was a short silence and then Martha said awkwardly, 'Sophie, what happened when Phoebe came to visit you at Christmas?'

Sophie crimsoned, and she shook her head. 'Oh, Aunt, it really is not important ——'

'I think it is, you know. You see — oh, let us not beat about the bush, Sophie. It seems to me that Freddy has more than a cousinly interest in you. I have watched him here watching you, and there is little doubt in my mind that he has found you — interesting.'

'Oh, no! Surely not!' Sophie said. 'I said I like him and am grateful to him, but as for anything further — why, he is so old!'

Martha smiled wryly at that. 'Not so old, my dear. But forty-three, you know. Not too old to feel the stirrings of passion.'

'Well, he must not, he really must not!' Sophie said strongly. 'I am in London for one purpose only — and anyway, he is married. It is all quite ridiculous ——'

'Ridiculous it is not. Possibly dangerous it is. I thought at first it would be best to keep you and the family well apart for I guessed that something had happened when you met Phoebe. She can be a difficult woman, and I cannot deny it, love her though I do. But she was rather spoiled when she was younger, and has too little now to occupy her mind. The boys away at school — anyway, tell me what happened at Christmas and then I will think of what we are to do.'

So Sophie told her, leaving out nothing of that embarrassing episode, and Martha listened, her face serious, and said nothing. Until Sophie had finished and then she stood up and walked over to her fireplace and stood there contemplating the glowing coals.

'Yes, I see. Phoebe was somewhat top lofty, and you were rather blunt with her. I dare say I would have been the same — however — the question now is, how do we repair this damage? It is now almost three months since she called upon you, and in not returning her call you have, in effect, snubbed her severely. So, when she meets you again, she will not be kindly disposed towards you — and now we are agreed, her husband has a softness for you! Oh, dear, deary me! This is a tangle ——'

'I am sorry, Aunt Martha,' Sophie said. 'Indeed I am, but not for snubbing Cousin Phoebe. She was abominably rude to me, you know.'

'Oh, I know,' Martha said abstractedly. 'But all the same, if you are to spend some time at Queen Eleanor's, and yet prevent Freddy from becoming even more — um — involved with you — we must find a way to make you close friends with Phoebe, must we not? But how are we to contrive — ah! I have it!'

Sophie said nothing, just sitting and looking at Martha. In these few weeks since her arrival in London, she had become more and more dependent on this sensible little woman's guidance, and treated her much as she would have treated her own mother. Indeed, she regarded her with much greater trust than she had ever felt for her own rather silly, feeble parent, although she would have been loth to admit that fact.

But trust her though she did, she was somewhat taken aback at Martha's decision.

'There is to be a ball next week, Sophie, for the London Ladies. It is being held at the Pantheon, and will be a most splendid affair! The tickets are being sold for an inordinate sum, and everything there will be quite dreadfully expensive — but never mind. We shall be there, you and I.'

'At a ball?' Sophie said. 'But Aunt Martha, whatever for? I cannot really say I enjoy the idea of balls very much, for truth to tell, there were very few held in Yorkshire and even those that were —— '

'It is not for pleasure that we shall be there,' Martha said firmly, 'but as a matter of policy. The whole family have taken tickets — they always do when it is the London Ladies, for it is a charity in which we have a peculiar interest, and this ball is no exception. I rarely go, and they permit this eccentricity in me, but this time I shall. You shall be my guest, and we shall contrive it so that you meet everyone, and I shall smooth over any unpleasantness with Phoebe, and so clear the way to your working with Freddy at the hospital. But once we have settled it, be wary, my girl! I would not for the world have any distress in my nephew's household.'

'And nor would I, Aunt Martha!' Sophie said with some indignation. 'Do you see me as one of those frightful characters in cheap novels who come between husband and wife and —— '

'No, of course I do not — foolish child! But I do think it is possible, if one is not fully aware of undercurrents, to allow matters to drift in such a way that trouble is inevitable. So, we shall, as I say, arrange matters so that you are on such pleasant easy terms with Phoebe that there can be no question of any problems developing. Now, that is all planned! Come here on Saturday, if you please, in a hansom, and then we shall go together to the ball. It will be shocking tedious for me, for I abominate such entertainments, I cannot deny, but needs must when the devil drives!'

*　　*　　*

It was not until she was safe in bed that night and almost asleep that Sophie realized that she was faced with a problem even greater than settling the unpleasantness between herself and Phoebe, and at this moment, definitely greater than arranging for herself to become a surgeon at Queen Eleanor's.

She sat bolt upright in bed as the realization of her dilemma came to her, and stared up at her skylight. 'Oh, heavens above!' she said aloud. 'What am I to *wear*?'

For she had never had any sort of ball-gown. Quite apart from the cost of such a garment, there was little use to be made of such things at home in Haworth, for such assemblies as sometimes took place at Bradford and Keighley were far from being fashionable affairs. Most of the local ladies contented themselves with day gowns suitably trimmed with extra ribbons, and indeed they could be quite scathing about any lady who over dressed in their opinion.

But here in London, Sophie thought, it is sure to be different. Here ball-gowns well trimmed with all the flounces and furbelows that fashion now decreed must surely be all the go. She remembered the vision of loveliness which had been Phoebe on Christmas Eve and threw herself down on her pillow and groaned into it. That had been but a day gown — imagine what Phoebe could do when it came to a full-dress ball!

She slept little that night, but woke next morning from her unrefreshing sleep with at least a firm decision. One thing she would not do was seek Martha's help. That that good lady would cheerfully arrange for her to have a ball-gown made forthwith was beyond question, but Sophie had leaned enough on her good will. On this matter she must contrive for herself, somehow.

It was at breakfast, listening to the girls' chatter — those who were out of bed, for many of them preferred to sleep late and miss the first meal of the day — that she realized that aid was available to help her out of her dilemma.

The girls were enchanted by her request for help. Jenny in particular threw herself into the provision of a ball-gown for their Miss Sophie with an enthusiasm that swept all before it. She scurried about among the other residents of the hostel, collecting ribbons and feathers and beads and then piled it all in the middle of the dining room table.

'Now, Miss Sophie, we can begin!' she announced. 'What we need to do now is choose one of your day gowns and then set about trimmin' it up to make it all the go! What do you have?'

'Nothing that would go with any of these,' Sophie said, dubiously, looking at the pile of trimmings on the table. They were a motley lot, ranging from gauze scarves dripping with sequins to feathers dyed purple and emerald green and crimson, together with as rainbow a selection of ribbons as she had ever seen. 'Quite truly, Jenny, I do not think any of these are — well, are precisely my style, you know!'

'Pooh to that!' Jenny said, and the other girls who were perched on the chairs about the room nodded vigorously. 'It's all to do with fashion, Miss Sophie, not what's your style, you know! You must wear what's in, you see, what's the regular slap up to the nines, like everyone else will! You show us your gowns what you got, and then we'll see what can be done with 'em.'

Their opinion of Sophie's gowns was clearly poor, and her heart sank as they rejected one after the other, of the few she had, as being 'too tame'. And then Maria, who was the tallest of the girls and so nearest to Sophie in size ran up to her room and came down with a heap of blonde taffeta over her arm.

'You borrer that, Miss Sophie,' she said warmly. 'It's the best I got — give to me by such a lovely gentleman, who never asked nothin' 'e shouldn't in return — a lovely man, 'e was and it'll fit you a treat. You try it ——'

Still very dubious, for the gown was far more vivid in colour than any she had ever worn, Sophie allowed herself to be chivvied into it, and then tried to expostulate as the girls took over.

'I cannot wear this!' she said. 'Truly I cannot — it is cut so low, and is so ——'

'It's a lovely gown, ain't it, miss?' Maria said, sitting back on her heels, for she had been pinning a green flounce on to it. 'Nicest I ever 'ad.' And Sophie said no more. The warm generosity that was wrapping her round forbade her to make any criticism; and after all, who was she to say? She had never been much interested in fashion, mainly because she could never afford to be, and these girls, working as they did in the most important theatres in London, must surely know more than she possibly could.

So, she swallowed her qualms, and allowed the fussing with needles and pins and flounces and frills go on busily for the next two days until her ball-gown was ready. And on Saturday evening at six o'clock allowed them to dress her, which they did with much glee, and then stood and surveyed herself with what equanimity she could muster.

She thought, privately, that she looked quite dreadful. The colours of the gown, being predominantly yellow and green, seemed garish to her, and she greatly disliked the exceedingly low décolletage, which the girls had framed with green-dyed feathers. The flounces on the skirt she felt to be much in excess of what was needed, and the shimmering of the gauze scarf which they set about her shoulders seemed to her vulgar in the extreme.

But they stood there and looked at her with such pride and

124

pleasure on their faces that she could say nothing more than, 'Thank you Jenny, Maria — all of you. Thank you very much.'

And set out for her first ball in London in as low a mood as she could ever recall experiencing.

CHAPTER THIRTEEN

There was a moment, standing at the entrance to the great Pantheon in Oxford Street, when she so much wanted to run away that she actually turned on her heel, but Martha seemed to divine her thoughts and put one hand on her arm and said cheerfully, 'Here we are, then. Now, we may be here for a purpose but that does not mean you may not enjoy yourself! Every girl should enjoy a ball — though truth to tell, I never did ——' and Sophie was swept along with the crowds into the great chandelier-hung entrance lobby.

She was feeling quite, quite dreadful. When she had arrived at Martha's house and been shown into her drawing room, Martha, herself wearing very sober dark brown silk, turned to greet her and had allowed an expression of surprise to cross her face. It had been a fleeting moment in which her eyes had widened and her lips had parted, but that had been enough for Sophie.

'Oh, I knew it was all wrong!' she wailed. 'They meant well, the girls, I know they did, but I should have been stronger and refused to wear it. I would have been better off in my old blue morning gown, with new cuffs and collar on it, rather than this — this monstrosity!'

'It is not a monstrosity at all!' Martha said stoutly. 'If I looked taken aback it is because I have never seen you looking so pretty and young and altogether — well, delightful! It is a somewhat vivacious gown, I grant you, but my dear child, it will fade into nothing, I promise you, against the other toilettes you will see tonight! Some of them will be so shocking vulgar that ——'

'This is shocking vulgar enough for anyone!' Sophie said tragically, and pulled at one of the flounces on her skirt with an almost vicious tug. 'It would not be so bad if I could take these off, perhaps ——'

'Oh, nonsense, child! There is no time to remake a gown now. You look perfectly splendid, indeed you do, and there is no need to distress yourself. Ah, Susannah! Is the growler here? — Good —

come along, Sophie — and remember to leave some hot milk and brandy for us when we return, Susannah. I believe we shall have need of it ——'

All through the journey to the Pantheon Sophie sat in misery, on the edge of tears. For one who had all her life been blessedly free of undue vanity it was a strange experience to be so cast down simply because of a gown — she who had been roundly berated by Bessie many times for tucking her skirts into her drawers when she climbed the moors, in order to give her legs greater freedom.

Bessie. The thought of that dear old friend nearly destroyed her, and tears slid out of her eyes and streaked her face, and she had to sniff hard and mop away the moisture with the back of her hand just as the growler arrived. A sadder and sorrier girl never went to any ball anywhere.

Not that in fact she looked as dreadful as she thought. The gown was undoubtedly far from being a good one. The stuff of which it was made was cheap, the colours were overbright, the trimmings too exuberant. But as Martha had said, the other people at the ball were a mixed lot, and many of the gowns that those others wore were much more vulgar and overtrimmed, if vastly more expensive, than Sophie's. But most of these excessive gowns were decking the backs of much older women than Sophie; her own sartorial shortcomings faded away in comparison with her face for her fresh country complexion really was charming and her narrow green eyes, for all the misery now lurking in their depths, had an enigmatic quality about them that was much more interesting than her clothes.

So Freddy thought as he saw his aunt and his cousin hovering at the entrance to the great ballroom. He had arrived early, uncharacteristically chivvying his wife and daughter so that they had left home in ample time — and indeed had been unfashionably early. Phoebe hated above all things to be among the first at a ball, and now she sat with her daughter Cecily beside her, her skirts of cream silk spread lavishly about her and her lace fan much in evidence, undoubtedly in a very poor temper as she observed the new arrivals.

'My dear,' Freddy said, with as insouciant an air as he could muster. 'There is Aunt Martha — we are rarely honoured with her presence at these crushes, and I am delighted to see her — and I believe — yes, is that not our little Yorkshire cousin with her? I am sure you will recollect her — you called upon her, did you not?'

'Indeed I did,' Phoebe said, kindling, glad to have an object on which to focus her general feeling of irritation. 'Fully three months ago, but the girl can have no breeding, cousin though she be, for she has not returned my call nor ——'

'Oh, come, Phoebe, you must not be too hard on her. She is a quiet little country girl, and possibly did not know the etiquette London demands in these matters ——'

'Quiet country girl, you say? My dear Freddy, *look* at that gown! Did you *ever* — good evening Aunt Martha. How pleasant to see you. I trust you keep well?'

'Excellently well, thank you, dear,' Martha said amiably. 'You recall Miss Sophie Lackland, I am sure — she is your Uncle Barty's daughter, you will remember.'

'We have met, I think,' Phoebe said frostily and bent her head slightly at Sophie, who reddened and bit her lip. 'Uncle Barty, you say? I cannot say I ever knew anything about him — ah, there is dear Felix! And does not Amy look enchanting? So refined and tasteful, as always. Do observe Cousin Amy well, Cecily, my dearest child. She has impeccable taste in her gowns, and would never appear vulgar in any circumstances — Amy, my sweet one! Come and tell me *all* your news!' And she made a space between herself and her daughter Cecily, a rather plain little scrap of a sixteen-year-old in white muslin, to make room for the newest arrival, a girl with dark curly hair and huge grey eyes and the most bewitchingly pretty face Sophie had ever seen.

She was wearing a gown which was extremely artful in its simplicity, being a confection of the palest lemon voile, trimmed with gathered frills, and Sophie, horribly aware of her vast green flounces, twitched awkwardly at one of them and seemed hardly aware of the studied way in which Phoebe was ignoring her.

'My dear Amy, you must meet your cousin! You too, Felix — this is Miss Sophie Lackland, from Yorkshire ——' Martha took over the situation with great smoothness and there was a flurry of handshaking and nodding, and Sophie tried to fix the names of the newcomers in her memory.

Amy, with a soft American accent, was the wife of Felix, and was, it appeared not only related to them all by this marriage, but also by blood, for she was a first cousin of Phoebe and Freddy. And then she remembered, as Martha went on explaining, that in fact Felix, a square stocky young man with a pleasant smiling face and closely cut curly hair and no hint of a fashionable whisker on his face was an adopted member of the family, and not a blood connection at all.

And no sooner had she got these facts clear in her mind, but more people came across the now rapidly filling ballroom to join them and more introductions confused her.

'Ah, dear Abby — Sophie, this is your Aunt Abigail, my sister, and Freddy's dear Mamma.' And Sophie obediently bowed to a decidedly stout lady with a very handsome face and greying hair and wearing a most sumptuous gown of deep green satin. 'And your Uncle Gideon, Freddy's Papa — well step-Papa, of course, but it makes no matter — Mr Henriques ——' And this time Sophie was faced with a tall spare man with very piercing dark eyes and a great deal of silky white hair.

Then there were more cousins, a most beautiful girl in a honey-coloured gown, introduced as 'Freddy's sister, Isabel — and her husband Jacob Da Silva — and here is Sarah and her betrothed, David Sassone — Sarah is also your cousin of course, since she is sister to Freddy and Isabel ——'

Sophie's head swam, but not so much that she was unaware of the sort of people these were and how she compared to them. That they were rich was undoubted; the gowns worn by both Isabel and Sarah were simple yet of an elegance that was unmistakable and clearly cost a great deal, and both they and their mother, like Amy Laurence, were wearing the most costly of jewels. Amy had a collar of garnets and diamonds and the Henriques sisters plain diamonds, while round Aunt Abby's throat were clasped several rows of the most lustrous pearls. Altogether Sophie felt as awkward and as poverty-stricken and undesirable as she had ever felt in all her life. Many had been the times when Mrs Brotherton, putting on her airs and graces, had tried to have this effect on the proud Lackland girl, but never had she succeeded as these rich, rich, rich relations were doing.

Which was partly why, Sophie later decided, she behaved as she did. No one had ever been able to regard Sophie Lackland as any sort of sycophant; no one had ever been able to accuse her of tuft hunting or social climbing in any way, and, she swore to herself, no one was going to be able to do so now, poor as a church mouse though she might be. She would show her pride in every aspect of herself. And so she did. She was cool, unresponsive, remote in every way, responding hardly at all to anything that was said to her.

'She is very unfriendly,' Amy said to Felix as he swept her off into the dance as the orchestra went into a lively galop to open the evening's proceedings.

'I agree she seems remote in her manner,' Felix said, and twisted his young wife's body expertly into the centre of the ballroom. 'But there, she comes from the North, you know, and they are famous for being dour there, are they not? Have I told you how delectable you look tonight?'

'I think she is most disagreeable!' Sarah announced, and smiled up at her handsome David. 'Do you not agree, my sweet?'

'I am not married to you yet, Sarah — when I am, I will comment on your relations. Not before, if you please!' And Gideon Henriques laughed heartily and slapped the boy on the back. A most witty young man, as well as being a very suitable one, with his excellent banking connections. 'Wise, my boy, very wise!' he said. 'But I can say as I choose, and I find her a most awkward female with no graces at all!'

'And that gown!' Cecily said, and tittered. 'Mamma, it is a dreadful gown, is it not?'

'What, dear?' Phoebe looked at her and then reached over and tweaked at her blue sash. 'Oh, the Yorkshire girl — I hardly noticed, dear. Dreadfully dull ——'

Martha said nothing. She watched Freddy and Sophie dancing — for he had taken her on to the floor as soon as Phoebe had refused him, as she always did refuse to dance the very energetic sets — and sighed. It was going to be harder to arrange matters than she had realized, but arranged they had to be. Quite apart from Sophie's own needs as a would-be student, there was this matter of the silly fancy Freddy had taken to the girl, and which had to be stifled as soon as possible — and that without Freddy's knowledge.

He was a dear good boy, Freddy, and Martha loved him sincerely, but she knew his character well. And it bore a strong and wide streak of great stubbornness, just as his grandfather Abel's had, and any attempt to manipulate him was sure to end in trouble. If that is, he realized he was being manipulated. So he must not realize ——

She turned to her niece and began to chatter, and Phoebe, fond as she was of her Aunt Martha, softened under these attentions, and as the set of dances at last ended, was sitting happily enough chattering as the dancers returned to the cluster of chairs that had become the family's own, there in the corner of the ballroom.

'Miss Lackland dances very well, Felix, and I insist that you share the pleasure I have just enjoyed ——'

'Thank you, no,' Sophie said sharply, perhaps a little too sharply, for she had intercepted an amused glance between Amy and Sarah and interpreted it as a criticism of herself and her dreadful gown — for by now the usually sensible Sophie was positively obsessed with her own appearance and thoroughly unhappy — 'No one need take *me* out, thank you very much, against his will! I am happy to remain standing up by myself!'

Felix raised his eyebrows at that. 'A prickly cousin, indeed,' he said lightly. 'Believe me, dear Miss Sophie, no one in this family would ever consider it possible that I could be forced to do anything against my will. I am much too set in my ways — ask my charming wife there!'

'Indeed he is!' Amy said and laughed. 'Hateful man, won't let a poor actress go to work as she should — but I will beat you down yet, you see if I don't!' And she made a little face at him, full of love and humour, and he smiled back. But Sophie, smarting all over from the pains this evening was bringing her saw only a snigger between them, and was sure it was directed at herself.

So, when Felix then turned to her and said with great charm, 'And I had already decided that I should ask you to dance with me once my wife had released me, and do so now ——' she responded with a chilly hauteur that was missed by none of them, saying aloud, 'No thank you,' and turning her back on him.

Felix did no more than raise an eyebrow and Amy stared at the tall awkward girl in the green and yellow flounces in surprise, but with no rancour, and after a moment the conversation started up again, and couples re-formed for the next set of dances, which were Viennese waltzes.

This time Freddy danced with Phoebe, who, Sophie had to admit with almost gritted teeth, moved as well as she looked. Many eyes followed her to the floor and Amy said cheerfully, 'Does Cousin Phoebe not look superb? She always does — and yet so tasteful, always, never pushing herself in that nasty way some women do ——' and again Sophie reddened, taking the innocently meant remark as a personal barb.

She had to dance then with David Sassone, as Sarah took herself and her sister away to talk to friends across the great ballroom, and enjoyed it little, for he was a poor dancer who had to concentrate on his steps, and even then frequently got them wrong, catching his foot on her gown several times. But she went through the motions of the dance doggedly, aching only for the end of this disastrous evening and the safe refuge of her little attic room in Villiers Street. Whatever else happened, she swore to herself, one thing was sure. Never would she seek any help or support from any of these hateful, dreadful relations. She loathed them all, the top lofty, purse-proud creatures that they were, and she yearned to tell them so.

The orchestra at last flourished itself into silence and David Sassone, with a somewhat stiff bow, led her back to their corner. The ending of the music seemed to have sharpened her hearing, and the general hubbub of voices from the crowded ballroom seemed to subside for a moment, as sometimes happens in noisy places, and just as they reached the palm in a pot that marked the cluster of chairs where the family were sitting she heard Phoebe's clear voice rise above it.

'My dear Aunt Martha, you must admit she is shocking boorish, and quite as awkward as any housemaid in our company! I understand your concern for her, since you are so good and sweet a person, who loves all who need you, but really, you cannot expect me to admit such a one to my friendship — we could have nothing in common, you must surely see that.'

Sophie's chin was high and her face white as she came round the palm. That this comment was about herself there could be little doubt, and she felt the anger bubbling in her very close to the surface. That she, Sophia Lackland, a Greenhalgh on her mother's side, should be treated so by these stupid Londoners — it was outrageous, and she would for two pins tell them so ——

'Oh,' squealed Amy as she came into sight. 'Oh, my dear, your gown — do but look at your gown!' and she pointed with one finger

132

at Sophie and the Henriques girls looked round and Sarah smiled and opened her mouth to speak.

But Sophie gave her no chance. She stood there in front of them, her head up and staring at the row of beautifully dressed women with their men standing behind them and let her upper lip lift as in a sneer.

'Yes indeed, it is a dreadful gown, is it not? Shall I tell you about it? It was provided for me by my friends — my *real* friends, the cheap little actresses who live with me in Villiers Street. They are but common working girls, of course — nasty creatures, I dare say *you* would consider them, since they lack your benefits. They have no money, no rich carriages and houses, and they have no nice manners and attitudes to defend. But they have warm and loving hearts, and when they heard that I was to come to this — this trumpery ball of yours and lacked such a gown as purse-proud creatures like yourselves can enjoy they provided me with this one. They provided it all and sewed it all for me, and did so with such — such real friendship that I count myself blessed to wear it! You may laugh and sneer all you wish, and consider me lower than a servant girl —' and she flashed a glance of pure loathing at Phoebe '— but I count myself very fortunate to know them, and most unhappy indeed to be related to any one of you — except Aunt Martha and Freddy, that is, who are the only decent ones amongst you. And now you can all — you can go to the deuce for all I care! I am going home. Good night!'

And she turned and went, marching away across the ballroom, her eyes blurred with tears, leaving them all speechless behind her, except for Amy who wailed, 'But I only wanted to warn her that she had torn her flounce and might trip over it, for it was trailing on the floor! Why should that make her so ——'

Freddy moved to follow her, but Martha put one hand firmly on his arm and looked up at him and he stared down at her, frowning and then followed her gaze to Phoebe, who was sitting erect and white-faced with fury, and after a moment he moved to stand beside her.

'You must not mind that little outburst,' he said awkwardly. 'The poor girl meant no harm, I am sure — it was simply a crisis of nerves.'

'And this is the one who wishes to become a surgeon?' Phoebe

133

said contemptuously. 'Why, she would not be fit to be a house-maid! I do not deny that I thought that was what she was when first I saw her, and now I am convinced no blame attaches to me for the error. Did you ever *hear* such talk from one that is supposed to be well bred. My Uncle Barty must have gone sadly to rot once he left his home in London.'

Across the other side of the ballroom, Sophie disappeared through the main doors, and Martha sighed and got to her feet.

'Now, hear me, all of you. This child is a good dear girl in many ways, and though I know she has not shown herself to advantage tonight, I would be most distressed to think you would think ill of her because of it. She has been under much strain, in many ways, and needs our support. I am asking you all to make every effort, now. Will you call upon her? Soon? Isabel? Sarah?'

'Oh, of course we will!' Abby said comfortably and fanned herself with some vigour. 'Poor child — I thought her quite justified in her outburst. I dare say we *did* look askance at her toilette — and it really was rather dreadful, was it not — and made her feel ill at ease. We shall certainly call upon her — and so shall you, Phoebe.'

'Why should I? Really Aunt Abby, you expect too much ——'

'No, I do not,' Abby said firmly. 'And it is rare indeed I offer you any authority, but now I do. She is a poor lonely child, alone in London and we are her relations. Of course we must treat her lovingly, and I insist that you do! So call upon her with Cecily — tomorrow. You hear me?'

'Oh, very well, Aunt Abby,' Phoebe said sulkily. 'But do not expect me to make a friend of her. You heard what I told Aunt Martha ——'

'Well, never mind all that,' Freddy said impatiently. 'I am more concerned to see she is well now. I shall go after her, I think, Aunt Martha ——'

'No, I shall,' Martha said and went. But by this time the music had started again and it took her some time to weave her way along the crowded edges of the room, and by the time she reached the lobby there was no sign of Sophie, and after looking about her for a while Martha sighed and returned to the family party. Tomorrow, she promised herself, tomorrow I will do what I can to put all right.

Had she gone a little further, she would have found her niece.

She had fled across the lobby, almost blinded with her own tears, and into the narrow corridor on the other side that led to the band room beyond, not knowing where she was going or what she would do when she got there, wanting only to be away from those hateful people, and out of the light and noise.

But as she plunged into the darkness, the tears now frankly falling down her cheeks, she tripped, for Amy had been quite right — the lowest flounce on her gown was badly torn, probably by David Sassone's very awkward dancing, and she fell headlong over it.

She lay there, weeping bitterly, too sore and angry and altogether miserable to make any attempt to get up. So that when Gilbert Stacey put his head round the corner of the corridor from the brightly lit lobby, he found her lying in a crumpled heap of yellow and green flounces with her face as tearstained as a baby's.

CHAPTER FOURTEEN

'Do you know,' Stacey said in a conversational tone, 'I believe you are going to have a black eye.'

'Oh, no!' Sophie wailed and put her hand to her face and then winced. 'And my cheek is bleeding — oh, I wish I were *dead*!'

'Oh, you are not so damaged as that,' Stacey said cheerfully. 'Come along — I shall call a cab and take you home. Then we can see what harm is done and put it to rights.'

'Who are you?' Sophie said suspiciously, peering up at him in the dimness. Her head was aching now, and her face was very sore, and as she again touched her cheek gingerly she realized that she had grazed it quite severely. And her eye indeed was puffing up and making it difficult to see clearly.

'Oh dear. I had hoped you would recognize me! Well, I think what I will do is apologize humbly to you first, because I know that I owe you a very definite amend, and then I will tell you that I was never more delighted in my life to see a lady in a ballroom as I was to see you this evening, and was debating with myself how to separate you from that huge party you were with so that I could both apologize and then talk to you. And then, in the hope that you would have accepted my apology and also the fact that I am now an admirer, tell you that my name is Gilbert Stacey and we last met at the Gaiety Theatre ——'

'Stacey!' Sophie said wrathfully. 'How dare you! How dare you come here and ——' and to her own horror she burst into tears again, and began to tremble so much that she could not prevent him when he set a friendly arm about her shoulders and said gently, 'You poor girl! You've had a dreadful shaking up. Come, no time now for talk — let me quietly get you out of here and safely home ——'

And he did just that, helping her to her feet and leading her out of the corridor and across the busy brilliantly lit lobby with such insouciance, chattering all the way, that hardly anyone noticed that his companion was wearing a gown so badly torn and bedraggled she had to hold it up in front with both hands, and a face so bruised and injured that she looked as though she had been attacked.

He obtained a hansom cab for them with equal skill, and she climbed in gratefully, and made no demur when he sat beside her with his arm still across her shoulders to support her and told the jarvey to take them back to Villiers Street forthwith. Which the jarvey, grinning hugely, did.

One comfort was that the house was quiet and peaceful when they reached it. The girls were still at their theatres and the cook and the maids had gone to bed, for they were never asked to wait up for the residents, so at least Sophie did not have to face any exclamations and murmurings. She gave Gilbert Stacey her door key when he demanded it, scrabbling in her reticule for it, and then allowed him to lead her in to the dining room where the fire had been banked up against the girls' return, and the tray with the milk and little rout cakes always left out for them was waiting on the table.

'There!' he said with satisfaction. 'That is better, is it not? Now let me look at you. Oh dear, oh dear! You did do yourself a mischief, did you not? I think a little care is needed here ——' and he left her sitting in an armchair, her head resting gratefully against the back of it, to go rummaging in the kitchen.

He came back with a piece of steak and some towels and a bowl of warm water and she allowed him to bathe her grazed cheek and set the meat against her eye, and said nothing. She was now, truth to tell, quite exhausted and beyond caring much about anything; the evening's tensions and the culminating tumble had left her quite wrung out.

He sat back on his heels at last, and contemplated her, and smiled. 'You know, you are a most interesting lady! I meet you first as a raging termagant, and now you appear as a tragedy queen, quite in disarray — what role will I find you filling next? You are clearly the stuff of which actresses are made ——'

She opened her uninjured eye then and glared at him. 'No, I am not!'

'Oh, and what is wrong with the stage as a career? You disapprove of it?'

'Of course not! Do I not look after twenty actresses here? But that does not mean that I am in any sort one of them ——' She closed her eye again and touched her face, wincing slightly. 'I have other plans. Fetch me a mirror please. There is one over there — take it from the wall ——'

'I would not look if I were you,' he said with mock earnestness. 'It will distress you dreadfully.'

'Nonsense! It is my face, is it not? And anyway, I wish to see what treatment I require ——'

'You will be better asking an apothecary tomorrow,' Stacey said, going to fetch the mirror. 'You will need an expert hand, I think, to deal with this. I have given what immediate aid I can ——'

She was looking at herself now, and felt tears rising in her as she stared, for her eye was already showing signs of bruising, as well as puffiness, and the graze ran from her nose to her chin.

'Oh dear,' she said, almost in a whisper. 'That will take much time — I must poultice the eye, I think — cold compresses. And a lanolin dressing for that graze ——'

'You seem knowledgeable on such matters,' Stacey said curiously. 'Every other girl I know who saw herself so injured would be weeping and wailing, not choosing dressings. You are indeed a strange young lady, Miss Lackland!'

She looked up at him, and frowned a little. 'Did I tell you my name?'

'When last we met. Of course you did. Have you quite forgotten me? Oh, I am so cast down — I had hoped you would recall a *little* about me ——'

She shook her head irritably. 'Oh, please, do not be tiresome. You were shocking ill mannered ——'

'But was I right? Did you find Miss Gunn flown and half your property with her?'

Sophie leaned back in her armchair again, and he took the mirror back to its hook on the wall. 'Oh, wretched man that you are, yes, you were! But that does not mean you were right to be so ——'

'I know.' For the first time he sounded serious, dropping the bantering tone that he had used almost throughout. 'But I was — well, I had a disagreement with John Hollingshead myself that afternoon, just before your arrival, and I was in a sorry temper. And in mocking you as I did, I was in a sense mocking him. It was

138

shocking bad behaviour, and well I know it and I do truly beg your pardon. When I told you at the ballroom that I was eager to apologize, I spoke no more than the truth. I hope you will allow me to be your friend now, and will forget the occasion of our first unfortunate meeting.'

Again the fatigue was overcoming her, quite vanquishing the little spurt of energy she had shown, and she looked at him almost dreamily. He had a most pleasant face, after all, she decided, deep in her weary mind. Easy and amusing and kind, and for a moment she saw Wilfred's face too, as though it were superimposed on Stacey's and closed her eyes against it, for thinking of Wilfred and home made her feel so lonely and tearful.

'My dear, you are at the point of dropping. Where is your room? Let me take you to it — no, forget about propriety! You are injured and need aid, and it is absurd to leave you in this state — and when I have taken you there I will rouse one of your maids and send her to you ——'

'No, please don't do that ——' She opened her eyes again. 'I am sure I can manage well enough, and the maids are the sort who will weep and wail and make such a pother that I will have to look after them ——'

He bent then and with a skilled easy movement, slipped one hand behind her shoulders and the other beneath her knees and almost before she knew what was happening, he had straightened up and was holding her across his arms as though she were a child.

'Oh, put me down at once!' she said, and tried to pull against his arms, but they were as hard and as tight as though they were carved of wood, and her struggles were feeble indeed against his strength.

'Oh, don't be so silly! You are injured and need your bed — now, where do we go? Upstairs, that much is sure ——'

She knew when she was beaten and stopped struggling, resting her head against his chest and enjoying the comfort of the swaying movement as he began to climb the staircase carrying her as easily as though indeed she had been no bigger than a child. 'The attic,' she said quietly, and suddenly yawned, and then winced as the movement hurt her face.

'Poor Miss Lackland,' he said softly and climbed on and she closed her eyes and allowed herself to enjoy the sympathy in his voice.

He left her almost abruptly, doing no more than setting her down on her bed, and then looking about him, by the light of a match he took from the silver matchbox he wore on his watch chain, to find her lamp and light it. And then he went to the door, bowed sketchily and said with great punctiliousness, 'Good night, Miss Lackland, I shall call again as soon as I may. I wish you a speedy recovery from your injuries.'

And she listened to his footsteps dwindling away down the stairs and yawned again, and thought sleepily that he was quite an agreeable sort of man after all — allowing for the fact that he had been right about the hateful Miss Gunn. And then she fell asleep with the suddenness of a weary child and didn't stir until morning.

*

She woke feeling a great deal worse than she had the night before. Her face was now uncommonly stiff, and falling asleep fully clothed had added to the underlying stiffness of her muscles. She almost groaned aloud as the light from her skylight moved behind her closed eyelids and dragged her into wakefulness.

The sight that greeted her inspection of the mirror was an even sorrier one than last night's. The swelling around her eye had increased, and it was quite severe round her face too, and she marvelled a little that such an amount of injury could have been done by just a fall, but then she recalled that the floor of the corridor had been of uncarpeted concrete, built in the new style; no wonder she had suffered so.

There was nothing for it, she decided, but to keep to her room until she should be fit to be seen again, and she dragged her aching body to the top of the stairs and called for Jenny, her favourite among the residents, for she was a helpful cheery girl and could be trusted to keep her tongue between her teeth when bidden to do so.

She came at last, a little bleary-eyed from want of sleep, but still her cheerful self and exclaimed and worried over Sophie's appearance no more than could be expected and then agreed to help protect her in any way she could. She took herself off to the kitchen to tell the maids that Miss was ill of a low fever and was to keep her bed, a statement which was quite enough to keep them well away from the attic, for they had an almost superstitious fear of the mere word 'fever'. And then, once dressed, took herself off to the apothecary's shop to purchase such necessaries as Sophie demanded.

And then there followed some of the dreariest days Sophie could ever remember. She poulticed and dressed her own injuries carefully, and had the gratification of seeing them heal well, with no signs of suppuration — which she had much feared — and for the rest of the time sat under her skylight and read such books as she had to hand.

There were many callers, but she steadfastly refused to see them all, sending down polite messages about being less than well, and looking forward to seeing them again when she should be fit enough. Even Martha was repelled by the determined Jenny, who stood at the foot of the stairs when any came, and would not be budged. So, Martha went away and sent delicacies from Robert Jackson's shop in Piccadilly, calves' foot jelly and fresh pineapples imported at vast cost, and beef tea in stone jars, all of which embarrassed Sophie mightily, but which could not be refused. Invalids could not properly refuse such tokens of others' good will, so she wrote polite notes of appreciation and begged Miss Lackland not to bother herself further. But still the offerings came.

And so did others. Freddy Caspar sent a pile of books, for which she was genuinely grateful, and wrote and told him so; there were treatises on disease, one on the growing science of anaesthesia, and a much-thumbed copy of an old surgery book that she fell on with great relish.

The gift cheered her greatly. It seemed to presage well for the future, for surely Mr Caspar would not send her such reading matter if he did not intend to help her further her ambitions? To do so without such good intentions would be cruel indeed, and whatever else Freddy Caspar might be, Sophie told herself, he was not cruel.

Unlike his wife, she decided, when she inspected the card that lady sent up when she came to call. She had written carelessly on the back, 'I regret to hear you are discommoded, and trust you will soon be restored to health.' Sophie scowled at it; such platitudes, she thought, when the woman had herself been in part the cause of her downfall! And then she scowled at herself, for she knew perfectly well, now that the heat of the moment had had ample time to dissipate, that her own temper and pride had had much more to do with it all. Mrs Caspar had been disagreeable, certainly, but she had not precisely *pushed* Sophie into that fall, had she? Sophie had to admit that, and hated Mrs Caspar the more heartily for that reason.

Gilbert Stacey, on the other hand, made himself more and more agreeable with his messages. On the first day after the fiasco that had been the ball, he sent her a pretty little parcel, which, when she opened it, proved to be a small heavily gilded mirror, into the glass of which he had pasted a cut-out picture of a simpering girl with blonde curls.

'I send you this to show you that you could look much worse than you do,' he wrote. 'For all your bruises and batterings, you appear infinitely more charming than this vapid creature, so peel her off, I beg of you, and admire the face that you will then see. It is in my estimation a much more agreeable one!'

This had been followed by all sorts of charming nonsenses: a doll wrapped in bandages, a set of ribbons 'to tie up your hair, the only uninjured part of you'; a little plant growing in a pot with the message, 'As this plant will shed its leaves and then flower again, so shall you shed your badges of war, and flourish again.'

Each time she laughed and each time she felt a little stab of warmth, for this was just the sort of comfort she needed. Martha's concern expressed in her gifts of invalid food made her feel even more low in her spirits, and Freddy's gifts of books made her feel restless and angered at the time she was forced to waste here in her room. But Gilbert Stacey made her laugh, and for this she was more than grateful.

She used much of her time to write letters home. She had been in steady correspondence with Haworth, of course, ever since her arrival, but her letters had been terse, for there was so much to be done, and so little time to spare for her own affairs. But now she had time, and she used it to scribble long epistles to everyone she could think of.

To Wilfred she wrote at length of the hostel, and how convenient it was that she could manage to earn her living so respectably, and also of the people in it. Bessie she knew would be bored by details such as that, and would criticize every one of her new-found friends, so bitter would be her jealousy, but Wilfred, she felt, would not, sharing with her real interest in her new life.

So, she told him of the girls at the hostel, of Aunt Martha, and Freddy Caspar — though nothing about disagreeable Mrs Caspar, scorning to waste ink on her — and then about Gilbert Stacey.

'Such a droll!' she wrote, 'I am sure you would enjoy his company, Wilfred, for he laughs at things in much the same way that we used to, and makes the same sort of foolish jokes, which are very agreeable to me. The way we met was unfortunate, I cannot deny —' and here she launched into an account of that dreadful afternoon at the Gaiety Theatre, and its outcome, and perhaps did not realize quite how much she dwelled on Mr Stacey's share in the proceedings. Until she read her letter over again, and realized that it did concentrate rather heavily on that young man.

But she folded the letter and sealed it, nonetheless. Wilfred, bless him, was not such a one as Bessie, jealous of anyone who interested her darling; he would be as amused as she was herself about all these new people, and take no offence in the world.

Or so she thought; and was less than her usual perceptive self in doing so, for her letter, when it arrived at Haworth, gave Wilfred much to think about and made him unusually terse with his workers at the mill, and most uncharacteristically sharp with his mother when she made some scathing comment about Sophie on seeing the postmark on his letter and guessing its origins. Which made that lady think rather more than she was wont to do, also; of all of which Sophie was quite blissfully ignorant, of course, as the week of her recovery dragged slowly by and she concentrated her thoughts on what she would do as soon as she felt herself fit to be seen in public once again.

On the last day of her incarceration, when she decided that the following morning she would, with the judicious use of a little rice powder begged from Jenny and a re-dressing of her hair to bring more of it about her face, be fit to move in polite circles again, she wrote yet another letter, this time to Freddy Caspar.

'Dear Cousin,' she started and then sat and chewed her pen for fully five minutes as she thought and started again. 'Dear Cousin Freddy, I first wish to thank you most sincerely for the books you sent. I have devoured them, I do assure you, not at all kept from them by the low state of my health, and they have fired me to greater than ever ambition. I now ask you, formally, if you please, to arrange for me to attend as frequently as may be at Queen Eleanor's Hospital to walk the wards and learn what I may in the guise of a lady nurse. I am an experienced nurse, and will not in any way embarrass you, of that I flatter myself I can be certain, and will learn much from observation and practice without pushing myself forward as a medical student in any disagreeable way or in a manner that would cause embarrassment with the Governors of the hospital. I know that in writing this I ask you to be mendacious, in a sense, and that is a wrong thing to do, but I am sure you will see that, placed as I am, I can do little else. I will call upon you at the hospital, if I may, on Monday of next week, when I confidently expect to be quite well again, and trust that we may come to a satisfactory arrangement. Your grateful cousin, S. Lackland.'

'And if that causes dramas with the puffed-up Mrs Caspar, I cannot be blamed for it,' she thought savagely as she sealed and stamped her letter. 'I am not at all interested in her husband, except as a mentor and helper in my career, and I am sure Aunt Martha is wrong and that he has no tenderness for me at all that need cause any difficulties. I will be a surgeon, in spite of them all, indeed I shall!'

And with that resolution, she went to her bed on that last night of her recovery from the ball feeling better than she had for a long time. In many ways, in fact, her injury had been good for her. It had forced a rest upon her that she sorely needed, and allowed her energies to fill her again and give her the impetus she needed to set out upon her new plans.

So she slept soundly that night, and woke refreshed and ready for all stops that might be put in her way, by anybody. And looking forward, also, to seeing people again, for a week with none but Jenny for company had been sorely tiresome.

And if she looked forward with most eagerness to seeing Gilbert Stacey, she did not admit the fact, even to herself.

144

CHAPTER FIFTEEN

One of the most useful things about her week of confinement to her room had been that it had shown her that her work at the hostel, vital as it was, did not need to fill the whole day. With Jenny's help she had dragooned the maids and the cook into taking over most of her domestic duties, and doing so with real satisfaction (Eliza, for example, displaying an unexpected talent for and pleasure in flower arranging). She had also used some of the time to devise a new and much more speedy method of keeping the books. So, when she finally sallied forth on that Monday morning to visit Freddy at Queen Eleanor's she felt confident that she would be able to accept whatever he had to offer in the way of hospital training time, and still would be able to perform her hostel duties adequately.

'Indeed,' she told Freddy earnestly, when she was closeted with him in his little shabby office, 'I have discovered that time is much more elastic than I would ever have thought possible. If one has important and valuable things to do, why then, it is possible to perform less interesting duties in a fraction of the time they once took!'

'I am sure you are right,' Freddy said and smiled at her eager face. She was a little thinner, he thought, as a result of her indisposition, but she looked rested and alert and filled with that eagerness he had first found so beguiling in her. And despite his own good sense, he found himself warming to the thought that he could see this pleasant face about his wards every day, if he so chose.

And he did so choose. Even up until this morning, he had not decided fully what he should do about her formal request. He had sat at breakfast, mulling over his thoughts as he mechanically chewed his way through toast and devilled kidneys, and longed to seek guidance from another on this matter. In past days he would

145

have talked to his Phoebe, the wife of his bosom, but that was before she had taken to these new lazy ways of hers, lying abed in the morning till all hours.

Or so he had told himself, as an excuse for not discussing Miss Sophie Lackland with her. In reality he shied away from mentioning Sophie at all in her presence, for she had clearly taken the girl in great dislike. So that left only Martha, who would be of little real help for she was clearly firmly on Sophie's side in this matter and would not counsel him, but add her cajolery. Which left only himself.

Now, looking at her sitting there with her neatly gloved hands folded on her lap and her plain straw bonnet surmounting that eager face, he let the decision make itself. For all the problems it might involve, and for all his own deep doubts about the propriety of a woman studying medicine at all, he would help her.

Her face lit with delight when he said so, and she jumped to her feet, both hands outstretched and took hold of both of his and shook them with great fervour.

'Dear, dear Cousin Freddy! I am so grateful! You will never know how grateful — for I am determined, indeed I am, upon this course and would have suffered much without your aid. If there is ever anything, anything at *all* I can do for you, please do not hesitate to tell me, for I am your servant always!'

'Oh, there is no need for such transports of delight,' Freddy said and laughed, but there was an undertow of embarrassed pleasure in him. To please this charming cousin was most agreeable. 'I am doing little enough in all conscience — simply giving you access to our wards. The manner in which you use that is up to you. I cannot give you formal teaching, you must understand that. If you happen to be nearby when I am teaching my students, and overhear, then of course that is no concern of mine. But I can do no more than that ——'

'That is enough, more than enough!' said Sophie jubilantly. 'And now tell me, to whom shall I be subservient? I imagine there must be somebody who will have charge of me?'

'The Matron — Miss Bishop. She is a very strong lady — well, any Matron of a hospital such as Nellie's must be — and I think ——'
He stopped and thought for a moment. 'I have not considered this point before, but now it occurs to me that we might do worse than

take her into our confidence. She is herself a lady of some ambition — well, she must be, must she not, to have achieved her present status —— Come! Let us take our fortunes in our hands and go and talk to her!'

Sophie followed him through the corridors of the hospital on their search for Miss Bishop with her head up and with her eyes, bright and enquiring, darting everywhere as she tried to take in all she could. And there was much to see, for the hospital was a large and busy one, with eleven wards — for over the years since its inception, it had encroached year by year on neighbouring buildings, swallowing them up and taking them into its own structure — and excellent accommodation for outpatients as well as two large and well-equipped operating theatres. The corridors were handsomely decorated with dark green paint on the lower parts of the walls, and a cream dado, and shining polished wooden floors.

The wards themselves she admired greatly, for each was a long airy room, with ample high windows, and the beds set in neat serried rows down the walls on each side, each with their brass foot- and head-rails polished to a satiny gleam and with curtains dependent on curved runners which ran round each bed, pulled back between them.

'We have the most modern system we could obtain,' Freddy explained, seeing her admire the curtains which were made of a serviceable cream rep. 'We found a cabinet maker who could devise the runners and charged us mightily for them and the Bursar purchased the fabric at great cost, but it is all worth it, for each bed can be separated from its fellows and give the patients the privacy they so sorely need. It is better for all, and not merely the ones who are most sick, for it is not good for those who are recovering to see all the time the appearance of those who are mortally ill. We are proud of our wards here, indeed ——'

'You have a right to be,' Sophie said fervently, 'and they are so beautifully kept! The linen looks so clean and the flowers so pretty and all is most ——'

Freddy laughed then. 'Well kept! I agree with you. It could not be otherwise under Miss Bishop's sway, I promise you. That is a lady of the most formidable kind. As you will see!'

They tracked her down at length in the sluice room at the far end of the women's ward. Freddy had been directed there by a frightened-looking nurse who had gone scurrying by bearing a large covered tray and had looked back over her shoulder down the ward at the door at the far end, and Freddy, smiling faintly, had marched there with a firm step.

They stood for a moment unobserved inside the little room. It had two large white sinks with taps above them on one side and on the other a great copper boiler steaming and bubbling softly. And against the far wall was a wooden draining board before which stood another nurse, this one with tears running down her pale cheeks, and a diminutive woman with her sleeves rolled up and her head bent over the work she was doing, which was scrubbing a large red mackintosh sheet with great energy.

'Good morning, Matron,' Freddy said loudly. The small woman did not cease in her scrubbing but said quietly over her shoulder, 'Good morning, Mr Caspar. I shall be with you directly. There, Miss Littleton! Now you see how I expect a rubber sheet in my hospital to be treated. If you cannot find it in you to do so simple a task as this properly then rest assured you will never be able to do any other task properly, let alone care for the fragile sick. First things first — now, do you set about dealing with those other sheets in the manner which I have displayed to you and I will return to inspect your work later. Now, Mr Caspar! What can I do for you?'

She turned, drying her hands briskly on a small towel and then pulling down her sleeves and fastening her cuffs. Sophie saw a neat round-faced woman, with her hair pulled back severely under a lacy cap which was firmly tied with bows beneath the chin, and a dark blue high-necked gown with a small white collar. She looked as round and as polished as an autumn nut, but her eyes snapped brightly from behind a pair of steel-rimmed spectacles and Sophie felt herself quail for a moment under their sharp regard, for there was indeed something very alarming about this small person.

'We would have words with you, Matron Bishop,' Freddy said easily. 'In private if you please. Can you spare the time?'

'Of course, if it be upon hospital business, Mr Caspar,' the small lady said equably. 'But not for any other affairs at present, for I am sorely put to it to see the wards well dealt with today, with two of

148

the nurses deciding to fall sick —' Sophie felt a moment of admiration for any nurse who would dare to fall sick when this important personage had need of her services, '— and the beds full, every one of them.'

'I think this can be called hospital business,' Freddy said, and held the door open for her and together they sallied into the ward.

'Is this private enough for you?' Miss Bishop said in her clear but quiet voice, stopping by the fire in the middle of the ward. 'I doubt that the patients can hear aught we say, and it will be quicker than going all the way back to my office. I wish to be at hand on this ward today, for the nurses here — tch — tch —'

'This will serve admirably,' Freddy said. 'Matron Bishop, I would like to present to you a young connection of mine — Miss Lackland.'

Miss Bishop flicked her eyes up at Sophie, towering tall above her, and compressed her lips slightly.

'How d'ye do, Miss Lackland,' she said and then looked fixedly at Freddy.

'She has a desire to be a lady nurse, Matron,' Freddy said and then smiled at Sophie. 'And yet not to be.'

'Come, Mr Caspar, I have no time for riddles today. On other occasions I enjoy a little chat with you, but I told you, today ——'

'I am not joking, Matron,' Freddy said. 'Far from it. I am about to tell you the truth of a matter which concerns Miss Lackland, and also me, and ask your aid. You will not, I think, like it entirely. But if you do not, I trust you to say no more about it than passes between us here this morning.'

Matron Bishop said nothing, just raising her eyebrows at him, and Freddy looked reassuringly at Sophie, and then plunged into an account of her situation, and told Matron Bishop clearly and succinctly of Sophie's desire to be a medical student.

The small woman stood there in the middle of her shining polished ward, never taking her eyes from Freddy's face, with her hands folded neatly on her blue gown, and listened. And Sophie felt her pulse begin to rise with anxiety until it was beating thickly in her throat. That this woman held the key to her hopes was clear and for a moment she wished Freddy had found it in himself to be a little more mendacious, and not expose her so completely to this formidable lady. Suppose she refused to co-operate? Suppose she chose to go at once to the Governors and expose Freddy's little plan to admit her as a nurse while training her as a medical student?

And then the little woman turned and looked at her, her eyes dark and inscrutable behind those round glinting spectacles, and Sophie looked back, her hope in her eyes and her lower lip caught between her teeth.

And then slowly, the little woman smiled. 'Miss Lackland, I wish I were you,' she said softly. 'I wish I were your age, and had your courage — for indeed, when I was young I had just such a mad ambition as this but did not even dare to give it voice! I have followed with more eagerness than you can imagine the exploits of Mrs Garrett Anderson and now Miss Jex-Blake and have yearned — indeed, I have *yearned* to be one of them! Well, I am past fifty and it is too late for me, but you — of course I will add my aid! But I tell you this, Miss Lackland — you have set your shoulder to a dreadfully heavy wheel. Never think it will be anything but hard and heartbreaking work that will be yours. If you make one step in the wrong direction, I will be upon you much more cruelly than I would if you wished but to be a nurse — and it is right that I should be so harsh. When a nurse cares for a patient she does so under a doctor's guidance. It is his responsibility to provide the treatment, to make the decisions. She is but the handmaiden of Aesculapius. This gives her a leeway, a freedom to be at error, on occasion. But Aesculapius himself — he is a different matter. He must never be wrong, so if you would be a female Aesculapius you must bend yourself to the most powerful of disciplines. Are you prepared for that?'

Sophie looked at her and, suddenly and with great sweetness, smiled widely. 'I will welcome it,' she said simply. 'Any teaching you can give me on this score I will welcome and I will, I promise you always bend my neck to your reprimands. And I have never been a meek person, Miss Bishop, ever. But to enable me to do as I wish, I will be meek when it is necessary.'

'Then that is settled,' Miss Bishop said briskly. 'I will add Miss Lackland's name to my register of probationer nurses, Mr Caspar, and she will be uniformed and treated as are the others. Do you live far away, Miss Lackland?'

'In Villiers Street, where I act as Lady Warden of a hostel run by the London Ladies ——'

'Ah, yes, I know of it. Well, you may maintain your residence there. The arrangements I shall make will not demand unusual working hours of you here, for I shall appoint you nurse to the medical school — how does that idea attract you, Mr Caspar?'

'Nurse to the medical school? Well, it sounds an excellent — but how will it serve, Matron Bishop? How can the Governors be made to see that ——'

'Oh, pooh to the Governors! They will do as I say in matters of nursing, as they always have. They are not fools, Mr Caspar, and know well that such matrons as I are hard to find. I do not speak in any spirit of self-aggrandizement but merely as a matter of fact. They pay me less than other matrons at London hospitals receive as their remuneration, and get the best service of which I am capable. Which is far from negligible — far from negligible ——' and for a moment the little lady looked so fierce that she was almost funny. 'And on this matter they will be pleased. Your tasks, Miss Lackland, will be to attend all rounds of the wards by medical students. To arrange for all dressings to be at hand for the students when they come, to maintain and provide at call all the patients' records that students require, to attend in the operating theatres when a student is being allowed to try his hand, and in general to act as handmaiden to the young men who are learning their profession. And if you cannot allow some of their teaching to rub off on you, then you are not the girl I take you to be.'

And so it was all arranged. An hour later, Sophie found herself outside the hospital, clutching a parcel of print dresses and white aprons and caps — for Matron Bishop was a whirlwind of activity, and had the girl in the linen room and fitted with nurse's uniform from the stock that was held there in no time at all — with firm instructions to present herself, suitably garbed, in the men's surgical ward at half past seven next morning. And there at the hospital she would have to remain until five in the afternoon, when she would be released to hurry back to Villiers Street, there to deal with the accumulation of daily tasks that had to be performed by the Lady Warden.

Standing there in Endell Street, staring up at the facade of the hospital and still smelling the carbolic and ether reek that filled its every nook and cranny, she quailed for a moment. For the next two years she had committed herself to a course of work that was huge, more than she had ever done in all her life. There would be free time, admittedly, on Saturday afternoons and Sundays when the students were not in attendance at the hospital, but on those days she must study. And on other days, she must pore over her books too if she was to keep up with her studies, when the accounts for the hostel had been drawn up and the stores checked — could she survive it all? Would she be able to pick up the challenge that little Matron Bishop had thrown at her? She could well imagine the scorn that diminutive person would pour upon her if she failed, and for a moment Sophie wanted to deposit her bundle of uniform on the steps of the hospital and run hot foot for King's Cross Station and the first train home to Haworth.

But of course she did not. Instead she took herself back to Villiers Street and set about making her own preparations, confirming Cook's and the maids' willingness and ability to carry on those of her tasks that she could easily delegate. And then she took a small luncheon and set out on a whirlwind of visits, for it would be many weeks, if not months, before she would be able to find the time again.

Martha, as she had expected, was delighted with her news and assured her that she need have no anxieties about Villiers Street.

'For my dear, you planned it well when you first went there and organized it excellently and now you may reap the benefit. I am happy to arrange for you to present your books and to deal with money matters once a month instead of once a week ——'

'Oh, but I should miss seeing you every Thursday, Aunt Martha ——' Sophie said quickly, and Martha smiled at that.

'You are a dear to say to — and I shall miss you. But you will be hard put to it to manage more often. And I was about to add that I shall come to you on the third Thursday of every month, which will save your time and energy. No, do not gainsay me. I will have it that way, and when I will it, so it is.'

'You sound like Matron Bishop,' Sophie said, and told Martha about that alarming lady, and Martha listened to her and watched the expressions flit about her face and was warmed by it all. To see this girl so happy and so hopeful was a great pleasure to her, and she remembered again, a little wistfully, her own girlhood and wished, not for the first time, that she was young now in the hopeful modern eighteen seventies, rather than watching her fiftieth birthday recede far behind her as the sixtieth came even closer on her horizon.

'I think, my dear, that it would be good in you, if you can spare the time today, to visit Cousin Phoebe,' she said when at length Sophie drew to a close, and they were drinking tea. 'Yes, I know that all is uneasy between you, and you will note I have said naught about the ball and all that happened there — but I am eager you should be friends with your relatives — and if not close friends, well, at least on nodding terms. Will you go?'

There was a little silence and Sophie said with uncharacteristic timidity after a moment, 'Will you come with me?' At which Martha laughed and assented. 'I suppose I can understand it. Phoebe can be tiresome when she gets up in her high trees! Very well — we shall go now, shall we? And afterwards, perhaps to my sister Abby.'

The meeting with Phoebe was not as unpleasant as it might have been, much to Sophie's relief, for when they reached her handsome house in Tavistock Square and were shown by the very lofty butler into the huge drawing room that ran the full length of the first floor of the house, Phoebe was not alone. Her Aunt Abby with both her daughters were sitting there, their bonnets off and teacups in their hands, and so was Amy Laurence, who greeted Martha with such pleasure and chattered so much about her own doings that the ice was quite broken and the awkwardness of the first meeting Sophie had had with them all since that dreadful ball soon passed off.

Abby drew her to one side after a while and began to quiz her, seeking information about her father, and after the first few awkward moments Sophie found herself chattering easily to this pleasant woman. She was large and comfortable to be with, and although she was dressed just as expensively as her niece Phoebe — indeed, perhaps even more so — there was no sense of posing about her, of which Sophie was very aware with the younger woman.

She listened with genuine interest to Sophie's reminiscences of her father and then sighed softly. 'Dear me, it is so strange to hear of Barty after all these years! Such a boy as he was — and then I wonder about Gussy and what happened to him and ——'

'Gussy?'

'Another of my younger brothers. We were a large family, you

153

know — there was William and Jonah — both long since dead, I am sad to say — Jonah being Papa to Phoebe and her brother Oliver — and then there was Rupert — ah, Rupert ——' and she fell silent for a moment.

'What happened to him?' Sophie was now interested, for she had never thought much about family matters — perhaps to protect herself from the pain of remembering the loss of Letty as well as her orphanhood — but now listening to Abby there was a charm in thinking about those who bore the same blood in their veins as her own.

'Oh, Rupert, I am afraid, was a sore rogue — he went away. I am told in fact that he went dreadfully far away — to Australia, no less. But that was but a rumour, and I have heard no news from him this many years. Ah well! One day, perhaps —— Now, tell me. What plans have you now you have come to live in London? Shall you launch yourself upon a social life with Martha? Or would you wish me to ask my girls to do so? They are both a little busy, of course, for Isabel, you know, is in an interesting condition, at last — for she has been wed these three years — and Sarah is to be married in three months' time. But ——'

'Oh, no, thank you, Aunt Abby,' Sophie said hastily. 'It is kind in you to be concerned, but there will be no time at all for such things as social affairs, by the time I get back each day from Nellie's ——'

'What was that?' Phoebe's voice came sharply across the room. 'From Nellie's, did you say? Each day? And what will *you* be doing there?' And the emphasis she put upon 'you' was slight but unmistakable.

Sophie went brick-red and could have bitten her tongue out. She and Aunt Martha had not discussed the matter, but she knew as surely as if they had that Martha would have advised her to keep her own counsel about her plans. But the damage was done now.

'I am to be a lady nurse there,' she said quietly, her cheeks still red but her voice steady. 'It was arranged this morning.'

'A lady nurse? How very — quaint,' Phoebe murmured, and looked at her sharply. She was looking particularly ravishing today in blue silk, and Sophie felt very gangling and awkward in her presence and this added a sharpness to her tongue.

'I need to earn my own bread, Cousin,' she said, 'and in due

154

course this will ensure that I am able so to do.' She pushed back the sense of guilt that her half-lie created in her. If Phoebe wanted to think she really was going to be a nurse, that was her affair. Sophie would not disabuse her of the notion.

'It is interesting, is it not, Phoebe, how family patterns recur?' Martha cut in smoothly. 'For there was I nursing at Nellie's during the cholera epidemic, you know, and you came out to Scutari with me ——'

'Those were different times and for different reasons, Aunt Martha,' Phoebe said coldly. 'But I take your point. Clearly Cousin Sophie is going to follow in the footsteps of the men of the family,' and she threw a satisfied glance at her own blue silk flounces and smiled a little.

'I could do worse,' Sophie said hotly, and then Abby laughed and said, 'Indeed you could, my dear. Had you but known your Grandpapa, my father, oh, dear me! How you would have been amazed!' And she launched into an account of Abel Lackland that had them all fascinated, and drew further reminiscences from Martha, until the younger members of the party became restless and got up to leave.

And so Sophie's visit to Phoebe passed off well enough, and they parted, if not on amicable terms, at least on speaking ones. But as they left, she and Martha, and made their way down Phoebe's rather splendid staircase, she watched them go with her eyes sharp and considering. Sophie Lackland at Nellie's! It was strange that Freddy had not mentioned it to her. Strange indeed. She would not, perhaps, ask him about it, but would wait and see what information he offered. There was something odd going on here, Phoebe thought, with some acerbity, and she was far from happy about it. But she would bide her time.

CHAPTER SIXTEEN

Sophie's last call of the day was made after considerable soul-searching and with not a little excitement. When they left Phoebe's house she saw Martha to her cab and, after promising faithfully to obtain one for herself immediately to take her back to Villiers Street, she instead turned and started to walk back towards the centre of London, thinking as she went.

To call upon such a person in such a place was not, she knew, the action of a well-bred young lady. Bessie would be horrified, for all her easy-going ways, and Aunt Martha, Sophie suspected, would be definitely disapproving. As for cousin Phoebe — well, the thought of her undoubted disapproval was quite enough to harden her resolve to make the visit anyway.

But still she doubted, as she walked briskly through the busy streets, making her way back towards the Strand; and if her steps carried more towards the eastern end of the Strand than westwards towards Charing Cross it was not fully intentional, for not until she reached High Holborn was her mind quite made up. She would have to take a cab now, of course, for newcomer to London that she was she did not know nearly enough about the city's geography to find her way about on foot as unerringly as most Londoners did, and to stop off on the way to Villiers Street — which was really all she would be doing — would not be so reprehensible. Not really.

So she told the cabman who stopped in response to her waving arm, 'The Gaiety Theatre', with what nonchalance she could muster and closed the apron over her knees as calmly as though she went in hansoms to visit young men backstage in theatres every day of her life.

This time the stage doorkeeper was awake, and she made no attempt to pass him illicitly, asking demurely for 'Mr Stacey, if you please,' and the old man looked at her suspiciously with one skewed rheumy eye, the other being tightly closed, sniffed unappetizingly and went shuffling off into the depths of the old theatre to find him. And she stood there half inside and half outside the building, wishing she were an errand boy or suchlike and able to whistle to keep up her spirits.

But then he came, almost running through the narrow corridors, his hands held out to greet her long before he was near enough to touch her, and smiling with that mobile twisting mouth of his in a most agreeable manner, and at once she felt comfortable again.

'My wounded friend!' he greeted her, his eyes wrinkled with pleasure. 'And how are you? Quite mended? Ah — almost. I detect, I suspect, the faintest hint of rice powder upon that innocent cheek! No, don't look so horrified. It is only because I am an actor that I can recognize these little subterfuges.'

He had taken her hand now, and drawing it through his crooked elbow, was leading her back through the corridors towards the back of the stage, and she did not resist him. Now she was with him she had to admit that he was a very beguiling creature and excellent company. He was still chattering, and she had time to look at him more closely and was a little startled to see his appearance, for not only was his face painted; he was wearing a suit of black which was quite unlike any other clothing she had seen on a man.

He caught her eyes on him then and laughed, breaking off his comments on the way rice powder could be used to hide a multitude of sins, but never the sin for which it was most frequently invoked, that of increasing age.

'You find my clothes strange? Well, so they are! You see, my dear Miss Lackland, I am a dancer. I act and sing as well, but I am above all else a dancer. And a tumbler. Which means I must needs have my limbs free and easy when I work. This suit I wear — let me show you ——' and he let go of her arm and moved ahead of her.

And to her amazement suddenly hurled himself forwards until he was standing on his hands. Then he twisted his body yet again and lo and behold, a series of cartwheels carried him down the length of the corridor with remarkable speed, and another series brought him back. He leaped and turned and then suddenly was standing on his hands again, his head poking forwards between his arms in a most droll manner as he peered up at her.

She laughed, and clapped her hands and he twirled himself lightly to his feet and stood brushing the dust from his hands and smiling down at her.

157

'Now, my dear Miss Lackland, did you observe? My clothes remained close to my body throughout, did they not? A mere hint of a flying coat tail perhaps, but at no point did my trouser legs flap back and display more ankle than any gentleman should ever show, and my waistband remained, I trust you observed, sleek and elegant at all times.'

'I did not look so closely,' Sophie said demurely. 'Indeed, sir, I had hardly the time, for you move so fast you seemed a blur! You are indeed an excellent dancer, are you not?'

'I do not know,' he said gravely, and came and stood close beside her, looking down at her. 'I never watched myself. Will you watch me tonight and give me your opinion?'

'Oh, my opinion would be worth nothing, Mr Stacey. I have seen few enough dancers with whom to compare ——'

'Your opinion on anything and everything would be of interest to me, Miss Lackland,' he said and there was a throatiness in his voice now that she found had a remarkable effect on her, for it seemed she was suddenly rather breathless. 'I listened to your indignation the first time we met, I observed your courage the second time we met, and now I admire your magnanimity the third time we meet — for many young ladies, having had two such uncomfortable meetings with a gentleman, would never wish to see him again. But you are different. So your opinion must be valuable, must it not, and quite untainted by others' foolish notions.'

She smiled uneasily. 'I came, sir, to thank you. You were most kind to me the other night, and sent me such — such amusing little gifts to while away my sickroom hours. I am indeed grateful, and would not wish you to think otherwise.'

'Do you know I came three times to call upon you while you were locked away there in your attic room?'

'Why, no!' She was startled. 'No one told me ——'

'Oh, I never knocked upon your door! For a start I came too late at night, after my performances here were over. And, anyway, I felt it would be unkind in me to expose you to a stranger's gaze. Were we already as good friends as it is my dearest hope we shall become, why, I would not have worried. But as it was I thought — well, even the most sensible and level-headed of young ladies — and I flatter myself that I am a good enough judge of character to know

158

you to be so — would be distressed at being seen in all her bruises! So I did not knock, but gazed up at your skylight only ——'

She looked at him, much struck by his words, for he displayed, behind his bantering tone, a genuine concern for her wellbeing that was very comforting, and she put her hand impulsively upon his sleeve and said, 'Thank you. You doubled your kindness in behaving so. I did look quite dreadful! And I would have felt ashamed to send you away, when you had been so kind to me, and seen my face when it was first injured.'

'Is it really all quite well now?' He took her shoulders in his hands, but with so gentle a touch she did not feel at all affronted, as she would have done had any other man as unknown to her as this one done so, and turned her so that the meagre light overhead illuminated her face. He looked at it searchingly and she followed the movement of his eyes as he looked closely at her cheeks and felt the hateful colour rising there, and tried to look away.

'Yes, almost well, heaven be thanked,' he said seriously. 'You are a little thinner in the face than you were, and a shade wan, but it does not misbecome you. You have perhaps less of that rosy country colour that I noticed so much the first time we met ——'

'Oh, Mr Stacey, please, can we forget the first time we met?' she said impulsively and moved enough to ensure that he had to let go of her shoulders. 'I am much embarrassed when I remember it and ——'

'Of course we shall,' he said heartily. 'For, to tell the truth, I am as much embarrassed by the recollection as you are. But I insist that I shall have some recompense for my loss of memory.'

'Oh?' She looked at him doubtfully.

'Oh, yes! I shall insist that you remain here to see our performance tonight — I will give you a seat in the stage box — and then, we shall sup together. How do you say to that? Hmm?'

'Oh, sir, I cannot! I must ——'

'Cannot? Or will not?'

'Well — you see, I have much to do tonight. Tomorrow as ever is, I am to start a new — well, I cannot tell you of it now, but it will be a most exhausting business and I do feel that after having been confined to my chamber for a week, it would be wisest to sleep early tonight ——'

She looked up at him again in the dim corridor and then to her

159

amazement heard her own voice speaking again. 'But, pooh to common sense! I would dearly love to see the performance here for I have seen few stage shows in my life, and supper afterwards would be delightful!'

'Ah — a woman of such infinite wisdom and good humour that she knows that pleasure must sometimes come before duty and hard work is a treasure above rubies!' he said and seized her hands and to her intense discomfiture kissed them one after the other. 'Miss Lackland, the day we met is one I should bless, and not attempt to forget! But forget it I will, and instead thank heaven fasting — well, over supper, then — for bringing you to me as she did! Come — let me see you to your seat, for it is getting late, you know, and I must be about my business!'

And indeed there was a bustle starting up around them. People in exotic clothes, against which his black suit looked quite sober and commonplace, were pushing past them, none of them seeming at all curious about them, and from somewhere deep inside the building there was a sound of scraping violins and ripples of notes from trumpets as an orchestra tuned up. The very smell in the air had changed, becoming thick with scent, and what she now was beginning to realize was greasepaint, and there was a faint hint of acrid lime as well.

'Thank you,' she said, a little breathlessly, for now he had seized her hand again and was hurrying her along the corridors, past the knots of dancers and singers, all with painted faces which were beginning to look to Sophie quite ordinary, so used was she becoming to the sight of them, and then, they were out into that great expanse that was the stage wings.

Now there was no hushed silence, no great pools of light in which people danced and moved, for the curtain was down. She could see it, a vast wall of crimson cloth looking as solid as bricks and she stared through the mêlée of people and the uncertain light thrown haphazardly about as workmen moved the big gas lamps about, and felt a great lift of excitement.

She had spent little enough time in theatres, in all conscience, but enough to catch the infectious anticipation that filled an auditorium of people waiting for a show. Here, behind the stage, where the faint hum of the chattering expectant crowds beyond the fabric wall made a counterpoint to the urgent voices and shouts

160

here on the crowded stage, the excitement was greater, much more raw and urgent, and she shivered slightly as the waves of it moved through her.

'Come along, my dear Miss Lackland,' Stacey said urgently and led her to a heavy baize-covered door, and held it open for her. On the other side, almost immediately, was another door, and he closed the one on the stage side first, so that they were crushed rather closely together in the small available space — an occasion she minded not at all — and then he opened the outer door.

Here all was very different. The rough wooden floors of the stage side gave way to deep-pile crimson carpeting, the dirty painted walls here were paper hung and handsome, and the lights everywhere were overwhelming; glittering, fluttering gaslight that made her blink and squint a little.

'That door there — do you see? That is the stage box,' Stacey said quickly. 'I must go now, for I am in costume and makeup and to be this side of the door where the audience may see me is most unprofessional. Please wait there after the show until I come. I shall not be long, I promise you. I hope you enjoy it!' And with a quick squeeze of her hand he was away back through the doors, leaving her to make her way as sedately as she could, for all her breathlessness, to the stage box.

And there she spent the most enchanted three hours she had ever known. She was alone, sitting on one of the six little gilt chairs which furnished the box, peering comfortably round its crimson curtains which were miniature replicas of those upon the stage, and so close to the stage that she felt she could jump out and be on it herself. Further below was the orchestra pit, with the musicians looking rather absurdly foreshortened sitting there in a tangle of instruments and music stands and sheets of paper and she gazed at them with great interest and then at the audience beyond.

They were well worth looking at. In the front rows of the stalls there were a great many men she thought at first looked rather foolish, so many of them seemed to have the same vapid stare upon their faces, and the same sort of monocle screwed into blank eyes above the same sort of whiskers. They sat and lounged and some picked their teeth with little gold toothpicks, and all of them seemed to have crutch sticks standing between their knees or propped up against the seat in front.

Further back in the auditorium there were more men heavily dressed and far less fashionable, and a few women, lavishly gowned and showing large areas of bare shoulders and bosom upon which jewels gleamed. She shrank back behind her curtains, very aware of her own rather dull green morning gown, though her velour mantle, of course, looked as good as any garment there. But somehow it seemed less than right for this setting and she was very glad to be here on her own, where none could look at her with any sort of sneer for her unfashionable appearance.

She lifted her eyes then to look at the galleries above and her lips curved, for up there the audience was quite different; cheerful family parties of the ordinary kind with children eating oranges and throwing the peel around — much to the indignation of those sitting below in the stalls — and women in exuberantly feathered hats and men with mufflers wound round their collarless necks. Good ordinary people, like her neighbour Mr Chamberlayne — much more interesting to look at than those bored mashers in their blank-faced self-importance in the front of the theatre.

The lights began to dim and she caught her breath as the orchestra swept into a cheerful lively tune, and her spirits rose almost perpendicularly. The place hummed with excitement and she herself positively rang with it. She was to see a show, and she was going to enjoy every moment, no matter what.

It was not hard to enjoy. The dancers were delightful, so energetic that they made her own muscles seem to ache in sympathy, and there were exquisite girls wearing the most beautiful of gowns who did little more than stroll across the stage and look statuesque, but they did it very well and with a scornfulness which well matched that of the first rows of dandies.

Then there was Nellie Farren, the little dancer and singer she had seen the last time she had come here, but been in no mood to appreciate fully; an enchanting creature who moved about the stage as though she were made of dandelion fluff and it was no more than a field on a summer day, and all her own domain; who sang her rather silly songs with a delicious lilt and a pointed drollery, rolling her eyes up at the galleryites — who shrieked their approval heartily — with such aplomb that Sophie found her face was wreathed in smiles of pleasure the whole time she was on the stage. And then there was Mr Toole, so funny in his silly clothes, so

162

adept with his jokes, so very wry in his many offerings!

And Mr Stacey, Gilbert Stacey, who danced, she thought, as easily as if he were made of sprung steel rather than human flesh and blood, who moved as insouciantly about the stage as did Nellie Farren herself, and who sang in a pleasing tenor voice with perfect pitch. How delightful to sit here and watch him and know he was her friend! And when he looked up at the stage box and very deliberately winked she could have swooned with the delight of it all, and embarrassment, for she was sure the whole audience had seen and known to whom that outrageous wink was directed.

The show ended all too soon for her, even the two intervals when girls with little trays went dancing about the auditorium selling glasses of fresh lemonade, because they too were fascinating in their way, as she watched the members of the audience and speculated about them.

But then came greater pleasure, for in no time at all Mr Stacey was there in her box with her, his face quite denuded of paint and wearing clothes of unimpeachable ordinariness, his arm crooked and his top hat rakishly on one side of his head, waiting to take her to supper. And though she tried to demur, because of her day gown, pointing out that she would look most odd among such lavishly evening-dressed people as those she had seen here tonight, he would have none of it. To Rules they would go, he told her in lordly fashion, and there enjoy the best supper ever. He had made up his mind to it.

And so they did. They walked the short distance to the restaurant in Maiden Lane, he talking all the while of the show and the things that had gone wrong with tonight's performance — none of which, she assured him, she had noticed in the least — and quizzing her most eagerly about her opinion of his dancing and singing. Had she noticed the vibrato he put into his voice when he sang 'The Lover's Farewell'? Had she recognized the great height to which his kicks had taken him in the second act? Had she noticed the way he had to catch Nellie Farren who had moved most awkwardly at the end of the first act? And did she not think Mr Toole's dancing grossly over-rated, for what it was? To all of which she assented, knowing that he was not really listening to her answers, and not thinking worse of him for that. He was clearly in a state of towering excitement, and she could well understand it, for she could quite enter into the drama of the feelings that must fill a man when he steps on to a vividly lit stage before an audience of many hundreds.

At Rules, a most elegant establishment with many fine etchings upon its walls and tables well furnished with the whitest of napery and the most handsome of silver and crystal, he ordered lavishly and insisted that she eat oysters. 'For soon, you know, it will be May, and then not an oyster may we have until September! I live only for those months which have an R in them, for I am a sad gourmand, and cannot deny it to you! And then, after our oysters, let me see — some mutton chops and a slice of Bradenham ham to speed them on their way. And a morsel of good Stilton to end with, hmm, Miss Lackland? Come, that will set us up well for the evening, do you not agree? That and a bottle of good Chablis, of course, to drink with our oysters, and a decent claret to accompany our mutton chops.'

She ate heartily, for so busy had been her day that she had expended much energy and become quite hungry, and as the meal progressed and the level in their bottles of wine went down she became more and more relaxed and comfortable with this pleasant, funny young man. He made her laugh, just as Wilfred had used to make her laugh, and he was as easy to be with as Wilfred, whom she had known all her life that she could remember; yet she had known Gilbert Stacey but a few weeks, and this was only their third meeting. It was a strange thing, that, she thought a little muzzily and smiled at him over the rim of her glass.

'And now, my dear Miss Lackland, you shall tell me what it is that you are to do tomorrow that filled you earlier with such trepidation when I suggested this supper!'

He was leaning back in his chair now, much more relaxed and far less full of his own doings than he had been at first and he smiled at her with genuine interest in his eyes. Emboldened by the comfortable way he behaved and her own good humour, and possibly by the wine a little, she launched into an account of her doings and plans while he listened with his face quite inscrutable.

'Well,' he said at length. 'So you are to be a Doctor Mandragora Nightshade, are you! No, do not look like that, my dear. I do but quote a joke drawing from *Punch*, you know! There have been several such published since there was so much in the news-sheets about the Edinburgh business. Some foolish female forced her way into the examinations, I believe, and bullied the wretched professors there to admit her to the faculty will-they, nill-they. Not the behaviour of a lady, I would have thought.'

A little chill had come upon her. 'So you are one of those who sneer at women who wish to better themselves?' she said, her chin up and staring at him challengingly.

He laughed then and was once again his comfortable self. 'Bless you, not at all! It is just that I am not used to the idea — and I cannot imagine that you, Miss Lackland, could ever be anything but a complete lady. So, if this is what you wish to do, then I bid you joy in it. My glass is raised to you, ma'am! To the future Doctor Lackland.' And she reddened as some heads were turned their way, and shook her head at him, but was well pleased enough.

He took her back in a cab to Villiers Street, and sent it away before handing her to her front door and opening it for her with her key, which he took from her hand.

'Miss Lackland, I trust we may now consider ourselves to be friends?'

'Indeed, yes, Mr Stacey,' she said with some fervour. 'I owe you much of gratitude for your help that dreadful evening, and now for such pleasures you have given me tonight. I trust indeed that we may be friends for many years.'

'It will not be easy, however,' he said gravely, and she looked at him uncertainly in the dimness of the street lamp that threw its poor beams across from the other side of the road.

'I am sorry to hear that,' she said. 'What is it that ——'

'Why, if you are to spend so many hours learning the skills of the doctor, you will have none for such poor wights as I, will you? And then you will be thrown so much with young would-be surgeons that you are sure to find your affections engaged many times over before the summer is upon us, and will quite forget your other friends.'

'Do you think me so inconstant, Mr Stacey?' she said quietly and at once he put his hand out to touch her again, a habit she was beginning to realize was very much a part of him.

'Oh, forgive me! I was jesting — but felt a little anxious, I cannot deny, for I cannot see how we are to prosecute our friendship when it is clear that time will be in great demand with you.'

'Of course it will, but I dare say we can make some arrangements,' she said, and frowned a little in the darkness. She had not meant to allot any time at all for pleasure, but his words had seemed to strike her with some pain, and now she found herself quite eagerly pushing against his view of her as a dedicated student. 'If you will call occasionally on a Sunday, perhaps we — I do not wish to make definite arrangements, you understand, but ——' she floundered and stopped; this wretched young man was upsetting her so much that here she was making actual assignations with him!

But her self-castigation came to an abrupt end with his response, for he was all smiles now.

'That will be delightful,' he bubbled. 'And be sure that I shall come on many, many Sundays. I am a wicked creature, am I not, Miss Lackland? I knew that if I asked you straight out when we might meet again you would swear you could not, for pressure of your studies, so I cannot deny I stage managed you into arranging it yourself! I am a sinner, am I not?' And he looked at her so roguishly that she could not help but laugh.

'There! All is well with us — I shall see you next Sunday, then, dear Miss Lackland ——' and he took both her hands and kissed them in that theatrical manner of his, '— and shall count the hours till then! A bientôt!'

And he was gone, leaving her to stand and watch his springing step take him back up the slope of Villiers Street past Charing Cross station to the Strand. He stopped at the top, and waved in the darkness before disappearing and she reddened with vexation. He could not have seen her standing there still watching him, but clearly he guessed she was, and to be so transparent irritated her a good deal, so she went into the house and slammed the door a little pettishly.

But all the same, she slept that night with a smile upon her face, and dreamed more of Mr Gilbert Stacey than of the onerous days at Nellie's which lay ahead of her.

CHAPTER SEVENTEEN

The first weeks of life at Nellie's went by in a blur of exhaustion and nervousness and downright physical pain for Sophie. The exhaustion set in early, by the end of the second day. She had not imagined it possible that any person could be so constantly, desperately, urgently busy. She went everywhere almost at a run, scurrying along the wards and the interminable corridors with her head thrust forwards as she tried to reach her destination without actually breaking into a trot — a piece of behaviour Matron Bishop would never tolerate from her nurses. She lifted patients in their beds, from chairs to commodes and back again, heavy ones, comatose ones, bony ones and awkward ones, and every time her own bones ached with sympathy as well as effort. She pushed heavy trolleys from place to place, poked about in great steaming coppers, made beds and unmade beds, and watched and listened and tried to absorb.

All of which was made much harder by the tension she felt in every part of her, for she was undoubtedly alarmed by all that was going on about her. She worried about whether the medical students would accept her. She worried about whether the other nurses would realize she was being treated differently from themselves. She worried about her ability to learn anything at all through the haze of weariness and anxiety that engulfed her.

And she hurt. Her feet ached dully. Her shoulders and arms ached heavily. Her back shrieked in protest at all the unaccustomed movements that were being forced on it. Her eyes felt sandy, her head buzzed and altogether she was stretched almost beyond endurance.

But not quite. By the end of the second week, when Saturday noon arrived and she was free to walk out into the early April sunshine of Endell Street, some of the edge had gone from the ache. She could lift her head and look about her and think of something more than just the way her own body felt, and she sniffed the smell of horses and rotting fruits from the market further over into Covent Garden, and a faint hint of drooping flowers from the Floral Hall further still, and felt that life could be after all more than just work.

She walked back to Villiers Street and enjoyed the rare luxury of a bath in the middle of the day, feeling no compunction in asking Eliza to carry cans of hot water to her attic, and afterwards, freshly gowned in lilac cotton, she came down to the dining room, which she used largely as her own sitting room since the residents tended to fill the drawing room with their chatter, to settle to the week's book-keeping, and then, with an energy that surprised her, opened the books that Freddy had given her in addition to those he had sent her when she was ill.

'You will have to work hard, my dear,' he had told her. 'For there is more to learn than just medical matters, you know. You must have an understanding of chemistry and mathematics too. It would be best if you could attend lectures for these subjects, like the other students, but this is not essential for I have here for you the notes the lecturer always uses. And since he is a prosy man who never departs by so much as a word from his notes, you will learn as much by private perusal. If you have problems with these subjects, tell me, and I will arrange what help I can for you.'

So, she spent her Saturday afternoon tranquilly sitting over her books, and agreeable she found the activity. For a start, to sit and not be rushing about was a pleasant change, and there was also a real pleasure in subjecting herself to discipline. She had taken deeply to heart Matron Bishop's words about the need for discipline, and had vowed to herself that not in any way would she ever allow anyone to suspect she had not in her the necessary will and power to succeed. That Saturday did much to help her feel she was at last on the road to such success.

The third and fourth weeks were a little easier, but not much. By now she was getting to know some of the people with whom she worked. The medical students, first, a loud and bawdy lot, in her opinion. They jostled each other a great deal, played stupid practical jokes upon each other, and generally behaved loutishly. However, they did not extend their ill manners to her, for which she was profoundly grateful. At first she had been in real fear that they would attempt to flirt with her, as she had seen some of them flirt with the ward maids, but one of the other lady nurses, a thin-faced thirty-year-old daughter of a Kentish vicar, observing her trepidation told her that 'they never speak a word out of place to the lady probationers, I promise you. Matron Bishop has warned them all that the least hint of insult paid to us will result in her refusal to have them in the wards at all — and of course she reigns supreme here ——'

It was in fact from the other nurses that her greatest problems came. The nursing staff was firmly divided into two; the ladies who paid for their training and were not expected to perform quite as many menial tasks as the others, who were known simply as 'the nurses' and who, in exchange for their teaching and the opportunity to obtain a certificate from Nellie's, worked longer and much more arduous hours than their more fortunate colleagues. The jealousy that simmered between these two groups was intense indeed. The lady nurses were constantly on the lookout for any infringement of their own rights, and the nurses were equally vigilant in case they should be put upon. Sophie soon learned that it was not politic, since she was wearing the distinctive blue print uniform of the ladies, to show undue friendliness towards the others, who wore a less elegant pink, and caps without any lace upon them.

She also discovered that she had been sadly misprepared for her encounters with the ladies. She shared her meals with them, and soon discovered that almost all of them lived in a house on the other side of Endell Street which had been obtained by Nellie's for their use alone. The only exceptions were the daughter of one of the hospital's administrators, who still lived in her father's house, and the daughter of the Vicar of the Church of St Martin-in-the-Fields nearby. They all evinced great curiosity about her own reason for not living in the special residence, for they soon discovered that she was not London born but from distant Yorkshire, and she could only mutter something about an aunt and being a distant connection of Mr Caspar.

Which made them even more curious, and the Kentish vicar's daughter, who had an eye and tongue as sharp and thin as her face even asked her outright if she had had to pay her premium like the rest of them. And they all sat and stared at her over their lunchtime bowls of soup and their pieces of bread while she tried to think of a safe answer. If they ever discovered that she was not in truth one of them, then indeed the fat would be in the fire, of that she was certain.

She looked back at them all and lifted her chin and essayed a light laugh. 'Now, why should you imagine that I should be treated any differently from anyone else? I cannot see the Bursar of Nellie's allowing any person to slip through his fingers when it comes to payment, can you?'

Which was safe enough, for she had already heard of the Bursar's cheeseparing mean-minded ways.

There was a little laugh at that, and the tension in the atmosphere lessened and she breathed again, and hoped God would forgive her for her mendacity; but her own curiosity was aroused and at the first opportunity she had spoken to Freddy about it.

'Mr Caspar,' she said, for she had herself decided that she must always address him formally within Nellie's wards, 'I would ask you — who is paying for me here?'

He flushed a dull brick colour which sorted rather ill with his sandy complexion and red hair, but it did not make him look at all disagreeable; indeed, she thought fleetingly, it makes him seem much younger than his years.

'Oh, that is of no matter ——' he said uncomfortably, looking over his shoulder at the students clustered round the foot of a bed. She and he were standing together beside a dressing trolley while she helped him prepare to perform an ascites tap on a man with a grossly enlarged belly due to liver disease.

'But it is, Mr Caspar,' she said softly. 'Indeed it is. I cannot be an object of charity to anyone ——'

'Say it comes from Maria Lackland's estate then. Are those trocars and cannulae quite sterilized? Have you rinsed off the spirit?'

'I have — you told me, Mr Caspar, that no moneys could be released from that estate for this purpose ——'

'We cannot discuss this now. Tonight, after my late ward round. Please to wait for me. I will talk of it then — now, will you ready the patient, please ——'

Obediently she turned to the man in the bed who was lying with his head thrown back on his pillows and his eyes half closed, only a rim of white showing beneath the lids. Gently, Sophie drew back the coverlet, and lifted his nightshirt to expose the great dome of the belly, so distended that the yellowish skin looked onion thin and glistening in the morning light.

Still the man did not stir, and Freddy set one hand on him to the right of the belly and said in a low but very clear voice, 'Now, gentlemen, we will to work. Here we have a case of severe hepatic enlargement. I consider it very likely that this patient has a tumour there of some dimensions, and there is little that can be done to lessen that — but we can alleviate the distress caused by the ascites — the excess fluid that has occurred within the peritoneum, which is, you will recall, the fine sac of membrane which encloses the abdominal contents ——'

'The old man's in his dotage,' one of the students behind Sophie muttered. 'He's told us all that before —' and Sophie wanted to smile, for it was clear to her that Freddy was repeating a lesson long since taught to his watchers for the sake of just one of them, herself. And she listened hard and tried to absorb all he was saying.

'— much of his distress comes from the pressure of this fluid upon vital organs, and the way it impedes easy movement of the diaphragm downwards, thus interfering with respiration. We will draw off the fluid with this apparatus and so lessen that pressure. Observe ——'

Sophie observed, and was grateful indeed that she had so much experience with Doctor Tom, for it was not an agreeable sight. Freddy opened his hands wide on the man's belly, splaying his fingers as much as he could, and then between the first and second fingers carefully thrust a long gleaming tube of metal tipped with a sharp point and crowned with a serrated knob.

The man winced, and cried aloud as the heavy needle went in, and Sophie put out a hand and rested it on his arm, murmuring softly, and the eyes opened for a moment and stared at her with a bewildered look and then closed again. Meanwhile, Freddy took the knob of the tube, now thrust right into the flesh up to its hilt, and with a slight and expert twist pulled it upwards and outwards. There was a sudden spurt of straw-coloured fluid, faintly blood-stained, and immediately Freddy held his hand out ready for Sophie to put into it a length of red rubber tubing, which he attached to the end of the now open tube as Sophie set the other into the cork of a large Winchester bottle, which she put upon the floor beside the man's bed.

171

'There, gentlemen, that is all there is to it. When passing such a cannula one must of course be always aware of the anatomy of the area. Vital organs, arteries and nerve trunks must be sedulously avoided — Mr Fletcher! Describe to me the blood supply to the right upper quadrant of the abdomen.'

Mr Fletcher, a sallow young man with protuberant eyes at once launched himself into a recital of the arteries; '— the abdominal aorta is at first related anteriorly to the coeliac trunk and its branches, the coeliac plexus of nerves and the omental bursa, which intervene between it and the papillary process of the liver and the lesser omentum. Immediately below the superior mesenteric artery leaves the aorta ——' and again Sophie wanted to smile, for Mr Fletcher was known as the star of the present group of students, being one of the few to work and study hard, and who consequently knew all the answers to everything. Clearly Freddy had called upon him in order to provide Sophie yet again with teaching. Dear, kind Freddy! And she began to think how agreeable it would be to meet him tonight anyway, and not simply in order to discover the answer to the question of who was paying for her.

'Now, nurse, we will ask you to observe this patient's progress closely, measuring the amount of fluid discharged, and telling us of any changes in his condition. What do you expect we will see?'

She reddened, feeling the eyes of the other men upon her and stammered, 'Er — why, sir, I imagine he will feel some relief as the distension goes down, will breathe more easily, and may lose some of the pallor he now displays, although I do not imagine the jaundiced tinge to his skin will change, since that is due, is it not, to his liver disease ——'

'You see, gentlemen?' Freddy said, looking at her with his brows raised. 'We have amongst us a lady as well able as any of you to observe and learn from the states of the patient we treat. Look to it, gentlemen, that you keep to your books that you may not be outstripped by a mere nurse!' And with a ghost of a wink at her he turned and went, his students trailing after him, for it was now the luncheon hour, and Sophie, now blushing hotly, was freed from her duties with them until two o'clock.

She did all she could in the time available to her, eating her own luncheon at great speed, and then hurrying back to the man with the tube in his belly. She was gratified to find that indeed he was much improved, some two pints of the straw-coloured fluid now having drained into the bottle, and she was able to hand over his care to one of the pink uniformed nurses with a clear conscience and remove herself to supervise the afternoon's rounds in the children's ward.

This was one round she already was finding particularly distressing. The children who were admitted to the wards at Nellie's were like creatures from another world when compared to the children she had known at home in Haworth. There, even the poorest had some sign of health about them, gained from the long hours they spent upon the moors; and also they were particularly hardy, for, as was often said in Haworth, 'any bairn that can survive a Haworth winter 'as a right tight 'old on livin' '.

But these London children were different. Wizened and old before their time, they sat in silence in the cots provided for them, or lay staring at the ceiling with an apathy that in a child was particularly painful to observe. Many had the protuberant ribs and rounded bellies that spoke of chronic undernourishment; many were clearly tubercular, with feverish bright eyes and hollow cheeks on which high spots of colour burned, coughing and spitting their young lives away with patient misery.

And then there were the babies, often pathetic scraps of humanity who had been found on neighbouring doorsteps wearing little more than rags, half starved and filthy. The mothers of Covent Garden and Seven Dials were clearly driven to greater despair than even those hunger-haunted ones from Town End Bottom.

But the children had to be looked after, painful though it was to see them staring at their helpers with their watchful dull eyes, and at two o'clock sharp she was ready standing by the door to greet Mr Caspar and his students.

This afternoon they were to lance a huge cold abscess on the hip of a girl who had been brought to the hospital the day before by her father. The child was barely five, but preternaturally aware, for she was the man's only surviving child. There had been, Sophie had discovered, six other children all of whom had died young, the youngest of all surviving his mother just half an hour, for his birth had killed her. So the little girl spent all her time in her father's carpentry workshop and watched and listened and became old well before her time.

173

That she was frightened of her father had been clear when she had come in. His protectiveness for the last surviving fruit of his loins took the form of a gruff and sharp criticism of the child at all times. No matter what she did, while they sat there waiting to be seen by Mr Caspar the day before, he had snapped at her, and slapped at her and altogether behaved in such a way that her cowed and watchful look was fully understandable, and Sophie had ached to reach out and take the small creature in her arms and comfort her.

Now, standing waiting for Freddy and his students, she watched the child covertly, as she sat in the usual stolid uninterested way staring dully at the bars of the cot and, obeying some deep-down impulse, Sophie went to her, and leaned over the cot and held out her arms.

The child looked at her, her eyes opaque at first and then with a slowly dawning suspicion, but Sophie stood firm, a slight smile on her face, her arms still outstretched, and saying nothing. And gradually the watchful gaze eased, became warmer, and the child blinked and moved one hand slightly towards her; and taking her cue Sophie leaned further and put her hands round the child's body and picked her up.

For a moment the little girl strained away from her, rigid with fear, but Sophie just stood quietly and again her stillness soothed the frightened child and she relaxed into Sophie's hold, and they stood there, the nurse and the child, quiet and peaceful in the middle of the ward.

She was dreadfully light, as light as a bag of dead bones, and Sophie could feel the small ribcage moving against her own upper arm with almost painful clarity and she set her cheek against the child's and crooned softly for a moment, and the thin body did not pull away.

'What is your name?' Sophie said after a moment, whispering into the ear so near to her lips. 'What do they call you?'

There was no response at first and Sophie repeated her question gently and then the child said in a breathy little whisper, 'Emmy. Emmy ——'

'Hello, Emmy,' Sophie said. 'I'm a nurse. Who am I?'

'Nurse,' came the whisper.

'Nurse likes Emmy,' Sophie said after a moment and laughed softly. 'Nurse likes Emmy.'

Again the delay and then the little girl moved in her arms and said rather more loudly, 'Emmy likes Nurse ——' and pulled her head back so that she could look at Sophie. And suddenly she smiled, a little stretching of her lips that revealed sadly rotted and broken baby teeth, but a smile nonetheless. 'Emmy likes Nurse,' the child repeated.

And then suddenly, all was a rough bustle and noise as the ward was filled with medical students who came thumping and shouting through the great double doors, for they were not yet accompanied by their mentor, and the child stiffened in her arms and cowered away from them.

Sophie glared over her shoulder. 'Be quiet!' she said sharply, almost without thinking, and several of the students turned and stared at her.

'What did you say?' one of them said, almost in surprise. 'Did you tell us to be quiet? And who do you think you ——'

'She is right,' Mr Fletcher, his usually sallow face a little flushed, pushed forward through the hubbub. 'Listen to those wretched children, will you — they were quiet enough when we first came in here ——' and indeed several of the children were crying in alarm at all the noise, their thin voices only just audible above the rough male voices of the students.

'That's as may be, pigface!' said one of the noisiest, rudely. 'But no damned nurse is going to tell *me* ——'

'I'd beware if I were you, Tanner,' one of the others drawled. 'She's one of the Bish's special ones — a blue nurse, not a pink! And Caspar has his beady eye upon her too, don't forget. I'd not say aught out of place unless you want trouble ——'

By now Emmy was stiff with terror in Sophie's arms, her body held so tightly that she shook and Sophie felt rage rising in her too. This child had an ordeal ahead of her for which she had tried her best to prepare her with soft words and gentleness, and now these wretched hulks of unfeeling brutes had made it worse for her. Hot words rose to her lips and she was about to burst into speech, when Freddy arrived, and almost magically the men fell silent.

He stood and looked about him for a moment, his sandy eyebrows raised and then nodded his head sharply and said, 'Well, let us about it. Are you ready, nurse, for this small operation?'

'Yes, Mr Caspar,' Sophie said and giving Emmy one more gentle hug set her back in the cot, and the child at once pulled her stick-like legs under her and crawled as far into the corner as she could, staring with real terror in her eyes at the cluster of big male faces looking over the edge of her cot.

'The child seems very alarmed, nurse,' Freddy said sharply. 'What ails her?'

Sophie looked up from the trolley which she had brought close to the cot side and caught the eye of Tanner, glaring at her. It would have been all too easy to tell Freddy that the students, especially Tanner, had been the cause of Emmy's anxiety, and for a long moment she stared at the big young man, her head up, and knew that he knew exactly what she was thinking. But she took a breath and said quietly, 'I do not know, sir. Perhaps it is that she is not used to seeing so many people at a time.'

'Well, we had best be about it ——' Freddy said gruffly and moving gently leaned over the cot and picked up Emmy, who broke into a thin wail of fear.

'Nurse!' she cried after a moment. 'Nurse — nurse ——' and leaned away from Freddy and held out her thin arms to Sophie who could not help herself; she took the child from Freddy and cradled her and whispered to her until the weeping stopped.

There was a short silence and then Freddy said equably, 'Well, gentlemen, the message is sent, and as far as I am concerned, received. This will be a painful experience for this little girl, and she will suffer less from it at the hands of a person she trusts. Our nurse shall open this abscess under my instructions, and all of you shall learn from her the need to treat a patient, especially a child, with kindness and peacefulness and sympathy. I shall hand the instruments myself, nurse. Sit you down here ——'

Almost in a dream, Sophie obeyed. That Freddy had intended to do all he could for her now that he had finally decided to help her in her studies had been clear enough, but she had not expected that he would be quite so eager as he was now showing himself to be. To open an abscess with so many would-be surgeons looking on? Could this be wise?

She threw an agonized questioning glance at Freddy but he smiled reassuringly and shook his head gently. 'You will manage well enough,' he said quietly, 'and my students will learn much. To work! And do exactly as I say.'

And she did. Whispering and crooning to Emmy all the time, so that the child obeyed her requests to lie down on her lap and allow her hip to be exposed, she swabbed the pale skin with a piece of charpie soaked in dilute carbolic acid. Then, as Freddy gently leaned over the child with his cotton pad and bottle of chloroform in his hand, she persuaded the wide-eyed Emmy to breathe deep of the nice smell. And Emmy did, and the small eyes blanked and the lids rolled back, and she began to breathe stertorously.

'Good,' Freddy said sharply. 'No time to waste! This child is too weak to accept much chloroform. Set the lancet at an angle so — aye, that is it. Now move it downwards and forwards — well done, precise and neat as any cut I ever made — now, the probe — aye, the probe, woman — that's it — insert it deep and follow with the sinus forceps and open out your wound. Ah! There's the pus — and enough of it in all conscience to make a woman ten times her age as sick as a dog — swab away, swab away — well done! And now the drain. Insert it deep as you can and splay the ends well, for we do not want the sinus closing on us. And now the dressing — so! And the bandage — a many-tailed will be best — and now I cease the chloroform and trust the child will not take ill from it ——'

It was over. Sophie sat there with Emmy on her lap, breathing more naturally now and with her eyes closed properly, and with the bowl of evil-looking pus beside her. Had she really opened so grievous an abscess? Had she actually sat at a child's bedside in a London hospital, observed by medical students, and performed such a task? It was not believable, and she lifted her eyes and looked about her. And saw again the glare of Tanner and some of his friends, and was suddenly jolted back to reality. They were angry, deeply so, and she feared would show their resentment in many ways in the future. Freddy had meant well to give her this excellent experience, but had he stopped to think, she told herself as she settled the little girl back in her cot, perhaps he would have been more careful. I think I really should speak of it to him tonight.

CHAPTER EIGHTEEN

'Oh, come!' Freddy said easily. 'I cannot believe that those thick-skulled creatures are aware of anything of the sort!'

'They cannot be so thick-skulled, Cousin Freddy, if they are your students. I grant you that they are rough and noisy but I for one do not belittle their understanding of the way things are about them. And I am sure that they observed your partiality this afternoon and were angered by it. I could not bear it, truly, if you were to be discommoded or embarrassed in any way by what you are doing for me — and also,' she smiled then and looked up at him with great candour, 'I lack the bravery of Miss Jex-Blake. She and her friends, I know, stormed a veritable phalanx of jeering ill-mannered medical students to enter the examination halls in Edinburgh, but I — for all my determination, I think I should quail if faced by any such thing. Truly, Cousin, you are treating me most kindly, and I dearly appreciate it. In only a month or two I have learned much and feel sometimes that I am absorbing information as a sponge does water. I do not need more opportunity than I already have to learn from you. Let me be just by you and hear you and that is enough ——'

She put one hand on his sleeve a little timidly and he looked up from his coffee cup and smiled at her. They were sitting in the hubbub of Gatti's restaurant, and enjoying some of the excellent cakes Signor Gatti provided for his before-theatre customers, and in the easy relaxed atmosphere much of the tension that had been in Freddy Caspar when they had arrived there was melting away.

'Well, if you say so, my dear Sophie. Perhaps I have been a little over eager, but I tell you truly, my dear, as a teacher it is so gratifying to have listening to one a student who shows so clearly that she is interested! In the present collection there is really only Fletcher who is any pleasure to teach, and I have, I dare say, in-dulged myself in treating you so particularly. I will watch and observe myself much more carefully in the future. A pity though —

you handled that lancing this afternoon with such skill it was a joy to watch. Oh, yes, I know you did do similar work with your old friend the doctor at your home — but all the same, it was a pleasant thing to watch. D'you know, my dear, I find myself wondering if we have got it all wrong, we men. I saw your hands at work, and thought — fingers so slender and so adept with needles and thread and scissors, as are those of girls who have been reared as ladies should be, are clearly much better suited to the art of surgery than our great paws ——' And he spread his hands wide on the marble table and looked at them.

So did Sophie and she had to smile, for they were indeed large square hands with spatulate fingers, and a strong growth of reddish hair on the backs and down the fingers.

'Well, I have observed your own hands at work, and marvelled at their delicacy,' she said and without thinking put out her own hand and set it over one of his, and as though he had been stung he pulled it away and, red-faced, thrust them both into his pockets.

Sophie too was suddenly embarrassed, for she had expected no such reaction to what had been to her but the touch of a friend, and she remembered then all too vividly what she had forgotten since starting at Nellie's — Martha's warning that Freddy had developed a tendresse for her.

'I — we really must speak, Cousin, of the matter that I mentioned earlier today,' she said hastily, and drank some of her coffee. 'I did not know, ignorant fool that I am, that the lady nurses at Nellie's paid for their training. I was quizzed, you see, by some of them, and that was what told me. Clearly someone at Nellie's is paying for me, and I find this most distressing. You cannot tell me it is the estate of Grandmamma Maria Lackland, for you were so adamant that that could not be done when first we met. And I cannot believe that you were being less than veracious with me then.'

'No. You are right. It is not the estate. It is not possible for that money to be touched by you — or by the London Ladies at present. I have notified the lawyers that you are attempting to obtain the qualifications that would make you eligible for the legacy — much to Mr Vivian's disgust I may tell you! — and Mr Onions, who has I think a fancy for the idea of a lady surgeon, has arranged that the matter be left in abeyance. I do not understand all the legal quibbles and quiddities involved, but I can tell you that the money lies waiting safely for you against the day when — and if — you are able to claim it ——'

'Cousin, you are prevaricating!' Sophie said firmly and smiled at him. 'Or at least procrastinating. I care not a whit for that legacy at present, and well you know it. I sought it when I did only as a means to an end. The day may come when I will gladly claim it, for I am not such a numbskull that I would scorn a fortune if it were properly available to me, but that is not the point at question just now, is it? I wish to know — indeed I demand to know! — who pays for me at Nellie's. For someone clearly is.'

'Oh, does it matter so much?' Freddy said almost pettishly. 'I begin to fear you are a very modern miss indeed and as obsessed with money as any of the flibberty girls that ——'

'Now, that is not fair,' Sophie said firmly and Freddy, a little shamefaced, grinned.

'Well, maybe not ——' he said and then stopped.

'Well?' Sophie said, inexorable in her determination and Freddy took his hands from his pockets and banged them on the table.

'Well, I am, damn it! And there — you made me swear, and I have never yet sworn in any lady's hearing! Perhaps having you learn my skill *is* defeminizing you as the opponents of medicine for women aver it must ——'

Sophie ignored that red herring. 'That is very kind in you, Cousin, but I am not sure that ——'

'Now, do not tell me you cannot accept it, for I will have no such nonsense thrown at me! If I cannot help a relation in whom I feel a natural family interest it is a poor thing indeed. You may regard it as a loan, if that will make you feel better, and repay me as and when you claim your legacy — for I am sure you will, one way or another ——'

There was a short silence and then, soberly, Sophie nodded. 'Well, there is nothing else I can do, is there?' she said. 'For to refuse now with the pride I would wish to display would be absurd, since I cannot exist and pay my way at Nellie's, and it would be poor thanks to all who have shown an interest to me to flounce off in an arrogant way now. And anyway, I know no other source of any pecuniary help. I can but thank you and say with all the fervour I have in me that I will repay every penny when I can, and as soon as I can ——'

'Thank heaven for common sense!' Freddy said with intense relief in his voice. 'If you did but know how anxious I have been on this score, knowing full well that one day you must surely discover that you are being paid for, you would pity me!' And he grinned widely and cheerfully at her and she smiled equally widely back and for a moment they sat there wrapped in a mutual regard that was warming and delightful.

'Well, well! I have sought you everywhere, and find you only when I have given up hope, and come to solace myself with cakes and ale! There must indeed be a moral in that!'

Her head whipped round and she looked up, blinking a little in the bright lights of the noisy restaurant and then her face broke into a wide smile and she jumped to her feet.

'Why, Mr Stacey! How surprising to find you here! I had not thought to — oh, I forget myself entirely! My cousin, Mr Frederick Caspar. Freddy, this is Mr Stacey, a — friend ——' and she sat down again, as Stacey pulled a chair from a neighbouring table, suddenly embarrassed and not knowing quite why. Was it because Gilbert Stacey was looking particularly outré tonight, wearing a wide-brimmed soft black hat and a cape of large proportions about his shoulders? Or was it because of the watchful expression that had appeared on Freddy's face when the introduction was effected? She did not know, and in her unsureness began to chatter rather absurdly.

Both men listened for a while and then Stacey said easily, 'Well, I feared, you know, that your work at the hospital would quite exhaust you, and wear you away to a mere streak, but I collect that I am very wrong. I have heard of no message sent by you this past four weeks and this too convinced me that you must be ill with over-work, for I had said — had I not? — that I would call upon you on Sundays, and did not. But you made no effort to enquire after me, although I had thought you might have guessed that the reason for my silence was indisposition — for what else could keep me from my promise?'

She was scarlet now with mortification and very aware of Freddy's eyes upon her.

'Oh, dear, I am so — I had no idea — I am sorry ——' she stammered and then subsided. What could she say? She had indeed thought many times in that first week of the agreeable Mr

Stacey, had in all truth looked forward to his promised visit on Sunday, and when he had not appeared had been quite cast down. But, with her usual common sense — and to be truthful also the exhaustion and absorption that Nellie's had brought her — she had buried those thoughts deeply indeed.

Until now. There he sat looking at her quizzically from under that mop of curly hair, his eyes as delightfully wrinkled at the corners as ever, and she was glad to be sitting down, for there was little doubt in her mind that her legs would melt beneath her if she stood up. An absurd situation to be in for such a one as Sophie Lackland.

He laughed then, and turned to Freddy. 'Oh, it is wicked, is it not, Mr Caspar, to so embarrass a lady?' He turned back to Sophie. 'Indeed, I have not been ill, and I am a wicked rogue for saying I was — I wanted but to make you suffer as I did!'

'You, suffer?' she said, looking up at him with some acerbity. 'You tell me lies, and then tell me you suffer? Indeed, Mr Stacey, you show too much easiness altogether! If that is the right way to behave in theatrical circles, why, I am glad that I do not spend much time in them ——'

'Oh, it is not a theatrical way at all,' Freddy said, with an edge to his voice, 'for both my wife and brother-in-law have been involved in theatres most of their lives — well, not my wife now, of course, but my brother-in-law certainly — and they are both as honest and sincere as any man would wish.'

'Of course they are!' Stacey said heartily. 'As well Miss Lackland knows. Your brother-in-law, Mr Caspar? Oh — of course — would that be Mr Oliver Lackland of the supper rooms in King Street? He is a man well thought of in the profession for his integrity. I much admire his productions, also. I should have connected the name long since, for I knew that Miss Lackland was your cousin.'

'How did you know that?' Sophie was momentarily diverted and Stacey laughed.

'Oh, I made it my business to know. Indeed, Miss Lackland, I may tell you that I have been quite obsessed with thoughts of you these past weeks, although you did not show the same courtesy to me!' He looked at Freddy and grinned again. 'I declare, Mr Caspar, I sit here making love to your charming cousin before your very nose! Is that not the action of a mountebank? I am sure you will agree that it will seem so! But it is not. It is in truth the behaviour of a would-be friend, for I am quite determined that Miss Lackland will, with her family's approval, of course, regard me as one of the people upon whom she can rely in any troubles that beset her —'

'Really, Mr Stacey, you are quite absurd,' Sophie said lightly and essayed a laugh, though it was, truth to tell, a rather shaky one. 'You will put me quite in dislike of you with all this nonsense.'

'Then I will forthwith be serious, and tell you that I have had to remain away from you, despite my promises to call, for a very good if tiresome reason. My employer, the occasionally difficult Mr Hollingshead — they call him Practical John, you know — sent me hot foot to France the very day after we last met to escort back here his newest star. The show you saw, you must understand, was the last of that production, and it was all arranged that we should go at once into rehearsal of a new and most charming burlesque with which to attract the early summer visitors, for May is hard upon us, and in that merry month there is a good deal of excellent business to be done. But woe was he — the French singer he had engaged had not arrived, and there was none, he swore on his hat, but I whom he could trust to fetch her. So, for the past weeks I have been making my way to and from Rouen on Hollingshead's business, for it was there that this veritable nightingale was said to be domiciled. I could send no letters, for believe it or not there was no time, as I rushed from train to ship and again to train and onwards yet, to do more than snatch the merest mouthful of food and drink! And then I had to return empty-handed for the wretched creature had chosen to go instead to America, I was told, and had sailed for New York from Boulogne the very day before my arrival. I tell you fairly, I am positively worn out by it all!'

'I think I can see that you are,' Sophie said after a moment, looking at him, and indeed he was pale and behind his bantering tones his voice seemed strained and his eyes were shadowed beneath the long lashes by violet smudges.

'I am forgiven, then, for telling such a taradiddle? I did but mean to jest — was I so wicked, Mr Caspar?' and he turned to Freddy then and smiled at him.

Freddy got to his feet. 'Not at all,' he said a little stiffly. 'I am sure that such badinage as yours is well understood by Miss Lackland. You young people are much given to it these days, they tell me. Well, I must be on my way, Cousin. I trust those matters we had under discussion are now settled to your satisfaction?'

Sophie smiled at him, putting all she could of her warm feelings of gratitude to him into her expression. 'Oh, yes, Cousin Freddy, indeed they are. And I will go on learning all that I can, in any way that I can, and trust you — well, we need say no more about the students, I think.'

She suddenly felt a pang of pity for him, for he was standing with his hat in his hand, and his face quite unshaded in the bright lights Gatti burned overhead, and she could see lines in his face and a weariness she had not noticed before. Cousin Freddy was not precisely old, she thought, but he is not really very young either ——

'No, indeed,' he said then, and turned to Stacey and gave him a slight bow. 'I trust you to escort my cousin to her door, sir. I know it is near enough, but it is a dark night and I would be perturbed to allow her to be alone in the streets at such an hour ——'

Stacey was on his feet at once. 'Of course, sir,' he said with a deferential bob of his head. 'You may rest assured that I will see to it that no harm comes to Miss Lackland. I am glad indeed to have met you, sir, for I am earnest in my profession of friendship, and will be happier to know that this is understood and accepted by Miss Lackland's family. Usually, of course, one would visit a young lady under the eye of her Papa or Mamma, but in this situation — well, I can only repeat I am glad to have met you, sir, and can now, I trust, enjoy your approval of my calls upon your cousin.'

Freddy blinked, and stared back at him rather bleakly. 'My dear Mr Stacey, Miss Lackland is her own mistress in every way, and more suited than many, despite her tender years, to take excellent care of herself. I do not stand in any way in loco parentis, you know.'

'Of course, sir, I agree — Miss Lackland is a most cool-headed lady. But as I say, a gentleman must always wish to behave — gentlemanly, must he not? And for me that means to be before the world with all, especially the families of any lady friends I may have.' He bowed again, and Freddy nodded rather frostily and went away, walking quickly between the little tables, and Sophie watched him go and again felt that small pang.

'You should not have spoken so to him!' she said sharply when

184

Stacey sat down again. 'He is right. I need no person's permission to choose my friends, nor do I ——'

'Well, forgive me again! I am afraid that I keep putting my feet in wrong places in all I say — but if you can enter into my feelings of fatigue and anxiety you will understand.' He put his hand on hers on the table. 'I was anxious, you know, and most put out at not being able to make contact with you, and as soon as I had spoken to Mr Hollingshead at the theatre I came at once to seek you, and was so cast down to find you from home I came here intending to while away the hours until you returned, whatever time that was, having quite set my mind to it that I would see you tonight — and to find you here — well, it set my wits awry! Forgive me? Please?'

And she laughed and nodded and gently extricated her hand and laughed again. She had to admit that she had missed him more than a little, and been annoyed at the silence that had stretched so long, and was glad to see him now and he seemed aware of her feelings and said no more, waving to the waiter to bring them more coffee and cake. And Pietro Pagani — for it was he — came running with plates on which he had set much larger slices than usual of the delectable cheese cake for which the restaurant was justifiably famous, and cups brimming with fragrant dark coffee. And he winked at Sophie with his usual impudence and murmured, 'Bellissima!' as he bore away Freddy's empty cup.

They sat for a long time talking, and she regaled him with tales of life at Nellie's and he riposted with absurd stories of his adventures in France, only half of which she believed — and he intended her to believe no more than that — and the evening wore on and the restaurant emptied and three times Pietro refilled their cups, until at last, Sophie yawned hugely and looked at the big clock high on the wall and exclaimed in dismay.

'Oh, no! It is near midnight! Have we sat and talked this long? It cannot be!'

'Indeed it can,' Stacey said softly. 'It is always so when one is with a person for whom one has regard. I have much regard for you, Miss Lackland. Have you some for me?'

'Oh, such a nonsense,' she said uncertainly. 'Of course you are my friend — I told you that ——'

'Ah, but there are friends and friends, are there not?' Stacey

185

said, and again took her hand in his. 'Are we friends enough for you to call me Gil? My many friends at the theatre do, and it would give me much pleasure to hear my name on your lips.'

'But we hardly know each other, Mr Stacey!' Sophie said, and then in spite of herself laughed and he did too.

'Precisely! We are not as other people, are we, Sophie? For so I insist I shall call you. My dear — friend — Sophie.' And he bent and kissed her wrist, turning her hand in his in a way that once again made her legs feel remarkably unstable. 'If we were as other people we would be most formal — but you and I — we are moderns! We are the new man and the new woman. You with your plans for the future, and I with my eyes on great success in the theatre. What do we want with silly rules about the way young ladies may address their friends, and be addressed by them?'

She looked at him for a moment and then nodded. It was true; she *was* a new woman, one of those late-century people for whom the bright new world ahead sparkled like a great jewel. Was she not going to be a surgeon, one of the first of her sex to embrace such work? Had she not this very afternoon opened an abscess under the eye of a crowd of loutish medical students, and done it better than any of them could?

Half drunk with fatigue and excitement and excess of coffee she laughed aloud and recklessly held out both her hands to him.

'You are right,' she said. 'We are different, are we not? So — you shall call me Sophie, Gil — and we shall be comfortable together ——'

'Oh yes, we shall,' he said fervently, and throwing some coins on the table for Pietro Pagani jumped to his feet, and held her chair so that she too could stand up, and crooked his arm to lead her out of the door and across the street to her own front door on the other side. And they laughed at each other the whole way, revelling in the pleasure of each other's company, and Sophie thought confusedly, 'Oh, it is so good to be here, and to be young and to be working at Nellie's and I hope Freddy is all right ——' and then yawned and laughed again. She was a very tired girl when at last she went to bed that night.

CHAPTER NINETEEN

Her good humour and high excitement buoyed her up for the next few weeks as April turned to May and June came laggardly warm — for it had been a sadly cold spring — into the sour London streets. She spent her days in a haze of work and busy-ness, enjoying herself more and more as she became ever more proficient, running the ward rounds with great efficiency and acting as instrument bearer in the operating theatres and outpatient clinics, and learning, learning, learning all the time.

That she had few friends among the other nurses worried her not a whit, and she put their cool attitude towards her down to the fact that they all lived together in the Nurses' House across the road while she lived in Villiers Street, and also that they worked different hours, for she was the only one who spent all her time in one occupation — accompanying the medical students on all their activities — while they worked sometimes at nights, and also moved about the hospital from one ward to another.

After all, why should she feel lonely? Had she not the girls at the hostel all too eager to chat to her when she came back at night, worn out if happy? It was indeed a small problem in her life that she had to hold them at arms' length, in order to have any time to perform her tasks about the hostel, and also to do her necessary studying. And then, of course, there were her monthly visits from Martha, and what had become weekly ones from Gil.

Gil. She enjoyed those Sunday afternoons she spent with him from three until six — which was all the time she would allow herself to take from the week's duties — more than she could say. Sometimes when the weather permitted they walked the broad cinder paths of Hyde Park, and listened to the music of the German bands that filled the post-prandial air with their silly bouncy trumpery tunes, while children ran between their feet with hoops and balls and tops; sometimes when rain came sluicing down the windows and filled the gutters with splashing miniature torrents and the horses went steaming along the streets they sat in cheerful Gatti's with its delicious smells of cakes and ices and hot coffee, and ate sweet things until she could eat no more and could not face her supper; sometimes they strolled along the Strand and gazed into the elegant shop windows at the beautiful jewels and laces and silks and furnishings garnered from half the world to tempt the pockets of the rich of London, pretending to be one of those rich and choosing their spoils.

He talked a great deal more than she did on these afternoons; about his dreams and plans for the future; about the plays and burlesques he wanted to write, but somehow never found time for; about the petty feuds and jealousies at the theatre and how so many of the people there seemed bent on tormenting him because they resented his greater talents. And then she would laugh and gently tease him, and he would sulk a little, his mouth making a mulish small-boy grimace that made her laugh even more, and he would sulk even more and she would have to tease him back to a good humour.

It was all delightful and funny and if sometimes she felt a little irritated that he was not as interested in her doings as his own, she put that down to the fact that few people found illness and surgery as fascinating as she did.

So it was not perhaps surprising, with all this to fill her thoughts and hours as the happy weeks went by, and June gave way to July and August, that she did not notice the storm brewing around her. Freddy was more careful now, she felt, to treat her like all the others, but still could not help sometimes betraying his interest, for he would occasionally ask her to give her opinion on a diagnosis or apply a dressing while the students watched, but she felt that this was rare enough not to matter. And anyway, she had become used to it.

So when she saw some of the students, always with the large Tanner among them, gossiping with their heads together, break off their talk when she drew near, she thought no more of it than that they were engaged on bawdy joking and were ashamed enough to stop in a lady's hearing. Even when she found that some of the nurses did the same, and almost insultingly turned their shoulders upon her when she attempted to join in their conversations, she shrugged it away. People who lived in an enclosed society like

Nellie's were very prone to such behaviour towards those they regarded as outsiders; she had learned that early. And living outside the hospital as she did, she was very much an outsider, and cared not a whit for that. Her future lay shining and exciting in the dark mystery of the years ahead, and nothing so trivial as this behaviour could now damage it.

So, when she set out to leave the hospital one late August evening she was not prepared for any unusual experiences. It was in fact far past her usual time for going home to Villiers Street, for Freddy had asked her to remain with a woman patient who had undergone an operation to remove a cyst from her uterus and who needed very intimate care for the first few hours afterwards.

'And,' he had said to her, his students standing clustered about him there in the operating theatre, 'she will take it more kindly from one of her own sex than from one of these gentlemen here. And I will not ask one of the other nurses to do this, for you saw the operation, and have an understanding of what was done and why, which must inform your care and greater skill. I trust you will not mind being so late tonight? You may leave at ten o'clock, for by then all should be well and the woman can settle to sleep with no further disturbance till morning.'

'Of course, Mr Caspar,' she had said, and caught a glance being exchanged between Tanner and his particular crony, another large young man named Massey, and thought fleetingly, 'I must warn Freddy again — he is showing his partiality ——' but no more than that.

Now, standing on the steps of the hospital, drawing her gloves on — for late summer though it was, the evening was cold — and looking up at the last shreds of daylight disappearing from the sky above the chimney tops, she yawned for she was very tired. But it had been well worthwhile, for the patient had recovered from the chloroform with little trouble, and had ceased her bleeding fairly early. Sophie had changed the pad she had to wear and swabbed her groins with warm soapy water at ten o'clock and found the blood loss was minimal, and it was safe now to let the poor creature sleep the night hours undisturbed. So Sophie had the agreeable feeling that fills one after a task is well done, and moved down the steps towards the street happily enough.

There was a faint movement in the shadows below and a voice

189

said softly, 'Miss Lackland!' and she stopped and peered, and said sharply, 'Who is that?'

'Why, no one to be alarmed about, Miss Lackland,' the voice said softly and now the shadows shifted and re-formed and there were darker shapes to be seen clustered at the foot of the steps. 'Only your fellow students, my dear young — *lady*.'

Her senses now seemed sharpened to a glittering point, and she stared at the darkness and slowly made out the shapes she saw.

'Mr Tanner,' she said uncertainly. 'Mr Massey — and Mr Baker, too, is it not? What do you mean, fellow students? I am a nurse, sir, as well you know!'

'Oh, no, you are not, Miss Lackland! You are not a nurse for all you hide behind the security of a blue uniform and ape the lady. You are no more than a trollop, Miss Lackland!' And the voice was as soft and superficially polite as ever.

She drew her breath in sharply, as though a bucket of water had been poured over her head. 'How — you shall not — how *dare* you ——'

'How dare I?' Tanner moved closer and now she could see the gleam of his eyes in the darkness and a hand shot out and seized her wrist in a vice-like grip. 'I dare anything when I speak the truth! And we have been watching, and observing and listening and learning, Miss Lackland, just as you have done. Oh, your loving cousin may dress you up in a lady nurse's rig and try to fool us, but we are not so green as we're cabbage looking. We know what you are about. We have listened and understood. You are treated as a medical student is, and no doubt plan to walk the wards here until you have learned enough and then inveigle yourself into an examination — got up in trousers, no doubt! — to steal our livelihoods from under our very noses like that other female abomination you no doubt admire. No decent *lady* would behave so, so do not expect us to treat you as one. You are no lady — you are a *trollop*.'

She took a deep breath, trying hard to think clearly. To scream? But what good would that do? The night porter at the hospital spent the long hours of darkness barricaded inside his lodge within the great doors and knew better than to venture out on to the streets of Covent Garden, where screams and fighting and arguments between brothel inmates and their customers were so

190

commonplace. And who else was there to hear?

To run? Nonsense — for she could never outrun these great creatures, long-legged though she was. And anyway, she knew herself to be filled with a fatigue that would soon wear down her speed.

There was only one answer for it, and she took it. She lifted her chin with what show of bravery she could muster and said quietly, 'Well, gentlemen, your opinion matters little to me. You have named me trollop, as though an interest in sickness and the care of it labels a woman as some sort of dishonourable creature when it does not so affect men. But I do not feel it to be so, so your ill-naming hurts me not a whit. If it gives you pleasure so to address me, so be it. I am a trollop. May I now return to my home, if you please?'

'Oh, dear me no! You must continue as you started, Miss Lackland. You would be a student of our craft and our art and our skill? So be it — you shall study *all* of it — we have determined on it — come along, Miss Lackland. There are splendours awaiting you that you will never forget!'

And the grip on her wrist tightened and another hand came out of the shadows to grasp her other hand and then she was being hurried along the street, in the middle of a crowd of panting, sweating men.

That they were afraid was clear; she could smell the fear in the acrid sweat that came from them, the same smell that patients threw out when awaiting painful treatment. But there was another smell about them, one that made her own face and body trickle with moisture, an animal musky odour. And suddenly, she was deeply, sickly terrified. They had called her trollop, and now they exuded this curious farmyard odour — were they going to ravish her? Was their anger enough to allow them to treat her as though she really were one of the raggle-taggle creatures of these Covent Garden gutters?

She opened her mouth to scream, for there was nothing else she could do, but Tanner seemed to be preternaturally aware of her very thoughts, and his hand let go of her wrist and seized the back of her neck and he hissed, 'One sound from you, and you will never have voice to speak again!' and she could not utter as much as a squeak.

191

Then, suddenly, the group veered and turned left and pushed her against the railings that ran alongside the hospital building. Someone said huskily, 'We are here — quick — the gate is open — hurry, for God's sake ——' and then her feet were slipping on iron steps and she was going downwards and now she knew just where she was as a door opened in front of her and a dim light could just be seen and she was bundled through the doorway into the corridor beyond.

The anatomy room. There, far below the wards, was the dark basement where the bodies of the paupers who died in Nellie's were taken, ready for the students' dissecting scalpels. Freddy had told her of the place, though of course she had never seen it, for no living woman ever set foot below there.

It smelled. She stood there, shaking, in the corridor as the cluster of men around her moved away and someone locked the door behind her with a sharp click of the tumblers. It was an odd smell, a mixture of the sweetish odour of physical corruption and another thick choking odour she could not identify, and in spite of her attempts at tight self-control she retched.

Tanner laughed. 'Sickens you, does it? Oh, you will be sicker yet, my dear young *lady*, my would-be medical student! It is sad to me that the odour that we greet you with here isn't worse, but this is a modern hospital and we have formaldehyde to disinfect our cadavers — that smells ill enough, but not as ill as the putrefying bodies upon which we had to learn our skills with our own hands. But never mind — you shall learn, you shall learn! Come along, Miss Lackland. Come and observe and teach us all how to do our tasks.'

She felt almost giddy with relief as she realized that they were not, after all, intending to ravish her. Tanner, now they had her in this narrow corridor and away from the street, was making no attempt to touch her, and indeed the other men too were keeping well away from her. One or two of them — there seemed to be perhaps seven or eight present — were in fact averting their faces from her, and she realized dimly that they were not as eager upon this adventure as were others, especially Tanner and Massey, both of whom were staring at her with a most disagreeable gleam in their eyes. But disagreeable though it was she knew it was not in any way a lascivious look. However else these men regarded her, it was not in any way as an object of desire and for a moment she wanted to laugh aloud, so great was her gratitude for that fact.

'Well?' she said as coolly as she could, smoothing her gown in front of her and pulling her alpaca jacket to rights, for their mishandling had sorely rumpled her. 'And now what? Speak up, gentlemen, for I have not all night to waste here with your childish japes!'

'Japes, is it?' Tanner said savagely, and put a hand between her shoulder blades to push her forwards. 'Such japes as this are rare indeed, madam high-and-mighty. Come you in and set about your studies!'

Ahead of her a door opened and she was propelled through it, and stood blinking in the sudden brightness of the light that filled the room they were now in. The other men were in there ahead of her, and now grouped themselves at the far end behind a row of broad low tables. Again she blinked and looked about her and now she could see very clearly indeed all there was to be seen.

On each of the tables lay a body. Naked bodies, with open eyes staring sightlessly up at the ceiling, the mouths drooping, lips apart, and the hands lying horribly lax at their sides. There were three men and one woman, and Sophie looked at the woman with a sudden surge of pity rising in her that glossed her eyes with tears and made her swallow hard, for she recognized her. She had been a patient in the women's medical ward, and when Sophie had first seen her had sat clutching her blankets to her, wide-eyed and terrified as the students stood around her. She had a cancer of the belly that had swollen it almost as badly as that of the man with the liver disease, and it had made the rest of her body sadly emaciated. She had died two days ago, Sophie remembered, looking now at the yellow creature naked on its bench. She could not have been more than forty years old but this poor thing lying so glassy-eyed and silent looked as old as time, with the flesh stretched across her bony cheeks and her hair lying rumpled on each side of the skull-like head.

'Look you, madam!' Tanner said, and put out his hand and with a contemptuous flick of his finger and thumb made the dead woman's left breast move lumpily and he grinned at the way Sophie's face reddened. 'Does that embarrass you, Miss Lackland? Surely not! What place has decent ladylike modesty in the sort of female that would make a doctor of herself? Why should *you* care what happens to dead bodies of other females, for you are not like one of them — are you? You are a *student* ——' and he took the dead nipple between his fingers and shook his hand so that the soft dependent flesh moved across the ribs; and still the dead face stared up at the ceiling. And Sophie could stand it no more, and she felt the rage rise in her and propel her across the room towards Tanner, her hands out and her fingers clawed.

'Hey, hey, a hellcat, is it!' roared Tanner and he laughed as he fended her off as easily as if she had been a fly, for tall as she was he was much taller and heavier, and had the table between them anyway. 'Does it upset you, madam student? Too bad, madam student, for there is worse to come!' And he whirled and seized from the table behind him a scalpel and then turned back to the dead woman and with one wide and sudden sweep, cut the abdomen from ribs to groins.

Sophie stood very still, unable to take her eyes from the great gape of wound that opened almost lazily in the wake of that savage stroke. There was no blood, just a faint serous oozing, and she could see yellow fat, a little, and then the glisten of a membrane, and she thought absurdly, 'The peritoneum. I have read of that — the peritoneum.'

The smell to which she had been becoming accustomed increased sharply and she had to open her mouth and compress the back of her throat to prevent herself from retching again. This time she succeeded, and looked up at Tanner's face and said as coolly as she could, 'Well? And what is that supposed to demonstrate? That you are as vicious and uncaring in your handling of the dead as you are in your care for the living? That does not surprise me! For my part, I would not have the sort of doctor you are likely to become to treat my sick dog.'

'Would you not, hellcat? Well, that is as may be — but at least I will become a doctor, which you will never do — for to do so, you have to be adept in the art of anatomy and to have dissected a cadaver for yourself. And that you will never do, for though you are no lady and dead to all feelings decent women have, you lack the courage to do as we do and take your knife to dead flesh!'

She lifted her chin and stared round at the watching men. Some of them looked, she thought, embarrassed, and she realized dimly that they were as frightened of Tanner's bullying as she was, and not at all united in scorn of her, however much their feelings may have been whipped up to start with. She almost smiled, so self-confident did she suddenly feel. It was as though a new wave of strength had come bubbling from deep inside her in the wake of her anger at Tanner's contemptuous use of the dead woman, and now she was going to use it, and use it well.

She turned back to Tanner and held out her hand. 'Give me that scalpel.'

He stared, standing there with the open abdomen in front of him, his hand poised above it, and for the first time looked uncertain.

'What did you say?'

'Give me that knife. You say I must study anatomy and dissect a body? Then I am grateful to you for the opportunity so to do. Give me the knife.'

'You damned hellcat ——' Tanner began expostulating, but suddenly one of the silent men clustered at the back of the room said sharply, 'Give it to her.'

Tanner turned his head and then another of the silent students found his courage and added, 'You heard, Tanner — give it to her!' and there was a murmur of assent and Tanner looked at Massey, standing beside him, who shrugged and made a face and let his gaze slide away from his crony's face.

'Oh, well, if you think we should punish her further, punish the creature further we shall!' he said with a somewhat blustering note in his voice and contemptuously he tossed the scalpel at her and with a turn of her wrist she caught it.

And then turned and marched away across the anatomy room with as steady a gait as she could, to stand in front of one of the other tables where a man of some sixty years, obese, and with purplish red patches across his pouched skin, lay in the same glassy-eyed way as the woman behind her.

She looked about her and then, after a second, took off her alpaca jacket, and moving quietly, laid it neatly across his groins.

'I see no cause to shame the dead,' she said quietly, and then took a deep breath, and turned the scalpel in her hands so that the blade pointed downwards, and looked at the abdomen before her.

It was not easy. Oh, she had opened many a dead body before,

195

but they had been of creatures for the table. Hens and rabbits and once even a pig, when they had been able to rear one at Tansey Clough and Bessie had allowed her to help. But this was not an animal, but a man. One who had once looked at the world through eyes much like her own, who had heard sounds through ears shaped as were hers, who felt and loved and hoped and feared as she did. This was different.

But yet it was not, for whoever or whatever this man had been, he was long since gone. What lay there before her was indeed so much dead flesh, like pork or rabbit. Regard it so and she could show these men that she was as good and as capable as any of them. So she moved slowly and easily and set her knife to the point where the ribs met above the belly, and using the same smooth stroke that Tanner had, began the incision.

She felt the men about her hold their breaths and remembered in time and opened her own mouth and pressed her tongue against the roof of it ready to repel the smell when it came, and slowly, just as it had on the woman's body Tanner had attacked, the opening gaped and parted, and she saw now much more yellow fat and the gleam of the peritoneum as it showed itself behind her moving knife. And she wanted to shout aloud, 'I can, I can, I can ——'

But she concentrated and at last the incision was complete and she looked up at Baker, the man who had first told Tanner to give her the knife, and said crisply, 'And what do I do now?'

There was a pause and then Baker said gruffly, 'I will show you,' and moved to stand beside her and took the knife and made two more incisions, this time on each side of the belly running down to the hips, so that there were four neat flaps covering the expanse of organs that lay beneath. He folded them back and with a different knife, which he took from a ledge below the table on which the body lay, he gently opened the peritoneum and with pins that one of the other men moved forwards to give to him, pinned it back over the superficial skin flaps.

And now she was no longer afraid, no longer brave, no longer aware even of Tanner and his threats. There before her lay a beauty that she would not have thought possible, as Baker, a neat and rapid dissector, bared first one and then another section of the abdomen.

'These organs that you see here,' he said quietly, 'are somewhat

196

discoloured but not so much that the tissue cannot be identified. See here — this is the small intestine and this the omentum and this the pancreas, and here, just behind, lies the spleen ——'

She listened and nodded and then, when he had identified the organs that could easily be seen, he seemed to become aware of the circumstances of this lesson he was giving and faltered and stopped and quietly put down the knife.

'This is all I can show you now, I think, Miss Lackland,' he said awkwardly and moved away to a sink on the far side of the room and began to wash his hands.

She followed him and did the same and then turned, the towel in her hands, drying herself carefully and said quietly, 'And may I go home now, Mr Tanner? The lesson from Mr Baker is one I have much appreciated and I do but wish it could have been longer — and could be repeated.'

Tanner said nothing. He was standing leaning against the wall with his arms folded and a sullen look upon his face and after a moment she bowed and turned and went to the door.

No one stopped her, but just as she was about to pass through one of the hitherto silent watchers called, 'Your jacket, Miss Lackland.'

She stopped but did not turn her head. 'I will not take it, thank you,' she said in a choked voice. The nausea had returned now and the thought of picking up that garment, and wearing it again, filled her with a revulsion so huge she could hardly encompass it. But for all that she managed to walk steadily out of the door and up the stairs and out into the street.

As she reached the street the clock on St Paul's church chimed. It was half past ten o'clock. Just thirty minutes since she had left the patient sleeping in the women's surgical ward. Thirty of the most terrifying minutes of her life.

CHAPTER TWENTY

'You dealt with it well enough,' Miss Jex-Blake said, cooly bending her head to her papers again, and Sophie felt a twist of anger. She had told her story with the minimum of histrionics, but even so she knew it to be a very dramatic one, and her own part in the affair far from negligible, yet this woman treated it all as very much a matter of course.

'I believe I was at very real risk for part of the time in that room, Miss Jex-Blake,' she said sharply. 'The man Tanner was very incensed against me and treated me with great callousness.'

'I am sure he did,' Miss Jex-Blake said, not lifting her head. 'But whoever told you that the path you had chosen was to be an easy one, or an agreeable one? I certainly did not. You have suffered no more than others who have gone before you.'

Now she did look up and for the first time a smile moved across those heavy features, lifting her face to a mischievousness that was very attractive. 'And you did at least obtain a short anatomy lesson from it, and actually set your knife to a specimen, which is more than most are able to do! Come, do you wish me to commiserate with you upon that?'

Sophie laughed then, and relaxed. 'I dare say I was fussing a bit. I am sorry. So, Miss Jex-Blake, what now? I cannot remain at Nellie's longer, that is certain. I do not see how my cousin could take me back, for I know the whole hospital knows of the affair. There were some of the men who were there that evening who talked much too freely. Stupid creatures!' she added angrily. 'I had won my point and could have gone on well enough if they had but held their tongues.'

'Aye, well, men are like that. Foolish blabbing creatures,' Miss Jex-Blake said, and grinned that friendly grin again. 'So, what to do? You have timed your little affaire well, my dear. I have at last settled upon a house at Henrietta Street in Bloomsbury which shall be used as the London Medical School for Women. We have far to go yet, for we do not have full access to wards at any hospital, except the London Free Hospital at Gray's Inn Road, which will give us some small access to patients. It will be some time — perhaps two years, I suspect — before we have all running as smooth as we would wish, but a start must be made somewhere. You shall be one of my first students — you have undoubtedly proved yourself to be of the mettle we need. I think that you may look forward to setting the word Doctor before your name by — oh, shall we say three years from now? In 1878? Not too long at all. It took me far longer ——'

'Three years,' Sophie said blankly. 'And that to become a physician? But it is surgery that I wish to make my profession, Miss Jex-Blake.'

'Walk first, girl, walk! It will be many a year longer before we can offer *that* at our medical school, I'm thinking. And we need physicians more.' She leaned forwards then and stared very hard at Sophie, her great dark eyes opened so wide that the white seemed to show all round them, and her heavy dark brows adding great power to her gaze. 'Understand this, Miss Lackland, I have no interest in those who seek to follow a career in medicine out of some taste for drama and excitement. The operating theatres are indeed full of such excitement as makes the blood sing in your ears, but what matters more is the humdrum day-to-day care of ordinary disease. The men and women and children — especially the women and children! — who drag their sick and weary bones about their daily business and need the aid of a concerned and thoughtful physician to diagnose their ills and treat them as best as possible. If surgery is needed, why then, we physicians can send our poor patients to those cutters and slashers — but for my part, a true doctor is a physician and worth any ten of those hard knife-wielding creatures. You said yourself that this Tanner — this student who treated you so ill — is one who is to be a surgeon. Do you wish to be such as that, as adamantine as some granite rock, with no care or heart in you?'

'Surgeons can be compassionate too,' Sophie said bravely — and it took much courage to gainsay Miss Jex-Blake — and stared back as firmly as she could. 'Mr Caspar is a surgeon but he is as gentle a man ——'

Miss Jex-Blake dismissed Freddy with a wave of one capable

hand. 'Oh, of course there are some who show the true compassionate approach. But by and large they are a harsh and hateful
lot! It is doctors I wish to help women become, not mere butchers.
If that is your need, seek elsewhere.'

There was a little silence and then Sophie said quietly, 'Well, we
will not argue as to the relative values of medicine and surgery. I am
glad to come to you to train as a physician. In time to come — well,
we shall see ——'

*   *   *

So it was that on the first of October 1874 Sophie Lackland started
her daily attendances at 30 Henrietta Street in Bloomsbury. There
had been much head-shaking and talking at Nellie's, following the
wave of gossip that swept the hospital after her experience in the
anatomy room, for many of the students turned against Tanner,
and made no effort to exculpate him, and in the ensuing hue and
cry, he left the hospital amid much rancour and enrolled at the
London Hospital. But it was clear to all, not least to Freddy, that in
spite of this, Sophie too would have to go.

'I did my best, my dear,' he said sadly to her, 'but it was not to
be. I must tell you that the Governors were not nearly as distressed
as I had feared they might be at my little masquerade, making you
a lady nurse, that is, but they feel that now we cannot go on as we
were after all the fuss. So — you must go to your Miss Jex-Blake,
though I cannot believe the teaching she can arrange will be as
good as that which you would have had here. There is nowhere,'
Freddy said loyally, 'as good as Nellie's! But I can offer you some
help — you may like to read my lecture notes, which I prepare most
carefully, and go over them with me, when I will try to enlarge
upon the material much as I do in the lecture room and the
operating theatre. Will that be of help to you?'

She had sat silently for a moment and then said abruptly, 'What
does Cousin Phoebe say about this affair, Cousin Freddy?'

He reddened. 'That is of no moment,' he said stiffly.

'But I think it is, you know,' she said as gently as she could. 'I
have a fear that — that she read more into the situation than was
justified.'

He stood up and began to walk about his little office, much like
a caged tiger at the zoological gardens. 'You have been talking to
Martha,' he said over his shoulder. She shook her head.

'I did not pry, if that is what you mean. But Aunt Martha did indeed tell me that there has been — that Cousin Phoebe was displeased.'

'Displeased. Aye, she was displeased.' He stopped then beside the window and stood staring moodily out into the street below and then sighed sharply and turned back to Sophie. 'Well, since you ask, you may as well be told. She took some maggot into her brain that — that — oh, it is too absurd!'

'That you and I were closer than cousins should be?'

'Something of the sort. But it is a nonsense.'

'Is it, Cousin Freddy?' Sophie said gently and then folded her hands tightly on her lap and looked down at them. 'I must tell you that I — that I was myself a little afraid that you — that your kindness to me was based on a more tender feeling than would be — oh, comfortable for you, under your circumstances. Had this matter of the students not supervened, is it not possible that Cousin Phoebe would have become distressed about some other matter? I am afraid, you know, that it would have been so.'

He stood there looking sombrely at her and then said suddenly, 'Tell me, Sophie, had I not been your cousin and a man much older than you — oh, this is a foolish question! You must forget I ever ——' and once again he turned away from her to stand and look out at the street and its passers-by.

'Could I have felt an affection for you, Cousin Freddy? Is that what you ask? A more than cousinly one?'

'I ask nothing.'

'Well, I will assume that is the question that is on your mind. And I must tell you that I have promised myself that I will not allow my plans to be disrupted by affairs of the heart. Men are more fortunate than we poor females. They may work and be ambitious and still enjoy the gift of love and — and marriage and family. But — such as I — I cannot. The time may well come when I will have to choose between my ambitions and my feelings, but at present I trust I am well enough in control to avoid that dilemma. So the question of tender feelings does not enter my mind. But I can tell you I have found you always charming and gentle and thoughtful and full of all those qualities I most admire in a man. Does that answer you?'

He turned back to her. 'Well enough — but you say you will not

201

allow tender feelings to deflect you from your course? That is a sad denial of your youth and — and undoubted charms. And what about Mr Stacey?'

Now it was her turn to flush. 'What about him? He is a friend, no more.'

'A friend? When he makes love to you so insouciantly that he can do so in another man's hearing? Even one he regards as — as a sort of *father* to the lady to whom he pays his attentions?'

She laughed loudly at that. 'Oh, you must not pay too much attention to Mr Stacey and his raillery. It is his idea of joking, you know, and means nothing!'

'Does it? Do you tell me you have no more interest in him than that of mere friendship? That the possibility of passion never enters into it?'

Flushing even more she shook her head. 'No!' she said strongly. 'Indeed, no. He is but a friend, just as — as Wilfred is ——'

'Wilfred?'

'A — a very old friend in Haworth who has much affection for me, and indeed I know would wed me tomorrow. But I am not interested in such things as marriage — only in the chance to follow the career I have chosen. So you see, there was no need ever for Cousin Phoebe to be anxious ——'

'There never was anyway,' he said heavily. 'She should know if anyone does that whatever may happen my love and duty belong all to her, however much I might find some pleasure and some comfort in the company of — of others. But, as you say, it is perhaps as well — I shall miss you, Sophie.'

She smiled at him with all the warmth she could. 'And I you,' she said quietly. 'Your kindness and generosity have been a shining example to me. I will of course repay your money when I can and ——'

'Do not dare ever to mention that again!' he said with a sudden uprush of anger, and she drew back in some surprise, and then, understanding, albeit dimly, she nodded.

'Very well. Then I will say only that I have been and still am deeply aware of your goodness to me, and thank you.'

'Shall I see you again?' he said after a little while, as she stood up and began to draw on her gloves preparatory to departure.

'I think not,' she said gently, after a moment. 'Unless perhaps at such family meetings as Aunt Martha may arrange. Do you not agree?'

'Yes,' he said heavily, and she smiled at him again and turned and left his little room and walked out of the hospital, and he watched her from his window as she walked along the street, her long back curving over the swell of her bustle, and felt some of the light go out of his day.

*   *   *

Gil Stacey, on the other hand, showed little interest in her new plans. He called as usual on the next Sunday, full of talk of his new play, and she listened and laughed and then told him a little of her adventure at the hands of Tanner and the students, and it was his turn to listen and then laugh.

'Such dramas, my dear! And you behaved admirably well, indeed you did. But then, who but my termagant would? Had that Tanner and his friends seen you the day you first spoke to me they would have thought twice before so setting about you! I am proud of you, indeed I am! Well done.'

And again she felt that little twist of the same resentment Miss Jex-Blake had aroused in her. Perhaps she was not as modern as she had fondly imagined she was, she told herself mournfully when Gil had taken himself back to his lodgings after the theatre. Truly modern people take such an experience as mine in their stride, while I make much of it. I have much changing to do before I am completely the New Woman, it is clear ——

The weeks between leaving Nellie's and starting at the Henrietta Street school were in many ways a holiday, although she was very busy, for these few days gave her time to chivvy the maids at Villiers Street into a prolonged and delayed spring-cleaning bout and to spend some time with Aunt Martha.

She was as perturbed by Sophie's experience in the anatomy room as Sophie had wished that Miss Jex-Blake and Gil would be, but with the usual contrariness of human nature, Sophie found the older woman's exclamations and head-shakings a little tiresome and pooh-poohed her anxiety.

'Anatomy I must learn, and will gladly, Aunt Martha. You must not think ill of these young men, for in a sense they were justified. I did not wish to study at Nellie's in such a deceitful manner, but it was forced upon me, and they, when they discovered the truth,

203

were perhaps entitled to feel put upon. They have had to do their hard work in studying anatomy and it seemed to them that I was escaping it, and yet claiming their privileges — well, let it be. All is now set to rights, and at Henrietta Street I shall be allowed to do my work and none will care that I am female. It will be quite wonderful!'

And Martha listened to her and nodded and said no more, but was slightly concerned, for it seemed to her that in some way Sophie had changed. The enthusiasm and energy were there in greater force than ever, but there was an edge to her that seemed to Martha to have something of hardness in it and she worried a little. Was it true, what they all said? That competing with men and working with men in their own avocations robbed a woman of the special qualities that only women have? Was her softness and essential gentleness being eroded by her experiences in the harsh world of hospital?

But then she looked again and listened again and changed her mind. Sophie was still Sophie, still had her femininity undamaged. But she was more watchful, and more careful now. The ingenuousness that had in part caused the problem with Freddy and with his Phoebe was burnished with town polish to a greater sophistication. She had learned, Martha decided, a little more about the way the world wagged, and was less vulnerable. Which was not a bad thing for a woman who was to make her way in such a hard and thoughtless world.

*   *   *

Sophie's letters home at this time were guarded. She had thought hard about what she should say, sitting in her attic and chewing the end of her pen, and then decided to say nothing to Bessie of what had happened. There would be little point in upsetting her and she would not be able fully to understand from a letter. So she told her only that she was now to go to be a student at a school of medicine for women, which news she was sure would warm Bessie's heart. And she wrote cheerfully of the hostel and the girls, for ever since leaving Haworth she had given Bessie news of her new life albeit carefully edited, knowing how much her old friend and nurse would want to share in it, and left it at that.

But her letters to Wilfred were different. Many were the times when she wished heartily that he were near enough to talk to, near enough to share with her her anxieties and dilemmas. Wilfred with his good sense and long knowledge of her would always understand and help her organize her own ideas, and now suddenly she missed him more than she ever had since coming to London, so many long months ago.

And she saw no reason not to let him know that, so she wrote him copious letters pouring out all her anxieties about her future at Henrietta Street — and there were many, for the new school was an unknown quantity, after all, and Miss Jex-Blake most formidable — and also telling him of all that had happened at Nellie's. And sent her letter feeling curiously comforted, as though she had indeed had a lovely long prosy talk with him, sitting in the firelight at Tansey Clough, their feet upon the fender.

His reply was all she could have hoped for.

'My dear Sophie. Your account of your adventures at the hospital first angered me — how dare such creatures treat you so? — and then made me proud, for despite your modest descriptions of what happened, it is clear to me that you were brave and sensible — and lastly, in a curious way, your account made me sorry for those louts. Does that seem strange? It is just that I feel they must have at some deep level of their hearts quite unperceived by them, I am sure, become conscious of your gifts and strength and been afraid of you. And no greater compliment could you be paid. I know you well and have been your friend too long to be afraid of you, but I can well understand that some men, lacking my good fortune in knowing your softer side as well as I do, could see in you a threat to their manhood. So, I was sorry for them. Let me know if that angers you, and I will try to elucidate further, but I think this will not be necessary. We understand each other well, you and I, do we not? I think you will have no difficulty in entering into the feelings I have here described.

'Now, as to news of Haworth ——' and he had gone on for several more close written pages to bring her all those titbits of information which made home rise before her eyes in such detail and with such vividness that her throat contracted for a moment with homesickness. And so engrossed was she with all he wrote, that she did not notice what was missing from his letter — which was any mention of Gil Stacey. Which was a little odd, for her own letter had been full of news of him and his doings.

And so at last October came, and Sophie enrolled as one of the first of the students at the London School of Medicine for Women. And in the succeeding months she buried herself almost ecstatically in her chemistry and physiology, her mathematics and anatomy, and learned as eagerly as any of her teachers could wish. Her days on the wards of the London Free Hospital, a small and rather shabby institution when compared with Nellie's, a much older hospital, gave her less satisfaction, perhaps, than the wards at Nellie's had, but even this became unimportant as the facts she learned slowly and carefully built themselves up into a body of knowledge and understanding that, added to all her previous experience, brought her close indeed to being the physician she had to be before she could be a surgeon.

Indeed, by Christmas of 1875, when she had been a student but fifteen months Miss Jex-Blake told her candidly that for some time in the future she would be wasting her time.

'There is no way we can arrange for you to be examined and admitted to the register of physicians yet, for we have not yet fully completed the legal arrangements to do so, although I am confident it cannot be long now. I think the time is approaching when we must set you to different work so that you do not waste either your energies or your talents. But we will see to that after Christmas. At present, go on as you are. I am well pleased with you.'

Which helped Sophie look forward to Christmas 1875 with much more than usual pleasure. Until the night, the frightening night, when she took one of her rare holidays and went to see the new burlesque at the Gaiety Theatre.

CHAPTER TWENTY-ONE

The theatre was alive with happiness that December evening. The family parties were much in evidence, even overflowing into the front stalls among the mashers, and Sophie, looking down from her special place in the stage box which was made available to her as 'a friend of the company' was mightily amused to see the way those elegant monocled creatures drew back their tightly trousered legs with fastidious care as large well-upholstered wives of suburban tradesmen came surging into their seats in a flurry of fringed bustles and gauze scarves and tinselly ruchings. Each gown at which she looked seemed to have more rouleaux and ribbons and passementerie and feathers and lace and broderie anglaise than the succeeding one. Each seemed to be in a brighter purple or crimson or shrieking green than its successor. Each woman's head seemed to have a greater chignon in a thicker fishnet snood than the one that had just passed before her bemused gaze, and she sighed a little at her own dowdiness.

For this past year she had been much too busy — and too poor in pocket — to give any thought to fashion. She had never been one to care unduly about clothes anyway for there was little chance to develop such a taste in Haworth, but she had cared enough to notice what others wore. Yet here in London where there was so much more to see she had, she now realized, shown even less interest, contenting herself with her few plain day gowns with their high necks and simple sleeves and most modest of bustles. And looking now at the glittering assemblage below her, all set to enjoy its Christmas entertainment with every possible sign of their increasing prosperity displayed upon their backs, she was not sorry. If being fashionable meant looking like these over-stuffed and over-dressed females, then she was glad that she was not, she told herself stoutly.

She leaned back in her chair then and stared down dreamily at the stage. She was tired, but not excessively so. Life at the medical school had been busy lately but far from arduous, for there were few patients available at present to the women students at the London Free Hospital's wards and the number of lectures had been heavily curtailed, because of Miss Jex-Blake's absence on a visit to her elderly mother. Even at Villiers Street life was peaceful, for several of the girls had been chosen to go on a tour of France with a new show, and would not be back until the New Year. So, she could look forward to two or three days of real peace, with the chance perhaps to sleep late in the mornings, as late as seven o'clock, a rare treat for one who customarily was out of her bed by half past five.

Perhaps she would ask Gil Stacey and Aunt Martha to eat their Christmas dinner with her at Villiers Street? And ask some of her friendlier neighbours like the Chamberlayne family and Robert Neal and Joseph Twigg as well? That would be an agreeable thing, to be a hostess in her own establishment, albeit one that was hers only by employment, and she began to think about what sort of entertainment she might be able to offer.

The orchestra had tuned up now, and swung into a very lively overture and the scent of the women and the men's macassar oil and the oranges many of the children were sucking with great enthusiasm drifted up to her in the warm moist air and made her yawn comfortably, and drift further into lazy plans for the holiday. She could perhaps obtain a goose, and persuade Cook to prepare it in the Yorkshire way that Bessie had taught her with a great deal of sage and onion forcemeat and a rich gravy to pour over turnips alongside. And a plum pudding and mince pies ——

The crimson curtain flushed into life as the footlights glowed, and the less sophisticated section of the audience 'aahed' and 'oohed', for John Hollingshead had installed the new incandescent gas mantles on the Gaiety stage and the effect was indeed stunningly bright. The orchestra became even more frenetic in its sawing and blowing and drum rattling and now the curtain shivered and rose on the usual Gaiety first number, with the stage seething with tall and beautiful girls looking ineffably bored in tunics of tinsel and diamond-trimmed tights and intricate coiffures that made them seem almost as eye-dazzling as the elaborate scenery.

As usual, Nellie Farren and J. L. Toole were well to the forefront,

208

capering their foolish enchanting way about the stage and the audience relaxed and laughed and cheered and roared their satisfaction at them over the footlights, which made the performers become even more frantic in their attempts to please.

Watching them from the stage box, still in that rather detached lazy mood that she had brought into the theatre with her from the raw December night outside, Sophie enjoyed them too. She did not shout or clap her hands but she admired the expertise of Nellie's singing, and the way Toole timed his jokes and droll gestures and glances to obtain the hugest laugh, and the beauty of the ladies of the chorus. They really were exquisite creatures, with their long shapely legs and magnificent busts and perfectly oval faces, but she was glad to have a more interesting way to spend her own life. She could think of little that would be more boring than strolling about a stage in nothing but feathers and paint.

So she told herself and then switched her attention back to the centre stage, for it was time for Gil's entrance. She had not seen this particular production, but every Gaiety show was much like another, and she knew the pattern now. It was time for Gil in his tight black suit of clothes, with his curly hair brushed up into an aureole around his head and his dark eyes gleaming as his mobile mouth stretched itself into a cheeky cheerful grin, to come capering on from the prompt side below her, to turn several of his amazing cartwheels and then launch himself into that sure-footed dance of his in which his feet moved so fast they seemed to blur and his long legs twisted themselves so fascinatingly that she would wonder, with her new understanding of anatomy, how his joints could stand the strain.

The music changed, becoming more rhythmic, and the girls on stage re-formed into new patterns as the comedians ran off to a tumult of applause, and Sophie leaned forwards to catch the first possible sight of Gil's entrance. But he did not appear and the music faltered and then with a skilful slide on the strings went back to the beginning of Gil's theme and began again as one or two of the less bored-looking chorus girls exchanged a glance and then peered into the wings on the prompt side.

Sophie was suddenly alert. All her detachment was gone and her eyes were wide as she stared down. Something was wrong — Gil had missed his cue, and that was something Gil had never been

209

known to do in any performance at the Gaiety she had ever seen, and she had seen many now. What was wrong? Would he miss his cue a second time?

But he did not. He came on stage, and the audience, well used to his appearance, gave him a noisy welcome, but Sophie frowned, her lower lip caught between her teeth. His usual ebullience was far from being in evidence. He moved well enough, seeming to keep time with his music, but to those who knew his usual standard of performance, this was not Gil Stacey, the dancer everyone loved to watch. This was a hollow simulacrum of him, a mere leaping automaton. There was no heart, no joy in a single step.

No one on stage seemed unduly perturbed, however, for the girls were moving in their well-drilled way, and the orchestra leader was bobbing his head happily enough, but for all that, Sophie felt anxiety rise in her. Gil was not right, for now he was actually missing his steps.

She looked at his face now, and it seemed to her to be white and strained under his greasepaint, and there was clearly sweat upon his forehead, and he was staring out front with a wide glassy look that was very foreign to him.

And his breathing, too, seemed laboured for he held his mouth partly open and she could see his nostrils flaring with each painful breath he took and now she was on her feet, watching him with her eyes narrowed with concentration. Flaring nostrils. She could hear deep in her memory Miss Jex-Blake's voice at one of her lectures: 'The accessory muscles of nostrils come into play when entry of air to the lungs is impeded in any way. It is an ability of limited value in mankind, although I have observed such animals as need to gain extra air when they run obtain benefit from the enlargement of the air passages which results when the muscles operate in this manner ——'

He was having trouble with his breathing. That was all she could be sure of, and it alarmed her, for Gil, although he usually enjoyed the rudest of health had suffered in recent weeks from a chill, caught one bitterly cold night when he had insisted on coming out of the theatre still in his sweat-soaked clothes from his performance, to find her a hansom cab to take her back to Villiers Street.

The performance went on, but now she was so alarmed that she

210

turned towards the door at the back of the box, determined to go down and back stage immediately to greet him when he came off, to see what it was that ailed him. She had just reached the door when a sudden huge sound made her whirl and run back to the edge of the box to lean and look over, down on to the stage.

The sound she had heard had been of a great concerted indrawing of breath from almost every member of the audience, and now it was superseded by a great babble of voices which quite drowned the orchestra, still working valiantly, if a shade raggedly, in the orchestra pit.

On the stage, almost in the very centre, Gil was lying, crumpled and looking strangely young, like a child who had fallen asleep at his play. His head was thrown back and she could see, even from here, that his eyes were not fully closed and that a line of white could be seen beneath the lids. Two or three of the chorus girls were bending over him and chafing his hands and fanning him and even as Sophie again turned to go down to the stage the curtain came whispering down to hide the interesting sight from the now clamouring audience.

By the time she reached the stage someone had come out before the curtain to make an announcement and soothe them; above the sound of her own rushing footsteps she could hear the audience quieten and the burr of a male voice, though she could identify no words. And then she was through the pass door, and running full tilt through the clustered people in the wings, pushing and indeed shoving rudely to force her way through.

On stage the chorus girls were still surrounding Gil and she pushed them roughly to one side as well, not caring a whit for niceties of behaviour in her anxiety, until at last she was kneeling beside him and with both hands was opening the shirt collar and cravat which was still tight around his throat.

The chorus girls seemed to accept her right to be there, for they fell back and formed a circle around her, watching and exclaiming to each other as she ripped his shirt open, too, and exposed his chest, and then bending her back and crouching even more, set her ear against his bare skin.

She had to hold her hand up then to enjoin silence and after a moment they stopped their chatter and just watched her eagerly and she moved her hand to cover her exposed ear, to shut out the sounds still coming from the other side of the wall of velvet that was the curtain — for the orchestra had struck up again — and listened hard, her eyes closed as she concentrated.

His heart was thumping heavily, easily audible and blessedly steady in its rhythm, albeit hurried and pounding. But it was his breathing sounds which alarmed her, and she sat back on her heels, and using her hands as Miss Jex-Blake had taught her, began to tap his chest, seeking for signs of what was happening in the lungs beneath.

She heard it all too clearly, even through the hum of noise that surrounded her; the dull flat tone of congestion. Again she bent her head and listened, this time to his breathing sounds rather than to his heart, and the rough intake of breath, the crackling sounds at the apex of each lung as well as the dull deadness at the base told her all she needed to know.

'Fetch me blankets,' she ordered, not looking up, and using the end of his ripped shirt to mop his sweat-damp face. 'He needs warmth — he has pneumonia. Blankets — at once, you hear me?' And now she looked up at one of the girls with such ferocity that the girl shrank back and then turned and ran to the wings, weeping as she went.

A couple of men came pushing through then, the stage manager following Mr Hollingshead himself.

'What's up?' Hollingshead said roughly. 'What ails the man?'

'Pneumonia,' Sophie said shortly. 'He should not have been working at all. Why did you allow him?'

'Now, don't you start on me, missie! You'll be the lady friend, I take it, that's learning how to physic folk? Aye. Well, let me tell you, missie, that he *was* told tonight — heard him coughing his heart out, I did, the moment he walked into the theatre, but you should know as well as I do that no one tells Gil Stacey aught. He does as he thinks fit, and he swore to me he was fit to dance and I believed him — so don't start your ——'

'Oh, I am sorry,' Sophie said. 'I dare say you are right — but we have no time now for argument. He needs care. I must take him to his chambers ——'

'No good there,' Hollingshead said. 'It's not a place where he'll get any nursing of any kind — his landlady is a slattern and a heartless one at that. Bring him to my chambers here, above the theatre. There is warmth there and we can rig a bed for him, and obtain the services of a nurse from somewhere and ——'

'No need. I shall care for him,' Sophie said firmly, and took the blankets one of the girls at last brought, and began very tenderly to wrap Gil in them. He was beginning to recover now and turned his head fretfully as she lifted his shoulders to set the blanket there, peering at her with bloodshot eyes.

'What is — where the — Sophie?'

'You are ill, my dear,' she said gently, 'and must be cared for. You are feverish, too, and need to be covered. Now do as I bid you — and all shall be well with you ——'

They had brought a disused piece of scenery now, a flat on which was painted a scene of an Italian garden, with statuary and exotic greenery and flowers, and at a jerk of the head from Mr Hollingshead the stage manager, with the aid of a couple of scene shifters, lifted Gil on to it, and he was carried from the stage to the wings.

'Get the performance going again,' Hollingshead called back over his shoulder. 'As fast as you are able. Toole can put in the fisherman sketch to fill Stacey's spot — and haste about it! And now, miss, we'll see you and young Stacey here safe bestowed. Come on ——'

With a man at each end of the makeshift stretcher — and Gil's restless head looked absurd framed as it was in painted garlands of foliage and with a simpering cherub's head alongside his own — and with Sophie walking alongside they made their way, not without some difficulty, along the backstage corridors and up the twisting iron stairway to the office where Sophie had first talked to Gil, that day so long ago when she had come hotfoot to the Gaiety to complain about their treatment of Madge Gunn.

Hollingshead bustled about, giving orders in all directions which were obeyed with alacrity, so that very quickly, the sofa to one side of the fireplace was covered with pillows and blankets, the desk was cleared of its heaps of papers, and a ewer and basin set upon it.

Then, tenderly, Sophie supervised the lifting of Gil's now restless body to the sofa, and she smiled at the stage hands and thanked them as prettily as she could.

'He is very ill, and you dealt with his needs most thoughtfully. I am sure when he is well he will thank you himself.'

'If he get well, missie,' said the taller of them, a thin man of lugubrious turn of countenance. 'For 'e looks sick to death if you ask me. My sister, she 'ad the pneumony, she did, looked just like that, gorn within the week she was, an' us pouring brandy an' all sorts down 'er, no expense spared. Gorn inside the week, an' looked just as bad as this.'

'Oh, he will not die,' Sophie said brightly, and with more reassurance than she felt, for as she began to clean his face with a towel wetted in the ewer of water she could feel just how hot he was, and how high his fever raged. 'There is nothing here that a little care cannot cure — I need some help, Mr Hollingshead, to remove his clothes. He needs to breathe as free as may be and he cannot in this constricting raiment.'

'Well, *you* cannot remove them, of course,' Mr Hollingshead said at once. 'And I have no skills in these matters — perhaps one of you?' and he looked at his stage hands, both of whom looked back at him very dubiously.

'Nonsense,' Sophie said at once. 'I am not too modest to do the task — just in need of aid. Come sir! Do as I ask you, and we shall have him free of these things in a trice. Have you such a thing as a clean shirt about the place? I have ripped this one beyond use in examining him, and he will need another ——'

'I will send for one,' Mr Hollingshead said with some show of resignation. Clearly he found Sophie a masterful person, and not one with whom he would willingly argue. 'Joe, take yourself to that linen draper's in the Strand — down by John Adam Street — and knock him up and tell him to send — what do you want, miss?'

'A couple of flannel nightshirts, cut loose about the body,' Sophie said, and slipped one arm behind Gil's shoulders, lifting him. 'Mr Hollingshead, come and hold him so — aye, that is the way — while I remove his coat sleeve — well done — and now, the other one. Splendid! And now his trousers ——'

Hollingshead, expostulating all the time, did so, and at last Gil was free of his clothes, and carefully wrapped in his warm blankets, and Sophie set about bathing his face and neck again with cool water, to bring down his fever, for this it seemed to her was the greatest risk that threatened him at present, for his skin was now burning hot to the touch, and his lips were drying rapidly as he rolled his head and muttered in his half delirious doze.

From far below she could hear the performance going on again and marvelled for a moment; for here lay one of the most important members of the company, sick to death — no, sick as he could be, she amended, for death was not to be considered — and yet the people with whom he worked and who were in some sense his brethren danced and joked and sang upon a stage before a great shouting, heedless audience. It is all wrong, she thought, patiently soaking her towel and wringing it out and again bathing the flushed and sweating face, that it should be so. They should all go home in decent silence, thoughtful for the sick man who had suffered so in order to entertain them ——

But then she dismissed the thought and shook her head at herself, for to expect such behaviour was not only absurd — it made it seem that Gil was far more ill than he was. He *was* ill, very ill, but he was not going to die, not he, she told herself fiercely, he was not going to die, and there was no need for anyone to behave as though he were.

The nightshirts came at last and she managed to get him into one, without help this time, for Hollingshead had gone back to the stage to see how all was going with his performance. Then as Gil seemed to settle into a less restless sleep she moved softly about the room setting it into the sort of order she felt a sickbed needed.

In addition to the ewer and basin and towels which Hollingshead had provided, she would need a slop bucket and extra linen, she decided and went hunting for them, and found to her great relief a housemaid's room at the end of the corridor, where brooms and buckets and above all a tap and sink were to be found. Nursing Gil here would not be too difficult after all ——

For herself she arranged in one corner of the cluttered office a couple of blankets, set on the scenery flat that had been used as Gil's stretcher. She would do well enough there, she told herself when she had finished, looking around with some satisfaction. It was not the ideal place to nurse a pneumonia case, but better than many she had seen in her work in Haworth at Town End Bottom, and she would manage well enough.

And so she told Hollingshead when he came up at the end of the performance to see what the situation was.

'I shall stay here with him until he is fit to return to his own chambers,' she said firmly, sitting beside Gil's sofa and staring up at the tall man who stood looking down at her so dubiously. 'And then I shall instruct his landlady in how to care for him, for slattern though she may be she must be fit to help a *little*. But first we must get him well, and that means we must remain here. I trust that will not discommode you too much.'

And Hollingshead, looking round his completely re-arranged office a little gloomily assured her hastily that this would not discommode him in the least and he was sure she was right.

'But what will you do for food, miss?' he asked them. 'For we have no kitchens here, you know — we go to the restaurant upstairs if we require aught, so have no need for kitchens or anything of that sort.'

Sophie looked blank for a moment. 'I had not thought of food,' she said frankly. 'I was more concerned about — well, we shall have to ask the restaurant kitchen to send down what is required, shall we not? Tell the man to come to me in the morning and I will tell him what is required for Gil. For myself they can bring what-ever they wish — I am not unduly concerned. But Gil will need nourishing broths and jellies and the like — I leave the arrange-ments to you, Mr Hollingshead, I am sure you will agree that we must all do what we can to make Gil well again.'

And Mr Hollingshead sighed and agreed and went away to do as he was bid. And hoped fervently that Gilbert Stacey's illness would run not only a satisfactory course, but a swift one.

CHAPTER TWENTY-TWO

To Sophie it seemed that time lost its shape. She had no awareness of its passage, no realization of yesterday or tomorrow. There was just now, and Gil's stertorous breathing and the need to mop his sweating face over and over again as the fever burned its relentless way towards the crisis.

She had nursed many people with pneumonia, was well aware of its classic rhythm, the way the illness seemed to get steadily worse until the moment arrived when the sufferer either gave way beneath the burden of congestion that filled his lungs and gave up trying to breathe altogether, or the miracle that was natural healing moved in and resolved the inflammatory process, loosening the mass of clogged tissue and allowing air once more to reach the starving lungs.

But it had never been quite like this with those other cases in Haworth. It was not that she cared more for Gil, she told herself, crouching there beside him and watching his flaring nostrils and painful indrawn breaths. I cared for all of them, I always wanted all of them to live, quite desperately. But this is different. Now it is *imperative* that he should live, for he is so vital, so different, so — so *Gil*. In him pneumonia is so much worse, so much more threatening ——

And then she shook her head in irritation at herself, aware that her mind was becoming woolly with fatigue, for she slept little in that first forty-eight hours. She could not, for Gil was a most demanding patient, rarely lying peacefully but tossing his head, and throwing his body about in ways that made his need for air much greater, and so made his breathing even more difficult. Unless she sat beside him with her towel, stroking, bathing, drying and bathing again, he developed this restlessness, and she felt the need that was in him as though it were a steel manacle tying her to his sofa.

But of course he slept sometimes, and then she would not move, for fear of waking him, but would sit there on the floor with her head resting on the edge of the sofa, to snatch what sleep she could. Sometimes, when the man came from the restaurant kitchen above with the trays of sandwiches for her and the cups of beef tea and calves'-foot broth that she demanded for him, he would rally a little, and behave more like himself, telling her in his weak voice to go and sit at the table and take her food there. He seemed then to be quite sensible, fully aware of all that was going on about him, but then, as the first two days melted into the third, and the theatre emptied — for now it was Christmas and there would be no performances until St Stephen's Day — he sank deeper and deeper into his stupor, and she became more and more alarmed.

She thought seriously of sending for a physician, but decided against it, for who was there that she could ask who could tell her more than she already knew? He had an infection of the lungs that must somehow heal itself, if he was to live. No physician alive could change that or advise any better care than she was giving, and well she knew it. It was not arrogance in her — though she did ask herself if it were during the particularly dark afternoon, when the fire had sunk low in the grate and the silence from the great building all around her filled her with foreboding — but common sense. She had in her early years in Haworth, and in her time in London since, learned enough of her skill to have the self-confidence that knowledge brings. She knew, and needed no one else to confirm her sureness.

And so she struggled on alone, doggedly living each moment as it came, thinking nothing about the one that had gone before or the one that was to come. There was but now, and Gil's noisy breathing and her own bone-deep fatigue.

By the morning of Christmas Day her spirits were at their lowest ebb. The restaurant had left enough food, the night before, to see her through, they said, and indeed they had left more than enough, for she had lost her own appetite and was subsisting on little more than bread sippets and cups of tea which she brewed over the fire in the small grate. Hollingshead had seen to it that ample coal was brought up before going off for the Christmas holiday, offering — with ill-disguised unwillingness — to remain and help her, but she had refused that at once, assuring him that they would sort well enough, she and her patient. And so he had gone, and all the actors and dancers and chorus girls and scene shifters and stage assistants, that whole great army of entertainers had gone leaving her feeling as alone as she ever had in the middle of the echoing emptiness.

It was curious, she thought, sitting beside Gil and watching him breathe his painful shallow uneven breaths, how at Tansey Clough, alone there on the moor, I could feel so comfortable, but here, with the noise of traffic just outside the window and a great city teeming all around me I feel as alone and as frightened as I have ever been in all my life. I must be losing control of myself. I must not let it happen, I must not be frightened. Please, Gil, please get better ——

It was at three in the afternoon that she felt the crisis was upon him. The room was dark, for she had not yet bothered to light the single oil lamp that served as her illumination, and the fire had sunk to little more than a sullen glow. She could just see his face in the grey afternoon light thrown through the window, and she sat and stared at him, trying to focus on his pale sweating face.

It was more than she could bear, then. She could not sit there any longer, and jumped to her feet and moved across the small room to press herself against the dulling window, to stare back through the shadows at the humped shape that was his body under the blankets and the faint blur that was his face against the pillow. This fight with his disease was one he must fight alone. She had done all she could and now she had to withdraw, to let the battle go on without her puny aid. For good or ill, he was alone, he and his disease, and they would sort out their differences in their own way.

She stood there, her feet braced against the floor, her knees locked, feeling the cold of the window glass through the fabric of her gown across her shoulder blades, and closed her eyes. She was not praying exactly, for although, like everyone else, she went to church and accepted that upright Christian behaviour was right and proper, she had no deep religious convictions, and had never found it possible to pray with any real feeling to a deity she could not know, let alone love. But for all that she was not praying, she was yearning for his recovery, begging whatever or whoever it was that controlled individual human destiny to regard Gil with compassion, to allow him to keep in his own hands the life he had had so short a time.

Perhaps she slept standing there; she could not be sure. Time again stood still, became an eternity, and after a while she opened her eyes.

The room was almost completely dark now, and her feet and legs were icy cold and she moved a little, straightening up, and pins and needles burned her toes and made her clumsy, so that her shoe clattered against something unseen on the floor.

She stood still again, and listened, straining her eyes towards the sofa but could hear and see nothing. No sound of breathing, no rustle of blanket as he moved, just an ear-ringing stillness that was ice cold with fear, and she had to force herself to move then, had to make herself fumble her way to the desk and find the box of vestas beside the lamp.

She stood holding the box in her hand for a long moment before striking a match, just standing there in the darkness and hearing her own pulse loud in her ears. Was he dead? Had she, in her weakness, left him to die alone on his sofa, without even the comfort of another human hand in his? Had she failed him at the time he needed her most?

She trembled then, feeling the tension in her muscles begin to shake her, and with a huge effort took a vesta from its box and struck it on the corrugated base and reached for the lamp. She could have looked at him then in the light of the match but she controlled that need, kept her eyes firmly on the lamp and, with every bit of concentration she had, took off the glass chimney and set the match to the wick. The matchstick curled and died and she put the chimney back on the lamp, and then its globe, fiddling with the wick with great punctiliousness, turning the little knob with tiny movements in order to set the flame at just the right height, enough to light the room, but not enough to smoke the chimney with smudges of lamp black.

And when she had done that she picked up the lamp and, moving with great care — for still her muscles shook and threatened to let her down — crossed the room, holding the lamp high, to come to stand beside the sofa and look down at Gil.

He had flung one arm up above his head and turned his head away towards the wall, and at first she could see nothing, no movement, no sign of breathing and she thought bleakly, 'He is dead. I left him and he is dead ——'

She leaned forwards, holding her lamp high and looked down on him and then, his head moved, turning towards her on the pillow, and she could see that his face was not beaded with sweat as it had been for so long, that the awful pallor with the high hectic flush on each cheekbone had gone. He looked more normal now, pale still, but with the pallor of life, not incipient death. And his breathing — his breathing, glory be, was normal. Easy breaths, silent and tranquil. The crisis had passed and he was sleeping as easily as though he had never been ill in his life.

And now the trembling set in in good earnest and she had to let her knees buckle so that she sat on the floor beside him, and she put the lamp down beside her, and bent her head and took a deep breath. The crisis was over and he had lived. From now on, all he had to do was regain his strength and he would be as well as he had ever been. He was not going to die. And for the first time she allowed herself to weep, the tears running down her face and dripping from the end of her nose as she luxuriated in all the fear and dread that had filled her, and which up to now she had not dared acknowledge.

*   *   *

She woke slowly, luxuriously, letting the last shreds of sleep ebb away, making no effort either to hold on to slumber or to force herself out of it, just natural, easy sleep, leaving her in its own time.

She opened her eyes slowly too, blinking easily in the cold morning light, staring upwards and was puzzled, for her skylight, that square of sooty glass in her ceiling that was the only source of light that her attic room had, was not there, and she frowned and turned her head to look about her.

She was lying curled in a blanket on the rag rug before the dead fire in the grate, and as she stretched and moved she felt the chill of the room creep into her. It was bitterly cold and suddenly, almost violently, she remembered, and tried to jump to her feet, but only succeeded in tangling herself in her blanket so that she tumbled back on to the rug.

'Oh, such a doctor as is my Sophie.' His voice sounded thin and a little weak, but blessedly, unmistakably his, and as she untangled herself and managed to get to her feet properly she looked at him and felt a grin of sheer pleasure stretch her cheeks.

221

He was lying on his side, one arm crooked under his head, looking at her. He was pale but not unduly so, and showing no sign of fever and his eyes seemed bright enough and she hurried towards him, her hands held out and said breathlessly, 'Oh, my dear, and how *are* you this morning?'

'How am I? Dear doctor, how can I tell? You must tell me ——' But he grinned and moved and with a little effort pulled his other hand from the blankets and held it out to her.

'I am well, my dear. I have but a hazy memory of what has happened, but I know I have been feeling quite dreadfully, dreadfully ill. I opened my eyes a half-hour ago and looked about me and knew that I was better. Not altogether — indeed, I feel as weak as a cat ——' and he grimaced and squeezed her hand. 'But better. Undoubtedly better.'

'You woke half an hour ago? Foolish Gil, why did you not wake me? You must be chilled to the marrow, and you need warmth and building up now ——'

'Oh, do not scold me! I had so much pleasure lying here watching you there in your rug, and remembering.'

'Remembering?'

'Indeed, yes. I have been ill, I know, and not always filled with enough energy to talk, but I have not been quite insensible. I have known what is happening, and how you have cared for me and — thinking of it this morning gave me so much comfort. That and looking at you.'

'I must light the fire,' she said, suddenly filled with an embarrassment she could not understand. 'It is bitter cold in here and unless I do, you will be ill again — no, do not stop me, Gil!' for he was holding her hand tightly still. 'But let me set about making you comfortable ——'

He let her go and watched her as she set about work, first riddling out the fire and relighting it, using papers she found in a drawer of the desk and which Gil assured her were of no significance, and some sticks she found in the housemaid's scullery at the end of the corridor, so that the room lit up with the flicker of new flames and cheered to the crackle of the burning wood.

And then she bustled more, filling the kettle and setting it to heat over the flames, so that she could wash him and make him comfortable, and while she waited, tidying the room.

He complained a bit when at last she bore down on him with a basin of hot water and insisted on washing him, but she would not be gainsaid, and he gave in, weak as he was, and admitted to enjoying the comfort of having his face washed.

'Although a shave as well is much needed, I expect,' he said, touching his chin which was indeed well covered in stubble. 'Or shall I grow a beard and be a patriarch?'

'You may stop wasting your strength on talking nonsense,' she said, 'and let me get to your arms and legs to wash them too ——'

Now he really did protest. 'I cannot allow — Sophie, where is your modesty — I cannot ——'

'Oh, pooh to such modesty,' Sophie said calmly and set to work, easily overcoming his attempts to prevent her. 'Who do you suppose dealt with all your creature needs this past two days? Ill as you were, your body still worked as it needed to, and someone had to deal with the matter! So I did. But when I have washed your legs, I shall give you this chamber pot and you can deal with that yourself this time. Then, while I empty the slops, you may wash those parts of yourself you will not allow me to! Though I have blanket-bathed many a sick man in my time, and find it not a whit disturbing, I would not distress you — there now, I will leave you with the pot while I go forage for some food for you. And when I return, and have removed all this and freshened your bed, we shall see about some breakfast.'

She found the kitchen empty of people and with most of the larders locked, after wandering through many corridors and pushing her way past many doors. Once there, however, she managed very well, finding in the only open cupboard bread to make toast at her fire, and some milk and some tolerable raspberry jam and took her spoils back to the office-cum-sickroom as proud as if she had procured a Lucullan feast of caviare and champagne.

He was waiting for her, his hands folded demurely over the blanket and looking more comfortable, and she smiled and said nothing, just quietly taking away the chamber pot and the wash basin and then making his makeshift bed as comfortable as she might, propping him up on extra towels, folded thick behind his pillows.

And then she made breakfast for both of them, toast and jam and hot milk and they ate and drank, and it seemed to Sophie that never had any meal tasted better. As for Gil — he wolfed the food and licked his fingers and asked for more, and laughing, she made more and watched him eat with as much pride as if she had been a mother and he a promising infant.

'There will be people here soon, I imagine,' she said when he had at last had enough, and she had cleared away the cups and plates and left all tidy in the housemaid's cupboard. 'I have enough coal to last us, I think, until mid-afternoon, and then, of course, we will need more food, and there is little enough in the kitchens — I imagine they have fresh food brought each day. I wonder if they will be there later on as well?'

'Oh, yes, they will,' Gil said lazily. He was lying back on his pillow now, sleepy and comfortable and he turned his head and looked at her, blinking a little. 'St Stephen's Day, you say? To think that I have missed Christmas altogether! Yes, they will be here. There is no matinee today, but an evening performance, so people will arrive at five o'clock or thereabouts to set all in hand. And the restaurant will open tonight as well, for the Gaiety likes to make money, you know, and misses no opportunity — why are we talking about such nonsense?'

'That is not nonsense, Gil, when we are alone here! Until people come, there can be no coals and no food and no ——'

'I have need of none while you are here,' he said and his voice was husky and he took her wrist in a would-be hard grip — though he was still very weak — and made her look at him. 'Dear Sophie, you have saved my life.'

'Oh, such rubbish,' Sophie said, awkwardly. 'I did but offer a little simple nursing. No more than that ——'

'Diminish it if you will — I know better. Sophie, you are the dearest, the gentlest, the strongest ——'

'It is not possible to be both gentle and strong, you know that — that is a contradiction in terms, is it not? And you really must not waste your strength in ——'

'I will not be stopped! Listen to me!' He was beginning to sound fretful, like a child, and well aware of how weakness after such an illness can upset the nerves, she subsided. His way of talking was embarrassing her and she wanted to stop him and yet — and yet she did not. There was a choking excitement in the intensity with which he was staring at her, and in the grip of his hand on her wrists. And she liked it.

'I want to tell you — I remember so much of what you did for me, of the tender care you gave me and — I can never thank you enough. But that is not what I want to say now. No — it is not. I want to say now — I must say now — that I love you dearly, Sophie. I love you more than I can possibly express and if you do not agree that you will marry me, and live always with me then my life will not have been worth the saving. It is all yours, Sophie, every atom of it. Please say you will take it because I could not bear it if you did not.'

CHAPTER TWENTY-THREE

'Gil, you must understand that I cannot do it to them. It is bad enough I have been away for fully two years and not been able to go home to visit. I cannot now tell them such momentous news as this in just a letter! You cannot expect it. I must go home. I will go home.'

'Why cannot they come to you? Who is there, after all? You have told me you are an orphan, and all the relations you have in the world seem to be here in London. Who is there in Haworth who can be so important?'

'Bessie, for a start. And I could never expect her to make so long a journey,' Sophie said. 'She reared me from my earliest infancy, and truth to tell. was more to me than my mother was, wicked as that may sound. My mother was an invalid, you see, and it was Bessie who had care of Letty and me — I must see Bessie. And then there is Doctor Tom. And Wilfred ——'

She stopped then and stared into the fire. In all the excitement of these past weeks she had thought hardly at all about what effect her news might have in Haworth. She had been too busy nursing Gil to full health again — and indeed he had recovered excellently, for it was now the last week in January and he seemed as fit and energetic as he had ever been — and arranging to have time free from her studies at the medical school, which had not been a problem, fortunately, so advanced in her work was she, and of course dealing with the hostel, where her usual duties still had to be performed. But now, sitting beside the fire in the dining room on this dull winter afternoon, she had time to think. Time to wonder how Wilfred would be when she told him.

It had been last night, lying in her attic bed and staring up at the skylight that she had decided she would have to visit Haworth. She and Gil had sat for a long evening, talking and murmuring and being generally lover like — and she had not fended off his kisses with quite as much propriety as she should have done, she had to admit — and Gil had talked of the day to come when they would wed.

And suddenly, for the first time, it had all come home to her. Ever since Gil had made his avowal there in John Hollingshead's office at the Gaiety Theatre and she, almost stunned by the sheer weight of his emotion, had accepted him, she had gone about in a sort of trance. She had told no one of her new status as an engaged girl, not even Aunt Martha, for whom she had so much affection. It seemed important to her to keep it all hidden and held close, to avoid any exclamations and discussion. But now she knew that someone would have to be told, and the first someone would have to be in Haworth.

But who was it in Haworth who mattered most? Was it Bessie and Doctor Tom? Or was it Wilfred, the boy with whom she had grown up, the sensible dear friend she had so long relied upon for good counsel, the man she knew loved her and who had had to be prevented so often from declaring himself and asking her to wed him?

She still could not be sure who it was she was most concerned about; but there was one thing about which she *was* certain, and that was that she must visit Haworth.

She turned her head now and looked at Gil with appeal in her eyes. She needed him to understand and to agree to let her go and to do so with a good heart. It would be dreadful if he did not, and they had a quarrel about it, they who had not quarrelled once since that first stormy meeting at the theatre.

He turned his head and looked at her, and his eyes glinted in the firelight, and his curly hair framed his face and shadowed it a little and for a moment she thought her appeal had not been heard. But then he leaned forwards and his face came fully into the firelight and he was smiling and her whole body seemed to fill with relief.

'Well, so be it. If you must go, then you must. But you shall not go alone. Hollingshead said I may take as long as I wish before returning to rehearse the next production, and I can spare a week or two now, I believe. I shall come with you and meet these special Yorkshire people of yours and tell them I have laid claim to you, and that they must let go, for now you are mine, all mine.'

'Gil! You will come too? But will not that — I mean, I did not think ——' She blinked at him and tried to push away the first thought that had come into her head; that she did not wish him to accompany her. Haworth was home, it was her childhood, all her past, and he had no part in it. But that was an ignoble thought, a very selfish one, for had she not promised to spend all of her future with him? Had he not a right to share her past with her? She must learn not to be so private. From now on she would be one of two, not herself alone.

'And we will do more than visit Haworth, my love. We shall visit Bedford! For I too have people who should be told our splendid news. I have a father and a mother there who will wish to see you and welcome you, as a new member of the Stacey clan.'

At once she was filled with compunction. She had been so selfish in desiring to make her journey home alone, and here he was, offering her his own family without being even asked! She had known he had parents, although he had not spoken much about them, and had not for a moment thought to ask if she could meet them. Yet he had thought about it ——

'Oh, Gil! That will be splendid! We shall make a tour, shall we not? We could go to Bedford first, and then on to Haworth — it will be a most exciting journey ——'

'When shall we start? Now? This very second, tonight?'

She laughed and leaned forwards and patted his cheek. 'Dear Gil! I think you know that we will need a little time to collect some necessaries and to buy tickets — and to let them know we are coming ——'

'No, let us not do that! I would much rather, indeed I would, that we surprise them. It will be much more amusing to do that than to send news ahead, for that will expose us to the risk of great formal welcomings. If word gets about in Bedford that I am to visit, half the town will be at the station to meet us. Let us, for pity's sake, keep it informal.'

'But I promise you no one at Haworth would do such a ——'

'Please, Sophie? I would much prefer it. I cannot bear to think that everyone will be expecting us, and talking of us, and trying to guess what sort of a man I might be, and surmising and, and — oh, you know how people are! Let me arrive unknown, to make friends in my own way. It is much better than having to overcome previously drawn conclusions.'

And Sophie had to agree that he spoke good sense. If she wrote ahead to tell Bessie that she was bringing her affianced bridegroom, the whole village would be in possession of the news in no time, and tongues would wag apace; Gil would undoubtedly be the cynosure of all curious eyes the moment he stepped off the train. He was entitled to ask protection from that.

So, she did not write ahead. She told Aunt Martha she was going home for a visit, and begged to be excused her duties in Villiers Street for the necessary time, and Aunt Martha willingly agreed, and looked at her closely and with such warm affection in her eyes that the words to announce her engagement trembled on Sophie's lips for a moment; but still she did not tell her. There would be time enough for that when they had returned from their visits. And the whole purpose of the visit was, after all, to tell her closest people at home first. No, Martha must wait for this titbit of news. And Sophie went away from Bedford Row with her secret still intact.

They set out, each bearing just one small valise, on the first day of February, taking an exceedingly early train — at seven in the morning — from King's Cross to Bedford. Sophie had objected at first at such an early start, for the journey took but an hour and a half behind one of the splendid new steam locomotives the Midland Railway had recently introduced, but he was adamant that this was the best time.

'I know my parents, my dear. My father is a most hardworking man — he owns a manufactory where engines are made, you know — and is busy indeed once the day has started. If we reach Bedford later in the day he will not have enough time to see us. And also I am most anxious that you meet him early in the day, when he is still fresh and cheerful rather than at the end when he is a little more likely to be fractious, for a tired man you know ——'

'Is he an — irascible person?' Sophie said, a little nervously. 'I am beginning to think he sounds most formidable!'

'Oh, he can be a little difficult at times, I suppose,' Gil said airily, but did not look at her, settling her in her seat in the corner of their second-class carriage with much careful arranging of her rug. 'But I am sure you will charm him ——'

The journey was pleasant enough, as the train steamed its majestic way through the frost-spangled fields, and they sat close and comfortable, while Gil amused her with whispered comments about their fellow passengers which were scurrilous in the extreme and made her giggle. But underneath she felt a pull of anxiety. There was something in Gil's manner and voice when he spoke of his father that did not quite ring true. His words painted him as a pleasant enough person, and yet there was a nervousness in him that made her wonder.

Her doubts, she discovered, were fully justified. At Bedford, a small and rather dull town but one that seemed comfortable enough, they took the station fly and were carried at a spanking pace out of the centre towards a clearly prosperous area where large redbrick houses, planted about with heavy shrubs that protected their privacy with some hauteur, bespoke residents of considerable affluence.

Gil's father's house was one of the largest and most prosperous looking, with white stucco pilasters in front of an imposing heavy oak front door, and windows swathed in large quantities of clearly costly Nottingham lace. The grass in front of the house was shaven as close as a monk's tonsure, and the laurel bushes had leaves so shiny and so tidy that Sophie wondered if gardeners spent their time polishing each one.

The door bell was answered by a maid in a very frilled cap and apron who stared at Gil for a moment and then put her hand to her mouth and looked nervously over her shoulder.

'Why, Mr Gilbert! We didn't know as you was expected, sir.'

'I'm not, Ellen,' Gill said easily, and stood back to allow Sophie to enter the house first. 'I chose to surprise 'em. Is my father at breakfast yet?'

'Yes, sir, they'm both in there — but Maister's a bit — well, sir, you know how 'tis.'

'I know!' Gil said cheerfully, but to Sophie there lay a hardness behind his light tone that made her more tense than ever. The house was dark inside, and again had the look of a great deal of effort with polish and soap. Heavy mahogany furniture, a great deal of engraved glass and thick red Turkey carpets made the entrance hall, with its thickly carved staircase, feel oppressive, and she shivered as the maid relieved her of her mantle.

'I'll go and see them,' Gil said easily. 'Wait for me, Sophie, my love. I shall return — perhaps you'd like to wash? Ellen, take Miss Lackland to set herself to rights ——' and he was gone, leaving

230

Sophie to follow the maid to a small bedroom on the next floor where a washstand and mirror were available for her to tidy her rumpled hair and she could wash her hands.

The maid had gone away by the time she was finished, and after a moment she took a deep breath and decided to go and seek Gil. However difficult a man his father might be, he would hardly expect any guest in his house to hide away from him. It would be bad manners on her part not to seek him forthwith, so with some trepidation she made her way back to the hallway and looked about her.

She had not noticed through which door Gil had disappeared; only that he had gone towards the back of the large entrance hall, and she moved in that direction and then stopped. She could hear voices, loudly raised and then a lower feminine voice that sounded appealing and anxious, and Sophie frowned. Were they arguing, Gil and his parents, and he in the house not above a few moments? She knew so little about Gil, for all that she was engaged to him, and standing there in the middle of all the rich furniture and with the heavy smell of soap and beeswax polish in her nostrils she wondered more than she ever had before about his background. That the family were rich enough for anyone was clear; this house was obviously the residence of a man of means. But there was another message here, a sense of heaviness and tension that must surely emanate from the man who owned it.

She lifted her chin then as the voices subsided and became just a faint rumble. Standing here wondering was going to get her nowhere; she must meet this mysterious Mr Stacey and see for herself, and with a steady step she walked forwards and set her hand to the door from behind which the voices had seemed to come, and opened it.

She was in a morning room, a warm bright room, well furnished with the same sort of rich furniture that the hall had, but yet not giving quite so overwhelming an impression. There was a bright fire burning in a burnished grate inside a most handsome marble fireplace, and a table in the middle of the room covered with a rich damask cloth and set for a most lavish breakfast.

Sitting at one end of the table, behind a magnificent silver tea and coffee equipage, was a thin lady in a white lace wrapper and cap and as Sophie came in she turned and looked at her with a

231

nervous glance that made Sophie think absurdly of the way sometimes the horses on the farms near Haworth would respond to a stranger coming too close. Her eyes seemed to become glaring and terrified, and then, even as Sophie thought it, the look had gone and the lady looked down and became just a quiet middle-aged woman at her breakfast table.

In front of the fire stood a thin man of medium height, but with a marked stoop, which made the way he thrust his head forwards seem even more pronounced, and Sophie thought, 'He looks like an angry tortoise —— ' and wanted to giggle. How could she be so wicked as to compare her betrothed's parents to animals in this way?

Gil was standing in the window embrasure, his legs apart and his hands thrust deep into his trouser pockets. Sophie glanced at him, but it was difficult to see his face clearly for the light from behind him dazzled her vision and she blinked.

'Sophie!' Gil said, and his voice was clipped. 'I had hoped you would wait until I came to fetch you —— '

'So! This is the — *lady* — is it?' the older man said in a high cracked voice. 'This is the person who is to bear my name, is it?'

Sophie looked at him and smiled. 'Yes, sir, I am happy to say I am. How d'you do?'

'Hmmmph. Happy, are you? Well that's as may be — no reason why you should be otherwise, is there? Every woman wants a husband, I suppose, and every woman must be happy to catch one —— '

Sophie's brows lifted. 'I am not every woman, sir, but myself. And I must tell you that husband catching has never been one of my ambitions.'

'Aye, ambition is a word with you, is it not?' The high voice seemed suddenly to fill with wrath. 'Goin' to be one o' these damned women doctors, Gilbert tells me! I never heard of such a crackbrained notion in my life! What does a decent female want with such things, hey? What sort of a female is it that so forgets her modesty and her manners as to even think of such things? Here's Gilbert, son of as respectable a lady as ever drew breath, who should have had more sense with such an example before him than to choose a female that talks of *ambition*. Hey, Louisa, ain't that so? Ain't it?' And he turned his head and glared at the silent woman behind the teapot.

232

'Yes, dear.' The thin woman did not look up. She sat with her hands crossed on the table before her and her eyes cast down.

'You see? No decent woman but isn't disgusted by one that takes such worms into her head as to think she should be a damned quack! You see, miss, that I make no effort to moderate my language for you, for I tell you straight I have a sickener of women with ambitions and do not regard them as any sort of ladies as need protection from a man's rougher tongue.'

'And what of your wife, sir? Is she not a lady needing protection?' Sophie's colour was high and now her own temper was seething just below the surface. Whatever else she had expected it had not been this attack, and she looked sharply at Gil to see how he was reacting to his father's use of her, but he was standing in the same posture, his face still shadowed by the light behind him.

'Don't you play at words with me, madam!' Mr Stacey thrust his head even further forwards, if that were possible, and glared at her. 'In my own home, I shall speak as I please and no damned man-woman is goin' to tell me what ——'

'Gil, I am sorry, but I think I must leave,' Sophie said quietly and turned to the door. 'I had hoped to meet your parents as — as a new daughter. I had not expected this attack. You must forgive me for being unable to remain longer.'

'I would not ask it of you,' Gil said, and his voice was now tight and very low, with none of the easy bantering tone that was usually so much a part of it. 'I will fetch your mantle at once, and we shall go.'

He came to the door and opened it, and then set one arm round Sophie's shoulders, and turned back to look at the silent woman at the table. 'Well, I tried, Mamma. Never let it be said I did not try. When we parted and he behaved as he did because I chose to make my life in the theatre, I put his behaviour and — and his abuse down to his disappointment. I was prepared to swallow all the cruel things he said and forget them, and hoped in bringing my chosen wife to see you that we could regain the semblance of a normal family. Well, that is not to be. I am sorry. Goodbye, Mamma. As for you —' and he lifted his chin and stared across the white breakfast table at the man still standing in front of the fire. 'May you rot in hell! On the day of your funeral, I shall celebrate in champagne ——' And then he turned and, pulling Sophie with him, marched out of the room.

Sophie looked back just once to see the quiet woman still sitting there at the top of her table, her head still bent and her hands still crossed in front of her. It was as though nothing had happened, nothing at all. The man by the fire was white-faced and opening his mouth to shout back at Gil, but Gil pulled the door hard to behind him and hurried Sophie across the hall to where the frightened-looking maid was standing, their wraps across her arm.

'I knew it would be so, Mister Gilbert,' she said in a low voice, barely audible under the great roar of shouting that was coming from the breakfast room. 'I knew as soon as I saw you how it would be — I wish you joy, Mister Gilbert, indeed I do ——'

'Thank you, Ellen. Take care of Mamma, poor weak creature that she is ——' Gil said. 'Come, Sophie.'

And less than half an hour after first setting foot in the house they were out in the frosty morning, walking down the gravel path and hearing the crunch of their boots against it, and saying not a word to each other. There seemed nothing useful to be said.

CHAPTER TWENTY-FOUR

'Well, I suppose I could have told you,' Gil said. 'But where would be the point? You might have said there was no sense in going there. I thought that perhaps, after all this time, the old fool would have realized that I was right to choose to live my life as I did, and would have been glad to see me about to be wed. But I was wrong ——'

'Why did he set about me so? I know that there are people who have a strong antipathy to the idea of women being physicians but he was — it was the outside of enough!'

'I know, and I have said I am sorry. But come, Sophie, you are one of the New Women, are you not? You are not like other women and unable to hold your own against your critics. You cannot tell me that you are distressed as that! I am angry with him, for being a pig-headed old fool, but no more than that!'

Sophie turned her head and looked out of the window. The train was fleeing north, leaving a great plume of steam behind it on the ice-grey sky and she should have been happy, for every second that passed was bringing her closer to Haworth and home and the joy there would be in Bessie's eyes when she saw her. But she could not be happy. She was still seething with anger at what had happened at Bedford.

They had walked back to the station, Sophie marching along with her chin up and a high colour in her cheeks, refusing even to talk to Gil about what had happened, and at the station, sitting in the warm buffet, drinking coffee and eating little biscuits as they waited for the next train north she had still been unable to talk about it all. But now, sitting alone in a second-class carriage — for trains in the middle of the day were far less crowded than the earlier ones — she had been able to put some of her confused anger into words.

Gil had, to her surprise, shrugged it all away. His father was a tiresome and very stubborn man, he told her. Always had been.

They had squabbled all his life that he could remember, and their years of simmering mutual loathing had erupted into a great and very noisy quarrel when Gil had announced he was going on the stage. His father had intended him for a career in engineering, expecting him to take over his manufactory in due course but, Gil said, he wanted nothing of such a plan.

'I am no engineer, and the thought of working with *him* — it could not be borne! So we parted bad friends, which I think saddened my mother, but she is so cowed by him it is impossible for anyone ever to tell what she is thinking and feeling. I have not seen them these five years, to tell the truth. But I thought, taking you with me, I could heal the breach. But — it is clearly not meant to be, so in taking me to husband, dear Sophie, you take no connections at all. And I feel that that can be a benefit you know, for I have heard enough stories of the miseries that mothers-in-law can inflict on young brides!'

'It is all too easy to make jokes, Gil. You should not have exposed me to it without warning — it was most unkind in you!' Sophie said wrathfully.

He shrugged. 'Come, don't make too much of it. As I said, my dear, if you are to brave the world as a physician, then you must be strong, and not expect to be treated as are other females. Do not fall into the trap of wanting to eat your cake and have it!'

At which she had to subside. For of course, he was right. That his father's attack on her had been as much born of the anger he felt towards his son as to any animus he felt towards herself was clear. And she should have been able to shrug it off, for Gil was clearly unhurt by it. He was sitting beside her now with his feet set comfortably on the facing seat and whistling softly through his teeth as he gazed out at the passing countryside; so why should she feel more than a passing irritation?

But she had to admit she did. She looked forlornly out of the window and told herself that indeed she did want to eat her cake and have it; to be able to follow a man's ambition in a man's world and yet be treated to the courtesies due to women; the careful protection, the tenderness. It was a disagreeable truth to face.

So she was far from happy as the journey stretched itself into its second hour and then its third, and Chesterfield and then Rotherham were left behind as Sheffield, with its great smoking chimneys, loomed on the far horizon. The soft south had disappeared, and rougher northern scenery fled past the windows and snow appeared on the fields and at last the memory of the morning in Bedford began to smart less and less, and her anticipation began to rise, filling her chest with excitement. She was going home, was going to see old friends, old sights, old joys. Home. The very word made her shiver with pleasure.

At Sheffield they had time to take a meal in the buffet, and Gil was in a towering good humour and teased and joked until at last she was laughing as heartily as she ever did with him. Now and again she found some of his jokes a little sharp-edged for her taste, for he poked a good deal of fun at some fat red-faced wool merchants, with their loud flat-vowelled Yorkshire voices, who were making a good deal of noise in the corner, but then she chided herself for being over-sensitive. To her ears, these Yorkshire voices were familiar and friendly, but it was understandable that one not used to them would find them funny. So she said nothing and allowed the jokes to roll over her head.

And then they were back in the train, and rushing onwards and ever more northerly as the short January afternoon melted into dusk, and the bright lights of the stations at Wakefield and Leeds and Bradford welcomed them into the bustle and excitement of shouting porters and grunting engines and hurrying nervous passengers. And now the anticipation that had filled her chest was consuming all of her, and cold as it was she wanted to lean out of the window and point out to Gil each familiar scene on the way to Keighley, the mills and the moors and the chimneys that had been part of her life as long as she could remember.

But he just grinned at her excitement and bade her sit tight and keep herself warm. 'For we shall die of frostbite, like a pair of sad Esquimaux, so far from home and comfort.'

'But this *is* home, Gil!' she bubbled at him, sitting down unwillingly and tucking her hand into the crook of his elbow. 'I could not be more happy to be here. And I can just imagine how dear Bessie will look when she sees me — eh, but there'll be a rare carry-on!'

He stared at her then, curiously. 'Can you speak in this local manner then? It sounds strange on your lips ——'

She laughed. 'Can I, lad? Eh, but tha's 'eerd nowt as yet! Just tha listen an' learn! Tha's i' Yorksheer nah, so think on!'

He grinned and shook his head. 'I'll have to practise it, sometime. You never know — the day may come when I can dance no more and must only act for my living and the ability to play a thick country bumpkin in a suitable voice will be most useful!'

'Not so thick, Gil,' Sophie said sharply. 'The local people may speak in a different manner, but never think they lack wits. For they do not, indeed they do not — oh, we are here! It is Keighley. Quick, my valise, and yours, and your rug — do hurry, for the train stops here only to take on new passengers before going on to Colne — and we must hurry to catch the connection for Haworth — the Worth Valley Line, you know ——'

They caught the connection, puffing hugely for they had to run, so long was Gil about collecting their valises and setting the rug to rights. Sophie sat in the little train on the edge of her seat, staring eagerly out of the window at every familiar thing she could make out in the gloaming, for it was now almost five in the evening, and the long winter's night was fast settling in.

'Where shall we go when we arrive, Sophie?' Gil's voice pulled her attention. 'To the inn? Or to your house?'

'I cannot say, Gil, as yet. Had you allowed me to write first, I know Tansey Clough would have been ready for us — but ——'

'Now, you must not blame me for that! I am sure that I did not mean to ——'

'Oh, I am not blaming you, my dear! Just explaining that I do not know how Bessie manages now. She is married, you see, to the ostler at the inn, and may not go to Tansey Clough so often. We must, I think, go up to the Black Bull and see what happens there ——' and she hugged herself with another surge of delight at the thought of arriving unheralded at the Black Bull.

At Haworth station the driver of the little battered fly peered at her in the dim light thrown by the lamp swinging over the ticket barrier as they made their way through and then beamed from ear to ear.

'Nay, but if it bain't Miss Lackland — eh, lass, but tha's welcome 'ome — an reet peaky tha's lookin! 'As tha bin all right in that theer Lunnon? 'Tis a mucky place, Ah'm thinkin', specially for a lass as 'ad the benefits o' livin somewheer better! Eh, well, yon Bessie'll soon have thi bonnie agen, when she gets some of 'er cookin' into thee. An' be this thi young man, then? Eh, but time do go on — it's nobbut a minute or two since thi was a little lass screechin' about t'moors like a peewit ——'

He talked busily all the way to the Black Bull, as the fly creaked and swayed up the cobbled street towards the inn, and Gil, holding on for dear life to the sides cursed softly under his breath.

'Do they all talk so much?' he whispered at Sophie. 'And is it always as bitter cold as this? That wind will take my ears off!'

'No they don't and yes it is!' Sophie said, and lifted her chin and took a deep breath of the icy blast that was whistling round them. 'And doesn't it smell marvellously clean? Not a trace of soot — Jesse, tell me — is Bessie there at the inn, do you know? Or in her own house? Or where?'

'Nay, lass, she could be any place. Tha knows Bessie Pighills! Or Bessie Oldenshaw, I should say — known 'er all 'er life, an' can't get used to 'er bein' wed to yon Oldenshaw. If tha likes, Ah'll go in an' ask for thee, an' if she's away at 'er own place, Ah'll tak' thee theer right away ——'

'No, don't do that, Jesse. Wait in the yard or have some beer while I seek her — I want to surprise her.'

'Eh, tha'll do that, lass, an' never fear otherwise! She'll be fair moithered ——' and the old man cackled in great glee as at last the fly turned into the yard of the Black Bull.

Sophie hardly waited for it to stop before she jumped down, and then turned and held out her hands to Gil.

'Do come, my dear — we shall soon have you warm again. Wait until you see the great blaze that waits you here in the parlour — William Sugden keeps as cosy an establishment as any you ever saw. And there will be mulled ale, too, if you feel the need of it.'

Gil, moving stiffly, climbed down, and at once she turned and hurried eagerly through the dark yard, and pushed open the door to the parlour.

She stood blinking a little in the light, and then Gil pushed her from behind and said a little fretfully, 'Please, let me in, my dear, before my frozen limbs drop off and clutter up the yard!'

'Oh, my love, I am so sorry,' she said and led the way in and he came after her decidedly blue about the cheeks and went at once to the huge fire that was blazing, just as Sophie had promised, in the deep inglenook fireplace.

He bent towards the flames, rubbing his hands and looked at her over his shoulder, grinning. 'Marvellous! I never thought to see anything so civilized this side of Birmingham. I always thought that in these parts men wore woad to keep their spirits up, but at the sight of this fire I grow more sanguine. Now, if there were some of that ale you mentioned ——'

'Nay, Ah doan't believe it — it canna be — nay, but 'tis — Miss Sophie, eh, tha wicked lass, not to tell me tha was comin' 'ome — eh, Sophie, lass, but it's grand to see thee — coom an' let me — eh, lass!'

Sophie whirled, her smile splitting her face from ear to ear, and holding her arms wide. Bessie was standing in the curtained doorway that led to the deeper recesses of the inn, her face red with pleasure and her square figure tense with excitement.

They fell into each other's arms in a great flurry of skirts, with Bessie half crying and half laughing and Sophie assuring her in a tumble of words that yes, she was well, and no, there wasn't anything amiss, she had just wanted to surprise dear Bessie, and yes they would like some ale and some supper; and how was Josiah and what was news of Doctor Tom? And on and on as Bessie first exclaimed and then tried to answer her questions and then exclaimed again. And Jesse, the wrinkled driver of the fly stood in the doorway and grinned proprietorially — for he had been unable to resist the chance to be the bearer of tidings and had hurried round to the kitchen to tell Bessie the momentous news of her Miss's arrival — and William Sugden busied himself at his bar, preparing mulled ale.

When the excitement had died down a little, and Jesse had been sent off with his foaming mug, Sophie drew Bessie towards the fire.

'Bessie, I want you to meet somebody,' she said and reddened, and Bessie looked at her sharply and then at Gil, now sitting comfortably in the inglenook with his feet stretched to the blaze. 'This is Mr Gilbert Stacey.'

'How do you do, Bessie,' Gil said easily but he did not get up and Bessie glanced at Sophie again and then smiled broadly.

'Well, lass, an' abaht time, too! I told thee to stop thi lakin' about an' get thissen an 'usband! Ah'm reet glad to meet thee, Mr Stacey,' and she held out one red hand to Gil who took it and shook it solemnly.

'I didn't tell you we were to be wed!' Sophie protested and Bessie laughed.

'Since when did I 'ave to be told owt about thee, lass? Coom away! Knew as soon as Ah clapped e'en on 'im as 'e were thy lad! I wish thee joy, I do that ——'

There was another little orgy then of hugging and kissing as Bessie threw her arms about Sophie and congratulated her most fervently. Then they settled to supper and Gil had his promised ale, and Bessie, after some pressure from Sophie, agreed to sit by the fire with them to give her all the news of Haworth.

By the time Gil had finished the last of his ale it was past seven o'clock, and Bessie jumped to her feet as the grandfather clock in the corner chimed the hour.

'Eh, lass, this won't do! I must be away up to Tansey Clough and get redded up for thee! Tha'll want to sleep in thy own bed toneet — an' Ah'll set the back bedchamber to rights — thy fayther's — for Mr Gil 'ere ——'

'We'll go up together, Bessie,' Sophie said at once. 'For I cannot have you going up alone on so bitter a night! There'll be too much to do, perhaps. Would it not be better if we stayed here tonight?'

'Nay, lass, there's not that much to be done. I've been up every day fettlin' — never think I'd let owt go wrong up at Tansey Clough! I've nobbut to light t'fire and set 'ot bricks to t'beds an' it all be as reet as ninepence. Come thi away up at nine or so, an' I'll be waitin'. There's no call for thee to come now, for Oldenshaw'll tak' me up — Mr Sugden'll let 'im go, I'm sure, for we're done w't'day's work — come along at nine o'clock, then ——' And she was gone after giving Sophie yet another smacking great kiss, leaving them together at last in silence.

'Well!' Gil said at length. 'You told me that you have an old nurse who loved you, but my dear girl, you did not tell me her love verged upon adoration!'

Sophie smiled. 'Well, Bessie reared me, I told you that. And there is never any love like that of a good nurse for her children, is there? Do you not remember yours with affection?'

'I remember nothing of my past with affection,' Gil said lightly. 'I think only of the present with you when I wish to wrap myself in felicity!'

'Oh, my dear, I am sorry!' Sophie was at once filled with

remorse. She had in the excitement of her own homecoming quite forgotten how disagreeable his had been, and she got out of her chair, on the other side of the fire, and sat at his feet, resting her arms on his knees and looking up at him. 'Forgive me for being so low in tact! I meant no harm. Indeed I did not ——'

There was a small sound behind her and she turned her head, peering a little, for William Sugden had turned down a couple of the lamps, leaving the pleasant little parlour lit mainly by the dancing firelight and the glow of just one oil lamp on a low table.

'Who is that?' she said quickly, and remained still, her arms still crossed on Gil's lap, peering in the dimness.

To Wilfred, standing in the doorway, she looked so familiar, and yet so different. Her hair still had that springing curliness but it was dressed in a more sophisticated style now, pulled back on to the nape of her neck in a thick knot and the tendrils that framed her face were soft and very pretty. Her colour was different — no longer the familiar wild rose look of the country girl, but a sharper, shadowed pallor that sculpted her face into planes and hollows giving her a look of considerable wisdom. And her figure, that lissom curving figure that he remembered so often with such delight — he could hardly see her in her bell of skirt that billowed up round her as she sat there on the floor, resting her arms so familiarly on a strange man's knees.

He stepped forwards. 'Hello, Sophie,' he said quietly. 'It is very good to see you home again.'

She jumped to her feet and ran towards him, both hands outstretched. 'Wilfred, oh Wilfred, my dear, dear friend! How did you know I was here? Oh, foolish question! Jesse Hearnshaw, of course!'

'My dear, he could never bear to let anyone carry news about Haworth but himself. He came all the way to the Hall to tell me you were here, and I could not wait to see you. My mother — she too wishes to see you, now you are home. I did not wait for her, for she wished to dress suitably for the journey, but she is on her way. I am sorry.'

'Oh, dear Wilfred, you must not apologize for her good thought of me! It is most charming in her to come out on so cold a night to greet me.'

'Well, to tell the truth, my dear, I fear she is driven more by

242

curiosity than by concern — but that is perhaps unjust in me and I beg you to forget I ever said it.' He looked over her shoulder then at Gil who was still sitting sprawled in his chair, and staring at them. 'Will you not introduce me, Sophie?'

She reddened and turned at once to Gil. 'Oh, I am making a sorry cake of myself! It is so exciting to see old friends that I forget my manners. My dear — let me introduce Mr Wilfred Brotherton, my very dear friend. Wilfred, this is ——' and then she stopped.

In all the high excitement the evening had brought and the unexpected pleasure of seeing Wilfred — for she had not thought to meet him till the next day — she had totally forgotten how sensitive a situation this was. There sat Gil, looking up at the big square Yorkshireman, with one eyebrow slightly raised and a faint smile on his wide mouth and there stood Wilfred, stolid and far from subtle, staring down at him.

'Wilfred,' she said lamely, 'I meant to take some time to speak to you alone, before effecting this meeting, but — well, Jesse meant well, I am sure, in telling you I was here, but it does mean that — oh, dear. I am being rather foolish, I think. I had best just out with it, I suppose. Wilfred, Gil and I are to — we are to be wed.'

There was a short silence broken only by the crackle of the logs in the big fireplace and still Gil sat there, his legs outstretched and his face bearing that faint smile, and Wilfred stood still and stolid as an ox.

Then he said slowly, 'I am — I wish you joy.' But his voice was husky and Sophie looked at him sharply. He seemed to be much the same as he always was, but there was a white line round his mouth that was different, and his eyes had a blankness about them that alarmed her.

'My dear,' she said timidly, 'I hope I did not surprise you too much with the suddenness of my news.'

'I — ' He swallowed and tried again. 'I cannot deny I am taken aback, Sophie. I ought perhaps to have guessed, from your letters, but I suppose I did not wish to think — well, as I say I wish you joy —' He looked again at Gil then, his mouth once more taking on that hard white line. 'I ask you but that you take good care of her, Stacey. She is a — she is a rare person, our Sophie. Rare ——'

Gil got to his feet, lazily, and grinned. 'Your Sophie? Such a

243

strange way to express it! I understood that all her relations were dead and there were none here in Haworth to hold her affection but old servants.' And his eyes slid down Wilfred's rough jacket — for he was wearing a simple set of tweeds of the sort that were most warm and serviceable in these bitter Haworth winters, '— and such-like.'

'Gil! You know quite well that I told you of Wilfred and that he is my dear good friend.'

'Oh, of course you did, Sophie! Forgive me that it had slipped my mind. But then, I am not one that was ever much interested in past experiences. It is the present and the future that always concern me most. And the future, of course, is ours. Is it not, *my* Sophie?'

And he turned and looked at her, almost deliberately lifting his shoulder to exclude Wilfred, and Sophie reddened and bit her lip. That these two men would be hardly likely to care much for each other was obvious. Wilfred who had, she knew, always had an interest in her, and Gil, her new love, must obviously regard themselves in some sort as rivals but she had not expected Gil to be quite so coolly metropolitan. Wilfred might look a solid and indeed rather dull countryman in his unpressed tweeds but he was a gentleman for all that, and should be treated as such.

She opened her mouth to say something expostulatory to Gil, but she was too late. Wilfred with a sudden anger born of his shock at hearing Sophie's news so baldly put out one hand and took Gil by the shoulder; no doubt he did not mean to be rough but he was a working man of strong physique and his grip was hard.

Gil looked down at the hand on his shoulder and then, very slowly, up at Wilfred's face.

'Take your hands off me at once,' he said softly, but there was an edge in his voice that made Sophie feel very cold deep inside.

'Now, we'll have none o' this nonsense,' Wilfred said, not letting go. 'I may not be one of your fancy London mashers, but I know what's right. And it's not right to mock the friends of the lady who is to be your wife before her face. You mocked me — and you should apologize to Sophie for that ——'

'I apologize to no one,' Gil said with a sneer in his voice. 'Particularly when there is nothing to apologize for,' and he twisted his shoulder with one of his lithe dancer's movements, shrugging off Wilfred's hand remarkably easily, and then, with some ostentation, took his handkerchief from his pocket and flicked it over his coat where Wilfred's hand had lain.

It was a studied insult, and more than Wilfred could take, and before Sophie could realize what was happening, his hand was out and he had thrown a blow at Gil that connected with the side of his jaw and made his head snap back. And Gil, his eyes snapping with fury, whirled, and moving with a great deal of speed and grace started to throw blows back at Wilfred, which he, now very conscious of Sophie's cry of alarm, tried to parry without hitting back.

Within seconds the room was in an uproar as William Sugden came running, a lamp in his hand, to see what the hubbub was about, and then another ostler came and one of the maids, and all were staring at the two men, who were now standing in front of each other breathing deeply and with clenched fists but not, to Sophie's intense relief, attempting to strike each other again.

'Wilfred!' she said, and her voice was as icy as she could make it. 'How dare you behave so to a man who is a guest in Haworth? He meant no harm —' she stifled a faint doubt that perhaps, in fact, Gil had indeed meant to be insulting, '— and to strike him as you did was outrageous! How dare you behave so — how *dare* you? I will not have such things happen to — to my friends, and I beg you will make amends to Mr Stacey forthwith.'

There was a short silence and the back of Wilfred's neck began to redden as Gil, smiling again, relaxed and brushed his hands delicately against each other.

'It matters not a whit, my dear Sophie,' he said, his tone light and amused. 'Put it down to experience. I have never travelled in these parts before, and I did not, perhaps, realize how to behave to — local inhabitants. It matters not ——'

At which point there was a clatter in the yard outside and a raised voice and footsteps and there was Mrs Brotherton, swathed in furs, and looking as majestic as ever, in the doorway.

She seemed quite unaware of any tension in the room, but swept forwards, one gloved hand outstretched towards Sophie.

'Well, my dear! This is a surprise! I understood you had quite given us up and gone to London to be a surgeon, or some such thing! What do you do in these parts again?'

'Good evening, Mrs Brotherton,' Sophie said, as calmly as she could, for her heart was still racing in her chest and the pulses thumping in her ears made it difficult to concentrate. The few moments that had gone before had filled her with a mixture of alarm and anger that was disturbing in the extreme. But she tried to be as relaxed as she could, and even managed a thin smile for Mrs Brotherton's benefit.

'Indeed I did go to London to become a surgeon,' she said. 'And I shall complete my studies, which go well, never fear. I came back to —— '

'To introduce her husband-to-be,' Wilfred said harshly. He had not moved, but was still standing in the middle of the room, but his fists were no longer clenched and he looked much as he usually did.

There was a short, tight pause and then Mrs Brotherton, very slowly, smiled. It was a look of such self-satisfaction, such pleasure, that Sophie felt her pulse speed up again. This hateful woman, who had done all she could always to make her feel low and not good enough for her son, was *rejoicing* — and not because Sophie was to be happy, but because she was to wed someone other than her son. And there was nothing she could say or do to show she knew or to stop that self-satisfied smirk from spreading even further over that jowly face.

But there was worse to come, for then Mrs Brotherton said sweetly, 'Well, that shows just how serious your ambitions were, does it not? I always said, my dear, that you would never succeed, and though I am glad to wish you joy, I must say I knew you would never finish what you started when you went to London.'

'Indeed?' Sophie said icily. 'And what makes you think that, Mrs Brotherton? I may be promised to marry but that does not mean I shall be like so many women and use a wedding ring as an excuse to sit about and do nothing but spend my husband's money.' She felt a little better at getting that gibe in, and went on more insouciantly, 'As for your certainty that I will never complete my ambition — you are quite wrong. For I shall do so, married or not! I have every intention of qualifying and Gil has no desire to stop me from it, have you, Gil?'

But before Gil could answer, Mrs Brotherton's voice cut in: 'Well, of course that is as it may be. But as I understood the matter, you were to qualify and claim a great inheritance as a surgeon

246

named Lackland at that hospital there in London. And if you marry, of course, you change your name. So you will never get the legacy, will you, even if you do qualify? Wilfred, dear, do take me home. The smell of beer in here is really making me quite qualmish.'

CHAPTER TWENTY-FIVE

'Wilt there be owt else tha'll be wantin', Miss Sophie?' Bessie lingered at the door, the lamp in her hand, and looked worriedly at Sophie, who was sitting on the edge of her bed brushing her hair.

'Mmm? No, I don't think so, Bessie — you've done a marvellous job, making all so comfortable so quickly ——'

And indeed she had. They had come up across the moor, Gil complaining more than a little at the effort of walking through the thick packed snow in his thin town shoes, Sophie silent and tense as she remembered the look that Wilfred had thrown over his shoulder at her as he escorted his mother out to her carriage, to find Tansey Clough as welcoming as it was possible for it to be. Bessie had used her time well, and there was a great fire glowing in the sitting room grate, burnishing the brass to a dancing glittering busy-ness that was very cheering, and both her bedroom, so dear and familiar that her eyes prickled as she walked in, and the back bedroom were warm and welcoming with their own big blazes.

'I do thank you, Bessie,' she went on now. 'You made Tansey Clough look so special that I am sure Gil understood at once why I have always spoken so warmly of it.'

'Don't thi' go thankin' me, my lass, unless thee wants a clout across t'ears as'll mak' thy 'ead sing ——' Bessie said, but she seemed abstracted, staring at Sophie with a faint line between her brows. 'What is't, lass?' she said then abruptly. 'I left the two o' thee down at t'Black Bull as chirruppin' as a pair o' blackbirds and thi cooms walkin' in 'ere not two hours later wi' thy chins on t'ground. What ails thee? Hast thi 'ad a lover's tiff, then?'

'Bessie, really!' Sophie began and Bessie smiled a little sadly and shook her head.

'Nay, doan't go tellin' me to mind me own business. Thy business *is* my business, and tha can call me an interferin' old besom if tha likes, but it won't make no nevermind. Tha's the last o' my nurslings, the only folks tha has to call thi own, and I won't

248

be told to 'old off. So, what ails thee, lass? Tha can tell old Bessie, surely!'

Sophie put down her hair brush and bent her head so that the mass of curls swung forwards and hid her face. 'I'm sorry, Bessie,' she said at last. 'I did not mean to hurt your feelings. It's just that — oh, I don't know. I —— ' She looked up then and managed a smile. 'Is it not strange how different people are in different places? Gil in London is quite different from Gil in Haworth. I find myself wondering how Wilfred would be away from here. Would he seem so ill at ease? No, that is not the right word. Gil is not ill at ease —— '

'He's different, Ah'll grant thee that,' Bessie said. 'A good lad, Ah've no doubt — well, if 'e's thy choice, Miss Sophie, then there can't be no doubt. But he's — well, it's like seein' a parrot flyin' around t'moors all mixed oop wi' t'larks and peewits and t'other birds. Exotic, like —— '

Sophie smiled more widely at that. 'Yes, I think you are right, Bessie. Yet in London he does not seem at all exotic. Well, not particularly so! But to think of Wilfred there — I cannot imagine it —— '

'There's no call to imagine any such thing,' Bessie said, and then after a small pause. 'Is there?'

Sophie looked up, a little startled. 'How do you mean?'

'Well, tha's got me fair moithered! Promised to be wed to this Gil, and now wonderin' 'ow Wilfred Brotherton'd be dahn there in London! Why should thi bend thy wits over any such thing? Unless Wilfred be planning to come to London with thee. Is that it?'

Sophie shook her head vigorously. 'Of course he is not. He belongs here with the mill — and that hateful mother of his —— '

'Oh, is that it?' Bessie's face cleared at once. 'Has that old bat been upsettin' thee? I 'eerd as 'ow she were comin' 'ot foot from t'Hall to see thee at t'Black Bull — eh, lass, tha should know better than to let that old besom upset thee! Far be it from me to say owt ill about anyone but Ah'll tell thee this mooch — 'er mother didn't give good butter neither!'

Sophie laughed aloud at that. 'Oh, Bessie, you are really very insulting! You must not call Mrs Brotherton a cow, you know —— '

'Why not, when it's what she is? Yon Wilfred's an angel to put oop wi' 'er, I'll tell thee that. Tha doesna' want to pay any 'eed to

249

owt *she* says, Miss Sophie. She's a right villain, and likes nowt better than upsettin' folk.'

'Well, she upset me a little tonight, I cannot deny. Oh, I dare say I will sort it all out in my mind, in due course. My dear, go to bed. It is late, and you must be very tired. I shall see you in the morning — good night, dear Bessie.' She held out her arms and Bessie came and hugged her warmly and went away, but still with a faint frown between her brows. Whatever it was that Mrs Brotherton had said, Bessie told herself, as she settled down to sleep in the little room behind the kitchen that had been hers before she married, it had upset her Miss Sophie sorely. And anyone who did that deserved nothing but ill from any source. So, Bessie, Godfearing good Christian woman that she was, fell asleep wishing on Mrs Brotherton a painful death and an eternity in hell.

Sophie did not fall asleep so easily, however. She lay there in her own familiar half-tester bed, staring at the square of window gleaming a soft ghostly grey because of the heavy snow outside and her thoughts spun in her head, going over and over the same ground. Gil and Wilfred, Wilfred and Gil.

And the scenes of the day kept re-enacting themselves before her sandy-tired eyes. The pompous angry little man in Bedford with his cowed little wife. Wilfred and Gil in the parlour at the Black Bull. The rattle of the train wheels in the background as Gil talked about his parents, and the way he had parted from them. Over and over again it went on, until she could have screamed aloud with the fatigue and frustration and anxiety.

But it was not only fatigue that was undermining her, and she knew it. As the clock outside on the landing struck its sonorous way through the small hours and her weary muscles settled to a deep heavy ache, she knew that the evening's experiences and the day that had preceded them had changed her thinking. All the plans she had made, the future she had seen beckoning her so clearly, had become shadowed and confused. She, who had known so surely what she wanted, had been so certain of all that life was to hold for her, was as vacillating and as silly as any schoolgirl. And she hated herself for it.

But, some time after the clock struck four she came through her confusion. She had given up trying to control her mind, had allowed thoughts to come into her head as they wanted and slowly

250

and in their own good time, they ordered themselves. So she fell asleep at last, knowing what was to be done, and how to do it.

And her resolve held, for she woke again at six, when the sky was still a deep grey and there was still no promise of dawn anywhere on the horizon. Moving quickly in her now cold room, for the fire had at last died down, she dressed herself and pinned up her hair and crept, shoes in hand, down the polished staircase to the kitchen.

It was warmer here, for the fire was banked up in the range ready for the morning's needs and the faint red glow across the stone-flagged floor was friendly and reminded her of many childhood winter mornings when she had come creeping early from her bed to coax hot toast and milk from Bessie before anyone else was awake.

But now Bessie was still sleeping; Sophie could hear the soft burr of her snores from beyond the door that led to her little room, and it behoved her to be very quiet. So she set a pan of milk on the fire to warm and then sat herself down at the table, and took a sheet of paper and a bottle of ink and a pen from the drawer where she knew Bessie kept such necessaries and set herself to write her letter.

It took her some time to get it right. She made many false starts, but at last she managed to complete one that seemed to say what she needed to say, and she read it over, her head bent as she held it to the firelight to make it easier to read her own firm handwriting flowing over the pages.

'My dear Gil,' she had written. 'I know this letter will come to you as a shock, but I am afraid I cannot help that. It must be written nonetheless. Gil, I am going back to London forthwith. There will be no sense in your following me in any rush, for it is my intention to leave the Villiers Street hostel immediately and go elsewhere to live. And it would be pointless to seek me for another reason — I have decided, my dear Gil, that our plans to wed were ill thought out. It is not that I lack sufficient feeling for you; that is not the source of my decision. The problem is one more complicated than that. First, I am more deeply distressed than I would have thought possible at your father's feelings about me. It seems to me that marriage to me will finally kill any family bond that may remain between you. I keep remembering your Mamma, sitting so still and silent while your father spoke so about my wish to become a surgeon, and it worries me. I know that your ties with your parents have been strained to breaking point these many years, but,

251

dear Gil, you cannot ask me to be the final tug that breaks them altogether. I am convinced that were we to wed, that would be the result, and I do not think that I could bear it.

'But that is not all. I know that Mrs Brotherton is a disagreeable person whose opinions should matter little to me. Indeed, they do not matter as a general thing. But, she spoke last night more truly than she knew. She made me realize that it is not possible for a woman of ambition to follow her own heart as another woman can. If I am to succeed as a physician, let alone as a surgeon, then I cannot be deflected by such things as marriage. That may be suitable for other women, and much to be welcomed by them, and I am enough like other women to know I will feel deprived if I do not wed you and live a happy life with you. But that deprivation is the burden I must bear, for as you yourself said, dear Gil, yesterday in the train, I cannot eat my cake and have it. And I have decided, after long thinking all night that I will have it, rather than eat it. That is, I shall return to my work. I shall qualify as a physician and in due course somehow will achieve the training of a surgeon.

'You may think I have decided so because of the inheritance. I have not told you a great deal about this before, for I did not think it important to us, but the facts are that if I do become a surgeon and am accepted as one of those who work at Queen Eleanor's Hospital, I shall receive a handsome legacy. But understand me well; I do not seek this legacy now in order to enrich myself, and I do not refuse to wed you simply because doing so will change my name and make me ineligible to inherit. I do so because it is the ambition that matters, not the money, although I have a glimmering of a plan about what I shall do with it when I get it. As I intend to do.

'I hope you can understand all this, and understand me, and will accept the truth which is that I remain ever your affectionate, Sophie Lackland.'

She folded the letter carefully and inscribed his name on the front with a steady hand, and then, with her hot milk in a cup beside her, settled to write another letter, this time to Bessie. She told her little; simply that she was returning to London at once, having changed her plans, and bidding her take good care of Gil.

'I will write to you again from London, Bessie dear, but I will not tell you where I shall be. I have my reasons for this, which are hard for you to understand, perhaps — suffice it to say that I do not wish to see or speak to anyone about my private affairs, and it will be better if no one knows where I am. But I will be well enough, and have sufficient funds to manage. So do not fret, Bessie dear, but remember that I love you well and always shall. Until we meet again ——'

And then moving quietly and easily and with a curious sense of calmness, she left her letters on the kitchen table and laced her shoes and wrapped herself in her cloak, and, with her valise in her hand, took one last look at the familiar kitchen. When she would return to Tansey Clough she did not know. What would happen when she got back to London and took herself to Aunt Martha to tell her she was leaving Villiers Street — which was as far as her plans took her at present — she did not know, though she trusted Martha to behave wisely and well as she always did. All she knew now was that she was leaving her home behind her, and with it what hope of personal happiness she had. For Gil was very dear indeed to her, and she knew that there would be long hours in the coming days and weeks when she would ache for him, and hate herself for casting him off in this cavalier manner.

But it had to be done. Of that she was sure and she closed the door on the warmth that was within and began the long walk down across the snowy moor to Haworth and so on through the cobbled streets to the station to catch the first train of the day to Keighley. With luck, she told herself as she trudged through the darkness with the hard dry snow creaking under her feet, they will not wake at Tansey Clough for another hour yet. And by that time she would be well on her way and beyond recall.

She slept most of the way back to London, so deep was her exhaustion. Her need for sleep even overcame her distress, which was running deep, but at least the journey gave her time to satisfy that need and she arrived at King's Cross in mid-afternoon, a little dazed and rumpled, but still with that curious calmness that had sustained her ever since she woke up in the dark February morning at Tansey Clough.

Her plans had been but half formed; to come back to London and remove her property from Villiers Street had been as far as she had thought. But now she seemed to know just what was the necessary thing to do, and she did it.

She went first to Villiers Street and packed her remaining possessions. She had added but a few gowns to her scanty store in the past two years, but they were enough to increase her luggage to two large valises and a basket, and when they were all filled and the little attic room made anonymous again, with all her most prized possessions — her drawing of Haworth Church and Parsonage, her etching of the moors above Stanbury — removed, she went to talk to the cook and the two maids.

'I am afraid I must leave at once,' she told them collectedly, as they stood there in the kitchen and gawped at her. 'But I know you will be able to manage well enough for the next little while for I had made arrangements, had I not, to be away for a longer holiday than I in fact enjoyed. Miss Lackland from Bedford Row will see to it that another replaces me soon, but until then, I trust you three to see that all runs smooth and well.'

And they nodded and looked puzzled, but content enough, and Sophie sent the youngest one to call her a cab, and to carry her luggage to it, and stood in the narrow hallway, looking out into Villiers Street as she drew on her gloves and having to bite her lips to hold back her tears.

She had not wept when she left Tansey Clough and Gil this morning; why did she want to weep now? Her two years in Villiers Street had been happy and busy and useful ones, and it was a pity they were over, but that was nothing to weep over. And she watched the people hurrying past in the narrow street, a couple of the waiters on their way back to Gatti's from a few hours of afternoon freedom to stroll about the Strand, and Mrs Chamberlayne bustling past on her way to the flower seller on the corner and returned their cheerful waves and smiles, and savagely bit down on her lip harder than ever. She would not, would *not* cry just because she was leaving Villiers Street.

And she did not. She managed to climb into the cab once her luggage was safely stowed and directed the driver in a composed voice to carry her to Bedford Row, and wave farewell to the cook and maids with a smile, and shed not a tear. And her own strength encouraged her and made it easier to maintain control.

Even at Aunt Martha's she managed to hold herself in check. She told her directly and simply that the time had come to leave Villiers Street, and that she must do so forthwith, even if it meant

254

discommoding the London Ladies, which she hoped it would not do too much.

'For,' she said, 'I believe that Cook and the rest of them can manage very well, as long as someone makes sure they have adequate money each day to do their marketing. I flatter myself I trained them well and they have been with me there for a long time — almost as long as I have, indeed — and they are good and hardworking women and entirely honest.'

'I am not unduly worried about the hostel, my dear,' Martha said quietly, looking at her over the top of her steel-rimmed spectacles. 'For I know you organized the place very well and it runs on oiled wheels. I am far more perturbed about you. You went off with such a spring in your step and such an air — of *satisfaction* that I was most happy for you. And yet a bare day later you return hugger-mugger like this, wishing to leave the hostel at once, and looking — well, far from the way you looked when you bade me farewell. Can you not tell me what the trouble is? I am your friend, you know, and not just a distant connection.'

'Not so distant, dear Aunt Martha,' Sophie said and smiled at her a little tremulously. 'I must tell you that in my — my anxiety, I thought first and indeed only of you. But even to you, I cannot speak easily — it is all so — please, may I just say that when I left here last I was promised to wed? I did not tell you then for I felt I should announce it at home first, and — well, anyway, I did not tell you. I would have done, soon, I promise — but now, well, I am now not to be wed. Do not ask me to say more, please, Aunt Martha. I am very cool and collected at present, and I take some pride in that. But I think perhaps that if I talk too much I will be — I will fly apart and be very foolish.'

And looking at her eyes bright with unshed tears Martha nodded and said no more on the subject. But she did turn her mind to more practical matters. 'And now, my dear? Where do you go?'

'I am going to go to Miss Jex-Blake and ask that I take my examinations now. She has said that I am ready to pass them — more than ready — and although the system for admitting women to the list of doctors is not yet complete, they cannot, I believe prevent me from taking the necessary examinations. After that, I must join the fight for admission to the ranks of the pro-fession ——'

255

'But the simple things, dear child — such as where you will sleep, and on what you will live?'

'I have thought of that,' Sophie said. 'I shall ask Miss Jex-Blake to allow me to live at the medical school and perhaps work from there. I do some teaching of the other students now, and I shall ask her to make that a more permanent arrangement from which I may receive some fees. The girls who come to be trained are *not* poor girls, like me, you know. Many of them are the daughters of very rich men, and well able to pay for their tuition. Miss Jex-Blake I am sure will be able to arrange this for me. And there is also medical work to be done, you know. There are sick people in those streets about King's Cross, near the Free Hospital there in Gray's Inn Road, who are desperately in need of care. I have a plan in my mind for caring for them — but I will not worry you with that now. I just wished to tell you that I was leaving Villiers Street and of my future plans, such as they are. And hoping you would approve them for I think highly of your wisdom, Aunt Martha.'

Martha took off her glasses, and leaned back in her chair. They were sitting by the fire in her sitting room at the top of the house in Bedford Row as they had so often in the past two years, their feet up on the fender, and Martha with her workbox beside her and her brown silk lap filled with her sewing.

'Two years,' Martha said reflectively, and shook her head. 'Oh, but you have changed, my dear.'

'Have I? In what way, Aunt?'

'Oh, you have grown, you know — I do not mean in stature, dear child — indeed, you are thinner and more spare than you were when you first arrived. Then you were a rather buxom country girl, of great charm, and now — well, you have become a much more town sort of person altogether. You have grown in your self reliance, I suppose. You seem to be more mature, more in command of your own life than you ever were then — although heaven knows, you were ambitious enough when you arrived, and sure enough of what you wanted ——'

Sophie smiled a little thinly. 'If you mean I have become more cynical — harder, Aunt Martha — then I think you may be right. I have learned much about the way the world wags since I left my home in Haworth. I am not sure I am a better person for that, however.'

'Nonsense,' Aunt Martha said vigorously. 'Of course you are! Never be beguiled into thinking that women are only agreeable when they are soft and silly. A woman of spirit and high determination is worth any six of the other mewling whining sort! I have much admiration for you, my dear, as well as affection. It is my belief you will go far — if not entirely in the way most people would expect. Your way will always be your own.'

There was a silence as Sophie sat and stared into the fireplace, her eyes wide and blank. She was still very tired, for all her sleep on the train, and it was getting harder and harder to think clearly. But Aunt Martha's warm approval was important to her, and made her feel much better, and when she got up to leave she leaned over and kissed the older woman and thanked her warmly for all her goodness.

'Oh, as to that, I say pooh!' Aunt Martha said stoutly. 'Where do you go tonight, my child? Could you not have stayed at Villiers Street at least till morning?'

Sophie shook her head. 'He will come there to seek me,' she said simply, 'and I do not dare to be found for if I am my resolve will, I know, melt away. And I must not allow that, for I must, I really must, do as I set out to do. I shall be a surgeon, one way or another — Aunt Martha — I know I have told you nothing of my affairs, and I have no right, after being so secretive to expect your help in this way, but please — if any come seeking me, will you tell them you do not know where I am to be found?'

'That will not be difficult,' Aunt Martha said equably, 'since I do not know. So wherever you go tonight, perhaps I had best not be told. But come to see me often, child, you hear me? I wish to know always of your wellbeing. Do not fail me in this.'

'I won't,' Sophie promised, and dragged herself and her luggage away to the same small hotel in King's Cross where she had spent her very first night in London, all that time ago, to fall at last into bed and to sleep. Tomorrow she would see Miss Jex-Blake and set her new life in motion. Tonight, it was sleep and only sleep she wanted.

She was just slipping into the state of drowsiness that comes before true sleep when she remembered that she had not seen Doctor Tom while she had been in Haworth. Then, for the first time, she allowed herself the luxury of tears and sobbed herself to sleep aching in mind and body for all she had left behind her.

257

CHAPTER TWENTY-SIX

It was surprising how easily she was able to put her plans into action. They deserved to fail completely, for she had made them on the wing, as it were, actually deciding what she would do at the very moment in which she explained it all to Aunt Martha. But perhaps there was a watchful Providence on her side, for had she spent hours on formulating her decisions they could not have been better ones.

For a start, Miss Jex-Blake welcomed her offer of teaching with open arms. One of her few really good teachers, a lady physician from America, had been called home to care for her ailing father, and had left the small and struggling London Medical School for Women sadly depleted of useful staff. So, for Miss Jex-Blake, having one of her own pupils to carry some of the load was more than welcome.

'I shall ask you to teach some of the practical work in particular, Miss Lackland,' she said. 'I have been much impressed by your grasp of some of the techniques we must use, and must congratulate you upon your teacher. He clearly gave you an excellent grounding.'

'He did indeed,' Sophie said warmly. 'Doctor Tom is a very fine doctor, with no nonsense about him, and under his eye I developed more skill than even I knew I had. I will gladly pass on what I can — and Miss Jex-Blake, I have another idea.'

'Well? Be quick about it, for I have much to do, and little time in which to do it, and you too, if you are to join us as staff rather than as pupil, must learn to use time wisely.'

'I am aware of that. Miss Jex-Blake, we have around the Free Hospital many mean houses where poor people live who cannot come into the hospital for their ills, for they lack sponsors to allow them entry — is there any reason why we should not go to them? I would like to take pupils with me into these houses and show them how to perform such treatments as are needed, there, on the spot.

Not all of them will work in hospitals at the end of their training, will they? Most doctors do what they have to do in ordinary bedrooms and I have seen many operations performed upon kitchen tables by Doctor Tom. Could we not train our people as they will need to work?'

Miss Jex-Blake leaned back in her chair and stared over her desk at the eager young face that looked back at her. The girl looked more tense and anxious than she used to, somehow sharper and more dejected, and it was a look of which Miss Jex-Blake approved. There had been a time when this same girl had looked much softer, had a sparkling-eyed gaiety about her that made her seem like other ordinary girls; far from the single-minded hardworking woman of ambition she ought to be. Something seemed to have happened to her in the past few days, for this demand for new responsibilities coming hard upon a request to take her examinations as soon as may be had been surprising. But it all suited Miss Jex-Blake well enough and approvingly she agreed.

And so started for Sophie one of the busiest years of her life. She had thought herself hardworking in the long years at Haworth when, with Doctor Tom, she had spent every spare moment among the poor sick of the village. But that had faded to insignificance when she had first come to London and run her hostel and followed her education at the same time. But now — now it seemed that all previous years had been high holidays.

She moved into a small room in a narrow house in a street that backed on to the Henrietta Street house and which Miss Jex-Blake had bought when the lease had fallen in. 'For you never know when it might be useful,' she had said. And useful indeed it became. With Miss Jex-Blake's aid, Sophie fitted out not only her own bedroom, but several of the others, for students who wished to benefit from the training she was to give them in the hovels around King's Cross had to be available at all times, for sickness waits upon no man, nor woman neither. The basement rooms were made into store rooms for the equipment they would need, and piles of charpie, and the new cotton wadding recently made available, and precious instruments bought out of Miss Jex-Blake's hard-pressed funds, and even some bedding and jars of preserved food were stacked there. 'For,' Sophie told her persuasively, 'in my experience many sick poor people need above all comfort and nutritious feeding, more than physic. If we can make their bodies feel cared for, their illnesses are less arduous to them.'

And Miss Jex-Blake agreed and let Sophie do as she thought fit, until she was once again deeply absorbed in her daily work, and had no energy left to pine over what had passed. Indeed, it was almost like the old Villiers Street days, except there were no more Sunday visits from Gil, and no regular visits with the books to Aunt Martha.

There was the deadly unremitting grind, however, and she revelled in it. Each morning she woke at seven, and after a snatched breakfast would pore over her books until nine, when she would take her first class of the day. Sometimes she felt she was only just ahead of the pupils, collecting facts from the great pile of medical books with which Miss Jex-Blake had provided her, and immediately transferring them into the heads of the six girls who sat before her, drinking it all in.

But she knew she did herself an injustice to feel so, for in many ways she was far in advance of them. Though she was still only twenty-five, she felt aware of her own maturity in comparison with them, despite the fact that two of them were very close to her in age, being twenty-four, and the others were all twenty-two or -three. But there was more to it than mere age. They, each of them, were the products of rich and pampered homes. As Miss Jex-Blake had once said sourly, 'It is only an unusually pampered miss who is likely to persuade an adoring Papa to allow her to follow such a career as this. I had enough trouble myself, heaven knows.' It was, Sophie decided, that which set her apart. She had been far from pampered and was far from rich now, barely earning her keep, yet these young women were casual about money in a way which she sometimes found quite shocking; they spent freely and easily and never counted the cost of anything.

They became very attached to her, her six pupils, and she enjoyed that too, for it helped to fill the gap in her life that had been left by the loss of Gil. She tried hard not to think about him, forcing memories of his laughter and funny twisting mouth out of her mind when they dared to intrude, especially in that vulnerable lonely time last thing at night before she fell asleep. Having the pupils to think about and deal with and worry over helped then, because she could force herself to think of young Margaret

Shepheard and her difficulties in grasping mathematics, or Miss Julia Caenwood and her complete idiocy when it came to chemistry. Anything rather than think about Mr Gilbert Stacey and how lonely life was without him, and how little there seemed to be to look forward to now that Sunday was just another day in the week.

But there were all the other days, when, after the morning lectures, she and her pupils would dress themselves in their practical dark gowns with white collars and cuffs and make their way to the streets behind the Free Hospital, hard by Holborn, and start their visits.

At first the girls had found it hard to cope with the smells and the dirt and the apathy of the people they saw. Women with sick babies would sit hopelessly in the middle of squalid rooms which were crying out for the attention of a stout scrubbing brush and plenty of soap and water; the pampered misses despised such laziness and said so — until Sophie pointed out sharply that a woman who lived at starvation level in order to give what little food there was available to her children lacked the energy that better-fed persons enjoyed. And she would set them to doing the scrubbing and cleaning themselves.

There had been complaints at first, and much moaning from the girls who thought that training to be doctors meant elegant book work, and certainly not filthy cleaning tasks of the sort set them by Miss Lackland; and one had even thrown in the sponge and gone home to Papa for good and all. But, to Sophie's intense relief, Miss Jex-Blake supported her in all she did, and told the pupils sharply that until they could make themselves subservient in every way, and deal with nasty tedious tasks like floor scrubbing a sick room, they could not hope to be fit to take full care of the sick person who inhabited it. And as the weeks went by, Sophie found her pupils warmed more and more to her philosophy of complete care, as taught her by Doctor Tom, and she revelled in it.

March and April, May and June went by, and then it was examination time. In addition to all her other work, Sophie had studied hard, using the tail end of the day after lectures and visits to the houses were over, to cram her mind with all she needed for her great day of reckoning, and when that day came she went, with Miss Jex-Blake marching beside her, to the Examination Halls to take her place among the many hundreds of young men who were also facing their moments of truth.

It was not an easy time; many of the students jeered and shouted as Miss Jex-Blake and her protégée made their way through the crowds to their places in the examination room, but none offered any violence. And then there was an episode that warmed Sophie greatly and seemed to her to augur well for her success.

Through the hubbub of noisy young men a tall man came pushing his way, thrusting with his shoulders and clearly quite determined to reach her side.

'Miss Lackland,' he panted as he managed to reach her at last, putting his hand on her shoulder. 'Miss Lackland!'

She looked round and then her face darkened with anxiety. 'Mr — Mr Baker,' she said uncertainly and looked appealingly at Miss Jex-Blake, who moved closer to her side.

'Who is this?' she said, her large eyes wide and very forbidding as she stared up at the tall man, while contriving to appear to be looking down on him from a great height.

'I — Mr Baker is a student at Queen Eleanor's,' Sophie said quietly. 'Miss Jex-Blake, Mr Baker.'

'How do,' Mr Baker said breathlessly, but did not look at Miss Jex-Blake. He never took his eyes from Sophie. 'I saw you — and I wanted but to wish you luck, if you are taking the examination, and to offer to escort you to your examination room and meet you and see you safe out afterwards. There are some here —' and he looked over her head at the milling crowds of medical students, '— who have less manners than they might.'

'Why, thank you!' Sophie said and put her hand out impulsively. 'Please, Mr Baker, do tell me — is Mr Caspar well?'

'Very well. He looks a little tired, you know, but at this time of year, when all are mad with anxiety about examinations — teachers and pupils alike — it is not so surprising! Shall I escort you, then, Miss Lackland?'

Gratefully she accepted, and even Miss Jex-Blake seemed to approve and she found her room with no more trouble, and there were no more jeers from the young men. So encouraging did she find this episode that she settled to answering the questions on her paper with a relaxed assurance, a comfortable sense of being well prepared. She knew, as she blotted the last sheet when the invigilator rang his bell, that she had acquitted herself satisfactorily, and it would be gross injustice if she failed. And since she had written on top of her paper only the initial of her first name before her surname, she had a hope that the examiner would never guess he was reading the work of a mere female, and would mark it on merit only.

The examinations lasted a week, and each morning Mr Baker met her at the Examination Halls and saw her safely to her destination, and afterwards escorted her safely out again, and at the end of the week, tipped his hat to her and wished her well in her future career as a doctor. '— For I am sure you will do well, Miss Lackland. You have all the qualities,' he said solemnly, and disappeared out of her life for ever. She never met him again. But she never ceased to be grateful to him, for he had made what could have been a much more severe ordeal bearable and even enjoyable.

And when in October the lists went up, and there she saw her name, S. Lackland, well up on the list of passes, her cup was full. She had always known she could be a doctor, and now she was. Not yet a surgeon, admittedly. There would be more training yet and more effort needed before she could be admitted to their august ranks, but she had come this far, and who would have thought that possible?

There had been some fears that she would not be permitted to be entered on the register of physicians, but even this faded away, for Miss Jex-Blake set to with a will, politicking and nagging busily at the professors at the University and the Royal College until, in late November of 1876, S. Lackland was permitted legally to sign herself 'Dr Lackland' and at Henrietta Street that night there was much celebrating indeed.

But for Sophie herself the victory seemed a hollow one. She had reached the halfway mark of her ambition; she had become a physician, and yet there was so little joy in it.

She wrote the glad tidings home to Bessie, and received in reply a letter written in such transports of delight as to be almost illegible. She told Aunt Martha of her success, and received her warm congratulations with quiet pleasure. Even when Freddy Caspar sent her a great sheaf of flowers by a messenger, 'To welcome the fairest of our profession,' she felt little more than an agreeable warmth.

And that was depressing. Where was the elation she had thought

263

she would feel when this time came? Where the towering sense of glory, the tears of sheer delight, the tearing excitement? There was none of it, and she would sit in her lecture room trying to concentrate on her teaching, or go through her day's visits demonstrating to her pupils how to apply poultices and to bleed and to put on leeches and open boils, with as little excitement as if she had been teaching them how to sew samplers.

It was Martha who at last made her see what was wrong with her. In the last few weeks, Sophie had taken to visiting Martha rather more often than she had been used to. Once the examinations were over, there was more time, for she no longer needed to spend all of the hours that God gave her glued to her books, and her Sunday afternoons hung heavy on her hands. And Martha was a welcoming and comforting solution to those dismal afternoons.

It was on one particularly rainy Sunday, when the water went sluicing down the windows and set the gutters swirling with dead leaves and street garbage, and they sat side by side at Martha's Bedford Row fireside, that Martha at last could bear it no longer. Sophie had been sitting staring silently into the glowing embers, and Martha had been covertly watching her, and then, sharply she sighed, and Sophie looked up.

'What is it, Aunt Martha?'

'I might as well ask you,' Martha said. 'I have been watching you, my dear, and I swear I have never seen so glum an expression on so young a face! What is it that worries you? You are a newly qualified doctor, much absorbed in your good work, enjoying the tasks of teaching your pupils — or so you tell me — and yet you sit here looking like Atlas with the weight of the whole world on his shoulders! I can bear it no longer, and you shall tell me what it is all about. And you shall tell me, too, who are these young men who pester me so often for news of you. No, do not look at me like that! I swore I would tell them nothing and nothing is what I have told them. But I feel, you know, that I am entitled to know something of what goes on in your mind. We are good enough friends by now, I would hope.'

'Young *men*?' Sophie said wonderingly.

'Never mind that! I will answer no questions until you tell me why you are so low. Come, out with it! I will wait no longer. I have waited nine months since your return from Haworth and said not a

264

word — not a single word. Now the time has come. So, speak!'

Sophie leaned back in her chair and smiled a little ruefully. 'You have indeed been very patient, dear Aunt Martha,' she said. 'I did not mean to seem secretive. Well, I will tell you. It is all to do with a young man I met at the Gaiety Theatre. We were to be wed.'

Martha nodded sapiently. 'Mr Gilbert Stacey, I take it?'

'How do you know that?'

'Because he came here seeking news of you! He keeps on coming here seeking news of you! We are becoming quite good friends, indeed. I have told him, may God forgive me for such falsehoods, that I cannot imagine why he keeps asking me for news of you, and why he imagines I should know your whereabouts, and why he cannot stop plaguing a poor old lady — as you see, I never tell the lie direct! — but still he comes. I believe he has a genuine affection for you, my dear. He shows every sign of missing you sorely although he is a cheerful enough young man, much given to joking. Still, he does persist, does he not, in hunting for you?'

Sophie was sitting up more straightly now, and looking rather pink. 'How often has he been here, Aunt Martha?' she asked, her eyes wide and bright.

'Oh, some dozen times or more! He is quite determined. He had been — let me see now, to the hostel, to Nellie's — where I may tell you, Freddy gave him short shrift — and ——'

'He also came to Henrietta Street,' Sophie said in a low voice. 'He came there very soon after my return from Haworth, and saw Miss Jex-Blake, but clearly she was better able to lie than you, dear Aunt, for she told him that she had no notion where I might be — and that was true too, for at the time at which they were speaking I could have been anywhere about the streets of King's Cross — and that he was on no account to come bothering her again, for she would not waste time on him. And he never came back.'

Truth to tell, Gil's willingness to accept his congé from Miss Jex-Blake had saddened her not a little. Miss Jex-Blake had told her of the young man's arrival and fast dismissal, and said no more on the matter, but knowing Gil had come to seek her, much as she assured herself she did not wish to be found, had warmed her. But his failure ever to try again had saddened her equally, and to discover now that he had in fact been more persistent in his attempts to find her lifted her heart more than it had any right to do.

265

'How did he look?' she asked as casually as she could. 'The last time he was here, I mean?'

'Very well,' Martha said, not at all deceived by the casual pose. 'I cannot pretend he looks lovesick. He is sprightly and cheerful and dances and tumbles with great skill ——'

'Here?' Sophie said, amazed.

Martha laughed fatly at that. 'Foolish child, of course not! At the theatre. He gave me box tickets and insisted I be his guest. He is a beguiling rascal, is he not, Sophie?'

'Yes,' Sophie said, and turned her head again and stared back into the fire. The animation that had filled her for a few moments seemed to die in her and Martha once again sighed and leaned forwards. 'My dear child, why, in the name of heaven, if you love the man do you not see him? He shows every sign of caring greatly for you. What holds you back?'

Sophie looked at her with miserable eyes. 'Can you believe that I do not know?'

'You can try to explain, for all that. Perhaps when you talk of your feelings you will understand them better. It is a truth I long ago discovered — that discussing one's confusions and anxieties is a signally successful way of putting them into a sort of order, and of shrinking them. So, talk away ——'

There was a little pause and then Sophie said awkwardly, 'I do not know the true validity of my feelings for him. He — he declared himself at a time of great emotion. He had been ill, and I had nursed him well, and we were both very — tired, I suppose and on edge. And I thought I loved him and accepted him. But then we went to Haworth and I saw — Wilfred, you see. Dear Wilfred. I saw Wilfred.'

She sat and stared broodingly at her hands in her lap, and then went on, talking more to herself than to Martha. 'And he was clever with Wilfred, and sharp and unkind with him, and then Wilfred's Mamma came in. She is a hateful woman, I know, but she is no fool, and she was so glad to see that I was not to wed her Wilfred that I felt — I do not know what I felt! As though I had till then underestimated Wilfred's — care for me. I knew he loved me in his own dull way, you know, but I did not think it was so — so powerful a love to make his mother that glad I was to wed another. And then I saw Wilfred's face and — it is all so ridiculous! Suddenly I did not know for whom I felt what. I found Gil so exciting and — and amusing and delightful, but he was unkind to Wilfred, you see — and I did not know what to think. And then Wilfred hit him, and that made me angry with Wilfred! It is all so bewildering. Perhaps I am not meant to wed at all. I am safer away from all these foolish feelings and concentrating on work. So I told myself. And then I thought — I have so much I could offer to sick people. I know this will sound — oh, arrogant and puffed up, but I have, Aunt, I know I have! I thought, I will not marry at all, and then I need not change my name, and I will obtain that legacy and use it to start a good visiting service for the sick in their own homes. Not another hospital — I have no wish to do that. A visiting service which will have good doctors and good nurses and will provide food and bedding and all that the sick need to be well again ——'

Her eyes had lit up with excitement as she talked and Martha sat and watched her and felt the old excitement stirring in her, the excitement she had once known long ago, planning to take just such care to people in need, the women and children who had followed the soldiers of the Queen to the Crimea in that dreadful Russian winter long ago. This girl, with her high hopes and dreams, had much of the young Martha in her and now the old Martha, her sixtieth birthday far too near for comfort, remembered.

She also remembered her own lost love. The man she had wanted and cared for so much, who had wanted to show his love in a Turkish garden in distant Constantinople. She had refused him, told him he must wait, but he had died and she sat here, almost sixty, as virginal as she had been the day she was born ——

She leaned forwards then, and put both her thin, lined hands on Sophie's smooth young ones. 'Sophie, listen to me. I speak to you not as an aunt should, but as one woman to another. Listen to your body, my child. You do not wish to wed this man? You are not sure that a life as a married woman would be enough for you whichever man you chose? That is no sin — but to waste your need and your — ability to love — that would be a sin. Go to your man, and share your love with him. Don't waste it ——'

Sophie was staring at her, her forehead crumpled. 'But, Aunt, I told you, I cannot be sure that I want to marry him! He is exciting and — and, yes, I dream of him and blush to tell you of the sort of dreams they are! But to marry now ——'

'I told you, Sophie. You do not have to marry. Not every woman does, you know, and not all that do not remain as I am. Look about you at the theatre girls, my child. They do not wed, do they? Nor do they sigh unsatisfied!'

Sophie shook her head and blinked and shook it again. She could not be sure that she had understood her aunt aright. How could she? What she seemed to be saying was so outrageous, so impossible, that it was unbelievable. Wasn't it?

Both she and Martha were so taken aback by the turn their conversation had taken that both of them completely forgot the mention Martha had made of young *men* who had been enquiring for Sophie. And even after she had gone back to her room behind Henrietta Street, Sophie did not think of it. How could she, when Martha's words had put so clearly so impossible a notion into her head?

CHAPTER TWENTY-SEVEN

It took her three days to make up her mind. Three days of confusion and self questioning and doubt and sureness and doubt again. Finally on the last Friday in November, when once again the rain was pouring relentlessly out of a leaden sky — as it had been doing for so many weeks that the Thames had flooded its banks in many parts of London — she reached her decision. It was not an easy one, but she felt it was the right one, and she wrapped herself in the heavy green mantle which was still her best and warmest garment for all it was now three years old, and put her galoshes on her feet and sallied out into the streets.

There were no cabs or hansoms to be seen anywhere, a circumstance which did not surprise her in the least, for she had long ago learned that London cabs always disappeared when they were most needed, and she pulled her collar up to her ears, and hurried through the streets as close to the houses and shop fronts as she could. All the same the water ran down the brim of her bonnet and dripped on to her face, and made her hair clump to her forehead in wet tendrils. However, she took a perverse pleasure in knowing she would arrive at her destination looking like a drowned rat. It made it all seem less reprehensible, somehow. Were she to present herself in the guise of a perfectly turned out young lady, intending to please a masculine eye, what she had to say to him would be particularly wrong. But if he listened to her and understood when she looked as bedraggled as she knew she would by the time she reached him, that would make it different.

At which absurd piece of illogical logic she shook her head at herself — spraying the water drops around with even more abandon — and hurried on. She was altogether behaving absurdly for a grown woman, and a doctor to boot. But now she had decided, she would carry her determination through, for good or ill, and absurdity must be controlled.

The Strand was humming with people and the shops threw

great swathes of yellow light over the streaming wet pavements, making themselves look even more tempting than they usually did. Crossing sweepers were doing a roaring trade, nipping busily between booted feet and under horses' hooves and dray wheels as insouciantly as children playing on a beach, and just as wetly. Umbrellas gleamed everywhere, and the traffic threw plumes of water up on to the pavements, to the rage of cursing passers-by, and horses steamed and drivers yelled at each other and altogether it was as exciting and as London a scene as Sophie had ever seen.

She stood in the shelter of a modiste's doorway for a while as a particularly heavy burst of rain came down, and watched it all and found herself thinking of grey Haworth and its steep cobbled street and huddle of slate roofs beneath the brooding moors, and wondered if she could ever go back there. Would it not be even more insupportably dull and stifling after these exciting three years she had lived in London? There was a sentimental pleasure in thinking about home, but would there be any real pleasure in actually living there?

She shivered suddenly; if what she was on her way to propose were to be accepted then she could never go back. Not on any account.

But that was not to be thought of, so she did not, and plunged again into the wet Strand and battled her way through the crowds and the streaming pavements to the far eastern end.

This time she did not hesitate outside. The first time she had seen the Gaiety Theatre there had been a dry road underfoot and a clear sky above it, not this torrential rain and flooded gutters, and she positively scuttled past the ornate front to the stage door, and in under the hissing gas lamp that surmounted it, to stand in the little corridor shaking her coat to get rid of the worst of the water.

The stage doorkeeper had gone off somewhere about his own ploys; since it was just half past five and the players would not be arriving for a little while yet to prepare for the evening performance that was understandable enough, and she stood uncertainly for a moment in the musty half-lit corridor, cogitating. He must surely have the same dressing room; she knew where that was from her many previous visits here, and she marched away down the corridor towards it, her chin up. He would be unlikely to be there yet, and she would have time to dry out a little before he arrived. And, it would be easier to face him if he came there after her and found her already ensconced.

His name was still on the door and she knocked first and then walked in. The room was empty though clearly ready for him, for a small fire was burning in the tiny fireplace on the far wall and costumes were hanging ready on a screen that cut off one corner. The table in front of the mirror was spread with sticks of grease paint and a pot of cleansing cream and a pile of old huckaback towels, and the mirror itself was reflecting the gaslight which someone had come in and put on.

She stood in the doorway for a moment and then stepped inside, closing the door and leaned her back on it, breathing deeply. She had thought a lot about Gil during these past weeks, and indeed he had never been far from her thoughts since the day she had left him behind at Tansey Clough, and disturbing enough had her thoughts of him been. Her dreams had been, as she had told Martha, startling in their powerful images. Sophie was a country girl, and far from mealymouthed about matters physical, but even she had blushed when she woke in the morning at some of the experiences she had shared with Gil in those dreams.

But disturbing though they had been, they had not disturbed her nearly so much as being here in his dressing room now did. She closed her eyes for a moment, hoping the wave of excitement and sheer animal feeling that had risen in her as she stood there would die away, and slowly it did, and again she opened her eyes and drew a deep breath, only to find the feelings rise in her again; and now she knew what caused it.

The room smelled of him. The thick scent of the greasepaint, the faint orange-flower effluvium of the pot of cream, the hint of heavy masculine sweat that came from the costumes hanging there — together they added up to as potent a trigger to her physical feelings as could ever have been imagined.

Fortunately, the sense of smell is an easily tired one, she told herself, and the effect will wear off soon — it must. And it did and she could move forwards to stand in front of the fire and hold out the skirts of her gown to the cheerful flames in a somewhat absurd attempt to dry it.

After a while she took off her mantle, feeling rather daring as she did so. That she was making herself at home in so familiar a manner was in itself an indication of how outrageous she was becoming. A New Woman indeed! At any moment, she told herself ruefully, I shall sit down and put my feet on his mantelpiece and light a pipe! They are right, the critics. Such ambitions as mine and such activities as mine do take away a woman's femininity ——

The door opened behind her and she stiffened, not daring to turn, standing there beside the fire with her skirts held wide in front of it, and then he spoke and she could stay still no longer and whirled and stood there staring at him.

'Sophie,' was all he said. 'My dear, dear Sophie.'

She had not meant to do it. She had planned it all so carefully. She would be cool, and very sensible and keep her emotions in close check. This was to be a sensible arrangement with nothing of silly sentiment or romance about it. But her resolve failed her and she held out her arms and said simply, 'Oh, Gil, I have missed you so dreadfully!'

He dropped his coat on the floor — he had been holding it over his arm — and he too held out his arms and came to meet her and then they were clinging to each other and kissing until she was breathless and had to pull away from him, and she looked up into his eyes and set her hands on each side of his face and smiled at him with all her feeling showing in her own face and without any hint of artifice.

'You looked for me, Gil, did you not? I am glad you did that. I thought you had given up after that one visit to Henrietta Street.'

'The battle-axe told me in no uncertain terms that you were not there and that I would be very likely transported to Australia or some such if I dared to come seeking you again, so I had to believe her! That such a one as that Jex-Blake should be a liar was inconceivable, so I did not conceive of it, and instead haunted your poor aunt. Did she lie to me, Sophie? Did she know where you were all the time?'

Sophie laughed. 'She did not lie, dear Gil, but she did not precisely tell the truth, either. I was in fact in Henrietta Street — well, let me amend that and be *quite* truthful — at a house behind the one where the medical school is. It is in a little street called Hayland Street — you would never have found it alone.'

He let her go and went and picked up his coat and hung it carefully on the screen.

'Wretched females, all of you! There was I eating my heart out in misery, and not one of you had heart enough to put me on the road to happiness! Such dire distress as I was in, and all lying, lying, lying to the tops of their bents! Dreadful, dreadful women ——'

'You do not look as though you have suffered too much,' she said, and smiled at him, for indeed he did look well. His curly hair was as lively and springing as ever, his eyes as bright and his step as jaunty, and indeed he had a glossy self-satisfied look that became him well.

'My looks belie me!' he said and struck a dramatic pose. 'You see before you but the hulk of a man, a mere shell, within whom the heart has died, the springs of human feelings have dried up, the beating pulse of love has faltered and faded — but one must keep up appearances after all! And I am a successful actor, my love, and must look the part. I play second leads now, you know! Old Hollingshead can't do without me ——'

'And I am a doctor, Gil. We have both come on in this nine months, have we not?'

He sobered then and looked at her with a lugubrious expression on his face that pulled at her conscience.

'Is that why you left me so abruptly, Sophie? Why you just disappeared from that bitter cold miserable place and left me to find my own way back to civilization?'

'Oh, I don't think it was that bad a place to be left in.' She was prevaricating and she knew it, and bit her lip. 'No, Gil, I went because — I was not sure. My feelings were confused and ——'

There was a rush of footsteps outside the door and then someone banged on it. 'Calling the half-hour — calling the half-hour,' bawled a boy's voice and then the footsteps rushed off again and she heard banging on the next door and the cry of, 'Calling the half-hour — calling the half-hour ——'

'Oh, dammit, I am later than I meant to be,' Gil said and began to peel off his jacket. 'I have a complicated makeup to do, and I must be about it, for I am first on. Dearest Sophie, we shall talk later — sit you down there by the fire and close your eyes while I dress, and then my man will take you to the stage box later, if you like ——'

'No, I don't think so — I am too bedraggled to be seen by any respectable persons.'

273

He glanced at her. 'Oh, you are wet, are you not? I had not really noticed — well, dry yourself there, and then we shall see. Perhaps you can watch from the wings ——' and then he pulled open his door and began shouting for his dresser. Sophie smiled and sat down by the fire.

Dear Gil! He did not change — and he could never imagine anyone would not wish to see the performance and above all himself in it. And it would be pleasant to watch him at work again, in all truth, for he was such a nimble and charming dancer, and had so much style about him.

He and his dresser went behind the screen to get him into his close-fitting first act costume, which was that of an incredibly richly decorated and elaborately uniformed count of some imaginary middle European country. Then, with only the jacket remaining to be donned, his dresser went away and he sat at his dressing table and began to apply his makeup.

She watched him, fascinated as the shadows and colours lifted his already pleasant face into a perfection of male beauty, with the eyes deeper and darker than ever, the cheekbones more elegantly modelled and even a dimple, which was not actually there, appearing in his pointed chin under the influence of his busy grease-paint-loaded fingertips.

When he had completed the painting he buttoned himself into the gold-braided jacket of his absurd uniform, and smiled at her and said lightly, 'Do you approve?'

'Yes,' she said and then smiled too. 'You look very pretty.'

But he did not see that she was joking and went back to the mirror and twisted and turned to see his reflection more clearly and nodded with a sober air of appraisal.

'Yes, I think so — well, I am ready in time —' as there was another knock on his door and a bawling of 'Overture and beginners — overture and beginners,' repeated next door and on down the corridor, '— although I had feared I would not be. Sophie, we must talk after the show. Will you take supper with me at Rules? Or we could go to Romanov's if you would prefer it there ——'

'No. Rules would be very agreeable. And by the end of the performance I may be dry and fit to be seen out with you.'

'Yes — I am sure you will. If you come to the wings quietly you will be able to watch from there — but do be quiet, for old Hollingshead gets very shirty when there are visitors back stage. Enjoy the show, now ——' And he kissed her briefly, leaving a smudge of carmine on her lips, and was gone.

She sat on beside the fire for a little while, as her gown slowly dried out and then, feeling a little guilty, went to his mirror and used his brush and comb to set her hair to rights. And then quietly went out into the corridor and followed the now familiar way that led to the stage.

She could hear the music, sprightly and a little tinny, and the occasional roar of laughter that came from the audience and as she reached the stage itself and the sound lifted and became much more heavy in her ears a little rush of ballerinas went hurrying by her in a froth of pink tulle and tinsel. The smell of greasepaint and patchouli that came from them made her head reel for a moment, and she shrank back against one of the flats standing stacked against the rough brick wall as they passed her, quite oblivious of her presence.

A strange world, this one, she thought, in which all that matters is the way you look. Were I standing here in pink tulle and tinsel they would acknowledge me and not push me aside so hugger-mugger; but I am wearing a dull stuff gown and so I do not really exist at all for them ——

But she brushed away such thoughts and slipped through the darkness of the rear of the stage to the wings, and reached her destination just as the cluster of ballerinas went fluttering on to it, all waving arms and twinkling legs, as the music lost its sprightly beat and became soft and romantic and dreamy.

Gil came off stage as they went on, and saw her and grinned widely, and his eyes seemed to gleam even more brightly in the confused lights of the wings. 'Did you see? That is a most successful piece of business — that with the sword? I devised it only a couple of weeks ago, and the audience go mad for it. And what do you think about the dance round the chairs? Droll, is it not?'

Fortunately she did not have to answer, for the orchestra leapt into a different tune yet again, and he was gone, rushing back on stage to twirl in the middle of the bubbles of pink tulle to the happy audience's evident approval. They were there beyond the lights on the stage like a vast animal, moving as one, shouting and laughing as one, not as several hundred individual and unique yet ordinary human beings, and Sophie gave a small shiver, almost frightened. Human illness in the individual she could understand and deal with; human excitement in the mass she could not. Yet she could see that for Gil it was what life was all about. For him that animal beyond the footlights was what he existed for.

But it repaid him warmly for his love and his devotion, for the shouts and applause that greeted him at every song and dance were huge and he came off at last at the end of the show sweating and flushed and supremely pleased with himself.

By the time he had washed and changed he had calmed down a little, but he was still in a state of high excitement as he took her arm and led her out of the stage door to the hansom cab that was awaiting them there, having been called up by his dresser.

The rain had stopped at last, but the dark streets still shone satiny black in the spilled lights, and the cluster of monocled mashers at the stage door, waiting for their favourite chorus girls to come out and be escorted to cosy little suppers in the fashionable restaurants around the Strand, glittered and shone as well from their well-brushed top hats to their gleaming patent leather shoes. Sophie was very aware of her own rather humdrum appearance compared with the other women coming out of that stage door. They were so fashionably dressed in their silks and laces, so haughty in their polonaise gowns and Dolly Vardens that she felt very subdued indeed, and sat beside Gil in the hansom in silence as they clattered down the Strand towards Maiden Lane and the bustle of Rules.

Not that he seemed to notice. He chattered on busily, talking about the show, about the amount of business they were turning away — 'We have the House Full notices up night after night,' he crowed — and the tiresome behaviour of Mr Hollingshead.

But just as the cab curved into Southampton Street, he squeezed her arm and said suddenly, 'I have not said enough about how glad I am to see you again, Sophie. I had almost given up hope of you when even that clod-hopping friend of yours, who had so much more time to search than I did, could not find you ——'

'What did you say? Who?'

'Oh, I am sorry! I did not mean to be ill-mannered, but you know, he is far from being in any sense a metropolitan man, is he?

An excellent man, in so many ways, and I know I offended you in being so — well, I was not as charming as I might have been when I met him that night! But I meant no harm and I was cold and tired, and there it is. But as I say, when even he could not find you I almost gave up in despair and thought you must have emigrated to America!'

'But how could he seek me?' Sophie said wonderingly. 'Wilfred — do you mean he came to London?'

'Indeed he did.' The cab drew up at the entrance to the restaurant in a clatter of hooves and a jingle of harness and he pushed upon the apron, and jumped down, and then handed her down with great care. 'Still is, as far as I know ——'

He paid the cabman with a flourish and led her into the restaurant, and for a while they could not talk easily as the head waiter led them with some ceremony to a table in the middle of the room, and Gil — who was clearly regarded here as very much a celebrated person and one to be toadied to — greeted friends, slapping men on the back and kissing ladies' hands.

But at last they were settled and menus were put in their hands and Sophie could say urgently, 'What do you mean, he still is?'

'As I say, my dear. He came down to London very soon after you ran back here — and we must talk more about that soon — and then went back North and has been back to London several times since. Indeed, one would think he has a private railway service, he comes so frequent! That he is determined to find you is clear — now, my love, what shall you eat? The oysters, of course, are splendid, and there is, I see, some of their special jugged hare and red cabbage, hmm?'

'Anything you please, Gil,' she said abstractedly, trying to imagine Wilfred in London, looking for her. 'Oh, I do feel so — I should have written to him. I told Bessie that on no account was she to tell anyone where I was, and clearly she obeyed me. She is the only one at home I have written to at all. Not even Doctor Tom, though I have sent them all good wishes, of course. But I should have written to Wilfred. Oh, dear, I feel so ——'

'Come, my love, there is no need for all this.' He leaned forwards and set both hands warmly over one of hers. 'You came to see me, did you not? You found me, rather than the reverse and this being so, surely it is me you are concerned about, and not this

277

—not your friend Wilfred? I will take it very ill if you go on about him now. It was because of him, I thought, that we parted last time as we did. Was it not so? Or am I wrong about that?'

She looked at him and then gently extricated her hand and folded them both on her lap out of reach. She kept her chin up and took a deep breath. What she had to say had best be said quickly and clearly. No sense beating about the bush, was there? None at all.

The words did not come easily at first, and he tried to interrupt her, to jolly her out of the mood of anxiety into which she seemed to have fallen, but she made him listen and at last he sat quietly, realizing the import of what she was saying.

'I am trying to tell you, Gil, that I cannot wed you. I do not think I can wed anyone. I have my work now, and it is important to me; also there is the matter of this legacy. I did not think that money mattered to me, but I have a use for it now. I want to start a visiting hospital service — well, I shall not bore you with that. But suffice it to say I will not take the risk of losing the legacy by changing my name — which I must do if I marry.'

There was a little pause and then he said, 'You have reappeared after nine full months of silence just to give me my congé? I cannot understand you, Sophie. Do you want to torment a man? What have I done to you to deserve such treatment? I cannot believe that you hate me so much that ——'

'I do not hate you, Gil,' she said and reddened. 'I have a very — I have a feeling for you which is very powerful. You — excite me in a way that I find very — it is quite shaming.'

He grinned at that. 'Don't be ashamed of it! There is no reason, surely, why a woman should not enjoy love as much as any man. You are a New Woman, are you not, Sophie? One who sees herself as equal to any mere male? Why then should you not have feelings like ours? I applaud them, my dear, and I would wish you did too.'

Her gaze shifted in embarrassment and she looked away from him, at the other diners, at the bustling waiters, anywhere but at that mobile mouth and those gleaming dark eyes.

'That is what I am here to tell you,' she said, and her voice was low. 'I will not wed you. But I will — I will not deny my feeling for you either. If you will consider we could enjoy a — a friendship on those grounds, then I am ready. That is what I will accept.'

'You will — what did you say?' He sounded genuinely dumb-founded.

'I said I will not wed you,' she repeated. 'But — but I will ——'

'You will be my mistress,' he said it quietly, as a statement and not a question.

'Yes. That is what I mean. My aunt — Martha, it was she who said — oh, well. Never mind that. It is my decision and I will abide by it. If that is what you want. Not that I saw myself as a mistress precisely — but what can I do? There is no other description, is there? So I must get used to it. I will be your mistress then, but I will not be your wife. I will keep my own name and my own in-dependence of movement — and my own money. Will you have me on such an arrangement?'

CHAPTER TWENTY-EIGHT

The rest of the meal went by in a blur. They set oysters and brown bread and butter in front of her and brought her lemons and red pepper but she could taste nothing. He ordered champagne and poured it with a lavish hand but it might have been water for all the effect it had on her. She ate jugged hare and let them pile her plate with red cabbage, and still none of it impinged on her awareness at all.

Quite what she had expected he would say or do she did not know. She had not been able to imagine anything beyond actually telling him of her decision, so she was not ready at all for the way he did react. He showed no surprise at all at her words. Nor, to her chagrin, any regret. Surely, surely, a man who had wanted a woman to be his wife should be a little put out when he is told she would not? So a tiny voice somewhere at the back of her mind nagged. Surely he should not be so rapturous?

But you have offered him yourself, and that is why he is rapturous, another voice inside her answered. He is paying you the greatest of compliments, is he not? But he does not care that I will not wed him, the other voice retorted, and she shook her head a little and applied her knife and fork to the food she did not want and could not taste in an attempt to shut out the clamour of doubt that was inside her.

Dinner ended at last, and when the waiters had cleared the linen, and left them with just glasses of wine in front of them he leaned forwards and held out his hands to her and she set her own in them and tried to find some of the old excitement such contact had once given her. But it did not come and she was puzzled. She should not be so numb, so coldly unfeeling, at such a time, when she had promised such — when she had made such a promise as she had made.

'Dear Sophie,' Gil said softly. 'You are a very remarkable lady, you know.'

'Am I? I do not feel myself to be so.'

'Oh, you are, you are. There is not one woman in a thousand, indeed in ten thousand, who could speak as you spoke, and then sit here composedly eating her dinner as though she had discussed nothing more momentous than the weather. I was not sure at first that you are up to all you said you were. I mean, that you wanted to be a doctor, and live your life your own way — to tell the truth, sweetheart. I thought it was all a hum. That the time would come when you would gratefully forget all about such silly ambitions and settle happily to being my wife and — not that I did not realize that there was more spirit in you than most! I knew that you could tolerate the occasional irregularities of an actor's life without too much fuss, that you would not demand a suburban villa with a fancy drawing room and a houseful of servants and your own carriage, but would be content enough with the bohemian life. But I never thought you would prove to be quite so bohemian as you have ——'

'You do not understand me very well, then, Gil? You misjudged my character, you think?' It was important that she should know he had, that he should admit to her that she was difficult to comprehend, but he leaned back in his chair and laughed.

'Oh, I am an actor, my love! We have to be good judges of character — and I am. I did not say that you completely upset my view of you — just that I was not sure about your intentions at first. But now I can see that you do indeed try to behave as you speak. Not, of course, my dear one, that I still do not suspect that the time will come when — well, let be! Let us not waste our time in speaking of the future. More to the point is the present. And a very special present it promises to be. Waiter! My account, if you please. And hurry — we have business of our own to be about!' And he smiled at Sophie, that twisting funny smile that she had always found so beguiling.

He hurried her out of the restaurant when the doorman told him that the cab he had asked for had been obtained, wrapping her solicitously in her still damp mantle, and holding open the door of the cab — a four-wheeler, for the hansom cab jarveys had all taken themselves home out of the rain, which was once more pouring down heavily — and then settling himself beside her in a flurry of cape and stick and top hat.

The cab rattled to the end of the street and then curved to the right to go down to the Strand along Southampton Street, and the movement threw her against him and he put his arms about her and laughed, a soft bubbling laugh deep in his throat, and would not let her go, although she protested or tried to. But it was not possible, for he was kissing her with a fervour he had never shown before, his tongue hard against her lips, and his grip almost violent in its intensity. Even in the heady early days of their engagement, while he was recovering from his pneumonia and had been ardent and loverlike to a marked degree, he had not shown this sort of passion, and it made her breathless and, deep down, a little frightened.

Not that she found it disagreeable. The sensations with which he was filling her were as intense as they had ever been; indeed, more so in some ways, and she found her own arms had gone up and hooked themselves around his neck and she was returning his passion with an almost equal ardour; but for all that she was uneasy. And when his hands began to move across her body, and she felt his fingers at the neck of her gown, tugging on the fabric, she managed to pull away from him and gasp, 'No — Gil, for heaven's sake — you must not ——'

He seemed not to hear her at first, and she took hold of his hand and pulled it away and heard rather than felt the soft rip of fabric and now she said more loudly, 'Gil — stop, for God's sake. Will you remember where you are ——'

This time he did hear, and lifted his head and looked at her in the darkness of the cab, and said after a moment, 'I'm sorry ——' and his voice was thick and rather husky. 'I was carried away — you are very exciting, Sophie, my love. And you are mine, and I forgot myself — but it will not be long ——' and he hugged her close, but this time without excessive passion, simply a bear hug; and she relaxed in the circle of his arms and took a deep breath, feeling with her gloved hands at the neck of her gown for the damage that had been done. But she could not tell in the darkness and gave up; later, when she was in the privacy of her bedroom at Hayland Street she would be able to assess and repair it.

The cab rattled on, and they swayed in the cold damp darkness, speechless, he still holding her close in the curve of one arm, she absorbed in her own thoughts, and then, after five minutes or so she roused herself as the cab again wheeled to the right, and tried to peer out into the darkness.

'Where are we?' she said after a moment. 'I cannot see — the rain is so heavy — which way is he taking us?'

Gil too looked out, wiping the steam from the window with his glove. 'We are nearly there — just the next corner — ah! Here we are — stay here, my love, till I have paid him, and then come down, or you will be drenched ——' And he opened the door as the four-wheeler drew to a halt in a clatter of hooves and harness, and then jumped out. She heard the clink of coins as he paid and then he was holding up his hand and she took it and stepped down and at once the cab man clicked his tongue at his horse and the animal, eager for its warm dry stable, moved off at a sharp trot, leaving them in the pelting rain on the kerbside.

'Come along, sweetheart — there is a fire and hot toddy waiting — we shall soon be as snug as birds in a nest ——'

'Gil, where are we?' she said, and tried to pull back on his hand, staring up at the façade of the house before which they were standing. 'I have never been here before! We have come to the wrong place, and ——'

'Of course you have never been here before,' Gil said heartily, and now succeeded in bringing her to the steps and up them to the front door. 'These are my chambers, my dear, and bachelor apartments though they are, cosy enough, you will find, for all our needs ——' And he bent and kissed her wet face and then put his key in the lock and pushed open the door.

She had no choice but to go in but as he closed the door behind him she whirled, and said urgently, 'Gil, I did not wish to come here! I want to go home — at once! I did not expect ——'

'Shhh! My landlady is the most inquisitive creature that ever drew breath and will come crawling up here from her basement as fast as a maggot out of cheese if she thinks I have interesting company. Come upstairs and we shall soon have you dry — shh.'

Suddenly she was shaking. The thought of an inquisitive land-lady creeping up the stairs from the basement to stare at her filled her with horror; she had never been a person to care unduly about others' opinions of her, but for all that she reacted to the thought of a stranger looking lewdly at her with the same revulsion that any milk-and-water parson's daughter would feel; so she dumbly followed him up the drugget-covered stairs to the floor above. She was not going to stay, but she was also not going to fight with him in the hearing of some harridan of a female who would be sure to put the worst possible construction on what she saw and heard. And anyway, she wanted to say a lot to Gil, a great deal. What was the man thinking to bring her to his lodgings at this hour of the night? Had he no sense of decorum at all?

By the time she reached the sitting room of his set of chambers she was seething with anger, and stood there in the middle of the room, almost glaring at him, but he seemed unaware of her fury, and hurried across the room to the fireplace to poke the embers into flame and to throw on more coal. It was a pleasant room, indeed, furnished heavily in mahogany and drab leather and with red plush curtains obscuring two tall windows, and there was clear evidence that the rooms were inhabited only by a man; the tantalus prominently displayed on one table, the box of cigars on another, and a total absence of the pretty fripperies that were so much a feature of ordinary drawing rooms.

Sophie was in no mood to admire domestic arrangements, though. As Gil straightened, brushing his hands together to rid them of the hint of coal dust they had collected, she opened her mouth to allow her wrath to escape, but again he thwarted her, for as his glance fell on his mantelpiece he said, 'Hello! I see I have messages!' He took a square white envelope from the shelf and slit it, and read the single sheet of paper it contained, and then, grinning, turned to Sophie.

'My love, this is too rich! I seek you for nine months and am almost in despair of finding you, and then you appear out of the blue, in my own dressing room — and now, d'you know what this is? Why, a missive from your Northern swain saying he has news of you that might lead to your whereabouts being discovered! Is that not rich, hey? Is that not the stuff of which melodrama is made? Indeed, if any of our writers allowed such a thing to happen in a play I would yawn with the boredom of it — but there it is in reality. Too rich, really too rich ——'

'That letter is from Wilfred?' Sophie said, at once deflected from her anger. 'He is in London now?'

'I told you, did I not, that he keeps coming here seeking you? I do not keep a watch on him but I am not surprised he is here again.

For all I know he has settled here —'

'But he cannot do that!' She was horrified. 'He could never be happy in London. And what about the mill? They are good people there, but without him to watch and judge they will never maintain it as it should be ——'

He came across the room towards her, pulling off his heavy top coat as he did, and throwing it with his hat on the sofa behind him.

'Dearest Sophie, I did not bring you here to talk of your friend Wilfred. I ——'

'You had no right to bring me here at all!' Sophie said strongly, all her rage coming back in a rush. 'It did not occur to me that you would even dream of doing so! I thought, as would any lady, that you were to take me back to my own establishment, and I take it very ill that you should dare to compromise me in this fashion and ——'

He was laughing now, standing very close to her, and looking down at her flushed face.

'Oh, Sophie, my dear heart, you are funny! In one breath you announce you will not wed me, but will bed me, and the next go off into a tantrum because I bring you to my chambers. What are you about, dear one? Do you think to captivate me with such girlish games? Come, Sophie, we are grown people, you and I. We do not play such tricks as these, do we? Of course we do not ——'

And he bent his head to kiss her, but she pulled away from him, twisting her neck almost violently to avoid his lips.

'I am playing no games, Gil!' she said furiously. 'Will you listen to me! I told you I — I said what I said in all honesty and I meant it, but not — I did not intend that we should go off in this precipitate fashion and — and ——'

He stood still, staring at her, his mouth a straight line and his eyes glittering.

'Then what did you mean?' he said and his voice was clipped. 'You really do confuse me, you know! On the one hand you tell me you are above the foolish conventions that govern the lives of others — or so you imply, at least — and in the next breath you berate me for believing you meant it and bringing you here! You did say, did you not, that you would share your love with me?'

'Yes, I did.'

'And you meant it?'

'Of course I did! Why say it otherwise? But I did not expect to be bundled off here like this, all unprepared to — to ——'

'Then what did you expect, Sophie? Some sort of ceremony? Are we to plight our troth in some way that makes it possible for you to do as you said you would, although without a wedding? Is that it? If you thought so then you are a foolish girl indeed, for there cannot be a way of eating your cake and having it, you know. Either you are free and ready to behave free, or you are as tied down as the rest of your sex ——'

She stood very still, staring at him. His face was straight now. None of the mocking laughter that usually filled his eyes was to be seen, and that mobile amusing mouth was but a line in the hardness of his face. To eat her cake and have it — was that foolish proverb to haunt her every action? Was she unreasonable in her desires, in her remedies for her problems? It seemed that she was, and for a moment a small part of her stood back, was apart from the real Sophie standing there in the middle of the room, and had become a little watching, jeering Sophie, perched high in the corner of the room staring down at her and laughing. She wanted everything, but wanted nothing, the little Sophie gibbered at her. She wants to eat cake until she bursts, and yet to have her larder full of it. She wants to take love but give none. Greedy, greedy creature! jeered the tiny watching Sophie, and the real Sophie, standing in the middle of the room in her wet mantle with her bonnet fallen back on her neck and held only by its strings over her rumpled wet hair, felt tears rise, needle-sharp, in her throat, and threaten to spill over to her cheeks.

'So, what do you want, Sophie?' Gil said. 'I put no compulsion on you, you know. You came to me of your own free will, after a long time apart and told me that you would be my mistress, and made me feel great — satisfaction. Now you seem to be pulling away and wishing to change your mind — what *is* it that you want, Sophie?'

She shook her head, hardly trusting herself to speak, and then managed to find her voice. 'I told you,' she said, quietly. 'I will — I will come to you. But not so suddenly. I need time, more time. If we were to be wed you would wait, would you not? So why be so hugger-mugger now? What is the urgency?'

'But we are not to be wed. And I love you, Sophie. That is why.'

She shook her head, miserably. 'I am sorry, Gil. But I must wait. I cannot rush into what is after all, a very important thing for a woman.'

'Don't make it too important.' Gil was still very controlled, and there was no hint of humour in him. 'It is never wise to allow such matters too much value.'

'I cannot help but do so. I may not be as other women are, in that I have — hopes and ambitions that are different from those most females have. But I am a female for all that and need to be treated as one.'

'Yes,' Gil said cryptically. 'I was right after all, was I not?'

She stared at him, puzzled, and he shook his head, irritably. 'Don't look at me like that — I really cannot be doing with any more of this ——'

'I would like to go home now,' she said, as calmly as she could, and he nodded briskly and went to the sofa and picked up his coat and hat.

'I will obtain a cab for you and see you on your way,' he said very punctiliously, 'and wait then until I hear from you again. I cannot, in all conscience, come to you, can I? I am sure you will understand that.'

'I understand,' she said miserably, and followed him down the stairs to the hallway below, feeling the tears very near the surface of her control again. She did want him; she wanted him very badly, and feeling him close enough now to be aware of the heat coming from his body, as they reached the small hallway by the front door, made her need greater and she put out one hand towards his back, ready to touch him, and tell him she was wrong and foolish, and of course she would stay. Now. They would be together tonight and she would stop this ridiculous shilly-shallying ——

'Well, there you is, Mr Stacey! An' me waitin' up this past hour an' more watchin' out for you so's I could tell you your message most partickler!'

A little woman in a grimy red wrapper was standing at the head of the basement stairs, peering inquisitively at them over the guttering candle she held in one hand. Her hair was tied up in curling rags, and she had the most pointed face Sophie had ever seen. Her chin, her nose, her very cheekbones seemed to be as sharp as pins.

'I tol' 'im as I'd tell you the minute as you was within doors, seein' as 'ow 'e said it was most important, an' 'e said as 'ow 'e'd be waitin' with his cab around the corner, on account 'e wouldn't want to 'ang round the door like, an' I must say 'e's a gennleman, ain't 'e, to be so careful? There's many as wouldn't care tuppence for what the neighbours'd say, an' when I said to 'im I didn't want no man 'angin' about my doorway like some bum bailiff, 'e understood right away, nice as pie, an' said as 'e'd wait around the corner, on the promise as I'd tell you the minute you was within doors. And there — if I didn't go and fall fast asleep over me bit o' cheese an' ale an' missed tellin' of you! But no 'arm done, like they say, when all's saved in the end. So I'm a-tellin' of you now, an' my dooties are done!'

Throughout this rambling speech the little woman kept her unwavering gaze on Sophie, taking in every detail of her, from her rumpled hair under her wet bonnet to her creased and sodden mantle, and the bright eyes seemed to Sophie to be jeering knowingly, and she felt the hot colour rise on her cheeks, and looked away, mustering what dignity she could as she drew on her wet gloves.

'What are you talking about, Mrs Stamper?' Gil sounded irritable.

'I *tol'* yer! That there big bloke what keeps a-comin' 'ere to see yer — 'e come again tonight an' 'e's awaitin' for yer round the corner so as not to discommode a respectable landlady like what I am, and wants to 'ave words with yer. Shall I go out an' tell 'im as you're 'ere now? I don' mind bein' 'elpful, even though I'm in my dishabile as you might say an' 'ardly fit ter be seen ——' and she giggled rather horribly.

'No,' Gil said shortly. 'I wish to see no one tonight. I'll see to the matter myself — thank you, Mrs Stamper, and good night.'

'No trouble,' Mrs Stamper said cheerfully and began to shuffle towards the door. ''E's a nice fella, comes from the country like what my poor old Mr Stamper did, afore 'e was called to greener pastures, an' ——'

'No!' Gil said loudly and looked sideways at Sophie, but she now had her chin up and was looking very directly at the little woman in the red wrapper.

'From the country, you say?' she said. 'And where did your husband come from, Mrs Stamper?'

'Why, from a little place miles from anywhere — Rother'am, it was — an' this gennelman friend of Mr Stacey talks much the same, if a shade more fancy, but then we can't always enjoy the benefits o' riches, can we? I'll go an' get 'im ——'

But Sophie reached the door first. 'No,' she said quietly. 'There is no need. I know who the gentleman is — do I not, Gil? And I shall go and see him.'

'It is none of your affair,' Gil said, his face pale in the dimly lit hall. 'Any person who calls to see me is surely no one else's concern ——'

'But it is Wilfred, is it not, Gil? Is there any reason why I should not speak to him? He is my friend, after all, and I have used him sorely, allowing him to come rushing here to London in search of me, when there was no need. I am in the wrong for not having written to him. I must put the wrong right ——'

'You are being quite absurd,' Gil said flatly. 'You cannot know that it is he.'

'Of course it is! You told me yourself that he had written you a message ——'

'I'd forgotten that!' Mrs Stamper said eagerly. 'Blowed if that 'adn't slid clean out o' my mind! O' course 'e left a message! Put it on yer overmantel, I did, Mr Stacey ——'

'Then it *is* Wilfred,' Sophie said. 'It is Wilfred!' And she felt herself fill with a great rush of relief that made her almost giddy. 'I must see him ——' And she scrabbled at the door knob awkwardly.

'If you go to him, then you will never come to me again,' Gil said flatly and she looked at him over her shoulder, as the door opened at last and she said uncertainly, 'Of course I will! But I cannot ignore Wilfred. He is my oldest friend — you must understand that ——'

'I think I understand more than you realize, my dear,' Gil said, and he sounded tired. 'Well, go and find your Wilfred. I am going to bed. Good night.' And he turned on his heel and went up the narrow staircase with never a backward look, and Sophie, after one worried glance after him, went out into the rainy night, and hurried along the pavement in the direction in which the eager Mrs Stamper pointed.

289

CHAPTER TWENTY-NINE

The sound of her own footsteps rushing along the narrow wet pavement was all she could hear above the steady drumming of the rain. There must be traffic out in the streets but the usual clatter of hooves and rumble of iron-rimmed wheels could not be heard in this weather and that made her nervous. Or so she told herself as she went along, her head down against the rain, towards the corner. There could be no other reason to feel anxious — could there? — for Wilfred was her friend, and seeing him would be a source of pleasure, not distress.

But when she reached the corner and turned it and saw the cab standing there with the horse with its head drooping and one leg bent so that it rested on the tip of its hoof, the very picture of wet misery, she stopped, a new wave of anxiety rising in her. To face Wilfred was not going to be agreeable, for she really had treated him very badly in not writing to him. And there was something so despondent about that tired-looking horse. But she took a deep breath and went on, and now she could see the shape of the jarvey up on the box, huddled in his mackintosh cape with a faint glow from a pipe in his mouth, and inside the cab, another deeper shadow.

She stopped at the cab window and the jarvey growled, without turning his head, 'Not fer 'ire. I'm took,' and she said a little breathlessly, 'I know. I want to speak to the gentleman within ——'

At once the door opened and she had to jump back out of the way, and then Wilfred was there, heavy and square, peering at her through the slanting rain.

'Sophie?' he said, and his voice was wooden as if he had expected her, as matter of fact as if they were meeting, as they so often had in past years, in the main street at Haworth. 'You'd better get in — it's not a fit night to be standing out here.' And he helped her climb into the cab and then followed her in and sat down heavily beside her.

It was warm in there and there was a faint smell of brandy and wet wool and steaming horse and she took a deep if somewhat tremulous breath and said simply, 'I'm sorry, Wilfred.'

'Aye, well,' he said after a moment. 'It wasn't kind in you to keep such a long silence, Sophie. Not with me. I'm not one to cause troubles for you, am I now? But I'm also not one to let a friend go lost in a city like London and do nothing about it. So it wasn't kind in you to keep such a silence and to forbid poor old Bessie to tell me aught of you. You must have known she'd do your bidding and that I'd try my best to get it out of her. She's not had it easy these past months, I'll tell you that.'

'Oh, dammit, dammit ——' Sophie said, almost sick with compunction. She had just not thought enough about what effect her silence might have on Wilfred, or how Bessie might suffer in obeying her injunction to keep silent. She had been much too absorbed in her own affairs, indeed selfishly absorbed, to think nearly enough about the people who loved her, and her shame and self loathing rose in her till the tears which had been so near the surface for so long could no longer be contained and came spilling over her cheeks.

'Well, there's no call to be using that sort of language,' Wilfred said, faintly reproving. 'I know you're a London lass now, and full o' town ways but to hear a woman swear — why, Sophie, if these are London manners, you can do without 'em!'

She sniffed dolorously and he peered more closely at her, and then, without a word took his big handkerchief from his pocket and put it into her hand, and gratefully she took it and wiped her wet face and blew her nose. The handkerchief smelt of soap and bay rum and, faintly, of raw wool and the smell took her back to her childhood, to the hours she had spent with Wilfred in his father's mill among the great bales of new wool, and she relaxed, comfortable at last, and leaned against his arm.

'Wilfred, I have been so — oh, there is so much to tell you! I am a doctor now, you know. I took the examinations and I qualified. Is that not strange? I am a doctor now.'

There was a little silence, and then Wilfred said quietly, 'Doctor Tom will be glad to hear it, Sophie. He has been much concerned about you, writing me letters to my hotel near every day to hear of any news of you.'

'Do not remind me again of how remiss I have been in treating my friends to such silence,' Sophie said. 'I know my fault and freely admit it. It was just that — oh, Wilfred, the last time I was in Haworth was all so — you and Gil and ——'

'I know. It was not easy. But the man was out of his own place, and ill at ease. He did not mean to be insulting, I dare say. I took no further umbrage, anyway. Indeed, I have seen something of him since I came to London seeking you. I thought that he would know ——'

'He did not. You must not think that I — that I put him before any of you at home,' Sophie said swiftly and tried to look up into his face for reassurance, but she could not see it, shadowed as it was under the brim of his hat. 'It was not until this very day that I saw him again, since Haworth. I do promise you that ——'

'You do not have to make speeches to me, Sophie,' Wilfred said. 'I do not quiz you as to your doings. You are free to do what you think fit, at any time. Had you been in regular contact with Mr Stacey I would not have taken that ill. I was only concerned that you had not been in contact with me. And I claim our many years of long friendship gives me the right to seek a reason for that.'

'I — because — oh, I do not know why because!' Sophie said. 'I was upset at what happened at home, and then — perhaps I needed to find my own way, without others to direct me, or — or interfere with me ——'

'Would I have interfered, Sophie?' He sounded as he always did, calm and reasonable, but she could feel the well of hurt that lay behind his words, and impulsively she slid her hand into his and squeezed his fingers hard.

'Of course not. Had I stopped to think, I would have known that, Wilfred. It was just that — oh, I was bewildered and confused, I knew I must write to Bessie, for she is — well, she has served me and my family these many years, and she has to be told I was well enough. But everyone else — I wanted just to be free. Can you understand all that?'

'I can understand,' he said woodenly. 'Servants must be told, but not friends.'

'That is unfair,' she said hotly and tried to pull her hand away, but he held on.

'Is it?'

There was a little pause and then she relaxed. 'No. You are right, of course. I can but apologize.'

'Then we shall say no more about it,' he said heartily. 'I am glad enough to see you safe and well and to know my long search is over. Come, we must take you to be dried and made comfortable again — and I would not say no to a little comfort myself! It has been a long evening and I am in need of some sustenance. Where shall we go? I will tell the cab man whatever you wish.'

'I would like above all things to go to my room and to bed, to tell the truth,' she said. 'I am so tired I hardly know what I am about — but there will be no sustenance there for you, for the medical school servants will long since have gone to bed — Gatti's! That is where. Tell him to take us to Gatti's in Villiers Street. There you will be able to have some food and all will be warm and comfortable. But Wilfred, I must soon go home for I must work tomorrow, and it is really getting very late.'

'You shall go home now, my dear,' Wilfred said. 'There is no need to worry about me — I can get a mutton chop when I go back to my hotel, I dare say. We can perhaps meet tomorrow? Could you be freed of your work for a little while, perhaps? It is time I returned to Haworth, for I have been away these past four days on this visit, and there are matters that need my attention. Maister's boots, tha knows, maister's boots! When they be absent, so's t'brass!'

She laughed at the sound of the old Yorkshire saying and relaxed against his arm again. To be with Wilfred was so comforting, so right, so very right, and she took a deep breath and felt the tiredness leave her bones, felt a new energy moving in her.

'I am not so tired that we cannot go to Gatti's now,' she said firmly. 'I will not go anywhere else, indeed, for I am determined you shall have your supper. Tell the man.'

He did, and the cab moved away, creaking a little, and turned the corner and she looked out for a moment as they passed Gil's house and looked up at the red glow of his pair of windows; and felt a little stab of — what? Anger? Or regret? She did not know, and somehow did not want to, and turned her head away deliberately as the cab moved on, gathering speed now, and she looked at Wilfred, trying to see what she could of his face in the occasional bands of light that came in from the houses and drinking dens they passed.

He looked drawn, she thought, and another stab of feeling, this time of compunction, moved into her. Poor Wilfred, to have spent so long seeking her, when she had been so heedless of his feelings; she did not deserve so good a friend, and again she moved closer to him and hugged his arm to her side. 'It is so good to see you, Wilfred!' she said impulsively. 'Not till now did I know how much I missed you.'

He said nothing, staring out of the cab window, but she did not mind. He was here, his usual comfortable self, and she was glad of it.

At Gatti's she was greeted with many exclamations and hand wringings and wide Italian smiles and her wet mantle and his hot and heavy ulster were taken from them and they were led into the small dining room at the back where a bright fire burned. There they were set to steam out while Signor Gatti himself prepared bowls of his best minestrone soup for the Signorina and her good friend — despite her protests that she had already dined — and they were left in peace to talk, with glasses of good red Chianti wine set in their hands and a bottle standing ready to refill them in the fender at their feet.

And now they could talk, and talk she did. He sat and watched her, his brown eyes warm and smiling above his sleek whiskers, and his square shoulders so straight in his chair, and she looked at him from time to time and smiled with the sheer pleasure of seeing him there, so familiar and comfortable and right.

She told him of her studies, of the long hours spent poring over books, and of her teaching chores, too. 'It was not at all like teaching the Sunday School children at home, as I used to do, Wilfred, of that I can assure you! I had to work every night and morning over my books to make sure I had enough information to teach them the next day! But it was good for me, for I learned as much as I taught, and I am sure that all that had much to do with my eventual success in the examinations. That and the great quantity of practical work I was able to do ——' And she launched into an account of the patients she had looked after in their hovels around King's Cross, of the diseases that had presented themselves, the abscesses that had to be lanced, the quinsies opened, the bleedings performed, the clysters administered.

'That sounds much like what you did at home, Sophie,' he said after she had finished a lively account of the setting of a broken bone for a child who had fallen on the railway line and miraculously survived with no more then a simple fracture. 'I remember you doing much the same for the Oldroyd boy when he tangled with the baler at my mill — do you remember that?'

'I do indeed — how is he? And the rest of his brothers — that wicked child Jonas — is he as troublesome to his poor mother as ever?'

'Indeed he is — nothing changes, you know. And I think from all you say that the people you look after here are the same as those you once looked after in Haworth. Their ills do not sound all that different.'

'They are not,' Sophie said after a moment. 'You are right, Wilfred. Perhaps in Haworth we have more accidents on the land and in the mills and fewer under horses' hooves in crowded streets, but life is much the same when people are poor. A hunt for food and warmth and comfort. It is no better at home than here in London ——'

'Then perhaps one day you will come to look after the Haworth people again,' he said looking at her very directly. 'I know there are more sick people here, and perhaps more excitement, but then, there are more doctors here, are there not? More hospitals, more dispensaries. In Haworth we have no hospital and no dispensary. But we have our sick people just as they have here in London.'

She looked up at him, a faint frown on her forehead. 'Are you telling me that I must not work here, Wilfred? That my duty lies in my own village?'

'I would not dream of telling you any such thing,' he said. 'You must be free to choose your own road. I was but saying that there is illness in all places. And some places have better care for their sick than others. That is all ——'

She turned her head to stare into the leaping flames of the fire and he leaned over and took the wine bottle and refilled both their glasses. She felt his eyes on her then, and looked at him and smiled and he leaned forwards and said, 'Sophie, please tell me ——'

But he could not finish his question, for Signor Gatti came bustling in, followed by two of his waiters bearing trays, and amid much clatter and chatter a table was pulled to the fireside for them and soup and bread and cheese put before the hungry Wilfred who

295

set to with a will. Sophie managed to convince Signor Gatti that she wanted no supper of her own, but he would not allow her, he told her firmly, to sit at his fireside with no refreshment at all, and though he took away her minestrone, brought her a dish of zabaglione, warm and frothy and sweet as he could make it, and she smiled and to oblige him ate a few spoonfuls.

And at last they went away, leaving them to the warmth and comfort of the food and the fire, and Wilfred, practical as always, ate his way steadily through his meal and said not a word, and she leaned back in her chair a little dreamily and watched him.

When he had finished, and the table had been pushed to one side he too leaned back in his chair and looked at her, and then he said sharply, 'Sophie — I must ask you. It has worried me ever since we came in here. Why is the neck of your gown torn? I have never seen you ever looking anything but neat since you ceased to be a child. To see you so now surprises me.'

Her face flamed red and she put her hand up to her throat and felt at her collar. She had in all truth quite forgotten the damage that Gil's ardent embraces had caused, but now she remembered in a great rush, and with the memory came all the confusion and shame that had so filled the earlier part of this momentous evening, but which she had been able to lay to rest, until now.

'It — it is not important,' she stammered. 'Will you have some of this pudding, Wilfred? It is a speciality of the place, and is made with eggs and sugar and Marsala wine and is very good — but I can eat no more ——'

'I think it is important, Sophie,' Wilfred said. 'For why else should you look so — look as you do?'

'I do not understand you. How do I look?' she blustered a little. 'Really, my dear, you should not quiz me so! I am not a naughty child who has been climbing forbidden trees ——'

'Precisely so. That is why I ask. You are not a child but a woman grown, and to see you with such a tear in your gown puzzles me. Has anyone tried to hurt you, Sophie? For I tell you, if that is the case, it will be dealt with, oh, it will be dealt with ——'

She looked at him and bit her lip. His square face, usually so lacking in expression and so calm when compared with the mercurial Gil's was more wooden than ever. But this was her friend Wilfred, the man she had known from his gawky boyhood, and she could see clearly what feeling lay behind the apparently blank canvas that was his face. He was no fool, and was well able to jump to a conclusion; she had a sudden vision of the parlour at the Black Bull at Haworth and Gil and Wilfred facing each other with clenched fists. Wilfred was not a violent man, but there were springs of anger in him that must not be lightly tapped.

She sighed, almost impatiently. 'Oh, no one has tried to hurt me, Wilfred! I am well able to defend myself, I promise you. I told you what happened in the anatomy room at Nellie's, and you applauded me and said you had no fears for my wellbeing. But this —' She felt her face redden again. 'This is different.'

'How different?'

'I would really rather not talk of it, Wilfred ——'

'No doubt you would. But I am as determined as you are that you will not, that you will. Must I remind you yet again of the many years of friendship that unite us, Sophie? You cannot shut me out of your concerns in this manner. Have I ever tried to do so with you? You are the only person in the world who knows how difficult I find life with my Mamma, for example. I have let you speak of her in such slighting terms that any other man would take very ill — however true such terms might be. We are friends, Sophie, and I claim the right of a friend to know what ails you, and who has torn your gown in that manner ——'

She shook her head in exasperation. 'Oh, Wilfred, stop being so — so *Yorkshire*! This stubbornness in you ——'

'Aye, well, the sooner you admit it is there and give in, the better for both of us. I will not give up that easily. Any more than I gave up seeking you. I have come to London times beyond count these past twelve months in my searches, and would have gone on twelve years more, had I not found you. So you may as well ——'

'Oh, all right! It was Gil. But it was not violence. It was — it was ——'

His face darkened at her obvious confusion. 'Has he behaved badly to you, Sophie? Has he forced his attentions upon you? For affianced though you are, I will not allow such ——'

'We are not affianced.' She said it loudly. 'How could you think we were when I have kept away from him all this time? I have not seen him, or communicated with him, any more than I have with you.'

'Then he has even less right — if ever he had — to so treat you that he tears your gown.'

She sat there and stared at him, not knowing what to do or say. His stubbornness, his determined picking away at the silly business of her torn gown had brought her to a precipice; either she had to think up some trumpery tale that would both convince him and prevent him from seeking out Gil and causing much trouble with him, or she would have to tell him the truth. And both prospects made her quail.

'Well?' he said implacably, and looked at her with his brows raised. 'Are you going to tell me? Or must I go there to Stacey's chambers and drag it out of him? For I shall, Sophie, believe me, I shall. No one treats a friend of mine in such a manner and does not pay the price for his effrontery. I will not have it.'

There was only one thing she could do, and she did it. She told the truth.

'I must tell you that — that I told Gil Stacey tonight that although I would not wed him, I would — I would share his life as though I were married to him. But that wed him I could not and would not.'

She managed to keep her head up and her eyes fixed on his face, difficult though it was. Every instinct in her made her want to hang her head as she said the words, but she could not do that. If she were going to behave in the way she had told Gil she would, then she must have the courage to do it openly, not hole-in-the-corner ashamed.

There was a long silence and then Wilfred said carefully, 'You will take him as a lover?'

'Yes.'

There was another long silence, and then he took a deep breath. 'Sophie, why? Why is it necessary that you fly so in the face of all that is — that is right and normal and ——'

She shook her head impatiently at that. 'It is not for the sake of being unconventional, Wilfred. I am not so foolish as to behave so for the sake of it. That sort of nonsense is for others, not for me. There are reasons — and you must not misunderstand them. There is the money, you see. The will that my Grandmamma left. I had not thought of it until your mother said it, I cannot deny, but she was right. If I wed, I change my name. If I change my name I am not able to claim the legacy. And I do not want the money just to enjoy it, but because I have a use for it.'

'Everyone has a use for money.' His voice was hard and flat and anger lifted in her.

'That is wicked and unjust! Have I ever showed any sign of being interested in money above other things? Were I that avaricious I would have allowed you to propose any one of a hundred times and accepted you for the sake of your mill and your fat income! But I never did!'

'No. You never did.'

She was silent then, uncomfortable in the face of his stolidity. That she had hurt him deeply she knew. It showed in his stillness, in the way his brown eyes looked at her so directly and without expression.

'My dear, try to understand, please. I have a scheme — I want to start a visiting service for the ill people in the poor parts of the city. The ones I have been looking after all these months. I thought — I could get nurses and teach them the skills needed to deliver babies in their homes in such a way that they and their mothers would not die like flies — as now they do. Believe me, they do. I want to find doctors who will work in such houses and not be ambitious for hospitals all the time. You see? That is why I need the money; and anyway — I am not sure that I want to be like other women and be wed. I have such — such *work* in me, Wilfred. There is so much I want to do! I wish to work and work and work — but does that mean I must deny — my physical nature? There is no sin in admitting that I have one, is there? That is why I said what I said to Gil. And why, in — in a moment of excitement this silly tear came to be on my gown. It is not important.'

Once again a silence slid into the room, broken only by the clatter of dishes and the rumble of voices from the big dining room beyond. Then he said stiffly, 'He agreed then? He said he would allow such a sacrifice on your part?'

'It is no sacrifice!' she said, furiously. 'Far from it! It is an arrangement whereby I gain much. I keep my name and obtain a legacy I can put to good use, and I hold on to my independence.'

He stood up and crossed the room heavily, and took his coat and hat from the chair where Signor Gatti had left them to dry.

'Sophie, he is the man you have chosen, and it ill becomes one

299

who is, as you so painfully reminded me, a failure in the fight for your affections, to speak badly of him. But I must say it. The man is a cad. He uses you as no man who loves a woman — truly loves her in every way, and not just — just desires her — should or indeed could. Had you offered me such an arrangement, Sophie, I would have told you that it could not be. I would have told you that marriage to me would not trammel you in any way. That you could live your life in any way you chose, and do the work that you felt called to do. I would have told you that I would aid you with it in any way I could. I would also have told you, Sophie, that in order to help you claim your legacy I would have changed my name to Lackland. For you I would have shed all I had — not only my father's name — to give you what you wanted. If you had asked me, that is what I would have said. I wish he had done as much for you. Goodbye, Sophie. I am returning to Haworth. There is nothing here for me to remain for now.'

And he turned and went, leaving her there beside Gatti's fireside staring after him without a word that she could say to stop him.

CHAPTER THIRTY

The rain stopped at about five o'clock in the morning. The sky was still black, but the heavy pall of cloud that had lain over London this past week at last broke up, and staring from her window Sophie could see scudding rags of cloud moving across the points of feeble starlight. The wind came up, too, and blew bitterly cold draughts through the ill-fitting rattling window and she shivered and pulled her woollen shawl closer about her shoulders.

She had been sitting there on her window sill staring out for over an hour now. At first she had tried to sleep, but it had been impossible, aching with fatigue though she was. The long evening that had led up to this dark night had re-enacted itself in front of her eyes over and over again; the show at the theatre, dinner with Gil at Rules, and then Wilfred's face, so expressionless and yet hiding such pain — she had tried to push it all away, but it had been impossible. So she had got out of her bed and with her shawl about her shoulders and a small blanket across her knees and round her bare feet, had sat down on the wide window sill to look at the world outside. Perhaps there she would find the answers to her dilemmas. Perhaps in staring up at those remote uncaring stars she would see how unimportant her own affairs really were, and would be able to see a way out of this sorry tangle of desires and needs and others' pains.

But it did not help. Still her head spun with it all, and not least the coup de grâce — the letter that had been waiting for her on her mantelpiece when she reached her room.

Miss Jex-Blake had been away from the medical school for some days, visiting Edinburgh, the scene of her first triumphs, and her letter bubbled with excitement and satisfaction in every word.

'— I have arranged all for you,' she wrote in her strong sloping hand. 'The professors here are not precisely putty in my hands, but they listen to me, especially since I have started the London Medical School for Women. And I have told them I have a newly qualified physician who wishes to become a surgeon and who has had considerable surgical experience of an informal kind. I have assured them that you will be an excellent person to enter for the examinations of the Royal College of Surgeons of Edinburgh, and require but a little more formal training, and this, I am more than happy to tell you, I have been able to arrange. You are to come to Edinburgh forthwith. I have written in this same post to Miss Hallsbury and told her she must take on your students and also your visits in King's Cross, and told the Bursar to arrange for moneys to be paid to you to make the journey. You will come to me here at the Royal Hotel on Sunday morning — you will take the overnight train tomorrow, Saturday, and that will bring you safe to me on Sunday morning — and then on Monday, I will take you to enrol at the hospital where you are, under Professor McIntyre, to have your first formal classes in the operating theatre. I know you will do well here, and may, with effort, look forward to qualifying as a licentiate of the College of Surgeons in two years' time. It will be hard work but you can achieve it ——'

It had been almost funny. She had stood there, still in her mantle and bonnet with the letter in her hand, and had laughed aloud. To have this thrown at her at the very time when she was in such turmoil about Gil and Wilfred — how could Providence so load her plate with troubles? What had she ever done to deserve it?

But then she had taken off her mantle and bonnet and sat down by the dying fire to reread the letter, and think about its contents. It was typical of the masterful Miss Jex-Blake to make arrangements in such detail without consulting the object of them, and for a moment she felt thoroughly annoyed at her would-be benefactor; but then had to admit that she was entirely wrong to feel so. Miss Jex-Blake had done much for her, had helped her on the road to becoming a physician, had listened with practical calmness when she had voiced her impossible ambition to study surgery, and now had made it possible. It was not her fault that Sophie herself should be such a foolish vacillating creature that she now no longer knew what she wanted.

For that, she had to admit, sitting now on her window sill and staring up at the black early-morning sky, was the root of her dilemma. She did not know what she wanted. Gil and the satisfaction of her physical needs? A working life spent in the

London slums? Or the excitement of a surgeon's busy training in Edinburgh? Or was it none of these that drew her, but the peace and certainties of life in Haworth?

That had been the surprising thing about all her ponderings. Round and round again it had all gone in her head; what Gil had said, what she had said, and what Wilfred had said — above all, what Wilfred had said. 'In Haworth we have no hospital and no dispensary. But we have our sick people just as they have in London.'

The vision of herself as she had been in the old days kept returning. Going round Town End Bottom with Doctor Tom, working with the women and children she had known all her life, hearing their familiar speech, seeing the familiar sights of the moors and the steep streets and the tall mill chimneys.

Then that vision would melt into a new one: of herself as she was now, qualified, experienced, with new knowledge to bring to the people she had always known so well. She kept remembering long ago cases; the child who had died of a quinsy, choking its small life away on a throat full of pus because Doctor Tom was away over the high tops dealing with a man who had fallen into the beck and fractured his pelvis, and could not be at Town End Bottom to lance the swelling. She had sat there and watched the child die because she could not aid it. Now, of course, she could. Now she would know what to do, and how to do it, and would have the confidence to do it. And the women who had died in childbed; could she not have saved them, had she known then what she knew now? Doctor Tom could not be everywhere; there was too much sickness for one tired man to deal with.

But if she were there — ah, if she were there, what could she not do? She did not need money to take care of those people in the village. Here in London, yes, a visiting service would eat up sovereigns, swallow gold like a greedy animal, but at home, all that was needed was a trained person. A trained *woman*. Herself.

Over and over again she tried to push it away, that vision of Wilfred's face, that memory of Wilfred's words, but it became more and more difficult, until at last she had to admit that, splendid though her new idea of future work at home was, it was Wilfred who mattered more than what he had said. It was Wilfred she was aching for, secure, sensible, comfortable, loving Wilfred.

He did not make her pulse race as Gil could. He did not remind her with every glance of wicked eyes that she had a passionate nature and physical needs. His mouth did not twist into a witty heart-wrenching curl when he looked at her. But for all that, the thought of him was what warmed her and comforted and supported her.

'I am a weak and foolish creature,' she thought mournfully as the clock crept towards six and the sky began, very slowly, to lift in the east. 'I thought I could break new ground, be a New Woman, but I cannot. I want to be safe and happy and useful — but not new. I have gone as far as I can go ——'

At half past six she dressed and went downstairs to the silent kitchen. The cook and maids would be stirring soon, hurrying to prepare breakfast for the students who would be arriving for the morning's work, and they would be in a hurry, for Saturday was everyone's half holiday, including themselves. Which meant, Sophie told herself firmly, that she could vacillate no longer. If she was to do as she knew she must, she must sort it all out now, so that all could be arranged before noon.

So she sat down at the kitchen table, very aware of the last time she had sat at a kitchen table to write a letter, and tried not to think too much about what she was doing. The time for thinking was past; she had sat half the night in her chilly bedroom staring out into the night and thinking. Now she must act.

Her first letter was not easy. It was to Aunt Martha. '— I hope you will not be too disappointed at what I have told you are my plans. I meant, indeed I did, to carry my ambition through, but sometimes matters are changed for one, however firm one's initial intentions were. I feel this has happened to me. I feel that I have been selfish long enough, putting my own desires before those of others. I have treated people who deserved better at my hands in a way of which I am now ashamed, and hope that I may be forgiven for it. Now, I ask *your* forgiveness. You have done much for me, and I owe much to you. I would not now be able to call myself doctor but for your kindness in giving me the haven of Villiers Street. At least I now have the comfort of knowing that my Grandmamma's money will be put to good use ——'

The letter to Miss Jex-Blake was even harder. To reject the plans of that iron-jawed and hard-eyed lady, even at a remove of some three hundred and fifty miles, was enough to make her pulse beat more thickly in her throat and her stomach churn; but she did it.

'— I trust you will understand that I mean no disloyalty in thus refusing your good efforts on my behalf. My reasons are good, although I will not disturb you with them; suffice it to say that my studies will not be wasted. I will work always among the sick and the poor, and bring to those who need it the aid of a physician whenever it is my power so to do. Please believe me when I tell you I am eternally grateful to you for all you have done for me this past two years ——'

The letter to Gil she had expected to be hardest of all, but it was surprisingly easy.

'Dear Gil,' she wrote baldly. 'I must say farewell. I will not see you again. Forgive me for any confusion I may have caused you, and accept my best wishes for your continuing health and success. Yours sincerely, S. Lackland.'

Then she went back upstairs and put her few belongings in her valise, and walked out of the house in Hayland Street as composedly as if she were going about her usual business in these mean and narrow streets. No one looking at her would have known the turmoil of the past night as they saw her lift her chin to the grey morning sky and take a deep breath of the sooty London air. No one would have guessed that she had reached a momentous decision.

But she knew that the turmoil was over and the decision was made. She had tried to reach a goal and failed — but in aiming for the sky she had at least reached the top of a tree. It was not the great height to which she had first aspired. She would never be a surgeon of the great Queen Eleanor's Hospital. She would not proudly carry her grandfather's name into the hospital's future with her crusading knife in her hand. She would not even inherit her grandmother's legacy.

She was not ashamed of what she had achieved, though, nor of the future she had mapped out for herself. It was not an insignificant height to have reached even if it lacked the full glory of her initial hopes.

She reached King's Cross station in time to catch the nine o'clock train to Keighley. The train was full, as Saturday trains always were, and she sat in her second-class carriage, a mother with a wailing baby on her lap on one side and a fat man smelling of cheap tobacco on the other. But it did not matter. She was going home to the high moors and the clean cold air and the dark grey stones of Haworth. She was going home to the sick people of Town End Bottom who needed her. She was going home to give back to Doctor Tom, who had started her on her path, some of the care and help he had given her.

Also, of course, she was going home to Wilfred. But she would think about that when she got there.